CW00468093

RETRIBUTION

PROTECTING CIVILIANS. PROTECTING
THE REGIMENT. CAN SAS: VIGILANT
PROTECT THEMSELVES?

SIMON DALEY

MYDOGFRANK PUBLISHING

This book is dedicated to the men and women of our armed forces and emergency services. Without them the world would be a much darker place.

So many acts of heroism and selflessness go unrecognised. They don't seek our thanks, and we don't thank them often enough.

The SAS are not superheroes. They are at times superhuman, but they are also very human. I hope I have captured some of that humanity in the characters of this book.

WE ARE THE PILGRIMS MASTER: WE SHALL GO
ALWAYS A LITTLE FURTHER: IT MAY BE
BEYOND THAT LITTLE BLUE MOUNTAIN BARRED WITH
SNOW.
ACROSS THAT ANGRY OR THAT GLIMMERING SEA
by James Elroy Flecker

CHAPTER ONE

He ducked instinctively, covering his head with his hands. He knew he was trapped. The sound of the approaching All-Terrain Vehicle's guttural diesel engine had warned him. The headlights pierced the slatted shell of the barn as he curled himself tight to try to avoid their reach. Gravel crunched and scattered as the vehicle skidded to a halt. Then the silence hit him and pinned him where he lay.

A fast moving shadow darted along the outside of the wall closest to his position. His heart hammered in his chest and he dared not breathe. He watched in horror as the shadow stopped and the dogs paws scraped at the earth. Its wet nose and muzzle tried to force its way through the mercifully too tight gap beneath the wall boards. Forcing himself to keep still, his eyes flicked between the dog and the door as he braced for it to swing open. He imagined the barrel of a shotgun appearing through the door and firing before he could plead with them not to shoot.

He'd been careful, only coming and going in the dark. Not riding his bike across the dirt patch in front of the door so he didn't leave tyre tracks. What he couldn't counter was his scent. It was hopeless, he'd been caught.

Just as he was about to give himself up, a man shouted something indiscernible in a thick accent. The dog reacted instantly and it's shadow sprinted back along the wall. The gear box clunked on the ATV, then it revved and the headlight beams spun across the wall to leave total darkness.

Lying on his back he clutched his backpack tight to his chest. He fought to get his breathing back under control. His bladder felt ready to burst but he lay there, staring into the dark, long after the sound of the ATV had gone.

Eventually he forced himself to stand up and swing aside the loose panel in the rear wall to squeeze out into the evening air. It was 7:50pm according to his phone. Time for him to try another location. To find them, before it was too late.

Recovering his mountain bike from a little copse of trees nearby, he set off down the bridle path. He thought better of switching on his lights until he was on the road.

Almost an hour later, stood in the shadows he scanned the car park. There were 4 vehicles, none of them stood out and gave no clue as to who might own them.

His fingers gripped the handle but he stopped short of pulling the door open. Looking carefully at the old wooden door he found himself counting the metal studs. He chastised himself for procrastinating, then took a deep breath, and pulled.

All eyes fell on him as he walked in through the door. The smell of fried food made his mouth water and compounded his feeling of not belonging. Scanning the room, he was hoping to recognise something, someone, despite not knowing who they were or what they looked like. He could feel the colour of his skin. It marked him out as foreign to this place. Foreign and unwelcome.

'Can I help you?' asked the woman, looking him up and down.

He cleared his throat, 'Please, may I have some water?' he asked.

She took a moment to think about his request, then shrugged and poured him a glass of water.

Ezekiel Olufemi slipped his backpack from his shoulder and took off his jacket. He was wearing a white t-shirt and turned on-the-spot meeting everyone's eyes as he did. Some looked away but others stared back at him.

Nobody spoke.

Chapter Two

The blurry edges grew darker and just as the lights were going out, he lifted his trigger finger. Rough, urgent hands dragged him from the water. A vicious thump to the back sparked an explosive light in his mind. Part retch, part cough, as much water as air erupted from nose and mouth as his lizard brain tried to kick start his breathing. Two more splutters followed two more thumps to his back. Then vomit splashed in the bath where he'd been submerged for almost six agonising minutes.

He was aware of people around him but he was only capable of processing a well-rehearsed shock routine. Blood had left his extremities as his body fought to preserve its essential organs. His brain was only too willing to sacrifice superfluous limbs and digits. As such, he was a rag doll as they threw him under the steaming shower. The hot water daggered his skin as it assaulted his near frozen scalp. His body offered no resistance as he was unceremoniously stripped. He felt the scalding water on his bare back and shoulders. He thought he heard a distant laugh as finally he succumbed and passed out.

Thirty minutes after being pulled from the bath, Captain Jonathon 'JT' St John-Templeman was wrapped in a duvet lying on his bedroom floor in London's upmarket Mayfair. He blinked rapidly trying to focus on the faces crowding into his vision.

'Come on boss, enough of the theatrics, the kettles on for one of your fancy brews.' The sonorous voice, in his sing-song Welsh lilt, could only belong to Sergeant Alwyn 'Taff' Michaels. The man wore a smile, even when knee deep in blood and guts. His good nature and fortitude had seen the friends and comrades through more than their fair share of scrapes. More than a smile, the man's size and strength coupled with a razor sharp mind made him the best of friends and the deadliest of foes.

Another voice joined in and was instantly recognisable as Trooper Patrick 'Posty' Harrower. As the team's Method of Entry and Demolition expert he handled explosives routinely. There was nothing he couldn't blow up or blow out. Posty's rough Northern Irish brogue cut through the ringing in JT's ears as he quipped, 'Fuck the tea, I've just found the drinks cabinet and it's full of real posh stuff. Stuff that would make for a lovely breakfast tipple, so it would!' He grinned, showing off the gap where his front teeth used to be. The rifle butt of an Iraqi guard had ruined his smile, but Posty had had the last laugh. Dislocating his thumb to escape his bindings he beat his captor to death, using just his one working fist. The regimental dentist had offered to provide new implants to repair his teeth. Posty turned down the offer saying they'd just get knocked out again, so he'd save it for when he retired from The Regiment – if he got there.

The Special Air Service aka the SAS were almost never referred to by other than *The Regiment* by its officers and men. There were hundreds if not thousands who had pretended to have earned the winged dagger. Very few, and only the best of the best, actually did.

The tea was hot, strong and served in a china cup, just as JT liked it. It signalled he was home. Two hours had passed since the bath ordeal and he was sitting in his father's wingback chair before the fire. The other five men in the room were relaxing, as only they could, sprawled on the sofa, across an easy chair and Posty sat cross legged on the Persian rug. The rug was worth more than a couple of years of the Trooper's salary and it pleased JT to see him sat there comfortably watching football on his mobile phone. There was no TV in the room, or indeed in the flat at all. Such frivolities, and all of the joy, had left the building with Esmé.

'Remind me again why you don't live here boss?' asked Trooper Rambahadur "Rambo" Gurung, the youngest and newest member of the team. The Grandson of a highly decorated Gurkha officer he had pushed back against special treatment when he joined the Gurkha Battalion. He earned a fearsome reputation among the Gurkhas before he applied for, and passed with flying colours, the selection process of *The Regiment*. Rambo was a talented climber and the best sniper in *The Regiment*.

'Rambo!' came the soft scold from Taff, 'Mind your manners boy.'

'That's ok, stand easy Taff,' said JT, in truth it was a question he'd asked himself while sat alone in the officer's accommodation at Hereford. Eventually he replied, 'Good question Rambo, for some reason I seem to like slumming it with you lot.'

'Sorry Boss, didn't mean to get personal,' said Rambo straightening a little in his seat.

JT nodded his admonishment and stared at the fire a few more seconds before standing and asking the room, 'who's hungry?'

The words had barely left his lips when a chorus of 'me', 'Boss' and 'yep' filled the air.

JT smiled and looked around at his men, his family. 'Risotto?'. The affirmative noises were music to his ears. He took pride in feeding his men, on the odd occasion he got to cook for them. 'Cooky, you're chopping,' he said to the biggest man in the room, Corporal Josiah Cook.

Cooky had already been getting to his feet and held up a huge hand as his signal of acknowledgement. The hand was missing its pinkie and the standard joke among the team was that he'd accidentally chopped it off while chopping vegetables. The reality was altogether more gruesome and Cooky never spoke of the torture inflicted upon him. It had left more than the livid pink scars across his ebony skin. Courtesy of his Caribbean heritage, his idea of flavouring food was to add as many fiery chillies as he could find to every meal. Thus, he had ensured he was not given a job in the team commensurate with his name. His knife skills however were in a league of their own.

The two men worked away in companionable silence, this was not their first duty as chef and commis and each knew their roles. When JT reached into the vegetable rack and threw the onions and carrots over his shoulder, he knew those huge safe hands were ready and always willing to catch.

The finely chopped onions and carrots sizzled in the hot oil as JT stirred them and Cooky carefully peeled the celery which was limp and past its best.

'Not our best work Boss,' said Cooky, not taking his eyes from his knife.

'No, just making do with what we have, as usual.'

The gentle sizzle and occasional tap of wooden spoon continued until eventually JT left the room before returning a few seconds later with a bottle of wine.

'One of Esmé's favourites, Pinot Grigio, not cold enough to drink but fine to cook with,' said JT, as he glugged the bottle over the arborio rice in the pan. He knew that on its own it wouldn't be enough to satisfy 6 hungry men. Checking on the 24 garlicky chicken thighs roasting in the oven he thought they'd be happy enough. None would go to waste, voracious appetites and a well ingrained habit of always eating whenever possible, as you couldn't always know when or where your next meal was coming from, would mean empty plates.

'Boss, yer phone's buzzing,' called the unmistakable Scottish voice of Trooper Joe Paterson. As the Comms and Engineering expert in the team he was always tinkering with something. If it could be fixed, he could fix it and if it could be broken, he could break it he would always say. He knew better than to get in the way of these guys in the kitchen so he placed the buzzing phone on the counter and retreated back to the safety of the lounge where his latest project was taking shape.

'Hello?' came a recognisable voice as JT held the phone to his ear.

'Hi Paddy, what can I do for you?'

'Hey JT, where are you and the team?'

'London, why?'

'Just checking, knew you were off base and there's a Fanboy come in.'

'Ah right, we're all here, well away from home. Anything of interest?'

'Probably not, Jake at the Old Bell called in a new face two days ago. It got logged as usual and marked *NO ACTION REQUIRED.*'

'Why the Fanboy tag then?' asked JT, adding a ladle of hot stock to the pan.

'It wasn't, not at first, but then Jessop down at the Prince of Wales, called this evening saying he thought he'd had the same new face yesterday. He hadn't seen him as it was his day off, but he checked the CCTV after Jake had sent the message round the pubs.'

'Just the one guy? Take it the plods have been made aware?'

'Yep, they've confirmed it was the same kid. Young black guy asked for a glass of water and sat for a couple of hours checking people out as they came in.'

'Nothing to link him with *The Regiment* though?'

'Not at first no, but 20 minutes ago the silly bugger was sat in The Coach wearing a t-shirt saying 'SAS Help!' staring at the CCTV camera. The civilian plod were busy dealing with a big crash on the motorway and when I called Phyllis at The Coach the kid got up and left saying he'd be back tomorrow.'

'Hmmm, interesting. What's the response from the brass?'

'They've said it's strictly Civvy plod jurisdiction and the troops are kept on base until he's been identified and threat assessed.'

'Well thanks for letting us know, glad to know our suspension hasn't seen us drop out of the loop completely,' JT said with just enough of a hint of humour to give Paddy a morale update.

'Damn stupid business' replied Paddy, 'and I told the brass that in person, got me a ticking off but I know they're not happy either. Bloody Whitehall and their political correctness, how dare they not take our word for what happens on the ground. Fucking desk jockeys couldn't- '

'Easy tiger!' said JT.

His old friend's vocal anger was a genuine gesture of support but JT assured him that his team were enjoying some feet up time and 'a game of Scrabble'. Both men knew that playing 'Scrabble' meant the very toughest sort of training that was usually kept to Escape and Evasion training for when it all went horribly wrong. Building minds and bodies to withstand torture and the harshest of conditions was what made these men the fighting elite.

'Take it easy on yourselves now, we'll need you fighting fit when this nonsense is sorted,' said Paddy.

'No worries, listen, dinner is ready to serve, let me know when the guy is identified. Ciao!' with that JT dropped the phone onto the worktop picked up a fistful of parmesan and threw it into the pan. 'Done, let's serve Cooky.'

The 6 men sat at the extended dining table and took up barely half of it. The Pinot Grigio might not have been at the required temperature to drink but the bottles of Heineken were, and the fridge was ready for them to make a night of it.

Taff made his customary toast before they started, he called it his 'Dis-grace'. 'Lordy, you have some hungry souls grateful to be alive and grateful for this food in front of them, keep them that way until it's time for you to serve them dessert alongside our comrades passed. This we ask in some bugger's name, Amen!'

As they ate, JT told his team about the Fanboy alert and relayed the message from Paddy. The men listened carefully while eating and drinking their beer. They'd had such alerts before, being away from Home meant none of them gave it much thought.

#

Two days later the new 'drowning' record for the ice bath was now 7 minutes and 23 seconds. The record, as everyone had known would be the case, belonged to Cooky. The man's ability to withstand pain was incredible and legendary among those who knew him. He'd emerged from the water after his tap signal to applause and with a chattering grin. He wasn't such a fan of the cold he said, as he was helped into the hot shower to recover his core temperature.

Pouring himself another steaming mug of coffee, Cooky heard Rambo return to the Mayfair flat and bustle into the kitchen carrying several thin blue plastic bags full of shopping. He was muttering away under his breath and Cooky waited for him to realise he was standing behind him. Cooky was about to clear his throat when Rambo said, 'I can smell you and your coffee breath, even over the coriander and timmur in my bag.'

"Let me know if you need my help," said Cooky with a mischievous tone, then left the room almost silently, which for a man of his size was quite a feat.

Rambo was proud of his traditional cooking and always sourced the most authentic ingredients possible. He insisted on cooking alone and as such had taken the first ice bath in the morning, so he could go shop for ingredients. His time of 4 minutes and 13 seconds was a personal best but was still more than a minute less than the others. This was probably why he was in a bad mood and why he had raised his voice at the halal butcher who tried to overcharge him for the goat meat he'd bought. The boss had given him plenty of cash to do the shopping but that wasn't the point, there are some principles in life that must be obeyed – treating a customer with honesty and decency was one such principle. He took a deep breath and a second to clear his mind before he emptied the bags and went in search of the biggest pot in the cupboards.

An hour later Rambo emerged from the kitchen in time to join the stretching session going on in the hallway, the hallway which was bigger than his parent's house in Kathmandu he thought. He slipped easily into the rhythm of the class. As ever, it was Posty who led the class; part yoga and part Pilates, it made for a full body workout and was especially handy in confined spaces. Rambo wished they could go outside into the beautiful gardens but he knew the sight of six men exercising together in such a way would raise eyebrows. He knew he was the smallest in stature but also that he was strong, the body weight exercises he did with ease belied the real power he could summon when required. Having been transferred into the team from the Mountain Troop he was an outstanding climber and skier. Navigation through mountains was second nature to him and it was this skill that had led him to JT's team. He might not be able to hold his breath as long as the others but he could carry his bergen and kit as easily as the rest. In The Regiment, and in his team, it was not the size of the dog in the fight, but the fight in the dog that counted.

At the end of the session, they all showered making use of all three bathrooms in the flat. JT mused that the water bill for these last two weeks would make up for the months the place had lain empty since Esmé left.

He tried but failed to think of the last time they had showered together. It used to be a ritual when he returned from a tour, as much a medical examination as an intimate embrace. She would undress him and inspect every inch of him for a new scar, bump or bruise. Then she would make him watch her undress and assess his physical reaction to her standing naked before him. Always, he would move to touch her and kiss her but she would push him away before leading him by the hand into the shower enclosure. She would grin knowingly at him as she soaped up the sponge and cleansed the war and action from his skin and from their world. Only once he was completely clean from head to toe, was he allowed to touch her, to devour her, and she him. They would often lie on the bathroom floor among the damp towels and make love again before robing in the kimonos they had brought back from their first holiday together.

His kimono now hung alone on the back of his bathroom door, it was limp and a little dishevelled, the same could be said of him he thought catching sight of himself in the mirror. He'd brought back his beard as a souvenir from Afghanistan. Even at 35 he sported more than his fair share of grey among the brown and auburn bristles. He picked up the clippers and held them against his throat. He savoured the thrum of the metal teeth on his skin but as he looked himself in the eye, he made a decision to visit his old barber and treat himself to a hot towel shave.

Brushing his teeth with the expensive sonic brush Esmé had given him for Christmas he stood back from the mirror and looked at his torso in the reflection. He was well muscled but not in a showy gym body way, rather he looked like he did hard physical labour, which was exactly what he did.

He touched his fingertips to the spidery scar down his abdomen. Tracing each bump and taut sinewy line, it told a story, in painful braille, a story of bravery, of good fortune, but ultimately, a story of loss. This particular scar, more than the bullet wound scar that neatly punctured his left pectoral where it had entered and, not so neatly, patched his left shoulder blade where it left. Or the ropey slice across his thigh, or the numerous scars across his hands and forearms. No, this particular scar was the straw that broke the camel's back for Esmé. She had braved out and survived all of his tours since they got together 8 years ago. Then it became too much.

Esmé's brother Peter was a Canadian Commando who JT had worked with in Africa on a UN mission. Peter had introduced JT to his beautiful kid sister at his wedding in Canada. They had spent the late evening drinking champagne on the roof of the ski lodge. Esmé was beautiful in a non-traditional way. Her hair was never 'perfect', she wore little to no make-up and was more comfortable in her favourite dungarees than a dress. JT remembered how at breakfast the day after the wedding she'd walked in wearing his shirt under her dungarees but had sat at another table and ignored him. Only he knew it was his shirt, he also knew she'd gone into his room to steal it. The night before she'd kissed him gently on the lips and whispered good night, before leaving him alone on the roof. He had barely slept, lying awake thinking over and over again about the feel of her lips on his.

When JT left later that day he hadn't asked for her number. She'd remained just beyond touching distance as guests mingled in the lodge, even when they'd gone en masse to the pebble beach to throw skimmers. Esmé had tried hard to avoid eye contact and on the occasions their eyes had met she'd kept her face passive, not unfriendly, not giving him any signals at all. When time had come for him to leave, Peter had hugged him effusively and Odette, the glowing new bride, had kissed him noisily on the cheek. As a soldier's wife she would get used to saying her goodbyes. Esmé had stood at the back of the group and bade him farewell with a nod and gentle wave before turning her back on him and walking back into the lodge. JT thought he'd never see her again.

When they did meet again 18 months later, JT found himself back in Canada. This time for his friend's funeral. Peter had been deployed on another UN mission, to another African country, where there was no peace to be kept. The news of his death had reached JT while training in Norway. It had taken a favour or two to be called in to get him flown to Greenland and then onto Banff.

The funeral was a formal military affair. JT had stood awkwardly with the civilians as he had no formal uniform with him. He had watched Esmé and her parents from behind. Her father sat straight-backed between his wife and daughter and appeared made of stone as they heaved and sobbed. Esmé sat with her sisters and parents at the other end of the front row. The rhythmical sobbing was interrupted with a quiet voice asking the same question over and over, 'Why?'

Esmé's hair was still short and JT found himself staring at the silver clasp of the string of pearls she was wearing. The silky white of the pearls sat in contrast to the black of her dress and the tanned brown of her slim neck. She was wearing matching earrings that hung from her lobes like opaque tear drops. The earrings jumped as Esmé recoiled from the sound of the rifle salute fired by the honour guard. The urge to put his arm around her, to somehow protect her from the noise was strong, but he knew it wasn't his place.

After the funeral the family and mourners retired to Esmé's parents' large house. It was warm for early May and little groups formed on the porch and by the boat deck. JT had offered his condolences to Esmé and it had taken her a second to recognise his bearded and snow burned face.

He'd found Peter's parents on the porch swing at the back of the house. They had met once before, at the wedding more than a year earlier, but Peter's father knew him. He shook JT's hand with a grip that belied his age and spoke of a life of hard physical work.

'I can't tell you how sorry I am,' he'd told them; it was true but felt woefully inadequate.

Another mourner came to pay their respects and JT took his leave. Accepting an offer of a cup of tea, he wandered down to the water's edge watching some male geese squabbling over a lone female.

Esmé appeared beside him. She stood close enough to smell her perfume. He imagined he could feel the warmth of her through the sleeve of his jacket. Neither of them spoke, she stared across the water to the far shore and JT followed her gaze honouring her silence.

JT had started to relax into the situation, stood there watching the light change the texture of the water, when she'd broken the spell with one word, 'Nine.'

'Nine?' he'd asked, not daring to look at her.

She stayed looking somewhere forward, her focus elsewhere, her mind in the past. 'Nine,' she repeated after a pause, 'nine skips.'

JT turned and looked at her beautiful eyes, reddened and puffy but with a blue iridescence undimmed by sadness.

'You made nine skips,' she'd told him.

There had been little time for them to spend together before he had to hitch a lift on an Canadian Air Force cargo plane and start his journey back to Norway. This time he left with her telephone number. The telephone number came with an email address that had been a lifeline between them when he was deployed and voice calls were impossible.

Once a month he'd written a letter, old fashioned ink on paper in his slightly scratchy handwriting. He'd practised using the Mont Blanc fountain pen his Godfather had given him until the ink splodges and scratches gave way to something legible, something personal.

In the end it took a job offer in London to entice her across the Atlantic and JT considered himself the luckiest man in England. Esmé was an art curator and JT had suggested her to a retiring family friend as a replacement in their gallery. JT never mentioned that his parents had been wealthy London socialites and as an only child he had been left a sizeable inheritance. She had known he was Army, and that he'd seen action, but it was when she'd moved to London and repeatedly pressed him that he'd admitted to her he was a member of the most famous and feared regiment in the world.

The day he'd been wounded was etched in his mind like no other. Not because of the shrapnel that embedded in his belly. It would have killed him had Taff not been on hand to stem the blood flow. Taff and Cooky had picked him up and carried him out of the rubble. It was a ticket home, and a retirement that Esmé had hoped for, but first a few weeks in hospital in Kandahar with sketchy reports from the hospital staff. They'd patched him up and sent him home. Not home to Hereford this time. Home to Esmé. Home to this very flat.

That woman and her child died that day. Two Royal Marines died that day. Five Afghan locals were seriously injured including two young kids, a brother and sister. The girl was blinded when blast material hit her in the face and her brother lost his arm. Her screaming was the first sound that breached the ringing in JT's ears after the blast. The image of her brother holding her in his one functioning arm, as the bloodied shreds of his missing limb hung by his side, was a clear image that harried him from that day on.

In the end it wasn't the injury that did it. It wasn't the scar. It was him. His decision to go back, to finish the job, was the last straw. She'd pleaded with him. Begged him. Begged him and then left him. Not the fault of the Taliban. Not the fault of the Army. No-one's fault but his. That self-inflicted injury was the hardest of all to bear.

#

A knock at the bathroom door dragged him out of his reminiscence and back from the precipice of self-pity, 'Yes?' he called.

'Phone boss, it's gone twice, thought it might be important,' said Cooky.

'Thanks, Cooky, be right out!' One arm into a sleeve of his Kimono, JT thought better of it and wrapped a towel around his waist.

Cooky waited for him silently outside the bathroom door. He held out a massive hand that JT considered made his phone look tiny. JT took the phone and nodded his thanks as he made his way to his bedroom. He closed the door and grabbed clean jeans and a t-shirt from their shelves, as he looked at the missed call screen. He recognised the Home guard house number, switching on the speaker phone function he pressed the dial key as he dressed.

After two rings a familiar voice answered, 'JT, thanks for calling back, thought maybe you had the guys out for a run.'

'We're suspended Paddy, just kicking back with a few beers and watching the football, you know the score.'

'Yeah, good one JT, meanwhile we've had them Thai ladies in and all had a pedicure!' he guffawed at his own joke before clearing his throat and continuing, 'Update on the Fanboy for you mucker.'

'Let's hear it.'

'The plods missed him.'

'Did the gate team go down instead?' JT asked, thinking he already knew the answer.

'No, like I said, confined to barracks, brass are looking to keep our heads down after...well you know.'

'Yes, I do know. This nonsense is getting silly. How long until they grow some bollocks and just tell the press to piss off and mind their own bloody business? Are the paps still hanging around?'

'No, they've got bored and left. Besides, some of the locals have taken to slashing the tyres of the media trucks and one of the reporters got a thick ear for asking questions down the pub.'

'Good to know the community still love us, even if the bleeding heart liberals and their human rights lawyers don't.'

'Amen to that.'

'What's the plan for the Fanboy?'

'Leave it until the plods do their thing. They've been struggling for officers apparently, I heard there's a few of them not so keen to be seen helping us out since the news reports.'

'Seriously? They believe that crap too?'

'They've got a new Chief Constable, some gay guy that loves the media apparently and they love him, always on the telly telling them how 'diverse' his force is. Sorry, strike that, he says they're not a force now, they're a 'service', like the Social Work service or some shit!' Paddy's voice conveyed a genuine concern about the situation. The Police had always looked out for the Regiment as they were an obvious target for terrorists from near and far.

JT considered this for a moment and thought about some of the good cops he'd met and worked with, from the uniform cops who called him to remove one of his team from a messy situation in a local pub, to DI Rory Maxwell from the Counter Terrorism Branch, a man he admired and called a friend. 'We'll sort it,' he told Paddy.

'Sort what?'

'The Fanboy. We need to come Home at some point, we left in a hurry to escape the press so travelled light. We'll come back up, sort out the Fanboy, and, if the brass don't mind, we'll get back to work.'

'Sounds like a plan to me mucker, not sure the brass will agree however.'

#

That night the team sat, on the floor, feasting on the goat curry Rambo had prepared. The ritual of sitting on the floor was partly a nod to Rambo and his Nepali heritage, but also as a memorial to the brave Afghan and Pakistani men they'd fought alongside and shared food with. During the meal JT updated them on the Fanboy situation. They listened without breaking from eating. That changed when he told them to pack, as tomorrow they were going Home.

Next morning the six men left Mayfair. Staggering their departures, they used different methods of public transport to reach the RV point. One slightly scruffy man walking in Mayfair wouldn't be noticed, but

6 together certainly would. Years of training taught these soldiers to blend in, but there's a limit.

Two were detailed to collect the 4x4s from the rear car park of a down at heel Travelodge. At exactly 1015 hrs, the two vehicles came to a stop as 4 men emerged from different directions and climbed in. The vehicles moved off into traffic and no-one paid them any attention, just as they liked it.

CHAPTER THREE

THE SPOT LIGHTS WERE bright and designed to dazzle approaching drivers. They were deliberately positioned low enough to obscure the guardhouse from view. A brick building with shuttered windows to the left of the main gate was easier for drivers to see. Anyone not acquainted with the base at Hereford would naturally assume that this building was the guardhouse. They would be wrong.

There were always two Military Police Officers positioned at the front of that small brick building. Their job was to protect the base and the 1000 personnel who called it Home. The MPs were well aware that they were never alone. Behind their little brick building stood a larger building that looked to all intents and purposes like a small warehouse. This was where the real defences lay. At all times two teams of six SAS soldiers were on duty and at the ready to repel an attack. These soldiers, the elite fighting force of the British Army, were in a constant state of readiness.

Tonight, the man in charge of these soldiers was Major Patrick 'Paddy' Kemp. Paddy had seen more action than most in his 25 years as an SAS soldier, but this role he took very seriously. Having spent time in Northern Ireland and been targeted by the IRA he knew the risks and threat were always real.

'Two vehicles approaching in convoy,' came the report over the radio.

'Known?' was the reply.

'Standby. Confirmed. Alpha36 and 37, appear 3 up and 3 up.'

Paddy was on his way to his desk when his phone rang.

'Evening Paddy, 36 and 37, almost Home, 2 mins out,' reported JT.

'Kettle's on, Lapsang Souchong on standby...and Tetley for the normal blokes.'

This exchange had happened so many times it was second nature to the two old friends and comrades. They had fought together. Won together. Lost together. Survived together.

'Good brew, thanks,' said JT 5 minutes later when he sat down opposite Paddy.

Paddy opened a manilla file and pushed it across the desk. 'That's the best screenshot from the CCTV. Plod say they don't know him, and the facial recognition guys at GCHQ came up blank too.'

'An unknown, huh? Looks young, what do you reckon, 18-19?'

'Sounds about right, mucker. He knows what he's doing. That "SAS Help" t-shirt and looking straight at the CCTV, guaranteed to get him noticed. Not too difficult to work out where the lads might go for a pint, and he's been in at least 3 of the local pubs.'

'Always alone, right?'

'Yep, same script each time, orders a glass of water and sits on his own watching all the customers.'

'Brass?'

'Still have us locked down,' said Paddy rolling his eyes.

'Anyone know we're home yet?'

'Not yet, just my team. What are you thinking?'

'I think it's time for us to have a chat with Mr T-shirt and send him back to whichever hospital he's escaped from.'

'You're going back out then?'

JT stood up and tapped his finger on the side of his nose then winked, 'We were never here Paddy.'

#

JT sat in the dark back seat of the Land Rover. It was parked under a tree that created a shadow from the security light. He had been sat still, in the same position for almost 90 minutes. A cold and drizzly evening meant there were just a few customers in The Coach. The time was 1855 hrs and if he was sticking to his previous pattern, Fanboy should be along soon.

'Double top required,' came the jovial Scottish voice of Joe in JT's earpiece.

'Double top required,' chimed in Posty.

JT responded with a double click response on the transmit button. He sat in silence watching the road for any signs of headlights.

'Pushbike on the bridle path, heading for the Coach,' said Cooky who was positioned in a barn half a mile away ready to cut off anyone trying to run away cross country.

'ID?' JT asked.

'Negative, too dark and wrong angle. Looks male, slim build, wearing a bike helmet...looks like...confirming he's wearing a backpack. It looks pretty bulky.'

'Roger that. Rambo?'

'He'll ride right underneath me boss, want me to rope him?' asked Rambo from his position in one of a pair of big oak trees that bordered the field behind the pub.

'Let him in Rambo, let's see what he's planning,' replied JT, 'Taff, once he reaches the end of the field, drive in and get your headlights on him, I want him ID'd.'

'Roger, 30 seconds out,' Taff responded.

A series of clicks on the transmit button told the team the bike rider had passed under Rambo. Taff rounded the corner slowly into the car park with full beams on. The lights dazzled the bike rider who covered his eyes with his arm, but not before JT confirmed this was their Fanboy. Taff reversed back into a space but kept his beams on which lit up the end of the car park.

The Fanboy dismounted and pushed his bike up against the fence just 6 feet from JT's vehicle. He took off his helmet and then his backpack from where he withdrew a padlock and chain. After locking the bike to the fence, he stood up and looked around.

JT watched him sniff the air like a wild animal, suddenly alert and nervous. Again, he reached into the backpack at his feet and JT felt himself stiffen. This time he stood up and JT could see he was holding a woollen hat which he pulled over his messy curly hair. JT watched him inhale a deep steadying breath, take one last look around and walk across the car park to the pub door.

JT said, 'Coming in...' but hesitated as the young man stopped and did a 360 sweep of the car park. He studied Taff's vehicle and watched as Taff spoke loudly pretending to have a conversation on his mobile phone. JT saw him lift his face slightly and sniff the air. Satisfied he couldn't be seen; JT observed him take another look around the car park and a short but deliberate pause over the 5 parked vehicles. This made JT think this guy had undergone some pretty basic counter surveillance training. He turned and opened the big old oak door to the pub and walked inside.

'Bullseye,' Posty confirmed ID and flicked off the flight from his dart to allow him to face the bar as he pretended to fiddle with it.

'Glass of water please ma'am,' the Fanboy said to the barmaid, who didn't look too impressed at the request.

'You're back then. Don't want to buy a drink, or maybe some food?' she asked him.

'Errm, no thank you ma'am, just some water, please.'

'You'll not be from round here then?' she asked him, not masking her suspicion, as she handed him the glass of tap water.

'No, I'm not. I'm just looking for someone.'

'Who might that be then? I knows most folks round here?'

'Actually, I'm not sure,' he said as he picked up his glass, then wandered over to a seat by the window.

Posty watched as the young man slipped out of his jacket and exposed his t-shirt with the words 'SAS HELP' written in marker pen across the chest. He went back to throwing darts and he and Joe made a show of it being a friendly game between friends.

Joe threw a double 11 and raised his arms aloft in triumph. 'You're not even worth playing, you're so rubbish!' His impression of a West Country accent was almost passable, as he jibed with Posty, 'surprised the boss even lets you drive a tractor!' he chuckled to himself.

'Cheeky bugger!' said Posty, giving his best toothless grin.

'Oi mate,' Joe addressed the Fanboy who was sitting nearby.

'Me?' he replied nervously.

'Yeah you. Any good with the old arrows?'

'I'm sorry, I don't know what you mean.'

'He's asking if you can play darts,' interjected Posty.

'Oh, no thank you,' he replied, trying not to make eye contact.

'Come on,' said Joe, 'my mate here is useless. I need a challenge!'

The Fanboy tried to ignore the two men and reached into his backpack. Joe tensed and had the darts held in a fist ready to strike. Posty gripped the back of a chair and lifted its feet just off the floor. They relaxed when the Fanboy brought out a book and placed it on the table.

'I think you've made a mistake,' Joe said, addressing the Fanboy.

'Pardon me?' he replied.

'Your t-shirt,' Joe pointed at the man's chest and took a step towards him.

The Fanboy sat bolt upright and looked suddenly frightened.

'It's spelled wrong, see,' Joe continued, 'it should be S.O.S for help. You know, like the Titanic and stuff. Save Our Sailors.'

'Souls,' replied the Fanboy, 'Save Our Souls.'

'Yeah, that as well,' said Joe taking another step forward, 'but you've got an A, instead of an O. Must be one of them cheap Chinese copies, you should get your money back mate!'

The pub door opened and Taff appeared, 'Right lads, if you want a lift back to the farm, I'm ready now,' he said, holding the door ajar with his foot.

'Oh, right, cheers boss,' said Posty, as he and Joe collected their jackets and left the darts on the bar as they left.

'G'night boys,' said the barmaid to their backs as they left.

#

Twenty minutes later the Fanboy walked out of the pub and over to his bike. He found the tyres were both flat and looked to the heavens muttering before unlocking the bike and pushing it toward the bridle path. He had no sooner gone beyond the light cast from the car park when Rambo dropped effortlessly from the tree in front of him landing in a crouched position. The Fanboy jumped and stood rigid. He didn't hear anyone approach from behind, as a cloth bag was placed over his head and a huge black hand covered his nose and mouth. He tried kicking out and struggling but was lifted off his feet and he felt his energy dissipate as he was starved of oxygen and lost consciousness.

CHAPTER FOUR

THE HOOD WAS STILL in place when he came to. Staying still, he realised his hands were bound behind him. He was sitting on a hard chair. It was cold, but dry, and he could tell he was inside a building. The smell of hay told him he was in some sort of farm building. The smell of hay was imprinted on him forever now. This last week he'd spent sleeping in an old barn while he tried to make contact.

The ache in his shoulders was gnawing and he tried to work out how long he'd been out of it. His body clock told him it was night and the lack of sound from outside supported his thesis. There were eyes watching him. Logic told him that would be the case, but more than that, he could feel them. Beyond the smell of the cloth covering his face, and the farm smells, there was something else. It was new, yet familiar. He unconsciously lifted his head a few centimetres to better sniff in the scent.

'Lapsang Souchong,' the voice startled him but held little menace, it was a statement of fact. 'Name?' The voice was steady, an English accent. 'Name?'

'Who are you?' he croaked, he had to clear his throat, 'who are you, and why have you done this to me?' He tried to sound confident and unafraid, but even he could hear the truth in his voice.

'Last time I'll ask. Name?'

'Ezekiel, Ezekiel Olufemi.'

'Well, Ezekiel -'

'My, my friends call me Easy,' he interrupted.

'Do they now? Well, "Easy", you have two minutes to answer my questions. If you answer truthfully, then you might just get to see those friends again. Understand?'

'Yes, yes I understand.'

'Where are you from?'

'I was born in Nigeria, but I live in London, since I was 5 years old.'

'Why were you in the pub tonight?'

'I was looking for you?'

'For me?'

'Yes, yes for you. Well, no, no not you. But maybe you, yes,' he spluttered.

'Explain.'

'I am looking for the SAS, that is you, yes?'

'Why would you be looking for the SAS?' asked the voice from behind.

'I, I need help.'

'Explain,' the voice had moved, coming close to his ear, making him lean away.

'Not just me, my family, my friends, everybody. We need the SAS!'

'You're not explaining yourself very well here Ezekiel Olufemi, and two minutes are nearly up.'

'Please, I can explain, they, they have my friend,' he said, almost in a whisper.

'Who has your friend?'

'The Bad Men,' Easy slumped in the chair and his head dipped, as if the saying of the words weighed heavy on him.

'What does that have to do with the SAS? It's the Police you need.'

'No, we've tried the Police but they do not help us. I think they are scared of the Bad Men. Please, you are the only ones who can help, they have my friend!' Easy sobbed beneath the hood.

The six men of the team looked at Easy, and at each other. Then they looked to JT. He was the Boss and would make the decision of how this would play out. It wasn't the first time they'd put the frighteners up a Fanboy and scared him off. They all instinctively knew that this was different. It was still a surprise to them when JT stepped forward drawing his combat knife.

Chapter Five

THE RELIEF OF BLOOD flowing back to his hands as his bonds were cut, was short lived as he tried to flex his fingers and the pain arrived. He shook out his hands and clenched and unclenched his fists. Eventually he felt he could control his hands again. He moved his hands to his neck and started slowly lifting the hood up and away from his face. He stopped before he uncovered his eyes. 'Am I permitted to take this off?' he asked.

By means of an answer the hood was ripped from his grasp and he was left blinking in the gloom. As he'd suspected he was within a barn and a wall of hay bales had been crudely constructed into a little room. He saw three men sitting on bales in front of him and instinctively knew there were more behind.

'Water?' asked a big man who offered him a tin cup. The man's voice was deep and friendly. His accent could be Cornish, like the lady in the library, he thought.

'Yes, yes please sir,' he took the cup and held it to his mouth, sipping gently and slowly, the way his Grandfather had taught him. The man with the brown hair and beard appeared to be the leader so Easy addressed him. 'You are the SAS, yes? I knew you would find me.'

'Ezekiel, do you understand who and what the SAS are?

'Yes, they are...you are, the best fighters in the world.'

'There's some Israeli and US soldiers who would argue with that!' said Taff with a guffaw.

'My Great Grandfather told me. He was in the Army, in the desert in Tunisia. He told me about the SAS, special men like gods of war he said. He called you invincible.'

'Look Ezekiel, how old are you?' asked JT.

'Sixteen sir,' he replied.

'Okay kid, here's how this works in the real world. The SAS are soldiers. Part of the British Army, and as such, are controlled by the Army to undertake military tasks only. The Police, and in your case, The Met, are responsible for civilian crimes. That's who you need to talk to,' JT spoke slowly and deliberately.

'I am not a stupid boy sir. I know what you say is true, but it does not work. The Bad Men took my friend from school. She is not the first girl they have taken. I know they took her to use her for sex, like a prostitute or a slave. The Police do nothing, they don't care. They say we are all like animals in our estate. The Bad Men treat us like animals but we are not.' Easy became increasingly indignant and as he began to raise his voice a large hand was placed on his shoulder. He composed himself before he went on, 'Perhaps I can show you some photos on my phone? Then you will know.' Posty handed him his rucksack and he fished out his phone, he fumbled anxiously at the buttons and then turned the screen to show a photo of an old lady, badly beaten with blood matted in her white hair.

'Who is that?' asked JT.

'Her name is Mrs Roberts.'

'What happened to her?'

'She tried to stop the Bad Men taking a girl from the grassy area beside the little houses where the old people live. They beat her to the ground. Some people went to help her, but the Bad Men said they would kill anyone who helped her, or called the Police, or even an Ambulance. Mrs Roberts lay there for nearly two hours until the Bad Men left. She crawled to her house. It was horrible.'

'You did nothing to help?'

'Please understand sir, we have all been beaten and a couple of the men disappeared after they tried to stop them before. The Bad Men make everyone too afraid.'

JT contemplated what he was being told. He had interrogated many combatants and civilians and felt he had a good grasp of when he was being lied to. So far, nothing this kid said made JT doubt him. The embarrassment or even shame of not helping the old lady was written all over the kid's face. JT had felt that shame. He'd seen that face in the mirror. 'What happened to the old lady and how did you get the photo?'

'I was with my friend Danny at his Grandmother's house when it happened. We watched and I called the Police... from his Grandmother's phone...' Easy looked down at his shoes.

'They found out?' JT softened his tone as he could see Easy was hurting.

'Yes, I did not give them my name but the Police went to Danny's Grandmother's door. It was obvious. The next day there was a fire and Danny's Grandmother was hurt. She lives in the hospital now.'

'A fire?' JT knew what was coming but asked the question. It occurred to him and not for the first time that gangs and criminals the world over must all use the same handbook.

'The Bad Men came. They pushed an old sofa against the door and made a fire. She was meant to die.'

'Why didn't she?' The question felt ugly and dispassionate in his mouth, but JT asked it in a matter of fact way. He felt Easy's judgement, the team had all seen and heard this before.

'You think she should have died...Sir?' Easy asked incredulously, but remembering his place and his manners he kept his emotions in check as best he could.

'If these Bad Guys, are as bad as you say, and wanted her dead, they'd have done it properly, no?'

'The Fire Brigade came quickly. They told Danny they were fitting fire alarms in the houses across the park and saw the black smoke. Danny's Grandmother was lucky.'

JT looked at Taff who simply raised an eyebrow and gave the slightest shrug. 'Back up a bit,' JT told Easy, 'the photo of Mrs Roberts, who took it?'

'I did sir, I waited until Mrs Roberts was back in her home, then I climbed over the back walls and her window was open so I went in and tried to help her. I have a first aid badge from when I was in the Scouts.'

'How is she now?'

'Terrified, this happened 2 weeks ago. She went to the hospital a couple of days later and said she had fallen down stairs or something.'

JT thought for a moment then said, 'Tell me about this missing girl.'

'Her name was,' he took a breath, 'no, her name is Dionne. We went to the same school but she's the year above me, she is a good girl,' he emphasised the *good*.

'Girlfriend?'

'No, we were friends in school. I would walk home with her sometimes. She played netball after school on Thursdays and I had IT club.'

'Go on.'

'Last Thursday she wasn't at netball, the other girls said she hadn't been into school for two days. I went to her house and her mother said she had gone missing. She said she had told the Police but they said she was 18 so could do as she pleased. They said she had to wait 48 hours before they'd take a report. I knew there was something wrong. I went and checked the CCTV from school and she definitely arrived on the Tuesday morning but I couldn't see her leaving at the end of the day. I asked one of her friends and she said she had seen her go out at lunchtime and the moped guys were there.'

'Moped guys?'

'They are some punks who sell drugs and rob people and stuff. There's always a gang of them. They hang around trying to look tough. They carry knives and hammers and steal peoples bags. I heard they robbed a jewellers shop and they all wear fancy watches and stuff. Everyone is scared of them.'

'Dionne knew these guys?'

'Everyone knows them, they come from the estate. They call themselves 'Crew B' They think they're gangsters because they're tight with the Bad Men.'

'They're part of the same gang?'

'I don't know, they're young, like 18 or 19 and the Bad Men are older. I think maybe the Bad Men use them to run errands and sell drugs.'

'You think they have something to do with the girl going missing?'

'I'm sure of it. It's not the first time. A girl called Des'ree started to hang out with them a few months ago. They were giving her drugs and stuff but then she disappeared. Just vanished. She was from the Social

Services Home up by the park. It's a place for 16 year olds kicked out by their parents. They go missing from there all the time.'

'Who else knows you're here Easy?'

'My Aunty, that's who I live with. She thinks I'm at Scout Camp. Danny knows where I am. He would have come too, but he's staying to guard his Grandmother.'

'Where have you been staying while here in Hereford?'

'In an old barn near the river. It has some hay and I brought my sleeping bag.'

'Food?'

'I have tins of peaches and sardines. I had some bread for the first days too.'

'Hungry?'

'Yes, yes sir I am ravenous.'

'Well, let's see if we can do something about that,' JT held out a hand to Easy and helped him out of his chair.

CHAPTER SIX

SEVEN PIPING HOT BOWLS of stew were served up in the old farm house. The building was used for exercises and had seen more replacement doors than anyone dared guess. Tonight, it was home to the six soldiers and a kid they'd known for less than 4 hours.

JT had been told in no uncertain terms he and his men were to remain on leave until the enquiry by SIB was completed in Afghanistan. The Brass were being pushed about by Civil Servants at the Home Office and a queue of Human Rights lawyers were doing their level best to embarrass the Government. The shit always rolled down hill. At the bottom of the hill sat JT and his men. All good, brave, honest soldiers. Currently they were considered guilty without a trial and without being allowed to defend themselves.

When pushed on timescales, the official message from the Brass was – as long as it takes. The soldiers were to remain on paid leave and off base until summoned. Under no circumstances were they to talk to the press or seek legal assistance other than that provided by The Regiment. The Brass also made it very clear that the men should be ready to deploy should an emergency arise. The irony of being superfluous unless the shit hit the fan was not wasted on them.

It was this state of limbo that saw the men contemplating the unthinkable. They had all been involved in sorting out bar room bullies, the abusive husbands of barmaids and the like. This they all knew would be another level.

#

Taff was first to speak as the dishes were rinsed under the outside tap, 'What are you thinking here Boss? This is some serious shit by the sounds of it.'

JT looked at his old friend, 'I know, but it doesn't seem right walking away.'

'I know the kid needs help, and the bastards need stringing up for what they did to those old girls, but we'd be on our own, no authority and the press would have a field day. We'd get court-martialed for sure, and not this made up crap from Helmand. They'd make sure we went down.'

'Can't argue with any of that Taff,' JT cupped his hands under the tap and splashed the cold water in his face. He was stalling, trying to work through the scenario and find a workable plan. After a few seconds of silence he continued, 'It's not my decision Taff. I can't order anyone to get involved, I'm not even sure I want to be involved myself. We'll put it to a vote. Let's sleep on it, then we'll drive the kid back to London. We can have a bit of a recce and then decide. Agreed?'

'Whatever you say Boss, that's good enough for me.'

CHAPTER SEVEN

SHIFTING HIS POSITION AWAY from facing the window, Easy turned to face Joe. Joe was looking over the shoulder of the bigger man who rode shotgun. Easy had noticed that all three of the men were constantly watching the road in front and the other vehicles around them. They seemed to be constantly alert and yet relaxed. Their eyes, he realised, were taking in everything around them but they rarely moved their heads. To an outsider they would look like bored travellers. His gaze fell on Joe's left hand. The knuckles of the hand looked like a boxer's, swollen hard lumps of bone that looked out of place on otherwise average sized hands. Easy was aware that at 5 foot 11, he was a couple of inches taller than Joe. Somehow Joe seemed to take up much more of the back seat than he himself did. Joe didn't look like the all action hero type that sprung to mind when he thought of SAS.

Come to think of it, none of the men did. The one they called Taff more than filled the passenger seat. He was a big man and looked like someone who had played rugby to a decent level. It was difficult to say how old the man was. His face was wrinkled in places but suntanned and healthy looking. Big as he was, he didn't look solid and muscled like one of the gym monsters who hung around the estate where he lived. Easy made sure that whenever possible he avoided those *silverback 'roid monsters* as he and Danny called them. No, he thought, Taff was like a friendly looking giant, someone who would enjoy a few beers after trudging round the rugby pitch. It was the eyes that told Easy the truth. Taff had looked him in the eye for a few seconds at most, that was enough. There was a menace in there, a menace that had shaken Easy. The big man might look affable enough to the unaware, but there was a darkness within that Easy did not want to disturb.

The driver was the quiet one. Easy hadn't heard him speak at all. He was obviously foreign but from where was unclear. Certainly, somewhere in Asia, but too soft featured to be Chinese. He didn't have the moon shaped face of the Kwon family. The Kwons were Korean and had joked with him that they all looked the same in family photographs. The Kwons were good people with open and friendly faces. The driver had a similar open face, he looked as though he had surveyed Easy without judgement, just registered his features to commit to memory but somehow in a disinterested way.

The three men in the car hadn't spoken since they set off more than an hour ago, a companionable silence which Easy found unnerving but also very interesting. His mind wandered to imagine these men holed up in a bunker for days on end standing guard and using the telepathy of a close knit team to say all that needed said.

The discomfort in Easy's belly was growing and he realised he would not make it back to London, especially as they seemed to be travelling at exactly 70mph on the motorway. Some lorries were going slower but every other car on the road was going faster. The 4x4 was an older type and pretty basic and it sounded as if it didn't want to go any faster. Eventually he mustered the courage to speak up, 'Please, I will need to pee. Please.' No-one answered him but he caught the eye of the driver in the rear view mirror for a split second. He might have doubted that he had said anything out loud otherwise and thought better of saying anything else.

A sign for motorway services in 2 miles gave him hope but when they drove straight past his heart sank. He knew they'd heard him, why wouldn't they stop for him? Another minute passed and as Easy braced himself to speak again he heard the driver put on his indicator. Looking over the back of the driver's seat Easy saw the other vehicle in front also had its indicator on. Telepathy he thought.

The two cars drove up the off ramp and turned left along an A road. They drove past a big lay-by holding a couple of lorries whose drivers stood outside a burger van. Another minute, that seemed more like ten, and they turned left into a small narrow road into a wooded area. The sign said something about fishing ponds but Easy was too busy focusing solely on his bladder to pay much attention. The vehicles stopped in a cool shady area of tall trees and thick bushes. The four passengers sat still saying nothing.

Taff turned to Easy and looked slightly bemused as he said, 'Go.'

Easy fumbled with the door handle and half ran, half hopped, into the bushes as he wrestled with his zip. The pleasure of release was immense. Easy had never taken drugs but he imagined this euphoria is what people sought. If only they knew he thought. He looked up to the sky and breathed a satisfied, 'ahhhhh.'

'Don't go pissing on your shoes now,' the voice came from so close to him Easy jumped and was lucky not to piss on his shoes.

'What...I mean how...how did you...?' He knew where the voice came from and he thought he should almost have been able to touch them, but he could see nothing but leaves.

'Steady now, just finish your business...and let me finish mine,' said the voice from the bush. The noise of a stream of urine hitting the soil was unmistakable.

Easy stood staring ahead and tried to work out how on earth some-one had managed to get into the bush that close to him and he not know. He was definitely first out of either car, he thought to himself. He pictured the scene as he climbed out and hot footed it into the bushes. Dismissing actual invisibility, he thought about how he'd read about these super-humans. The men he had met looked and sounded like ordinary men. Maybe that was one of their superpowers too.

As Easy approached the vehicles, he noticed his seat was taken by one of the other men. JT stood beside the front vehicle and motioned him to get in the rear of that one instead.

Climbing in Easy felt naked without his backpack which was still in the other car. 'I just need to...' JT closed the door on him before he could finish the sentence.

Joe watched from the rear vehicle. He got a nod, from JT as his boss walked around the rear of the car and climbed in the front passenger seat. After the two vehicles re-joined the motorway, Joe reached back and picked up the backpack. He knew what was in there as he'd been through it the night before. As he pulled out the iPad and iPhone, he looked them over. Both had protective covers and he noted the precision with which the screen protectors had been applied. He'd had barely 20 minutes with them last night and was surprised by the level of security. Joe had not been able to overcome the log on for either device which intrigued him almost as much as it irked him. The kit Joe had used was supplied by the Regimental boffins and had proven effective in getting them into the phones and laptops of countless War Lords and more recently Taliban commanders. Why would any kid have high level security software on his devices?

Joe's instincts had instantly told him there was something not right with this kid. Instinct had kept Joe alive this long despite working in some of the scariest places imaginable. After transferring from the Regiments Signals Unit into his Sabre Squadron, Joe has been on active duty in all 6 of the inhabited continents. His team was part of the Air Troop in A Squadron. As an Air Troop, the team had parachuted into enemy territory countless times. Joe loved to jump and he never lost that feeling of excitement in his gut when he left an aircraft. Helmand had been different. Choppered to within a few miles of a target then yomping cross country trying to avoid Taliban patrols. He'd survived. He'd killed. He'd avoided boobytraps and IEDs. He'd listened to his gut. He survived by listening to his gut, and right now, his gut was talking to him.

Joe switched on the encryption service on his own phone and di-alled a number he knew by heart. On the second ring a female voice said, 'What do you have for me Joe?'.

'I got an iPad; 5th Gen and an iPhone 13,' Joe replied.

'Status?' the voice asked.

'Status? You cheeky cow!' Joe laughed. 'Sandra, you know full well I'd only come to you if- '

'That's Captain Cow to you, Trooper!' Sandra cut him off before she joined Joe in his laughter.

'I beg your pardon... Ma'am,' sniggered Joe.

'We'll discuss a suitable punishment for your insubordination when I see you next.'

'Okay, okay Sis, just don't tell Mum, ok?' He laughed again. Joe was immensely proud of his big Sister Sandra, not just one of the first ever women to join the Regiment, she was also the smartest person he knew. Her computing skills had been spotted when she joined the Navy and she'd been head-hunted by the Special Reconnaissance

Regiment. Her tech skills surpassed his own and Joe often remarked he was used to being the smartest guy in the room – until Sandra came in.

'This would be easier if you brought them to me,' Sandra told him getting back to business.

'I know, no time, and we're rolling,' said Joe.

'Rolling?' Sandra had lowered her voice instinctively despite being alone in her office, 'You guys are still on gardening leave, what do you mean rolling?'

'We're just giving a Fanboy a lift home to East London. The Boss just wants to check out his story, but there's something a bit off with the kid,' he informed her.

'Mental Health? Why not just give him to the Plods?'

'They were too busy to track him down apparently, so we're checking him out. Gives us something to do while we're grounded, I guess.'

'Ok, my advice would be to walk him into a Plod station and go somewhere nice for a holiday. Back up home Joe, to see Mum maybe?'

'We'll see what happens when we drop him off.'

'Ok, so what's off with this kid?'

'He's 16, lives with his Nigerian Aunty on some estate in East London, Barking. He came looking for us saying some 'bad men' had taken his friend and tried to kill some old lady by setting her house on fire.'

'That's all Plod business Joe, why is JT getting you involved?'

'The kid says the Plod won't help. He thinks they're scared of them. Maybe they're getting paid to turn a blind eye, who knows. JT hasn't said we're getting involved, we're just going to see if this kid is full of it. You know about the t-shirt in the pub yeah?'

'Yes, ballsy stuff, I'll give him that. You sure he's not missing from some institution somewhere?'

'He doesn't appear on any systems at all, no Police records or anything,' Joe confirmed.

'Clean skin?' Sandra used the term for a person without a criminal record and unknown to authorities. They both knew that such people were used by Crime Gangs and Terrorists alike to do their bidding.

'That's what my gut is asking me,' said Joe. 'There's no way a standard Nigerian school kid can afford a new iPad and iPhone, much less some Gucci level security.'

'You definitely can't bring it to me?' Sandra asked him.

'Don't think so.'

'Ok, then if your 'can opener' can't force it,' said Sandra referring to the security decoding gizmo she'd helped develop for front line use, 'you'll just have to go route 1.'

'Route 1?' asked Joe, unsure what she meant.

'*Persuade* him to open it for you.'

Joe considered this for a moment then replied, 'I'll ask the Boss, and if he says go, I'll get my persuasion hat on!' He chuckled and said goodbye to Sandra promising to keep her updated if possible.

CHAPTER EIGHT

'YES, YES, I KNOW, I have to cook for myself Carol,' Stacey rolled her eyes and blew on a hot chip before pushing it into her mouth. She held her phone away from her ear and looked around at the other customers in the burger shop.

'I can come help you with shopping, and to plan your budget Stace. We will be there to support your tenancy until you're properly settled in. You know the local Social Workers are available 24 hours if we're not around.'

'Yeah, like I said, I'm 16 now and can look after myself. I don't need your help so stop phoning me.'

'Stacey, I helped lots of girls move on from care and I know it's daunting...'

Stacey was no longer listening as she watched the mopeds ride into the car park. The guys on the mopeds were laughing as they parked in front of the window where Stacey was sitting. They spotted her and gave her the sort of look that made her blush slightly. They gestured to her to come outside but she held up her tray of food to show them and shook her head.

One of the guys came into the takeaway, 'Alright sweet stuff?' he said and smiled at her. Stacey pretended not to be paying attention but watched the reflection in the window as the guy walked up to the counter and lifted a can of coke out of the fridge. She watched him open the can as he turned and walked out without paying for it. He winked at her as he left.

Stacey turned to look at the owner of the take away. He had definitely seen the guy take the Coke but hadn't said a word. Whoever the moped guy was, he was definitely somebody pretty cool, she thought. He was quite good looking and the big sparkly ear-ring he wore must have cost a packet.

Leaving her half-finished meal, she picked up her phone and heard Carol still speaking. 'I told you; I don't need you no more, stop calling me and don't come to my flat neither!' She hung up and slid the phone into her back pocket. Her jeans were tight and she was glad she was small enough to still fit into children's sizes. She checked her image in the window reflection. Her false eyelashes made her look older, she thought but her flat chest meant people thought she was 13 or 14. She took a deep breath and prepared to try to walk out in her new heels. They'd been cheap and she loved the way they made her taller, but her feet were already cut and blistered. Determined not to wince at the pain, she walked slowly but mostly steadily out onto the pavement. It wasn't far to the bus stop and thankfully it was one with a bench seat. She started walking that way without paying attention to the moped guys.

A few steps later she was excited to hear a moped coming up slowly behind her. She looked back and saw the guy from the takeaway smiling at her. He wasn't wearing a helmet but he had his hood up. She smiled back but then stumbled as her heel caught a crack in the pavement. Managing to stay on her feet she felt the rush of blood redden her neck and face.

'Steady now!' shouted the boy on the moped.

Stacey stopped and turned her face away from him wishing the ground would open up and swallow her.

'Hey sweet stuff, you need a ride?' he asked, stopping beside her.

'No ta,' she said, still looking away from him.

'Hey, what's your name?' he asked.

'Stacey.'

'Hey Stacey, I'm Felix. You go school here?'

'I'm not in school, I'm 16,' she said, turning round to face him, 'Are you in school?'

'Nah, not me. I've not seen you round here. You new?'

'Yeah, I just got me a flat up Gascoigne.'

'Nice, me an' my crew are from Gascoigne. You should come hang out.'

'With a bunch of boys? No thanks!' she said, trying to sound more confident than she felt.

'Oh, you a lezza, prefer the ladies huh?' Felix laughed as he said it.

'No! That's disgusting, I like men, not boys.'

'Oh yeah, you think maybe I'm man enough for you.'

'Maybe. Do you think you're man enough?' she said, cocking her head.

He laughed and said, 'Who you live wiv, at your flat?'

'It's my own place.'

'You got your own place at 16, how come?'

'I was in foster care. Family don't want me no more so the council had to give me somewhere.'

'Cool,' he said, looking her up and down. 'Listen, me and some of Crew B are having a bit of a party tonight, you wanna come?'

'Crew B?' she asked, trying not to sound too keen.

'Me and my boys. There be some girls there too. None sweet as you mind,' he grinned at her, 'so what d'ya say?'

'Sure, but I have to go home to change first.'

'Gimme your number and I'll come get you about 9 yeah?' He typed her number into his phone as she dictated it. He didn't offer her his.

The bus rounded the bend and Stacey hobbled in the direction of the bus stop. She laughed as Felix rode his moped zig zagging in front of the bus to slow it down until she reached the stop. She waved to him as he rode off and boarded the bus unable to contain her smile.

At 8.30 Stacey sat folding a sheet of loo roll and using the wad and some Sellotape as a makeshift plaster for her red raw heel. She slipped on her trainers, and wished they didn't have the glittery hearts on the sides. Her make-up was thick as she tried to cover her spots and she wished that she'd taken the iron Carol the housing lady had offered. Her dress was made of a stretchy fabric but the top was strapless and she had to wear her denim jacket to cover up her lack of boobs. Her phone buzzed and she let out a little shriek as she read the text message; "outside".

Grabbing her keys, she stuffed her lipstick and blusher into her jacket pockets. This is the grown up life I've been waiting for, she told herself as she ran down the stairs, her sore feet a distant memory.

Felix wasn't on his moped, instead he was standing beside a shiny black car with blacked out windows. He smiled at her and said, 'Looking good sweet stuff.'

'Is this your car?' she asked, wide eyed.

'Nah, it's a friend of mine's. She wants to meet you,' he said, indicating the rear door.

'To meet me?' asked Stacey bemused.

'I told her about you,' said Felix, maintaining his smile, 'told her you're a sweet one.'

He opened the door and ushered Stacey inside. As she sat down, she found herself looking at a glamorous woman with black hair and deep brown eyes. Stacey could see she was beautiful, her makeup perfect and her clothes looked like something from a magazine.

'You must be Stacey,' said the woman giving her an appraising look. There was no friendliness in her voice.

'Yeah, I'm Stacey. Who are you?'

The woman ignored her question and asked another of her own, 'Felix tells me you live here alone?'

'Yeah, that's right, it's my own tenancy. Where is Felix?' she asked, trying to locate him through the darkened windows.

The woman answered the question with a question, 'Where is your family?'

'I don't have a family; I haven't spoken to my Mum for years. Why?' asked Stacey as she felt with her fingers for the door handle. It moved but the door didn't open.

Stacey felt a sting in her leg and saw the woman retract her hand holding a syringe. Panicking she grabbed again at the door handle pulling hard at it but the door didn't budge.

She saw her hand fall from the door handle and realised she wasn't controlling it. Turning her head as she slumped in the seat, she saw Felix's face at the car window accepting a pile of cash from the lady. He smiled at her and gave a little salute. Then everything went black.

CHAPTER NINE

AT THE SAME TIME as the 4x4s were travelling in tandem south east toward London, another little convoy was preparing to leave. The ostentatious display of two Bentley Continentals, one black, the other white, was incongruous amongst the scruffy facades of the high street shops. People crossed the road rather than get too close as they shuffled along with their blue plastic shopping bags. The cheap vegetables from the market stalls that filled the pedestrian precinct were like everything else in Barking, ugly and past their best. Everyone knew that you shouldn't walk too close to one of the Kosanians' cars.

A menacingly big man wearing a t-shirt stretched tight over his muscular frame stood between the two vehicles, smoking. A mother and child walked out of the launderette and stopped as she searched in her bag for her ringing mobile phone. The ringtone was Bill Withers ``Lovely Day' and got louder as she retrieved it. Her little boy wearing a cheap replica Spurs football top, stood staring at the beautiful cars. His mother had let go of his hand and was talking animatedly and giggling. She had been too preoccupied to notice the cars. That was her mistake. The sight of the gleaming cars was too much for the 4 year old boy. He wandered innocently toward the closest car, the highly polished black paint acted like a mirror and the boy reached out and high fived his reflection. His giggle alerted the big man and his sudden movement caught the attention of his mother.

She dropped her phone as she ran forward screaming 'Ryan. No!'. Ryan was turning toward his mother when his body was twisted violently backwards as the massively muscular security man grabbed his little hand. An ear-piercing shriek and howl stopped the other pedestrians in their tracks but they quickly looked away. No-one dared look. The mother ran to grab up her son who lay sobbing on the ground. The Kosanian security man growled as he struck her open handed across the face as she reached down for her son. She was knocked to the ground and instinctively wrapped herself around her son to protect him. A big tattooed hand grabbed a fistful of her hair and she was dragged back to the launderette doorway. The woman and child were temporarily saved by the Kosanian leader's appearance as his entourage walked out of the next-door bookmakers shop. The security man jumped and ran to the first car to open the door for his boss.

His boss was Viktor Liriazi and he wore a black suit and black open-necked shirt. His dark sunglasses matched his black hair and neatly trimmed black beard. This was something of a uniform for him as he was never seen in public wearing anything else. Two big men got into the front of the black car once their boss was safely seated in the rear. Four men got into the white car and the engines started in unison. Before they pulled away, the boss man looked at the woman and child where they were huddled in the doorway and smiled. Then the cars were gone. The big, angry security man was not.

The young woman got to her feet and put herself between the man and her son. She backed away through the propped open launderette door. He followed her in. An elderly Chinese woman stood folding her washing at a table and quickly tried to pile it into the blue Ikea bag as she saw the look on the man's face. She couldn't see the face of the young woman but could see her shaking. The man pointed at the old lady then turned his hand and used his thumb to point at the door. She didn't need to be told twice and grabbed up her bag and the loose washing as quickly as she could. As she passed the man, she saw he was sweating and could almost feel the excitement emanating from him. She consciously looked at the floor and muttered 'I'm sorry' as she left. It was said in an attempt to mollify him but her heart was saying it to the poor young woman and child.

The man kicked the door closed and turned the sign from *OPEN* to *CLOSED*.

'He, he didn't mean any harm, please, please don't hurt him!' she pleaded as the man walked slowly toward her. She looked around desperately but already knew she was cornered. There was no escape. 'Please, I have money, you can have it,' she pulled a handful of coins and a ten pound note from her pocket and held it out toward the man, he batted it away and grinned at her.

'No money', he growled at her, 'you pay.' He close enough to her that his aftershave overpowered the laundry detergent smell. He got closer still and she saw several gold teeth among an otherwise dirty looking mouth. His breath was rank from stale cigarette smoke. She looked down and away from him and at her terrified son who had wet himself. His little trousers were soaked and a yellow puddle was forming where he stood wide eyed and shaking.

The man laughed a deep menacing laugh as he grabbed Ryan's little hand with his right hand. His left hand he used to grab a fistful of the mother's hair. 'Knees!' he barked at her as he pushed her head downward. She fell to her knees and tried to look at her son, but the man used her hair to force her to look up at him. 'Suck,' he told her, his face amused and his body shaking slightly as he felt all powerful.

'No, no, you can't...' she said incredulously, her shocked brain trying to make sense of what was happening. She tried to look out the open door, desperately seeking help.

He laughed out loud when he saw her pleading look toward the door. 'No-one comes to save you. Now suck!' He pushed her face into his groin which was swollen with his excitement.

'No, no I won't. I won't!' she shouted at him in defiance.

He squeezed Ryan's hand in his and the child screamed out in pain.

'Stop it, please don't hurt him!' she cried out feeling the agony of her son.

'You suck now, or I have fun with kid.'

Tears ran down her face as he let go of her hair and undid his zip pulling out his erect penis and snarled at her. 'Now suck, you or the fucking boy.'

'Look away Ryan, look out the window' she croaked barely forming words.

'No, he watches!' growled the man. 'Now. Suck good and I don't break your boy.'

She knew there was no choice, defeated, she closed her eyes and opened her mouth. She had no idea how long it lasted before he was finished, she gagged and spat his cum onto the floor wiping her mouth with the back of her hand. Looking her son in the eyes she saw his eyes were blank. His little face was ashen white and he rocked slowly moving his weight from foot to foot.

The sound of a zip being pulled up made her look up at the man. The satisfied look on his face made her feel wretched but that feeling was made a thousand times worse as she realised that he had filmed her on his mobile phone.

'We can go now?' she managed to ask.

The man walked toward the door and unlocked it without speaking. He walked out and didn't look back.

Reaching for her son, she pulled him, trembling, to her and held him tight against her. He stood silent and unresponsive. Eventually she got to her feet and looked down at her beloved son. He lifted his little hand to her and showed her his deformed and broken fingers that had been crushed. Her animalistic cry stopped people in the street outside. No-one came to help. No-one dared get involved.

Bill Withers' soulful voice caused her to jump as her phone began to ring. There would be no more *Lovely Days*. There and then she vowed, somehow, someday, she would kill this man.

CHAPTER TEN

IN THE SECOND 4X4 Joe sat upright, 'Here we go.' He lifted the iPhone which had just buzzed an alert. 'What the fuck?' he said as he looked closer at the thumbnail preview of a video. That it was porn didn't surprise him, the kid is 16 after all, he thought to himself. What bothered Joe was the face of a young child watching the sex act. Some skinny young woman giving a bloke a blow job was one thing. A kid watching was just plain sick. 'Seems our kid Easy is maybe a bit of a paedo. Time to have a chat with our Fanboy.'

The 4x4s turned off the motorway at the next exit and drove until they reached an old church which was being renovated. The site was empty as the workmen had obviously finished for the day. After a sweep of the areas for CCTV cameras, the vehicles parked at the rear of a shipping container and portacabin.

Easy had sat watching what was going on and assumed this was a toilet stop but soon realised his mistake as his door was opened and Taff dragged him unceremoniously from the vehicle. He struggled to stay on his feet as the big man half dragged, half marched him into the vestry at the rear of the old church. He was pushed down to sit on the floor with his back against a broken sink. Sitting up as straight as he could, he watched them nervously. The space was eerily blue as tarpaulins covered the gaps where the windows had been. It smelled of damp and disturbed earth. Easy's mind started to wander and he imagined his body being thrown into the crypt, or worse buried alive. Still, he didn't speak, he didn't want them to know he was scared. He knew it would be written over his face but he wouldn't give them the satisfaction of begging, or so he hoped.

JT came into the vestry and looked around before opening the creaky old oak door that led into the chapel proper. He gestured with a head movement and Easy was lifted to his feet and pushed through the door. Inside he saw two pews sat facing each other. Joe was sitting on one with Easy's backpack at his feet and his phone and iPad in his hands. Easy was shoved onto the pew opposite and he was aware that Taff took up position and stood behind him.

After what felt to Easy, like an eternity, JT spoke, 'Time for confession,' was all he said. His voice was calm and measured as it had been the night before in the barn. This time though he walked back and forward behind the pew where Joe was sat. Joe said nothing, he just stared at Easy in a way that he knew was designed to unnerve him – and it was working.

Easy watched him pace slowly back and forward and waited for him to say something else. Nothing more was said and Easy felt the silence start to weigh on him. After a minute or so the silence became physical. It sat on his shoulders, in his lap, he felt it press. Another minute passed and his head became heavier, he felt the effort increase just to keep his head up. It was easier to look down and avoid looking at the staring Joe. The man didn't seem to blink. He just sat, staring. Easy thought Joe seemed to be growing bigger, or maybe he was shrinking? The air pressure was building and trying to force the air from his lungs. Trying to force him to speak. A darkness seemed to be pushing at him, it crept in from all around him and the edges of his vision started to disappear.

The hand placed on his shoulder seemed to explode, such was the fright it caused him. The jump caused an involuntary question from his lips, 'What do you want?' he croaked. His throat had been so constricted his voice was broken and raspy. 'What do you want from me?' He managed at the second attempt.

'Truth,' replied JT. He had stopped immediately behind Joe and Easy found his brain fighting over which threat to focus on, the man speaking to him, or the man staring at him as if he wanted to kill him.

'I told you the truth,' he said, still unsure who to address.

'Did you now?' replied JT, 'We're not here to be fucked about. One lie and we leave you here. Understood?'

Easy nodded.

'My friend here will ask you some questions,' continued JT, 'You will answer all of them. Hesitation will be taken as a lie. Understand?'

Another nod.

'First though, your name and date of birth.'

Easy looked JT in the eye as he replied, 'Ezekiel Washington Olufemi, I was born on 4th July 2005 in St Nicholas Hospital, Lagos.'

JT walked out of the room without saying anything else. As the big oak door to the vestry closed Easy saw him lift a mobile phone to his ear.

'Look at me,' said Joe, his voice low and with more than a hint of malice.

Easy looked at him and tried to focus on his forehead, then his chin but the eyes demanded his attention. Once the eyes were locked, Easy felt them burning him and he blinked hard. He lifted a hand to wipe his face and realised he was shaking.

'Passwords.'

'What?' asked Easy, he had heard the word but his frightened brain was in lizard mode, ready for flight or fight and was not computing properly.

'Last chance. Passwords,' said Joe glancing at the iPad and Phone in his hands.

Easy got the message loud and clear and started a stream of letters and numbers, 'S,Z,D,3,P,9,W,8,5....' after 24 characters he stopped and looked at Joe.

'Again,' replied Joe, his stare never wavering.

'S,Z,D,3...' Easy continued, all 24 characters. Easy watched Joe sit motionless, he didn't move a muscle and certainly made no attempt to take notes.

'Again,' Joe said.

'What...?' Easy's response was met by the hand on his shoulder. It didn't explode like the first time but it contained the message succinctly.

'S,Z,D,3,P...' 24 characters and still no movement.

A moment passed before Joe finally moved. His staring eyes finally shifted to the gadgets in his hands. Easy closed his eyes and gently rubbed at his face with his hands. His alert state was exhausting and had just come off the boil when a shout startled him back onto full alert.

'Lying bastard,' shouted Joe and he sprung from the pew toward Easy.

'No, I'm not lying!' he yelled as he ducked and covered his head with his arms.

'Wrong fucking password,' came the voice. It was said quietly but uttered from a mouth so close to his left ear it propelled him along the pew.

Easy looked through squinting eyes trying to judge where the inevitable blow would come from and saw Joe's hand containing the iPhone. 'iPad' he squealed, 'it's the iPad password!'

Joe stood over him and he had a slightly amused, quizzical look on his face. 'You have a different password for your phone?' he asked.

'Yes, of course,' Easy replied.

'Let's have it then.'

Easy uncurled himself and sat upright, he took a breath and started rhythmically, 'Asterisk,W,6,7,X,U...' 24 characters. Joe looked at him impassively and Easy took the hint without prompting he began again, 'Asterisk,W,6,7,X...'. He waited a moment before he asked, 'Again?'

Joe didn't respond and instead started typing on the iPhone screen. Easy watched in amazement as he realised that Joe had correctly remembered all 24 characters, after hearing them just twice. He hadn't taken notes. The iPhone sprung to life and Joe sat it down on the pew beside him. To Easy's amazement, Joe picked up the iPad and started typing, again from memory and recalling the 24 characters perfectly. The glow of the iPad screen shone in Joe's eyes as they scanned the page. A few taps on the screen and he sat it down on the pew.

'What's with the security?' Joe asked.

'I live in Barking; they robbed my old phone two years ago.'

'That's not what I asked, and you know it,' came Joe's response, the menace returned to his eyes.

'Everything I own, or nearly everything, is on there. I can't let it be stolen.'

'How does a kid from Barking get their hands on the latest iPhone and iPad? Stolen?'

'No!' Easy said indignantly. 'I bought them.'

'How could you possibly afford these?'

'I have money, plenty of money.'

'Oh, have you now?' JT entered and took over the questioning. 'What do you mean plenty of money?'

'It's not all money or I mean it's not all cash,' offered Easy.

'So, what is it, and how did you get it?' asked JT.

'Bitcoin mostly, and some other cryptos. I have a flat and a café too,' he said without emotion.

'How much are we talking?' asked JT, failing to hide his scepticism.

'I'm not sure what the prices are today as you've had my phone- '

'Roughly,' interjected JT.

'Roughly...800,' said Easy.

'800 pounds?' asked JT.

'800,000 pounds.' Easy felt the men's gaze. 'I trade Bitcoin and Crypto. Last year I made a lot of money by utilising an arbitrage between the prices in the UK and the prices in Nigeria.'

'You're a fraudster?' quipped Taff, still standing behind him.

'No, I am not!' replied an indignant Easy.

JT looked at Joe, who gave a slight shrug and nod, confirming this could be true. 'And you own your Aunty's flat?' asked JT.

'No, it is a council flat. I offered but she would not let me. I do pay the rent though.'

'So, this flat is where? Nigeria?' asked JT, taking a seat on the pew next to Joe.

'Clapham,' replied Easy.

'Clapham, London?' asked JT.

'Yes, Northcote Road.'

'Northcote Road!' exclaimed JT, 'are you taking the piss?'

The other men in the room all looked on expectantly not understanding the significance of the address.

'72 Northcote Road.'

'That would have cost about... at least 500k,' said JT.

'I paid 750 thousand pounds, but that included the café beneath the flat.'

Taff let out a low whistle, 'Christ!'

A stunned silence descended. It was broken by Easy, 'I wanted to move my crypto profits into property and Danny' he looked at the men in turn, 'I told you about my friend Danny,' he said looking for recognition before carrying on, 'well, his Uncle was working on the flat and the café for the developer. Danny and I had gone with him one Saturday to help clean up after the plaster men had finished.'

'How does a 16 year old kid buy a property? Is that even legal?' asked JT who still considered the story to be unlikely.

'I had to use a lawyer in Nigeria, he set up a company for me. I bought the flat and café together direct from the developer.'

'And you don't live there?'

'No, my Aunty doesn't want to move.'

'It's empty?'

'Yes, but I will find a tenant if I don't go live there.'

'What about council tax and rates, bills and things?'

'I rent out the café and the rent takes care of all the bills, and pays the rent on my Aunty's flat,' he said, proud of what he'd achieved. Not the property he owned, but ensuring that his Aunty's rent would always be covered.

'Interesting story,' said JT, not quite believing what he was hearing. He knew Northcote Road well and had often frequented the café's and boutiques there with Esmé. The memory of it stung a little and he shook them from his mind.

Joe cleared his throat and changed the topic of conversation, 'What about the kiddy porn?'

'Kiddy porn?' asked Easy in response, he felt the atmosphere change again.

Joe picked up the iPhone and turned the screen to face Easy. The still image was of a woman apparently with a penis in her mouth and in the background the face of a terrified little boy.

'Ryan,' said Easy, the name catching in his thickening throat.

'So, you know him, you sick fucker!' said Joe, his anger palpable.

'He lives on the estate. That lady is his Mother, her name is Michelle,' he said sadly.

'You get off on this kind of thing then, sicko?'

Easy paled and could not suppress his own anger. Angry tears rolled down his face as he blurted out, 'How dare you? You know nothing about me. I do not like that, that stuff. It's disgusting. How could you even think…?' his voice trailed off as he held his head in his hands and sobbed.

Joe was unmoved by the tears and continued, 'so you just happen to get sent a copy of the paedo video then huh?'

Easy sniffed loudly as he wiped his eyes and looked defiantly at first Joe and then JT. 'I am not a pervert. I did not get sent that image. I hacked the Bad Men's group chat; I can see what they share.' He paused, his face twisted slightly as he remembered images that scarred him mentally, 'they are why I came to you for help. They are monsters.'

'Wait a minute, you 'hacked' their chat? How exactly did you manage that?'

'The big guy who is always at the bookies is called Igor. He is like a bodybuilder or something. He is always angry and likes to hit people. One day about two weeks ago I was at the launderette and I saw Igor drag a man out of the bookies. He punched the man to the floor and was kicking him. A woman, I think it was the man's wife, tried to stop him and he punched her too. He stood there and undid his trousers then pissed on the man and woman.'

'He just pissed on them in the street?' asked JT.

'Yes, I told you he is a monster.'

'How does this lead to you hacking his phone?' asked Joe.

'After he pissed, he took his phone out of his pocket and started filming them. I remember he was laughing. When the man started moving, he got to his knees, he was begging Igor. Igor went to put his phone back in his pocket and kicked the man. The man fell back into the road, and Igor's phone fell out of his pocket. Igor didn't notice and he went back inside the bookies. I went to see if the people were ok and found Igor's phone in the gutter. So, I picked it up.'

'What happened to the man and woman?'

'I helped them up and they went away, they were bleeding but could walk. I asked them if they wanted an ambulance or the police but they said no, they said it would make things worse.'

'So, you kept his phone?' asked JT

'Only for a little while,' replied Easy, keen to show he wasn't a thief.

'Explain.'

'I went back to the launderette and I had an idea. I took the SIM card out of his phone and downloaded all of the data onto my phone. The phone is quite new but I retrieved about 3 weeks of data. I was able to use the IMEI number from his phone to make a clone. At first, I thought I would start phoning Nigeria or something and it would all go on his bill but then I thought it might be useful for the Police or something, if I could just hack the phone. Igor is 4467 on the keypad so I tried that for the code. He is not so clever. I downloaded some spyware onto his phone, then dropped it into the doorway at the bookies. Now I can see whatever he does on his phone.' Easy looked at JT expecting to see some acknowledgement of his skills but was met with a blank look.

'Who is this Michelle? Is she one of them?' asked JT.

'God no, she is a nice lady. She lives with her son. I think his father died soon after he was born. He was a Deliveroo guy, he got knocked off his bike and killed.'

'So why is she in this video?' JT asked.

'I don't know, but I think she must have been forced,' he thought for a moment before asking, 'can I see the rest of the video, you can crop the bit with Michelle. I know where her house is so I might recognise it,' he reached out for his iPhone.

Joe looked at JT, who nodded, and the phone was handed over. Easy took the video and altered the screen. The clip was some 30 seconds long but that was long enough for Easy to recognise the location.

'This was filmed in the launderette. It is on the High Street beside their bookies. It was filmed this afternoon at 2pm. Broad daylight.'

'You said 'their bookies'?' said JT

'Yes, it is the Bad Men's place, they are there every day. I think it's like their Head Quarters.'

'Oh, is it now?' said JT, and he stood up and walked out. The others followed him and they all climbed into their vehicles to head to London.

CHAPTER ELEVEN

'NESSUN DORRRMA. NESSUN DORRRRMAAAA, da dum da dum dum, da da, da dum dum...' DI Rory Maxwell stopped singing as he heard his phone ringing. Switching off the shower he reached over and clicked the answer button for speaker phone. 'Maxwell" he said as he stepped out of the cubicle and grabbed a towel.

'Rory, it's JT.'

'Urgent or can I get dried?'

'Pardon?' laughed JT.

'I was enjoying a shower with my good friend Luciano and now I'm dripping over the bathroom floor.'

'Ah, I see. I'll bet nobody is sleeping after hearing you screeching!'

They both laughed.

'Wow, this getting kicked out has made you funny, you should have left years ago!' Maxwell chuckled to himself safe in the knowledge that he was one of the few people who would get away with saying such a thing.

'Suspended from active duty, temporarily,' JT countered, 'As well you know.'

'Yeah, yeah, I know, just pulling your leg. What's up, you back in London?'

'En route as we speak.'

'Beer and a curry or did you fancy another lesson on the squash court?'

'I'll give the squash a miss this time but thanks for the offer. I need to pick your brains about something.'

'Fire away,' said Maxwell his interest piqued as he realised this wasn't a social call.

'Can we meet, don't want to do this over the phone.'

'Sounds ominous.'

'No, just need to run something by you.'

'Ok, where and when?'

'Tonight, Draught House, Northcote Road. 2130 hrs?'

'Bit late, no?'

'I've an errand to run first, see you there?'

'I'll have a pint of Moretti waiting for you.'

'Thanks Rory,' said JT and he hung up.

'Where we headed boss?' asked Rambo as he signalled to overtake a lorry.

'Mayfair,' replied JT, 'but first you can drop me and the kid in East London."

#

JT watched the 4x4s head off into the remnants of rush hour traffic. Turning to Easy he said, 'Ok kid, now we're in your manor, where does a man get a decent pie and mash around here?'

Easy smiled and replied, 'I wouldn't know, I don't eat such things. Come, my Aunty will cook you some real food.'

'Nice of you to offer but maybe some other time. Tonight, I want to get a feel for the place.'

'So, you are going to help me?' asked Easy grinning.

'Didn't say that kid. Let's just go eat.'

'Oh ok, I will take you to Samir's, he makes the best Moroccan food.'

'On the High Street?'

'Yes, but at the far end, we can take a bus or an Uber?'

'No, we have time to walk, besides I want you to show me the bookie shop.'

'And the launderette,' said Easy.

JT wasn't sure if it was a statement or a question but he nodded, 'Which side of the street are they on?' he asked.

'This side,' replied Easy pointing down the footpath.

'No pointing kid, we don't know who's watching. We'll cross here and have a look from across the road. Just follow my lead. If we bump into anyone you know just tell them I'm a stranger you're showing the way to Samir's.'

The two set off and once shown an appropriate pace, Easy walked as casually as he could alongside JT. Twice JT stopped and pretended to look in shop windows. He explained to Easy that he was noting the CCTV positions. Easy told to him that the Bad Men had systematically broken the cameras until the council refused to replace or repair them. The Bad Men could operate freely without prying eyes.

Fifty yards short of being directly opposite the bookies, JT stopped and knelt down to tie his laces. He told Easy to keep walking and wait for him at the next junction. JT looked from between parked cars and could see the bookies was in an old bank building. A solid stone structure that looked out of place among its red brick and concrete neighbours. In the windows there were numerous posters that blocked the view of the interior. It was the tiny, barely visible from this distance, flash of red light that snagged his attention. Inside the window, in the top corner was a CCTV camera and it was pointing out onto the street at the front door. The council might not be able to see who was going back and forward, but the Bad Men certainly could.

#

Igor Stasse stood behind the desk in the back office of the bookie shop. From here he could watch the CCTV monitors fitted to the wall. He was watching the girl at the payment desk counting cash. The bundle of notes was placed back into the envelope and she nodded to the man stood before her. Igor recognised the man but did not know his name. He was one of the Arab types he despised. These dirty people who wiped their arse with their hand and didn't know how to use cutlery, were animals to his mind. He sucked at his teeth trying to dislodge a sesame seed before reaching into his pocket for a toothpick. He always kept a toothpick at hand, not only were they good for shifting food, but they had other uses.

Back in Albania he had found that inserting a toothpick under the fingernails of the girls meant he could cause them just enough pain to be compliant, but not leave a mark. He had learned his lesson after slapping one of the whores too hard and bruising her face. The boss had been angry and made Igor apologise to her. He, Igor, had to apologise to that bitch! It made him angry at the thought of it. He also remembered the beating he had to take from the boss. He had lost two teeth, but that didn't matter, he could afford to buy better teeth, gold teeth. The boss had punched and kicked him but the blows didn't hurt. What did hurt was the fucking apology. He felt the blood rise in his face at the memory. Then he remembered how he'd had his revenge. The woman had a daughter, she must have been 14. Ugly little bitch as he remembered. She had begged him. Begged him to stop. Kept saying she was a virgin. As if that should matter to Igor! He snorted at the memory of her pleading. She was the daughter of a whore, she would be a whore, she might as well get started he had told her.

The door to the office opened and the girl from the payment desk came in. She placed the envelope of cash on the desk without speaking and without looking up at him. She knew better. Picking up the envelope he sniffed the cash inside. Cash, his favourite perfume. This money wasn't his though, it belonged to the boss. Talking of the boss, Igor thought, he would be pleased with how Igor had punished that bitch who let her kid touch the car today.

The thought of the punishment caused a stirring in his groin, he let himself remember and felt himself become erect. The blow job was pretty average, she wasn't actually trying, but the look on the kids face as Igor crushed his pathetic little hand was just perfect.

CHAPTER TWELVE

ACROSS LONDON THE TWO 4x4s were parked facing the canal. The five men were eating fish and chips and talking through the open windows.

'So, we're doing this then?' said Rambo between inserting chips into his mouth.

'Doing what?' replied Cooky.

'The boss hasn't told us what he's thinking yet, let's not go jumping the gun boyo,' said Taff without looking at them. He was watching a mother walking hand in hand with her child walking along the path on the opposite side of the canal. She was smiling and joking with the kid who was giggling. A swan swam toward them and the kid tried to move closer to the edge, the mum held tight to the kid's hand and put herself between the kid and the water's edge. Taff wondered whether she was protecting the kid from the canal or from the swan. Both most likely he thought.

He had seen mothers throw themselves over their children to protect them many times. In Afghanistan the mothers were the same as the rest of the world. The men folk might shout "Insh Allah" and let their God decide who lived or died, but the women behaved in a much more primal way. His own mother did the same for him, in her own way. She would go hungry to make sure there was enough on the plate for him and his brothers. It shamed him to think of it now, but it's how she'd wanted it.

He was shaken out of his memory by a blur of white and a splash as another swan landed on the canal. It honked and chased away the original swan as it looked to the mother and child for food. The kid was throwing bits of bread into the water and pulling the mum along to where the original swan was sitting dejectedly. The kid threw the last of the bread to this swan. He smiled at the thought of the kids' innate sense of fairness. He knew what the boss would say when he returned. He knew how he would vote, in fact, he knew how they would all vote. They'd all seen the video and that little boy's face.

Cooky crumpled up the newspaper that had wrapped his fish and chips and gave a satisfied, 'Ahhh.'

In response Posty gave out an almighty elongated belch and they all laughed. 'Sorry, lads, bloody Vimto, so it was,' he sniggered. 'What about this Easy kid being fucking loaded?'

Joe responded first, 'Bloody clever boy that Easy. I can't help but think there's more to him than meets the eye.'

'Well, when the boss gets back, he'll hopefully fill in some of the gaps,' said Cooky.

'Let's get these motors stashed and back to the boss's place, I could murder a good brew,' said Taff, winding his window back up. He watched the Mother and her kid wander along the canal path and just before the engine started, he caught the sound of them singing a song, '...I can sing a rainbow, sing a rainbow too.' He knew how he was going to vote.

#

Easy ordered the Maroc King Special for them both before joining
JT at a table near the back of the little café. The table was old, and its
Formica chipped, but it stood level and steady thanks to the folded
napkins under one leg.

'You'll like the food here; Samir is an excellent cook,' said Easy. He
watched as JT scanned the premises and misinterpreted that as disap-
proval. 'He is always clean in the kitchen,' he offered as reassurance.

'I'm sure he is, smells good,' said JT still looking around. 'You're
sure these Bad Men don't come in here?'

'I've never seen them here; I don't think they like people who are
not Kosanians.'

'Kos-what?' asked JT.

'Kosanians, it's what they call themselves. I think they must be part
Kosovan and part Albanian.'

'Interesting,' said JT.

An old man with leathery brown skin and a short white beard
approached them carrying a tray of tea. 'Here you are, some tea,' he
said as he slid the tray onto the table.

'I didn't order tea, Uncle,' said Easy using the familial title in a
respectful way.

'It is to welcome your new friend, who you have brought to my
kitchen,' replied the old man with a smile. He placed his hand over his
heart and bowed his head slightly to JT and said, 'as salaam u alaikum,
welcome.'

'Wa alaikum as salaam, and thank you,' replied JT, nodding his
thanks to the old man.

The old man smiled at him and wandered back to his kitchen
muttering happily to himself.

'You speak Arabic?' asked Easy, impressed.

'A little,' said JT, who was alert to some activity outside the café's front door.

Easy looked around and saw two women wearing short skirts and high heels arguing. They were speaking in a language he did not recognise.

'Ukrainians,' said JT, as if he'd read Easy's mind.

'They work for the Bad Men,' said Easy.

'Prostitutes?'

'Yes, they used to work outside the Benefits Office at Wakering Road, but now, now they stand along the end of this row of shops. The Police don't even tell them to move away.'

'Why here?'

'At first, I thought it was because Uncle Samir let them come in to have a hot tea or coffee when it is cold, but now I think it is because the Bad Men are at the bookies shop. They can keep an eye on the women, I think.'

'The Bad Men are at the bookie shop at night too?' asked JT.

'The lights never go out and people are always going in and out,' Easy paused as a customer came in and ordered a take away shawarma. He lowered his voice before continuing, 'I think the people have to pay them money there. I see many people go there, people who own these shops. Those women go there too. I think that is where the Bad Men collect their money.'

'You're very interested in their money,' JT told him and fixed him with a steely gaze.

Easy was initially confused and then laughed as he understood what JT meant, 'I have more than enough money. You asked me about the bookies, I just told you what I know.'

Their meals arrived on old earthenware plates and were heaped with grilled chicken and lamb on a mound of cous-cous and salad. Samir placed a bowl of chilli sauce in front of them and a bowl of minted yoghurt. He shook his head and retrieved the bowl of chilli sauce with a waved apology and returned it to the kitchen. He brought back a bigger bowl and placed it in front of JT, 'Very hot, very good, keep your stomach strong!' he said, patting his own flat belly. His smile was infectious and JT and Easy returned the happy gesture.

'Thank you, Uncle,' they said unison.

Uncle Samir walked back to his kitchen a happy man.

'Good food, huh?' said Easy, 'like I told you.'

'Yep, like you told me,' said JT, 'but, there's a lot you haven't told me.'

'What do you want to know?' said Easy, lifting some pitta bread into his mouth.

'How'd you get involved in dealing in Bitcoin and stuff?'

'My Aunty does not like me to go out. Most of the time when I'm not in school, I'm on my computer. Mr Kuczak, my IT teacher, runs an after school club for coders and things. I help with the younger kids, and he teaches me stuff.'

'Go on,' said JT

'Well, we set up a bitcoin mining rig and we got lucky,' said Easy, excitedly.

'Lucky?' JT's deadpan face suggested he didn't share the excitement.

Easy ploughed on, 'Yeah, we solved a block in the first month!' his volume had increased with his excitement in the recounting of the story. JT motioned with his hands that he should calm down. 'Sorry!' Easy said conspiratorially, 'We got 6.25 Bitcoin as our reward and we split it 2 each.'

'2 each?' asked a confused JT.

'Yes, we took two each and sold the rest to buy more ASICs,' before JT could ask the question, he continued, 'ASICs are little computers that mine for the bitcoin. The more you have the more chance you have of winning the block rewards.'

'And you've kept winning?'

'No, well yes, we did win another block a few months later.'

'2 blocks doesn't account for the money you've been spending though, does it?' JT asked the question but thought he already knew the answer.

'No, of course not. But I also traded the bitcoin I got,' Easy didn't enjoy being questioned this way but knew he had to explain himself.

'So, now you, a 16 year old school kid, are an FX trader?'

'Sort of, yes.'

'How does that work? Last time I checked they don't teach FX Trading at High School.'

'More's the pity,' replied Easy honestly. 'It was an accident really. I wanted to send some money to my cousin in Nigeria. He is 14 and doesn't have a bank account so I sent him some Satoshis. Do you know what a Satoshi is?'

'Yes, 100,000,000 per bitcoin, right?'

'That's correct,' continued Easy, he could feel his adrenaline rising and forced himself to keep his voice down, 'well I soon realised that Bitcoin in Nigeria costs more than here in the UK. I looked back over a few months of charts and there is always a premium paid in Nigeria and a few other countries.'

'How does that help you? Surely that's better for your cousin,' asked JT his interest now piqued.

'My cousin was mega happy, yes; he was able to buy a bicycle and that lets him get to school much faster.'

'Stick to the trading part,' said JT.

'Well, I realised that I can sell bitcoin in Nigeria for cash, transfer the cash here to the UK and buy more bitcoin. Then start the cycle again.'

'How much more expensive is a bitcoin in Nigeria?'

'It varies but somewhere between £3000 and £5000.'

'Ok, but you only had a couple of bitcoin to start with.'

'True, they don't teach FX trading in school but they do teach compounding in Economics and Mathematics,' he smiled at JT, then frowned. 'Do you know about compounding interest?'

'I've heard of it certainly, but not my field. So, let me see if I got this right; you and your teacher mine bitcoin. You then trade Bitcoin in Nigeria and use the profits to buy more Bitcoin, then trade that too?'

'Essentially, yes,' said Easy.

'Wow, no idea how you managed it, but well done kid.'

'Thank you, some luck and some hard work. Now you know I have money and how I earned it; you know I can pay you to help me.'

'Pay?' JT was bemused by the very suggestion; it had never occurred to him. 'I haven't said I'm going to help you Easy, and I don't need your money. We are not mercenaries.'

'No, no, of course not, but you will have expenses, for bullets and things…' The look on JT's face prevented him from finishing the sentence.

'Christ kid, you've been watching too many movies!' JT smiled at him without humour and shook his head. JT looked at his watch and stood up. Easy went to stand up too but JT motioned for him to stay seated.

'You'll need your bike back I expect?' he said.

'Eh, yes.'

'It'll be chained outside here on the railings. Come pick it up at 1730 hrs tomorrow, understood?'

'Yes, yes, 1730 tomorrow. And then?'

'1730,' said JT and he stepped to the counter and shook the hand of Uncle Samir, before he walked out of the café without looking back.

JT walked quickly up the road to the tube station and caught a tube going West. He had an appointment with a pint of Moretti, and with a man whose life he'd saved a long time ago.

CHAPTER THIRTEEN

WALKING ALONG NORTHCOTE ROAD, JT could feel the understated opulence. The area had undergone something of a transformation since his last visit. The road being closed to traffic meant all of the cafes, restaurants and pubs had tables and chairs outside. Even on a Thursday evening the tables were full of healthy looking, casually well-dressed people. The upturned collars of the foppy haired men shook as they guffawed at each other. Their women folk sported a mix of gym gear which showed off their lithe yoga bodies. Other women wore floaty light coloured dresses and held glasses of wine while gossiping with their girlfriends.

This had been Esmé's world. A world that she'd dragged him into and that he'd muscled through the discomfort of. It hadn't been all bad. He walked past *Umbra* which had been his favourite brunch spot. It was run by a Czech woman, who was blissfully unaware of just how beautiful she was, and treated everyone like a long lost friend. The table where he would wait for Esmé, while she did Pilates, sat in the corner by the window. He remembered the time her class was cancelled and she'd beaten him there. She'd taken up his position, back to the wall and with a clear sight of the front and back doors. Challenging him to sit with his back to the room, she'd promised him a night of unbridled passion if he lasted the whole meal. After 45 seconds she'd relented at seeing how uncomfortable it made him and they'd swapped seats. The night of passion had followed regardless and he could feel the touch of her smooth skin, it was visceral and real, even after all this time.

He passed one of the little coffee vans, parked and locked up, and the *Draught* came into view. This was safer ground. Esmé hadn't liked the *Draught* with its big screen football coverage and bit of a 'lads' atmosphere. No, this was where men came to be with men and escape the wife and kids.

Rory Maxwell was a tall, handsome man, with chiselled features and the broad build of a swimmer. He'd played semi-professional water polo in Australia in his younger years and still swam most days. The training pool he'd built in his basement had a current system you had to swim against. He could spend an hour swimming off the stress of his job he'd told his ex-wife Siobhan. The reality was, he'd explained to JT, he did some of his best thinking in there. No phone's, no disturbance, just him and the water. Something about the rhythmical breathing and motion induced a bit of a trance like state for him, and then he could think, really think.

JT understood exactly what he meant; he had the same sort of head space when he ran. I don't *jog* he would say, I *run*; *jogging* is for fat people.

Maxwell stood at the end of the bar exactly where JT thought he would be. It was the position he would choose himself. Solid wall backstop and a good view of the TV showing the football. Just as importantly it gave a good view of the front and, via the big mirror, side entrance doors. This was the best position in the place and Maxwell stood relaxed sipping his beer and watching the last few minutes of the match between Barcelona and Dortmund.

'2-1, 3 minutes plus injury time to go,' said Maxwell without looking at JT as he slid a full and freshly poured pint toward him.

'Many injuries?' JT asked, as he lifted his beer to his lips and completed his scan of the pub.

'You'd think a couple had been shot the way they rolled around, but then got up and ran about as soon as they won a free kick. It's like a pantomime at times,' he chuckled to himself while shaking his head at the latest theatrical dive.

'More prima donna than Maradona then?' JT was no football fan, but he knew the basics and the language of the spectator.

'Bloody right,' said Maxwell turning to face JT for the first time. 'Seat? Or are we standing like real men?' The final whistle ended the game on the TV and the three men who'd been standing further along the bar pulled on their jackets to leave.

'This'll do,' JT said.

Seeing his friend's face was all business Maxwell asked, 'So, what do you want to know?'

JT paused and leaned in slightly toward Maxwell, 'Kosanians.' He registered the recognition in Maxwell's expression and so went on, 'where do they operate and what's their gig?'

'Nasty buggers,' said Maxwell, 'arrived here after the Balkan wars. They run drugs, prostitution and everything else that makes money up East.'

'How nasty?' asked JT.

'Extremely,' said Maxwell, 'some of them are ex-military. After the war they took wet work on for anyone who would pay, Russian and Italian mob used them for the rough work they didn't want to dirty their own hands with. They have a fearful reputation. They got fed up with taking orders and came here where they could run their own game. Ousted some of the local gangs, they butchered a few Yardies and even a few Tri-ads. Got the place to themselves.'

'If you guys know all this, why don't you close them down?' asked JT.

'Not that easy,' snorted Maxwell, 'bloody human rights lawyers have our brass shit scared to be called racists if we target any certain group. The local uniforms know there's no-one going to be a witness against them or they'll end up falling off the roof of the high flats.'

'Yeah, sorry, not an accusation,' said JT apologetically.

'Do you know why they're called the Kosanians?' asked Maxwell. JT shook his head as he took a mouthful of beer. 'The cheeky bastards pretended to be Kosovans when they arrived here. Her Majesty's Government was keen to help the poor undocumented Kosovans, we gave them houses, benefits, set up a Community centre, all the usual bollocks. We weren't going to be so welcoming to Albanians, but they knew we're a soft touch and think we're stupid.'

'Maybe they're right,' offered JT.

'Abso-fucking-lutely!' Maxwell lifted his glass in a mock toast.

JT thought for a moment, assimilating what he'd just learned.

'Why the interest?' asked Maxwell, 'or shouldn't I ask?'

'Can you check something for me?' asked JT, bringing out a slip of paper from his pocket and handing it to Maxwell. 'The address is a bookie shop in Barking. I think it's connected to these Kosanians. Another thing, I'm told an old lady got burned out of her house a couple of weeks ago on the Gascoigne Estate. Can you check that one out for me?'

'You think it's linked to the Kosanians?'

'I don't even know for sure it happened, but yes, yes I do,' said JT.

'Anything else?'

'Yeah, there's a young woman called Michelle, a widow with a little boy called Ryan. Lives on the same estate. Her husband was killed in an RTA. She was the victim of something nasty yesterday and so was her kid. Can you get me an address?'

'What kind of nasty?'

'The kind of nasty that an evil bastard films on his phone to show his mates,' JT closed his eyes and paused a second, 'while making the kid watch.'

'Understood,' was all Maxwell said in reply.

The two men had seen more than their fair share of atrocities and the evil that men did to each other but neither were immune to the impact of kids being involved. JT instinctively touched his abdomen where the scar was a visual reminder of just such evil.

#

As arranged Maxwell appeared at the Mayfair flat at lunchtime the next day. He carried with him an old tatty sports bag which looked out of place against his smart suit, shirt and tie.

JT introduced him as Rory to the rest of the team and they all sat around the dining table as Maxwell produced photos and several manilla files from the sports bag.

He arranged the photos in two groups, firstly the crime scene of the fire at the old lady's house. The black scorch marks were across the door and up the front of the building and the remnants of what appeared to be a sofa. Next was a group of eight photos, they were a mix of mug shots and what appeared to be surveillance photos.

'The old lady?' asked JT

'Elizabeth Roberts, known as Betty to her friends and neighbours. She's in hospital, unlikely to come out. Fire brigade were on scene in 3-4 minutes, seems they saw the black smoke while out on another job. Saved the old girl. Uniforms canvassed the neighbours, no-one saw or heard anything. Sofa and some pallets just appeared and caught fire without anyone noticing.'

'What did she say about it?' asked JT.

'She said something about a bad man doing it but wouldn't say anything else,' said Maxwell in full professional flow. 'The girl you asked about, Michelle Kowalska, 25, she has a son, Ryan aged 4. Her husband Lucas Kowalski was killed in a hit and run, 3 years ago. She lives at Desmond Tutu House, flat 73. No criminal record, nothing on social work records re the kid either.'

'Ok thanks, any family?'

'When her husband was killed his family went back to Poland. They asked to be kept up to date on any progress with the case.'

'Her family?'

'None that were mentioned anywhere in the records I could see. A neighbour was asked to come and sit with her when the uniforms gave her the bad news.'

'Poor lass,' said Taff.

'Aye,' said Joe, 'poor kid too.'

'Do you guys want to tell me what's happened and how you are involved?' asked Maxwell as he looked around the table before settling on JT, 'It's obviously nothing to do with the Regiment.'

'Best not ask,' replied JT. 'We were told a story and wanted to check it out.'

'Okay, let's pretend I didn't ask,' said Maxwell as he reached toward the photos on the table. Cooky placed a big 4 digit hand on top of the photos without looking at Maxwell.

'Tell us about these guys,' said JT nodding toward the photos.

'There's a line gentlemen, you know that,' started Maxwell, 'Civilian and Military roles are clearly defined. If something is going on and you're involved with these Kosanians then you need to back out, it's a Police matter.'

'Didn't say we were involved Rory,' said JT, 'and we're very grateful for your filling in some gaps in the story.'

'Aren't you guys in all sorts of shit already? Isn't that why you're, you're 'suspended'?'

'Just a bit of Politics Rory, we followed our orders. Some folks just don't like the reality of our work,' said JT, softly. 'Look if you don't want to tell us about these guys then don't, but I think we both know you didn't bring this stuff here just to take it away again.'

Maxwell looked his old friend in the eye and then with a wry smile said, 'Okay, have it your way, but remember intel goes in both directions.'

'Just like Belfast Rory,' offered JT.

'That was an official job, bit different but yes, just like Belfast.' Maxwell selected the one photograph and set it above the line of the others, 'This guy appears to be the Boss. We think he is the leader of the Kosanians in London and heads up the council. They call themselves 'Luan' or Lions. The council as we understand it are the 3 UK based Albanian gang lords all reporting to a bigger boss. The others are smaller outfits in Liverpool and Newcastle. Between them they control a chunk of the UK Cocaine trade. They also run a huge ring of people smuggling, prostitution and illegal firearms. They make millions out of those people they boat across the Channel from France. The National Crime Agency reckon these guys have brought enough arms into the UK to supply a small army. They have a few assassins on their books that are available for hire, I understand they did jobs across Europe and into Russia before they came to the UK. They were marked men back home and were working out of Istanbul before the Russian mafia raised an army against them. An Oligarch was drowned in his bath but these guys couldn't help themselves and they left their calling card.' He reached into one of the manilla folders and brought out another photo. The photo was from an autopsy. The photo showed a star slashed into the skin of the forehead of the dead Oligarch.

JT looked closely at the photo, 'I take it there's some symbolism involved here Rory?' 'I don't have a photo but I'm told that the Russians carved Roman Numerals into the foreheads of the Albanian men they killed in Istanbul,' he replied, 'I think it was revenge and they wanted to show they could get to the men calling the shots in Russia.'

'The Russians who chased them out of Istanbul, do we know anything about them?'

'Not much, we know the Turks had issues with a load of Chechens and the Solntsevskaya Bratva hacking bits off each other in a running battle up and down Istakal Cadessi. The Bratva are big time Russian Mafia, the Chechens were mercenaries. The Turkish MIT – that's their Intelligence guys, reckon it was a battle over who was taking over after they'd cleared out the Albanians. Friends turned foes, and they spilled a lot of blood.'

'Who won?' asked Posty

'Good question,' said Maxwell, 'the Bratva are scary but the Chechens kill for fun and don't seem to have any fear of dying themselves. My money was on the Chechens but apparently, they all packed up and moved out. Word is that pressure was put on from Moscow.'

An ember of an idea came to JT as he listened, he had met the Russian Mafia before and knew how ruthless they were. 'So now the Bratva are finished fighting battles in Istanbul, they've got time on their hands...interesting.'

'Seems that way, what are you thinking?'

JT didn't answer the question, 'Some of these have been taken with a long lens. Surveillance?' he asked Maxwell, without looking up from the photos.

'Yes, the Met Organised Crime guys had been watching the Yardies and set up a few cameras. They were set up just before the Kosanians took over so they got a bit of the transition.'

'They're still in place?'

'Sadly no, budget cuts mean there's only so much kit to go around and it was moved in to bolster the coverage around Parliament. As you know the Islamists take priority,' Rory paused and took a breath before he continued, 'something else happened.' He looked as though he was trying to find the right words.

'Go on,' said JT looking at his old friend and trying to read the look on his face.

'They took a cop,' he said eventually.

'Took a cop? What the hell does that mean?'

'Just that, a young cop was walking in the High Street in uniform. Apparently, he'd nipped round there on his own to get his wife a birthday card or something. He radioed in to say he'd heard shouting coming from a shop and he was going to take a look. Then he disappeared for 2 days.'

'Disappeared?' asked JT.

'Literally disappeared. When he didn't answer his radio, they sent a couple of cars round there. He was gone. The guy in the shop swore blind he hadn't seen a cop. No CCTV, no witnesses, nothing. As you can imagine all hell let loose but they couldn't find him. 48 hours later someone drives a car into the middle of a shopping precinct over in Tottenham and he's tied up in the boot. He says all he can remember is a pair of big eastern European looking guys grabbing him, then he gets hit from behind and wakes up in a dark room. He's no idea how long he's in there, a lot of shouting outside in a language he doesn't recognise. Then the same two blokes tie him up and hood him. He's put in the back of the car and driven around, he thinks, for a couple of hours. He's unharmed and after a medical, gets sent home. He lives up in Leighton Buzzard. Next day he's at home recuperating and the door goes. Wife answers the door and the taxi driver hands her a bunch of flowers and an envelope. The envelope contains £10,000 in cash. There's no card with the flowers. We tracked down the taxi driver, says some guy gave him £50 to do the delivery. Says he never saw his face.' Maxwell looked at his hands and took a long slow breath before continuing, 'embarrassingly the brass decided they didn't want to risk the public scrutiny of storming the place with cops and instead withdrew. There's barely a cop that goes near the place now, and even then, they have to be in minimum of 4s.'

'Jesus,' said Taff and looked at Maxwell, 'your guys have thrown in the towel.'

'Seems that way,' said Maxwell, 'I've only found this out last night and this morning, can barely believe it myself.'

'Not your fault Rory,' said JT putting a hand on his shoulder. 'Let's get a brew on, this is a lot to take in.'

JT clicked on the kettle and pushed the button on the coffee machine moving it from standby to element heating mode. As he reached into the cupboard for a box of coffee pods, he asked the question he was confident he knew the answer to, 'Double espresso?'

'No, best not, I've had four already this morning,' said Maxwell as he leant his hip against the worktop.

JT turned to face him and responded with questioning raised eyebrows.

'Yeah, ok, bugger it, I see you still keep Yirgacheffe, much better than that Starbucks muck I've had all morning. My machine in the office didn't have an up to date PAT check and they condemned it. Can you believe these people? We can't solve crimes, never mind prevent them, but no one can ever say we have unsafe coffee machines!' The exasperation in his voice was no real surprise to JT, his friend had lamented the demise of the once great Metropolitan Police Service many times.

'The world is a messy place my friend, that's why they need folks like us,' said JT comfortingly.

'Too right,' sighed Maxwell, 'this politically correct and woke bollocks will be the end of us. They want me to do another Diversity Course, apparently, I'm not recognising my privilege enough. I've put them off so many times they're threatening to discipline me. As if I've got time for that nonsense. Some Transgender, Lesbian who identifies as a fucking duck going to tell me I should feel remorse about slavery or something. Honestly, if I didn't know how much the shit would hit the fan, I'd jack it all in. Christ knows what'll happen when me and my lot retire, the new breed think terrorists just need a cuddle!' he snorted.

JT busied himself with the teapots, a big old silver version for the team's brew and a cast iron pot for his Lapsang Souchong. He waited for Rory to make his usual joke about his choice of tea but when it didn't come, he knew Rory had more to say.

'These Kosanians are bad news JT,' he began, a gravity to his voice, 'I don't know what you're thinking, but you need to know this is not your battle. You're already under the microscope. Your SIB lot will have been told to find as much dirt on you and your team as possible. You're their sacrifice at the progressives' altar.'

'I know, but we did nothing wrong. Dangerous people died and they're no longer a threat, to the locals or to the boots on the ground. That was our mission. We followed our orders.'

'I hear you, but the Politicians want to be seen to be holding you to account. They've got the media whipped up too. Death squad assassination headlines are turning the public against the military.'

'They want an excuse to pull out before finishing the job, they can't think beyond the next election,' said JT lifting the tray he'd assembled. 'Grab the biscuit tin will you,' he gestured with his head to the battered and chipped biscuit tin on top of the fridge.

Maxwell grabbed the tin barrel and opened the kitchen door for his friend. He looked at the tin in his hands as he followed JT back to the dining room. It had looked out of place in the smart modern kitchen but he knew it had sentimental value. The images around the side were of the Charge of the Light Brigade, the Crimean War. Ridiculously brave men following orders from inept and duplicitous commanders. That was their mission. They followed their orders.

#

Maxwell sat listening to the chat at the table. Joe was briefing the team on all of the open source information he had found on the internet. Reports in newspapers of dead Yardie drug dealers being found around the estate. Four Tri-ad affiliated premises suffering synchronised arson attacks. Gun battles and drive by shootings. Body parts being found in dustbins near a primary school. Complaints of Prostitutes soliciting in broad daylight. Calls for action from the Police and the Mayor with reassurance messages galore. Then things seemed to settle down. The number and frequency of reports had lessened and the public uproar seemed to have given way to acceptance. In the last 6 months there was no mention of any gang activity in Barking. He knew they wouldn't find any mention of the kidnapped Police officer, it had been hushed up and it was as if it had never happened. To an outsider it might appear the Police had gone in and tidied the place up. If only that were true, he thought.

Maxwell felt something shift in him and though he didn't want to give the idea oxygen, he knew it was there, planted in his mind and demanding consideration. A day job of 10-12 hour days that often extended to 16 hours, just trying to keep on top of things. The terrorists he dealt with felt emboldened by the hysterical hand wringing that the progressive politicians wrapped themselves up in – a battle he knew he could not win. 26 years ago, he had sworn his allegiance to the Queen and to uphold the law, without fear or favour. Without fear or favour, what did that even mean, he wondered. Prisons were overflowing with convicted criminals for whom the Police were no deterrent. The newspapers seemed to carry headlines of new lows in depravity, kids killing other kids, old people being attacked in their own homes by junkies, rape gangs operating with impunity as everyone was scared to be called a racist, car jackings in the middle of London. The list went on and on in his head and he had to force himself to set it aside.

JT was speaking to him, '...for bringing us the intel Rory.'

'Um sorry?' he asked looking up at JT, 'I was just thinking about something.'

'I was saying thanks for the intel. We'll go drop the kids' bike off and see if he shows. We can take a look around, see the lay of the land.'

'You think he might not come back for it?'

'We'll see. The kid seems genuine enough and the things he's told us, check out,' JT realised he hadn't told Maxwell about the kids finances, but thought that could wait.

'Can I meet him?' asked Maxwell.

'Why would you want to meet him?' JT asked, looking at him quizzically.

'Because, I'm involved now, aren't I?' he looked JT in the eye.

'You've done your bit, I'll stay in touch and we can share intel, but we haven't decided what our next move is, if any,' said JT flatly.

'Bollocks you haven't decided!' snorted Maxwell, 'you might not have voted yet, but no way you're going to just walk away.'

'As I said-'

'Vote now,' suggested Maxwell, 'go ahead, don't mind me.'

'There are things we need to discuss. Each of us gets a free vote, after we discuss the options,' said JT.

'I'm in,' Taff interrupted, 'I'd fancy a shot at sorting these bastards out if the coppers can't.'

'Me too,' said Posty as he, Rambo and Cooky all held up their hands.

'Say the word boss,' said Taff.

JT nodded and looked at his team, he'd known they would all volunteer for anything he'd put to them but the ramifications of what might happen to his men was eating at him. He realised that all of the men were now looking at Maxwell who was holding up his hand. 'Count me in,' he said with sincerity, 'count me in.'

'Thank you, gentlemen,' said JT, 'I was never in doubt that you would want to do the right thing. Let's have another chat with Easy and see exactly what this right thing is going to entail. Then we can vote.'

'I want to have a proper run through his tech kit with him boss, the kid's got some skills.' said Joe, 'maybe get me some financial advice while we're at it.'

'Financial advice?' queried Maxwell

'Long story,' said JT. 'You in a Police vehicle Rory, where are you parked?'

'No, came in my Prius, parked at the back of the Connaught, Parker the Concierge is ex job.'

'Ok, can you take Rambo and Cooky over to collect our vehicles and we'll RV 1640 hrs at New Beckton Park?'

'New Beckton?' asked Maxwell.

'Yes, will give you time to go get changed, you look like a cop in that suit.'

'I am a cop,' protested Maxwell looking down at his clothes.

'Not where we're going, you're not,' said JT.

CHAPTER FOURTEEN

HALF WAY ALONG THE road the second 4x4 sat at the junction of Campion Close. The silver bodywork hadn't seen polish in a long time, if ever, but like most 4x4s in London there was not a speck of mud to be seen. The number plates it bore related to a much dirtier and harder worked version of the same Toyota Land Cruiser model. That particular vehicle was currently parked up outside a cowshed in Cumbria, its owner checking on his animals.

JT glanced up from the iPad he was using and could see 4 passengers as they passed the Landcruiser. His team was together and they had Rory Maxwell in tow, he wasn't yet sure how he felt about that.

'Cooky, we'll drop you here at Abbey Playing Field,' said JT leaning forward, and pointing to the park on the map filling the iPad screen, 'the bike gets locked to the railing outside the café, here,' he continued pointing out the second spot.

Cooky looked at the screen, then traced his finger along a route from park to café. 'Roger,' he said, 'Code?'

JT handed him the bike lock with the padlock combination set, Cooky memorised it and rotated the tumblers to activate the lock.

'Drop the bike off, then get yourself a seat in Samir's café. Get a view of the bookies and of the launderette across the road,' JT told him.

'Roger that, you want updates on movements?' he asked.

'Any vehicles, any of the faces from the photos, see if you can get images on your phone, it's at distance but better than nothing.'

'Roger all that. What about the kid?'

'Let him take the bike away, Joe's put a GPS tracker inside the seat post so we'll see where he goes.'

'You don't trust him boss?'

'Not yet I don't. I think he's telling us the truth about what's going on, I just don't know why,' said JT, as he sat back to contemplate that very question.

#

Cooky locked the bike to the railings and stood up to remove his high-vis vest. He'd had a quick look at the bookies and launderette as he rode past and then doubled back after a hundred yards or so to return to the railings outside the café. Standing and turning slowly he appeared to be looking for someone or something without his gaze settling on any one place. Satisfied he had the lay of the land fixed in his head he went to the window of the café and pretended to read the menu. In the reflection of the glass, he could see the roofline of the building opposite. The launderette was on the ground floor of a two storey red brick building. Launderette, charity shop, estate agent and a nail salon completed the four retail spaces. There were no doorways from the front street to the flats above which meant stairs at the rear of the building, he noted. The roof was pitched with slate but was too low to cover the depth of the building; parts of it must be a flat roof. Another mental note and a piece of the mental map he was building. The building opposite had looked of the same age and design as the one he was stood in front of but he couldn't be sure. Cooky walked the forty-one steps to the zebra crossing and waited for an older man to start using the crossing from the opposite side. When the traffic had stopped, he walked out looking left and right and checking the roof lines as he went. The building beyond the bookies confirmed what he'd suspected, the roof was made up of two pitched sections to the front and rear with a channel of flat roof running between. Stopping outside the estate agent's window he looked at the reflection of the building opposite. He saw immediately why the roof was designed the way they were. The 60s architects hadn't wanted to ruin their design by having rainwater down pipes down the front of the buildings. Like doors to the flats above the retail premises, they must be at the rear or the gable ends. Another detail to add to his mental map.

Having spent enough time to feign perusing the estate agency window ads, Cooky turned and headed back for the crossing. He was aware of an old man watching him from the doorway of the café. Samir? Still looking relaxed and moving more sluggishly than he would naturally, he crossed the road and wandered back to the café.

The old man smiled at him with genuine warmth as he approached and stepped back saying, 'Welcome, welcome my friend. Would you like to eat something?'

'Just some tea please,' said Cooky as he stepped into the café. Two women sat at a table in the rear bent close to each other chatting conspiratorially. Their Hijab's were brightly coloured and spotlessly clean. Neither paid him any attention as he took a seat on a stool at the little shelf table in the window.

A moment later the old man appeared with a tray and set down a glass into which he poured steaming hot mint tea from an admirable height without spilling a drop. 'You are looking for somewhere to live?' he asked, gesturing with his eyes toward the estate agent across the street.

'Yes, well sort of. Thinking about it. What's this area like?' Cooky asked him.

'Oh, you know, there is trouble for those who seek it and those who are not careful to avoid it. But there are good shops, good food,' he smiled and gestured to his own café, 'there are mostly good people here.'

'Mostly?' asked Cooky, raising an eyebrow.

'There are bad men everywhere my friend,' said the old man, a little sadness and resignation in his voice. Cooky noticed the old man glance at the bookie shop as he spoke.

'I keep myself to myself, don't want any trouble,' he told the old man, then held out his hand to introduce himself, 'I'm Cooky,' he said.

'As Salaam u Alaikum Cooky, I am Samir,' he said, offering the slightest bow.

'Pleased to meet you, Samir,' Cooky smiled back at him.

Another customer came into the café and Samir greeted him with a smile and a hug. The two men chatted in Arabic as Samir prepared some food.

The smell of the food and sizzle of the meat on the grill made Cooky think of another café he'd sat in and drank tea. He thought about the bag he'd left under his seat when he left and how he'd felt the heat of the explosion on his back after he'd been ushered out by the café owner. The premises had been used by a warlord to plot the killing of US troops across the border in Mogadishu. The café owner had been part of a chain of informants spying on the UN troops, especially Americans. He'd deserved to die.

'Are you sure you don't wish some food?' Samir called to him from behind the counter, my chicken is extra fresh and good quality.

'It certainly smells good,' said Cooky. From his pocket he fished out some coins to count, 'What could I have for £3.75?'

'That is all you have?' asked Samir.

'Yeah, I don't get paid until tomorrow,' said Cooky, with a shrug.

'Then that will be enough,' smiled Samir.

The customer he'd greeted with a hug watched the conversation, then spoke to Samir in Arabic. Cooky pretended not to understand as the man chastised Samir saying he was not a charity, and how he'd always be poor if he gave his food away.

Samir held open his hands and with a warm smile said 'Inshallah!'. He deftly sliced open a pitta bread and used it to slide the chicken pieces from the skewer. He added chilli sauce and salad before wrapping it neatly in paper. He handed the parcel to the man who placed a £10 note on the counter. Samir opened the till to extract the change but the man held up a hand and nodded toward Cooky.

As the man left, he put his hand on Cooky's shoulder and said, 'Enjoy your food brother.'

Cooky nodded to the man and turned to see a grinning Samir approach him with a plate of food. 'God provides,' he said holding up a hand to decline Cooky's handful of coins.

'You are too kind,' he told Samir.

'What goes around, comes around,' said the old man happily, heading off to clear the table of the two chatting women.

Across the road Cooky could see Easy walking. He was approaching the bookie shop and would have to pass both it, and the launderette, to get to the zebra crossing. As Easy reached the bookie shop the door opened and a big man built like a bodybuilder stepped out and stood on the top step. He lit a cigarette and took a deep drag before coughing and spitting onto the pavement. Easy had to check his step and moved out closer to the edge of the pavement. The big man's face showed no recognition of the fact he'd almost spat on someone. He lifted the cigarette to his mouth as Cooky snapped photos of him while pretending to type a text message. As Cooky zoomed in to check the images he'd captured he saw the big cigarette holding hand was tattooed. There were gaudy gold rings to match the chunky gold bracelet. A chill ran through Cooky as he realised where he'd seen that hand before. It had been holding the hand of the little boy in the video. Sick big bastard thought Cooky, and went back to eating his food.

Easy crossed the road at the zebra crossing and walked up to his bike, he was 5 minutes early but it was already chained to the railings as JT had said it would be. He examined the padlock and tried it but it was secure and needed a combination. Cooky watched him from the café window and realised Easy was facing a quandary. He didn't know the combination of the new bike lock. The puzzled look on Easy's face changed to recognition as he turned and looked into the café. Cooky gave him an almost imperceptible shake of the head and, after a second of eye-contact, he looked away.

Cooky watched as Easy paced back and forward and turned his gaze up to the sky as he racked his brains for what the code might be.

Come on kid, you can do it, he thought to himself and realised he was willing the kid to work it out. He knew this kid was super smart but wondered if he would pass this test, if indeed this was a test, as JT had deliberately not told him the code.

Easy took his phone from his pocket and looked at it, he seemed to be debating who to call and Cooky wondered if JT had given him a contact number. He didn't dial a number but stopped and stared at the screen for a couple of seconds before he looked up, smiling. He was careful not to look at Cooky but had turned to where he knew he could be seen. He was still smiling to himself and approached the bike with a confident swagger.

Cooky knew he'd worked it out and watched with something approaching pride as the kid bent down and turned the tumblers to the code. 3-2-7-9 spelled E-A-S-Y on a phone keypad.

Movement shifted his attention to the front of the bookies, the big man was leaving and walking toward the zebra crossing. Cooky reckoned the man to be 6'5', a good two inches taller than himself, his steroid induced physique was the classic inverted triangle. His powerful biceps made the short sleeves of his deliberately tight t-shirt ride up so the world could see this guy liked to curl. Cooky saw the guy, like all of his sort, had skipped leg day. His huge frame made his rather average sized legs look positively bird-like. When Cooky saw the guy's shoes, he knew for certain this was the guy from the video.

Igor reached the zebra crossing and stepped out without looking to see if cars were stopping. Of-course they would, they wouldn't dare otherwise he thought to himself, and not for the first time. He remembered with relish how he had dragged the young guy off his motorbike and kicked him unconscious at this very spot when the young guy revved at him for crossing slowly. His mere presence, he knew, could make grown men piss their pants.

Outside the café he saw some black kid fiddling with his bike at the railings. He paid him no heed, these kids needed to man up and get themselves a car he thought. At the door of the café, he stopped and looked inside. There were two women wearing those stupid Muslim outfits that he hated, sitting at the back. How was he supposed to know if they were worth taking, when they covered themselves up in these tents? Stupid cows, they didn't know what they were missing, he thought to himself and grinned. His grin changed to a frown when he saw the big black man sitting on a stool at the window. This was not a face he recognised and he was sitting in the seat Igor used on the odd occasions he visited this Arab cesspit.

He walked to the counter and said in a deliberately loud voice, 'Old man, grill me some chicken, I want fresh chicken not the shit that sits out all day, fresh.'

'Yes sir,' said Samir, 'all of my chicken is fresh, I prepared it...'

Igor interrupted him, 'Enough of the chitter chatter get cooking my fucking chicken like I told you, and hurry up,' he said, still in the loud voice he was using for effect.

Cooky was using his phone propped against the wall at the corner of his shelf cum table. He watched Igor turn to look at him as if waiting for a reaction. Igor walked to the door and spat on the pavement, his huge bulk filling the door frame. Cooky repositioned his phone and reverted to his peripheral vision as he made a show of ignoring Igor.

'Hey black boy, you are in my seat,' he said, still looking out at the street from the doorway.

Cooky ignored him but gripped the fork he held in his right ready to stab Igor should he approach.

'I'm talking to you Blacky!' Igor hissed at him, as he kicked the nearest stool against Cooky's.

Cooky looked at him as if seeing him for the first time. He pushed back his stool and stood up, he looked Igor in the eye and waited. He glanced at the man's throat and knew that's where he would thrust the fork he held at the ready. He knew his second move would be a vicious kick to the inside of the man's knee, from experience he knew the man would never walk quite the same again.

'Please, no trouble, no trouble!' said Samir as he rushed out from behind the counter. He stood between them, dwarfed by the huge men. Turning to Cooky he said, 'Please my friend come, sit at this table over here, I have for you some more tea. This way please,' the pleading voice sounded pitiful, and he placed his hand over the fork in Cooky's hand, 'no trouble, come, come sit over here.'

Cooky allowed himself to be guided away to a table beside the women at the rear of the café.

'Yes, Blacky, go sit with the other women,' snorted Igor from the doorway.

Samir went back to the counter and retrieved his cleaning spray and cloth. He removed the plate and glass then sprayed and wiped the surfaces.

'Do it properly old man, I don't want to catch no Monkey Pox from the Blacky ha?' He roared with laughter at his own joke.

Samir gave an extra spray and wipe then retreated back behind the counter. The two women took the chance to collect their bags made their way to the counter where they each placed some coins and headed for the door.

'Hey, honey, why do you wear that big bed sheet? Are you fat and ugly under that thing?' snorted Igor.

He watched the women stop, frozen wide eyed with indecision, to run or stand. 'Maybe you should show me what you got under there, maybe some nice lingerie huh?'

Samir appeared with a tray of tea and a can of coke and brought them to the window table. As he did so he gently pushed the women out of the door, 'Goodbye my sisters, safe home.'

He placed a can of coke on the table. 'Your usual sir,' he said to Igor.

Igor looked at the tray, 'I didn't tell you to bring me tea,' he growled at Samir.

'It's not for you sir,' said Samir, 'it is for the other gentleman.'

'Gentleman? Gentleman? You mean this is Blacky's tea? Let me see it.' Igor picked the teapot up and lifted the lid. He looked back at Cooky's table but Cooky did not look back. Igor grinned and then spat noisily into the tea pot. 'There,' he said, 'now the tea is ready!' He fixed Samir with a look that dared him to complain.

Samir stepped backward and moved to go back behind the counter.

'Give the Blacky his tea. Now!' screamed Igor, loud enough to make Samir jump.

Samir composed himself and turned toward Cooky and looked at him apologetically. Then he dragged his foot and hooked the leg of a chair tumbling forward and spilling the contents of the tray over the floor. Cooky jumped up to help him and lifted Samir back to his feet.

'A thousand apologies my friend,' he whispered and placed a hand on Cooky's arm.

Cooky nodded his reply but said nothing then retook his seat as Samir picked up the tray and teapot. He watched Samir take them behind the counter then return with a mop.

Cooky saw that Easy had been watching the events from outside and he gestured to him with a sideways nod that he should go. Easy gave a little nod back and walked off pushing his bike.

Noisy dance music blasted out from the window seat as Igor's phone rang. He answered with, 'Yes Boss,' as he stepped outside.

Cooky couldn't hear what was being said and from his seat spoke to Samir, 'You ok?'

'Yes, he will go soon enough. It is always the same, shouting and demanding.'

Igor walked back in still speaking into his phone, '...I make collection and get food then back in 5 minutes.' He hung up the phone and glanced at Cooky before saying, 'hurry the fuck up old man, I am hungry, now!'

'The chicken will take two more minutes to be cooked sir, just two minutes more.'

Igor picked up his can of coke and drained it, almost absent-mindedly he crushed the can and threw it onto the floor. 'More Coke,' he said without looking at Samir. Samir took a fresh can from the fridge and placed it on top of the counter along with a pile of napkins. Igor stood in the doorway, and lit a cigarette.

Samir did his thing with the pitta bread and wrapped up a pile of grilled chicken. 'Chilli sauce?' he asked the back of Igor's head.

'Of course, lots,' said Igor as he turned and stepped to the counter with the cigarette in his mouth. 'I take payment now,' he said to Samir as he picked up the can of coke.

'But payment is always on a Saturday,' answered Samir, sounding nervous.

'I said I take payment now. Don't piss me off, old man.'

Samir opened the till and retrieved £35 in notes, 'this is all I have. On Saturday I will pay all.'

'You try to take piss old man, maybe I burn your café huh?'

'No, please. I will get the money for you. Take this £35 and I will get the £65 to you tomorrow. I will have customers tonight. Tomorrow, please!'

'I take this now,' said Igor, pocketing the money, 'you have £100 ready Saturday. Or else I bring Mr Zippo,' he grinned as he flicked his lighter open and closed. He picked up the food parcel still grinning and walked out.

Cooky checked his phone, the line to JT had remained open since Igor had entered the café. He tapped the phone 3 times before ending the call to let the others know it was over. As he stood up, he saw Samir leaning back against the counter with his fingers clasped behind his head looking at the ceiling.

'You ok Uncle?' he asked gently. When he got no response he touched the old man's arm, 'Uncle? You ok?'

Samir brought his hands back down by his side and turned to Cooky. His face seemed somehow more wrinkled as if he'd aged in the last hour. 'Yes, my friend I am sorry you had to listen to that, that animal.'

'Why don't you tell the Police?' asked Cooky.

'No Police. They cannot help. I spoke to an officer once and he said I must make a statement but they could not watch this place 24 hours a day.'

'You think he'd burn your café?'

'They did it to the nail bar around the corner. The Chinese man, he would not pay. They burned the shop. Four women slept in the flat above the shop and there were bars on the rear windows. The chemicals in the shop they...the fire brigade could not save them.'

'They all died?' asked Cooky.

'Yes, it was terribly sad.'

'The Police launched a murder investigation?'

'No, they said it was an accident. The Chinese man ran away, I think the girls that worked for him were illegal.'

'How much money do you give that guy?'

'£100 per week, but it is not always him, there are others,' said Samir.

'Others?'

'Yes, there is a boss man, he does not come here but I have seen him go into the betting shop over there. Actually, he came here once when they first arrived and asked about my CCTV.'

'What about your CCTV?'

'They wanted to see the tapes. To see what was covered. It pointed at the counter. I get some drunk people at the weekend, sometimes they can make trouble.'

'And the cameras are a deterrent?' asked Cooky.

'They were, sometimes. But...'

'But?'

'Now I am not allowed to operate them. I said I would only point them in the shop but they said no. They said they would protect me instead. £20 a week for them to make sure no trouble. Then £50. Now £100. The café barely takes £200 some weeks, I will not be able to continue I think.'

'That's bad news Uncle, I'm sorry.'

'Thankyou my friend,' said Samir, then brightening up he went on, 'enough of my troubles. God will know what to do, he always does. Now you, what is your situation, you need somewhere to live?'

'Yeah, I'm thinking I might be doing some work around here.'

'What sort of work?'

'A bit of driving, manual labour sort of work. There's a team of us. My boss is checking out an opportunity nearby.'

'Ah, I see,' said Samir, 'I may be able to help. My landlord Mr Choudhury, he is a good man. He has returned to Bangladesh and asked me to look after the flat upstairs. The old tenants moved out and it's a bit of a mess but perhaps it might suit your needs until you find somewhere better?'

'I could pay you some rent?' suggested Cooky.

'We will see what you think first, as I say, the old tenants left a mess. Perhaps if you could do some repairs and tidy then Mr Choudhury would let you stay without rent?'

'Sounds good to me.'

'Excellent, I will fetch the key and you can go through the back door here, from the lane there are steps up to the black door. Go have a look and tell me what you think?'

Cooky opened the door and was hit by the stale smell. Rubbish in a black bin bag sat in the kitchen as if someone had started tidying after a party but gave up. Empty cans and bottles covered every kitchen surface and a fair bit of the floor. Cooky opened each door as he passed. Two bedrooms, one with a double bed, the other with bunk beds and all with filthy mattresses. Pipes sticking up from the floor and out of the wall above the broken bath were all that remained of the sink and the shower. A seatless toilet and a lidless cistern stood defiantly against a background of peeling 1970s orange and brown wallpaper. The living room faced onto the front street and Cooky used a broom handle to push open the faded and dusty curtains. Dozens of dead flies littered the window sill. When he tried to open the window, he discovered the catch locked and no key obvious. A check of the bedroom window provided a key and Cooky opened each window to let some air through the place.

Back in the living room, despite the outside of the window being filthy Cooky found as he'd hoped he had a perfect view of the bookie shop and the launderette. Closing the window, the traffic noise was cancelled and he realised he could hear Samir speaking with a customer downstairs. The voices were muffled but he couldn't quite make out what was being said.

After using his phone to take a video of the flat interior and of the views afforded from the windows, Cooky sent them as encrypted files to JT. His accompanying message read, 'Room with a view'. A few seconds later the reply came, "Reserve it."

Cooky went back down stairs and used the lane to get round the block to an ATM to withdraw £100. He returned the key to Samir saying he'd price up the repairs to make it habitable and let him know. He handed him the £100 saying he'd found it on the floor upstairs. Samir did not wish to accept it but Cooky insisted saying, 'It must be the will of god.'

#

At the same time as Cooky had been looking round the flat above Samir's café, two mopeds each carrying two youths, rode along the footpath near the fishing pond in the park. They wore the urban uniform of grey hoodies and tracksuit bottoms. The youths were oblivious to the men watching them from the parked 4x4s sat side by side on the opposite bank. Each of the moped pillion passengers climbed off and walked up behind two fishermen sitting facing the murky grey water. The youths looked at each other, before simultaneously kicking the fishermen from behind, pushing them into the water.

Picking up the bags of the fishermen, the passengers jumped back onto the rear of the mopeds and laughed and jeered at the fishermen scrambling to get out of the cold water. The shouts of the fishermen were indiscernible but their meaning was clear. The laughing youths took off along the circuitous path that would bring them to past where the team were parked.

'May I?' asked Taff.

'Be my guest,' replied JT, 'but cover your face.'

'No problem,' said Taff, before covering his smile with a snood.

Taff left the vehicle and Posty said, 'I think maybe I could stretch my legs too Boss.'

'Make it quick, and quiet please.'

After Taff had climbed out of the vehicle, Maxwell climbed ungainly from the back seat into the front beside JT. 'Elegantly done,' said JT as he watched Maxwell wriggle his legs into position beneath the steering wheel.

'What are they going to do?' he asked JT when he was sitting comfortably.

'Deliver a life lesson I should think,' said JT without emotion.

Taff walked toward the path and stooped to pick up a hefty fallen branch. Posty caught up with him and did likewise. Posty then jogged ahead and into some dense bushes that skirted one side of the path. Taff walked past him toward the approaching mopeds and then made out that he'd seen them and turned around to walk away. He reversed his route back up the path and held the branch in front of him, hidden from the youths.

Seeing another potential victim, the youths laughed and revved their whiny engines as they sped up toward Taff. One pairing never made it that far. Posty swung his branch into the face of the moped rider nearest him and knocked him and his passenger clean off the moped. The other moped carried on building speed and the pillion passenger was looking back to see what had happened to his mates. He didn't see Taff turn, but the rider did. He was too close to evade Taff and instead rode straight at him. Taff stepped aside, agile as a matador and struck the rider to the side of the head.

'Bullseye!' said Taff, as he walked toward the tangle of moped and youths.

Blood was already showing through the hood of the driver and Taff used the stick to push it back from the youth's face. A terrified looking youth of 18 or 19 stared up at him, the blood seeping from the split under his eye trickled down pooling in his ear and dripping onto his hood. The crimson blood shone against the matt brown skin. The passenger was trapped under the moped, pinned against the protruding roots of a big tree. The tree glowered over them and so did Taff.

'It's burning me, mister,' whimpered the passenger.

Taff thought he could smell the singe of the painfully hot exhaust where it rested centimetres from the youth's face. 'So, it seems,' replied Taff, he was still wearing the snood up to his eyes but he spoke using an accent that he thought sounded somewhere between Polish and Pakistani.

'Do you know who we are man? You in deep fucking shit!' hissed the driver, who had found some misplaced bravado.

'Yes, it so happens I do,' replied Taff ,struggling to maintain his assumed accent, 'you're no good pieces of shit, is who you are.'

'I'll fucking kill you!' shouted the driver reaching for his pocket. He seemed to have forgotten he was still on the ground and Taff stood on the youth's arm. His elbow was resting on a tree root and his hand trapped in his pocket. Taff shifted all of his weight onto his foot and was rewarded with a satisfying crack as the bone in the arm broke.

Ignoring the yelp, Taff bent down and stuffed the blood stained hood into the youth's mouth. Reaching into a pocket he removed a long silver handled flick knife, 'Oh, pretty knife,' he said to no-one in particular. He ripped out the waist cord of the youth's trousers and made a noose. Slipping the cord around the neck of the driver Taff stabbed the knife into the tree above and used it to secure the rope. It wouldn't kill the kid but he was going nowhere in a hurry.

Posty appeared beside him and gave a mock round of applause for Taff's handywork. Then showed him the phones he'd taken from the other two youths before letting them run away.

'Good idea,' said Taff, in an accent that made Posty snigger.

Posty lifted the moped off the passenger and took the phone which was obvious in the tracksuit pocket. He also saw a hammer jammed in the waistband which he removed before letting the moped fall back onto the wailing youth. He threw the hammer into the pond behind him before examining the phones. Both required fingerprint activation and he used the fingers of the prone youths to open the phones before changing the settings to keep them open. He'd done the same thing with the first two phones and now had four new phones to play with.

Maxwell could see the fishermen who had been pushed into the pond were making their way around the path and in their direction.

He looked at JT who was reading something on his phone. 'Time to go,' he said and pointed to where the fishermen were on the path.

'Yep,' said JT.

Maxwell gave a short beep of the car's horn and started the engine ready to leave. Taff and Posty got into the rear of the vehicle and Maxwell drove them out of the car park and toward town with the second vehicle following.

'Let's go get Cooky,' said JT, 'it's time to vote.'

CHAPTER FIFTEEN

After driving north for almost an hour, the vehicles pulled into the car park of a large pub and the seven men found two tables they pulled together in the otherwise empty conservatory. They ordered food and pots of tea and made small talk about a camping trip whenever the staff came in and out to serve them. JT sat quietly as Cooky filled them all in on what he'd learned.

'Easy?' asked JT when he'd finished.

'Bright kid boss, as I said he got the padlock code. He looked scared of the big guy and didn't look like they knew each other. He hung about to see what happened in the café, but took the hint and buggered off on his bike.'

JT sat contemplating what to say before looking round the team. 'I had a message from the brass earlier. We're persona non grata, until the SIB investigation is complete. Who knows how long that will take. Meantime we're on *Gardening leave.*'

'Gardening leave?' asked Maxwell.

'They can't sack us, and they can't court martial us until the SIB are finished with their Whitehall sponsored witch hunt.'

'We did nothing wrong boss,' said Joe looking dejected.

'I know Joe, we followed our orders, we did our job.'

'Bloody right we did,' said Taff, his usual smiley demeanour missing.

'They expect us to keep our heads down, but stay match fit in case they decide to invade some other hell hole and need us to go do their dirty work again,' he looked at them each in turn. 'Which means we have some time to kill. Whatever we decide to do we are on our own, no back up, no kit and no protection. So now gents, we have to decide. Do we take these Kosanians down a peg or two? And if we do, how do we make sure it doesn't come back on the Regiment?'

'Or the Met,' said Maxwell, 'I just watched some rather entertaining vigilante shit go down. Not only did I watch it, I did nothing to stop it. Like it or not I'm part of this too.'

'You can always walk away Rory,' said JT.

'No chance, besides I'd have access to some useful intel, and maybe some kit too.'

'Okay, my friend, thank you. Gentlemen, show of hands...'

CHAPTER SIXTEEN

JT turned on the spot looking around at the state of the flat. He realised he'd instinctively put his hands in his pockets to stop him touching anything.

'It's going to be like the Ritz in no time!' chortled Cooky as he ripped the corner of the filthy carpet up.

'Evidently, your idea of the Ritz is different to mine!' replied JT.

'How long are we renting the place?' asked Rambo, who had just returned from yet another circuit to the skip outside, 'Is it worth our while stripping it all out?'

'We'll see. It's the ideal OP and saves us travelling back and forward to Mayfair,' replied JT as he pulled on a pair of gloves.

JT knelt down at the opposite end of the carpet from Cooky and they rolled it neatly. Cooky threw it effortlessly over his shoulder and walked out of the room heading out to the skip.

An expletive laden curse from the bathroom was followed by the sound of laughter. As JT approached, he saw Taff bent double in the doorway with tears of laughter dripping from his nose.

'What's so funny?' JT asked.

Taff stepped back to clear the doorway and pointed, 'The...Posty...has shit himself, boss!' his laughter making the words a struggle.

'Very fucking funny!' came the disgruntled response from within the bathroom.

JT popped his head around the corner and saw Posty slumped back against the bathtub with the broken toilet between his legs and a smattering of brown sludge down the front of his boiler suit. 'Something you ate?' asked JT, before ducking his head out of the way as a handful of sludge was hurled in his direction.

'Movement!' came a call from the lounge.

'What are you seeing?' asked JT as he made his way through the flat.

'Two vehicles just pulled up outside. Four up and three up. The same set up as yesterday,' reported Joe.

JT looked at his watch, 1130 hrs, same time as yesterday and the day before. 'They keep a tight schedule,' said JT as he stood behind Joe at the window of the flat.

'Big goon is out babysitting the cars again. He looks like he's wearing his wee sisters t-shirt, or it was sprayed on,' Joe spoke without ever taking his eyes off of the target.

'Guys from the cars tooled up?' asked JT.

'All wearing loose jackets certainly. The one with the shaved head can't help himself and has to keep touching inside his jacket with his left hand. Shoulder holster judging by the way he stands. Pretty amateur goon by the looks of him. The guy minding the boss looks a bit sharper. He checks the street and when he gets out the car and is much more attentive than the others. He's another big bugger and I think he's wearing some Kevlar under that shirt.'

'The boss?' asked JT.

'He's cock of the north. Expensive clobber, well groomed, and that silk shirt isn't hiding anything. He obviously trusts his security team big time, or he's too stupid to think of any threat.'

'He certainly is confident that he's untouchable,' said JT picking up the notebook Joe was using. He read back a few pages and nodded slowly as he confirmed what he was thinking. 'So, the marked Police car drives past at 1115 hrs, each of the last 4 days, then these guys arrive at 1130 hrs. That's not a coincidence, that's a pattern and a deliberate pattern.'

'I was thinking the same thing Boss,' said Joe, still watching the building across the road. 'Those coppers either have a rigid designated patrol matrix that the Kosanians know about, or they're clearing the way.'

'They appear from the same direction each time?'

'Yes Boss, coppers from the West, they don't stop but go pretty slowly and they follow the High Street until they turn North toward the train station. The Kosanians come in from the East, they're not in a rush either but they go straight to their parking spots with the big ape guy standing waiting for them. He stands guard over the cars until the boss guy leaves by 12. He's never stayed longer than that.'

'Other visitors?'

'A pretty constant flow.'

'Gamblers?'

'Some maybe, but it follows a pattern again. Someone shows up every 10 minutes like clockwork from 0900-1100 hrs. Regular looking folk, a proper mix but they all stay less than 2 minutes. I checked the racing post for horse racing and dogs but none of the timings fit. I'm thinking it's like that place in Fallujah, remember that old school where the locals had to pay the Taliban their taxes?'

'I remember it well,' said JT remembering the heat and dust and the roof they'd been observing from. He also remembered the mother they'd watched being flogged in the street when she'd been raped by her husband's brother, as if it were her fault. He could hear her screams that gave way to a pitiful sobbing. Then he remembered her terrified face three weeks later when she appeared out of a doorway and walked towards his position, how he'd called to her over and over to stop. He remembered it all so vividly, but a slowed down version of the real time events, as she'd opened her coat to show him the bomb vest. From 30 yards his three round burst had hit her in the face, they'd smashed her jaw and teeth and exited the back of her head in an explosion of skull fragments and brain matter...

'Yeah, well it's just like that but without a load of Taliban trying to kill us.'

JT cleared his throat and shook the memories from the front of his mind, 'What happens after 1200hrs?'

'Somewhere around 1500hrs 5 or 6 young guys turn up and do their best gangster impression. They're all hooded up and wear scarves over their faces, but get this, one of them has a plaster cast on his arm.'

'Our friends from the fishing pond? Very interesting! How long do they stay?'

'10-15 minutes, they swagger in but when they come out, they're bouncing.'

'Drugs.'

'Yeah, I reckon so, looks like they've all had a snort of coke and they're heading out to a party.'

'Where do they go?'

'They head East, but cut round the back of the block, beside the hairdressers and the Oxfam shop. I reckon they must keep mopeds round the back, you can hear them start up and rev the noisy bloody things. They don't come back out onto the road so there must be a path up there. I've not had a chance to eyeball it.'

'Okay Joe, thanks. I'll take a walk up there myself later. Want a brew?'

'Cheers Boss, that would be pukka.'

#

JT had watched the Kosanian vehicles leave and then went out to recce the area where the wannabe gangster youths parked their mopeds. He found the narrow alleyway beside the Oxfam charity shop, at just over 3 feet wide and a rubbish strewn floor it wouldn't be easy to ride a moped through, certainly not in a rush. When he found a few broken glass bottles lying in a pile he took the opportunity to spread the broken glass in a haphazard strip from wall to wall. A few bits of litter and leaves scattered across the glass made it less obvious to the untrained eye. At the rear of the buildings was a small service yard. The concrete surface was less messy than the lane and it was easy to see the skid marks of narrow moped tyres. This was the moped parking area.

A bigger derelict warehouse made up the back of the service yard and it had a tunnel for delivery vehicles from the road running parallel to the High Street. JT walked through the tunnel and crossed the road. He turned to look at the old warehouse and saw the metal fire escape running down the right hand side of the building. The peeling paint on the front of the building read 'Thos. Wolfe & S'. The graffiti that covered the bottom half of the three storey building obscured the rest of the name and JT wondered whether Mr Wolfe had more than one son. He scanned the building and saw that all of the windows had been boarded up apart from the two long windows of the top floor. Maybe they were two high for the stone throwing vandals to reach. The fire escape had a metal door to prevent access and a liberal arrangement of barbed wire covered the top. Checking no-one was in the street or overlooking the fire escape, JT reached up from underneath the metal treads and worked his fingers into gaps. Getting a decent grip, he walked his hands upwards and backwards to climb the stair from underneath monkey bar style. At the top of the flight, he swung his feet up and over the handrail then pulled himself over and landed in a crouched position. He waited for a few seconds listening, before moving up the stairs to the second floor. He found the door had been previously forced open and it was braced in place with a piece of 2 by 4 wood. A few kicks at the wooden brace dislodged it and the door swung open far enough for him to slip into the building. Long tables lined the room, each with 4 sewing machines fixed in place. JT saw a set of faded plans on the wall, it showed various sections of cloth that made up canvas bell tents. That's what Mr Wolfe made here he thought, they were coming back into fashion but like everything nowadays they were made cheaper in China. Locating the stairs at the end of the room he walked up to the 3rd floor. This had been the management level and glass partitions separated 5 rooms of different sizes. The corrugated glass distorted the views and he opened each door to see inside.

The biggest office had been Mr Wolfe seniors and inside was a heavy wooden desk with a big green leather chair behind it. The filing cabinets were also dark wood with brass curved handles under a layer of dust. JT lifted a hand to pull open a drawer that was slightly open, his training made him automatically check for wires. He paused and remembered a day when he'd gone shopping with Esmé in a Bordeaux flea market. She'd found a lovely old bureau and was about to open the drawer when he'd grabbed her hand. She'd gotten angry at him and stormed off. Even then it should have been obvious she wasn't cut out to be a Special Forces wife. Or maybe he just wasn't cut out to be a husband. Pulling himself away from the uncomfortable memory he slid open the drawer and found a sales brochure for Wolfe Tents. It was dated 1978, before he was born. He moved to the window and confirmed it had a clear view of the yard at the rear then dusted off the big old leather chair and made himself comfortable.

At 1450 hrs he heard the mopeds whine as they raced up the street. They drove through the tunnel with a noisy engine rev and squealing brakes as they came to a halt. 3 mopeds each with a driver and passenger. They all wore the uniform of every self-respecting youth, grey jogging bottoms and hoodies. JT watched them park and could hear them speaking thanks to the courtyard acoustics.

'I can out shoot you any day bro!'

'Fuck dat man, you ain't never shot shit!'

'Nah, I've shot plenty of times.'

'Yeah, like when?'

'Like last night, in your Sista!'

Uproarious laughter made it sound like kids having fun, but JT knew there was a dark undertone of violence between young men when they tried to find a pecking order.

'Hey Dylan, how about I put a cap in your ass?' said one of the hooded youths. He was taller than the rest and skinny. He was holding what appeared to be a Glock pistol in the ludicrous horizontal fashion like American movie gangsters. Another kid walked up to him and put his forehead against the barrel of the Glock. JT could see this was the kid with his arm in a plaster cast. So, this was Dylan, JT could see he had a bit of a screw loose. The group was silent for a second, before the kid with the Glock put his arm around the kid with the plaster cast.

'Funny you should say that Felix, that's exactly where I did your Sista!' cried Dylan laughing. The whole group laughed and the tension was broken.

'Now, come on, don't want to be late for big bad Igor the mon-ster, we've got supplies waiting,' said Felix tucking the Glock into the waistband of his trousers.

JT watched the group head off down the alleyway before checking the photos he'd taken on his phone. 20 minutes later the group were back and as Joe had said they were all hyped up and bouncing. They jumped onto their mopeds and screeched off through the tunnel and away.

CHAPTER SEVENTEEN

Rory Maxwell climbed out of his training pool and peeled off his swim cap. Reaching for his towel he glanced at his mobile. He had missed a call from a withheld number but the caller hadn't left a message. Can't have been that important he thought as he dried his body. Pulling on his robe he slipped his phone into the pocket and instantly it started ringing. He glanced at the screen and saw it was from an unknown number. Swiping the screen to answer the call he waited for a voice at the other end.

'Detective Inspector Maxwell?'

'Who is this?'

'You are, Detective Inspector Rory Maxwell?'

'I'll ask again, who is this?'

'My name is unimportant, Detective Inspector, however, you may call me Hamilton, if you wish.'

'What can I do for 6, Mr 'Hamilton'

'Ah yes, very astute of you...may I call you Rory?'

'As long as you tell me why you're calling my personal mobile, you can call me whatever you like,' replied Maxwell steadily.

'Hmmm, quite. Then, Rory, I wonder if you care to get dressed and come to meet with me.'

'Get dressed?' asked Rory looking around him wondering how he could be seen.

'I am led to believe you are an accomplished and regular swimmer Rory, the background noise and the echo suggests you are by the pool in your basement.'

'You are making me uncomfortable Mr Hamilton; I think I may just hang up and you can contact me at the office,' Maxwell showed no emotion in his voice as he tested the stranger on the phone.

'Not my intention at all, I assure you, my good fellow. Perhaps if I tell you that one of my team who you know as Phillips speaks highly of you, you might feel less put upon? I have a car outside your house at the moment, Iversen, the driver, will wait another 10 minutes. If you should choose to meet with me, then he will bring you to my club. I would ask 15 minutes of your time to discuss matters of mutual interest. If you decline, I will not be offended, but will be...disappointed nonetheless.'

'Care to tell me what this matter of mutual interest concerns.'

'Not on the telephone, no. Hope to see you shortly,' replied Hamilton airily.

Maxwell didn't get a chance to speak again as Hamilton ended the call. Running up the stairs from the basement Maxwell went to the front window and saw a grey Jaguar parked on the opposite side of the road with the engine idling. The driver sat motionless, eyes forward.

Maxwell showered and dressed quickly. He stopped midway down the stairs and returned to his wardrobe to grab a tie, better safe than sorry, he knew some of these Gentlemen's Clubs had strict rules.

He crossed the road and climbed into the rear seat of the Jaguar. The driver made brief eye contact, but didn't speak, as he pulled away and drove Maxwell unhurriedly away from home.

25 minutes later Maxwell was shown into the St James's Square dining room of the East India Club. In the corner farthest from the window sat a tall straight backed man wearing tweed. He was difficult to age but the salt and pepper of his hair made him look a distinguished late 50s and every bit the quintessential British gentleman spy.

The room was empty and as Maxwell approached, he saw a plate of kippers and eggs sat waiting for him. The man looked up from his newspaper and placed his pen down before standing and offering Maxwell his hand.

'How good of you to join me Rory, please take a seat,' he gestured to the seat opposite his, 'I took the liberty of ordering us some breakfast, I hope my choice is agreeable?'

'Can't beat kippers,' said Maxwell, looking behind him before taking his seat.

'We will have the place to ourselves,' assured Hamilton, 'Coffee? I believe it's Ethiopian as you prefer?'

Maxwell nodded, slightly dumbfounded by how much this man knew about him.

Hamilton poured them both steaming hot coffee from the silver pot. Maxwell noted that Hamilton poured a touch of milk in the coffee he placed before him but that he took his own black. Something else he knew about him without asking.

Hamilton lifted his newspaper and turned it to show Maxwell the crossword he'd been completing, 'I'm a little stuck today, it's a new setter of the cryptic today. 6 across, 14 letters. The clue reads, "Unchanging Sn, undivided by continental name changes, Cupid's stone".' He looked at Maxwell with a raised questioning eyebrow.

Rory took a sip of his coffee and glanced at the newspaper, 'Constantinople?'

'Oh, you think so?' smiled Hamilton.

'I know so,' confirmed Maxwell, 'Unchanging is constant, Sn is the chemical symbol for Tin, and Cupid's Stone is Opal.'

'Ah yes, well deduced sir, well deduced indeed!' said Hamilton, dropping the newspaper onto a spare seat. He made no attempt to fill in the missing letters.

'Perhaps, you could explain why you have brought me here, other than to pretend you can't complete the crossword. Perhaps you can also explain the significance of Istanbul?'

'Istanbul?' asked Hamilton, with the questioning eyebrow raised.

'Please, let's not play that game,' said Maxwell, meeting his gaze.

'Let's eat, before the food gets cold and I will explain myself fully,' smiled Hamilton, the eyebrow still raised. Without waiting for a response, he shook out his napkin placing it across his lap and then picked up his cutlery. 'The food here is rather good. They bring their seafood from Loch Fyne, you know,' he said and lifted a forkful to his mouth. Maxwell copied the gesture and was instantly impressed by the eggs Arnold Bennett.

'Well?' enquired Hamilton.

'Excellent,' nodded Maxwell.

'Have you visited Istanbul, Rory?'

'I've transited through Ataturk, but never been into the city, no,' replied Maxwell, before adding, 'but I should imagine you already knew that?'

Hamilton ignored the question and carried on, 'Oh you should definitely make the effort, Sultanahmet is simply glorious. The Hagia Sophia is still breath-taking despite the ravages of Islamisation. The Blue Mosque is exquisite but a tad touristy. I would recommend the

Dolmabahçe Palace, the architecture is wonderful but perhaps my favourite is the interior with those enormous chandeliers – British made I might add – each weighing almost a ton.' He looked at Maxwell who remained impassive before going on, 'We have had strong links in the Byzantine world for centuries and of course we were instrumental in the downfall of those nasty Ottomans.'

'Thank you for the tourist information advert, but perhaps you can move on to what this has to do with me?' said Maxwell, pushing his unfinished plate away from him.

'Yes, quite, I was coming to that. Rory, it won't surprise you to know that we, her Majesty's Government, take an interest in goings on in areas where some of our friends and enemies congregate. Istanbul being just such a place,' he looked at Rory holding his gaze, the eyebrow flying at half-mast.

Maxwell ignored the invitation to fill the silence and waited until Hamilton went on.

'You have taken an interest in an area which we... monitor.'

'Monitor?' asked Maxwell, trying not to show his irritation at how long this was taking to get to the point.

'As you are well aware, my department and the Police Service share information and intelligence.'

'When it suits you,' said Maxwell.

'Yes, indeed. We share what we can, and what we deem suitable, but I'm sure you understand that there needs to be some...some separation?'

'Mr Hamilton, please get to the point, what exactly does any of this have to do with me?'

'Forgive me, please Rory, some matters need not be forced, but I can see you are impatient, so allow me to get to the point,' he smiled at Maxwell before continuing, 'Your database at New Scotland Yard –

Nemsys I believe you call it, was installed with a *back door*. That *back door* allows my people to monitor the intelligence on that system.'

'It's a shared system,' said Maxwell, 'your guys get to see the same intel we do. That doesn't require a "back door".'

'Yes indeed, we can access the intelligence database but our "back door" also allows real time eyes on the searching of, and input of intelligence. In doing so, it allows us to remove toes, before they are trod on, you might say.'

'There's a flag system in *Nemsys*, to prevent such things,' replied Maxwell but he was already understanding that this was something else.

'Indeed, however, flags are a very public symbol. I'm sure you understand that we would not always wish our interest to be known.'

'You spy on the Police,' said Maxwell.

'Of-course we do, we must root out the bad apples and protect the Police from yourselves – so to speak.'

'My colleagues and I are all vetted to the highest levels.'

'There is vetting, and then there is vetting Rory. There are also levels above levels,' Hamilton smiled his best disarming smile, but Maxwell was in no mood to be charmed.

'Where are you going with this?' he asked, looking Hamilton in the eye and mirroring the eyebrow raise.

'You have been enquiring about a group operating in Istanbul and here in the UK. I would like to know why.'

'Okay, but first you can tell me why you are interested,' replied Maxwell, reaching to pour himself some fresh coffee, without offering any to Hamilton.

'As I have explained, we take an interest in many things.'

Maxwell stood up and wiped his mouth with his napkin, 'You have obfuscated, not explained anything. I'll be at my desk tomorrow at

0730 if you wish to contact me about work.' He took one step and saw the driver who had brought him here stood in the doorway.

'Please sit down Rory, I will endeavour to satisfy your questions and I believe we may be able to help each other,' Hamilton picked a folder up from under his newspaper and offered it to Maxwell.

Maxwell took the folder and took his seat before opening it. Inside were several photographs of rough looking men. Each photo had a copy of a passport page beneath it. The photos were of Kosovan and Albanian men. Maxwell had seen the first 4 before – these men were known to be living in London.

Hamilton then handed him a second folder. Maxwell opened the folder and found another set of photographs. This time the men were all Russian and sported the tattoos of the Mafia. 'Not all of these men are subjects on the *Nemsys* database,' said Hamilton.

'Why are you showing them to me?' asked Maxwell.

'You showed an interest in these Albanian chaps, they may claim to be Kosovan but they are ethnic Albanians. They are all living and working here in the UK. I need to know, what is your interest in them?'

'They came up in a Police enquiry.'

'A "Police" enquiry?' asked Hamilton, using the eyebrow to full effect.

The emphasis on the word 'Police' was not wasted on Maxwell and rang alarm bells but he fought to keep his expression neutral. Not for the first time he was aware that this man, calling himself Hamilton, knew or perhaps pretended to know much more than Maxwell thought he should. 'The Russians?' He asked the question and took another sip of his coffee trying to look as casual as possible while his mind raced trying to work out where all of this was leading.

'Perhaps, it would be beneficial to all parties if we laid our respective cards on the table?' said Hamilton as he lifted a third folder and placed it in front of him.

Maxwell looked at the folder but it offered no clue to its contents. 'You first,' he replied and sat back in his chair.

'Very well, but first you might do me an obligement and answer a few questions to let me know how much detail I will require to impart, in order to help the telling, as it were?'

Maxwell remained perfectly still and gave no response. It was his turn to leave a silence for the other man to fill.

'Excellent,' said Hamilton, apparently happy to assume Maxwell's silence was tacit agreement. 'Your "enquiry" is based in London, yes?'

Maxwell gave a short perfunctory nod but maintained his silence.

'These Albanian chaps refer to themselves as 'The Kosanians' and are set up in East London with the usual business of drugs and prostitution. You are, of course, a decorated Detective operating in Counter Terrorism. Do you believe there to be a link between these criminals and terrorist activity?'

'My enquiry is at an early stage,' offered Maxwell.

'My dear Rory, while I understand your circumspection, it would speed things along if you accepted that we are on the same side,' he offered a smile that did not reach his eyes. 'When we are finished here today, I am meeting with Ronnie and the Home Secretary. Forgive me, by Ronnie, I mean your Commissioner, Sir Ronald Fowler. I'm sure he would be able to furnish me details on any new threat that you are investigating. I do, however, find him a bit of a bore. As such, I would much rather the details come from your good self – the horse's mouth, as it were. You were doubtless surprised that I am aware, or interested in your investigation, but as I say, we are on the same team, and I feel we will be able to assist each other. What do you say?'

Maxwell paused as he considered that he was in the dark about the MI6 interest. He understood that they had access to much more information than he currently did. That information could be useful and it might just stop JT and his team getting mixed up in something they shouldn't. 'I was made aware of these Kosanians operating in East London as you say. They are a particularly nasty breed of gangsters. I was told of young women going missing, children and old people being hurt, and for whatever reason, the local officers don't seem to be interested in the criminal activity. As for Terrorist links, I don't have any information to suggest that – so far, beyond the usual fundraising links and connections somewhere down the line,' he stopped and looked at Hamilton, then at the folder sat on the table. 'Your turn, what is MI6's interest?'

'By way of a gesture of good will, allow me to give you this,' said Hamilton handing over the folder. Maxwell opened the folder where he found two photographs of Police officers, neither of which he recognised.

'That young woman is Chief Inspector Ermonella Misu, known as Ella. Bit of a rising star, been with the Met for some 8 years and seems destined for high office.'

'Never heard of her,' said Maxwell, examining the photograph of an attractive young woman with dark Mediterranean features.

'Pretty girl, smart, extremely ambitious and unusually rapid at climbing ranks wouldn't you agree?'

'She ticks a few boxes and if she's as smart as you say it's not unfeasible, but yes unusual nonetheless,' said Maxwell, turning his attention to the second photograph. This face he recognised, 'Steve Harper.'

'Indeed, Chief Superintendent Steven Harper, Area Commander for East BCU. Ella Misu has been Harper's right hand person, since he plucked her out of her probationary period to work directly with him. He has been quite the mentor. You know him?'

'Know of him. He was DCI in Human Trafficking when we did a joint operation with them and the French, a couple of years ago. You're saying they're bent?'

'Not my terminology but yes, they are 'bent' as you put it.'

'That would explain a few things around there,' said Maxwell shaking his head.

'Indeed.'

'It might also explain how things came together on that operation.'

'Operation Chimera,' replied Hamilton, a statement rather than a question.

'Yeah, Chimera. We took down a Turkish/Kurdish network working out of Calais, Dunkerque and Kent.'

'Yes indeed, Chimera, the three headed monster. Steve Harper was Bellerophon?'

'Beller who?' asked Maxwell.

'Bellerophon, hero of the legend, slayer of the Chimera,' Hamilton looked out of the window as he spoke as if remembering something from a long time ago.

'I don't suppose he did it single-handedly but yes, he led the Operation and his star was certainly ascending afterwards,' said Maxwell, watching Hamilton looking lost in thought.

'You didn't think he deserved the accolades?' Hamilton returned his attention to Maxwell.

'Such things don't interest me personally. He was just, just a bit cocky for my liking. He was almost bragging about it before the job was even done.'

'Perhaps that was because he was certain of the outcome,' offered Hamilton, 'and with good reason.'

'Go on,' said Maxwell, his interest piqued.

'Are you aware of another mythical creature, the Hydra?'

'Yes, you cut its head off and it grows back.'

'Not exactly. Hydra was a multi headed sea creature, legend would have it, that if you were to cut off a head, then two would grow back in its place. Of course, the legend has it that Heracles, or Hercules if you prefer, killed the creature by removing all of its heads. His second labour. A less well remembered aspect of the legend is that he was only able to secure victory with the help of his nephew Iolaus. While the better known hero Heracles was cutting off the heads, it was Iolaus who had the idea to use a burning torch to cauterise the severed necks and prevent the re-growth.' Hamilton stopped to sip at this coffee and winced as it had become cold. He held up a hand and a member of staff appeared a moment later with a fresh pot. She placed it on a table by the door and retreated as silently as she'd arrived.

'Let me guess,' began Maxwell, as Hamilton walked to collect the coffee pot, he noted a slight limp as the MI6 agent crossed the room, 'you guys are Iolaus while the public get to see the Police as Hercules?'

'Not exactly,' replied Hamilton, as he poured fresh coffee into both cups, 'you see, Iolaus is perhaps less well known, but his name is still known to those who study the detail. We on the other hand much prefer to operate anonymously. Besides, the real strength in fighting these monsters is not always from the Police or even the Service now, is it? No, our Special Forces friends supply the muscle for heavier lifting.' He lifted an eyebrow, and the faintest of smiles, before continuing, 'sometimes only our Special Forces chaps can get the job done. Especially when lawyers and activists scrutinise everything our Police Service do. You might even think they have an agenda and would prefer anarchy. They really are terribly tiresome. Sadly, our Special Forces are not immune to the attentions of mud-slinging do-gooders. Please do take your coffee, it is Ethiopian Yirgacheffe, the club brought some in for you especially.'

Maxwell, picked up his coffee cup and held it savouring the aroma. He was realising that Hamilton must know about JT and the team, but how, and why, he could not yet work out.

Hamilton went on, 'Just like the Metropolitan Police Service, the British Army is scrutinised on behalf of the British people by our elected officials. There are actions that must be undertaken to protect the people and the interests of the country. Some of these undertakings do not sit well with certain politicians or the public. That they all benefit from the results does not interest them, they are either oblivious or outraged but in either case they are also benefactors.'

Maxwell waited patiently; he could feel the pitch was getting closer.

'So, you see,' continued Hamilton, 'there is a necessity for our Heracles and Iolaus to slay the monsters, but better that the public and politicians are unaware of the heroic acts carried out on their behalf.' He paused to take a sip of coffee and wiped his mouth with his napkin before continuing, 'I am aware that your friend Captain St John-Templeman and his team of 5 SAS troopers are currently in Barking, East London and have taken an interest in the aforementioned Kosanians. I am aware, and now you will be aware that Chief Inspector Ella Misu is a distant cousin of Viktor Liriazi. Liriazi is a crime lord in his homeland but also attempted to ply his trade further afield. We understand that he was empire building but came up against a bigger and more ruthless rival – the Russian Mafia.'

'Constantinople,' said Maxwell, as things started to become clearer,

'Yes indeed, Istanbul was a bridge too far for Liriazi. The Soltnsevsya Bratva took exception to his attempt to set up shop in what they see as their city. The Albanians thought they could simply kill the incumbent Russians and take over without realising that Moscow might not be too happy. Liriazi has since disappeared, a badly burned body was found in his residence and the local Police concluded it was Liriazi. We however, know he is alive and well, here in the UK.'

'What makes you think that?' asked Maxwell.

'We picked up some details of one of the men who had arrived on a small boat across the channel 6 weeks or so after Liriazi's alleged death. The man had no fingerprints. He had burns across his fingertips and told Border Force officials he'd been working on a boiler. He had fresh injuries to his face as if he'd been beaten. We believe this was a rather painful disguise to prevent facial recognition software identifying him.'

'I'm guessing he's not in a Detention centre?'

'Sadly not, two days after he arrived, he miraculously disappeared from the holding centre and Border Force have not seen him since. There are several disappearances per month from these centres and it appears enough money buys you the keys to our green and pleasant land.'

'So now you're looking for Liriazi, why?' asked Maxwell.

'Let's just say that Liriazi is a little Pawn on a bigger board. We have been trying to identify and remove the Queen for quite some time. Every time we think we are getting closer to identifying her, she clears the board with a literal slash and burn technique which destroys any evidence of her very existence.'

'But you're sure she exists.'

'Oh yes, we are quite sure. You see, the myth of Hydra didn't end with Heracles and Iolaus removing the creatures heads, there was one immortal head they could not kill. Legend has it that they placed a rock on top of it to keep it from doing any more harm. We believe that somehow the rock has been removed and the immortal head is back, bringing terror with it.'

'The immortal head is the Queen?'

'An awkward mix of analogies but yes, that is what we believe.'

'Where do I fit in this story?' asked Maxwell.

'You, and I believe your Special Forces friends can choose your parts,' Hamilton smiled and gestured expansively with his hands, 'you can be Hercules and Iolaus, or you can consider yourselves pawns on the board.'

'Mere pawns?' asked Maxwell.

'Never underestimate a pawn dear boy, they are just as capable of taking down a queen as any other piece.'

Chapter Eighteen

By 1630 hrs the flat had a new functioning toilet and running water. As the boiler was condemned it would mean cold showers but none of the team would complain. The electricity was back on just as Easy arrived with a box full of goodies.

'Your kettle Gentlemen,' said Easy with a grin, 'and a box of cookies from my Aunty.'

'Excellent, I'll take that kettle and get a brew on,' said Rambo taking the brand new kettle from the box.

Posty entered behind him wiping his freshly washed hands on his t-shirt, 'Did you say cookies?' he asked, as he reached into the box and extracted the Tupperware box.

'Aunty says she needs the box back when you're finished with the cookies.'

'That won't take long lad, your Aunty is a great cook!' chortled Taff, 'take a seat,' he gestured to one of the camp beds against the wall.

'I could get you a sofa you know?' said Easy, as he looked around the room.

'That's a kind offer, but no need, I don't think we'll be here too long, will we Boss?' said Taff looking at JT.

'When Rory gets here, we'll see what else he's been able to dig up, maybe he can persuade the local plods to get off their arses and do something about this lot,' replied JT, though he was already fairly certain this was going to be left to them to sort out. He looked at his watch and decided to call Paddy back at the Hereford Barracks.

On the second ring, the guard house phone was picked up. 'Home.' It was the one word answer that was always used when that particular phone rang.

'Captain JT St-John Templeman to speak with Major Paddy Hildersley.'

'Good afternoon, Captain, Trooper Salter here Sir, I'll find him for you now.'

'Thanks Salter,' replied JT.

A few moments later a slightly out of breath Paddy picked up the phone. 'JT, how's it going my friend.'

'All good Paddy, just checking in.'

'Glad to hear it. Your team ok?' he asked.

'Yes, we're all good. Still with me, and we're training our civvy skills.'

'Don't go getting fat on us now, we might just need you back.'

'Some movement?' JT asked, with a touch of excitement in his voice.

'Oh no wait, sorry, didn't mean like that. Listen, I know this isn't the sort of news you were looking for, but one of the clerks overheard that smarmy bastard Symmons saying they've got a decent case against you boys, and he's looking for a court martial. He's obviously trying to make a name for himself, sooner he fucks off back to Whitehall to push some paper the better. He's been here three weeks and not been out of the Generals' arsehole. He's a fu – '

'Steady now Paddy! I don't like him either, but if it takes a court martial to put an end to this nonsense then so be it. What's the Colonel saying to it?'

'He's still being advised to have no contact with you, but he calls me regularly to check you're all ok.'

'Okay, thanks Paddy. Listen, I'll be doing some urban training with the team rather than sitting around in Starbucks, so we might need some kit.'

'No worries, I cleared that with the Colonel before, let me know what you need and I'll have it dropped down.'

'Cheers Paddy, I'll sort you out with some Jameson's when we're finally allowed Home.'

'Deal,' said Paddy, 'now if you'll excuse me, I'll get back to leathering this Brazilian Jiu-Jitsu instructor with some Ballymena Ju-Fucku!' he laughed, as he hung up.

#

When Maxwell arrived at the flat, he asked Easy to give them 30 mins to talk in private. Easy offered to go order take away food from Uncle Samir. Maxwell then spent 15 minutes describing his strange meeting with Hamilton.

'Can we trust him?' was JT's initial response.

'I don't know,' replied Maxwell honestly. 'He knew so much that if he wanted to screw us over, he could have done so already. Besides, he seems to think we can use this Liriazi and help to find the Queen.'

The six soldiers looked at each other then back to Maxwell.

'There's more,' he said, 'I spoke to an old pal who worked out here in East Command. He was promoted out of there, to a job he didn't particularly want and knew he wasn't qualified for. He reckons they got rid of him as he'd started asking questions about this Chief Inspector Ella Misu. He'd suggested she was untrustworthy and interfering with investigations. The Chief Superintendent told him to his face he was just racist and a misogynist. Next thing he knew he was getting a promotion he didn't apply for and well away from East Command. Seems they have two Albanian cops on secondment to the Met. They're under direct control of Ella Misu and have full access to all of the Intel systems here and back in Tirana.'

'Handy,' said JT.

'So, what do we think?' asked Maxwell.

JT's team looked to their leader, whatever he decided they would follow his instructions and he had to consider them. 'This Hamilton, is he asking us to take these guys out and try to locate Liriazi for him on behalf of MI6?'

'Pretty much, yes. Anything we choose to do will be on us, he can't protect us acting here on British soil. We can't be acting officially, you as SAS or me as Police. We will be on the outside. If it goes wrong...' he left that hanging and looked at the men's faces. None of them gave anything away.

It was Taff who spoke first, 'Boss, forgive me but I reckon I know you'll be considering how to look after us. Me and the lads are ready to go take these horrible bastards out. I keep thinking of that wee boy's face in the video. We've all seen some shit, but that's in war, this was different somehow. Then there's the old ladies and the missing girls. The coppers aren't going to stop them, if we don't nobody will.'

JT looked at him and said, 'Thanks Taff, I'd expect nothing less from you guys. I'm also keen to put an end to these guys hurting people, but we'd have to do it in a way that doesn't come back on the Regiment, on Rory, or on any of us.'

'I've been thinking about that,' said Maxwell, 'I have an idea on how you can be verifiably not here.'

CHAPTER NINETEEN

'You checking to see I didn't kill the Jiu-Jitsu guy?' chuckled Paddy as he answered the phone.

'No, not at all,' laughed JT, 'but, you didn't, did you?'

'Nah, he's a hard bastard, I'll give him that. He's just not dirty enough for real fighting!' Paddy finished his chuckling and asked, 'something changed?'

'No, all is good here still. Decided we should do some surveillance and counter surveillance work.'

'Always good to keep the skills sharp,' said Paddy.

'Going to try somewhere new, we all know London too well, in fact any of the UK cities. Thought we'd try Paris,' said JT.

'Paris? Does this mean you're taking the team to Disneyland?' he chuckled again.

'You never know!' laughed JT. 'Thought we'd do some E and E training too.'

'I'd always try to Escape and Evade Disneyland myself, too many screaming bairns for my delicate ears.'

'I know what you mean. Listen, can you run it by the Colonel and if he says yes, I'll get a list of kit to you. We'll all need our passports too obviously.'

'Yeah, remember this Brexit stuff means you need a stamp on the way back out or they don't let you back or something.'

'We'll make sure they stamp us in and out.'

'Good stuff, gimme an hour and I'll get the okay from the Colonel then call you back.'

#

The driver of the van also handed over a thick brown envelope containing the 6 passports of the Team and a few thousand Euros. A note inside from Paddy read, "Persuaded the man upstairs you would need to buy some Croissants and a glass of wine to blend in!"

JT checked off the items on the list before signing for them. He packed the two way radio sets and covert earpieces into a waterproof holdall along with the parabolic microphone that could listen to a conversation from more than 300m away. These would be difficult to explain if they were to be stopped at customs. The capture and interrogation kit was full of strong cable tie type quick-cuffs, tape, recording equipment, lighting, headphones to blare music into the ears of the unfortunate listener, some ordinary tools and kitchen equipment which in the right hands could be extremely persuasive. That said, French customs were less interested in things arriving into France than their UK counterparts. He considered leaving the kit here in London but for this plan to work some of it would have to be seen to be deployed in France.

With the team packed and ready they headed for Kent, but before the ferry there was a stop they had to make. The rented motorhome was big and wallowed on the road but for this part of the plan speed was not of the essence.

CHAPTER TWENTY

The windmill stood gleaming white in the afternoon sunshine as the team approached. The sails had long since been removed but the cylindrical building still housed the old mill workings. It also contained the home of the man watching the motorhome struggle along the narrow approach road that he'd deliberately let get overgrown.

'That'll teach the bloody idiots!' he said with a grin to his companion. His companion was a German Shepherd named Monty and the dog stood on his hind legs to get the same view from the window of his best friend and master.

As the motorhome got closer Jacob 'Walter' Raleigh descended the narrow staircase with his usual grimace at the pain in his arthritic knee. He collected his walking stick from the stand by the front door and made his way to the locked gate. The only way to turn a vehicle was in his yard. The alternative was an excruciating mile long reverse. Walter had planted bushes to obscure the old passing places along the lane, after all he wanted to make this place as unappealing as possible to visitors.

He was standing at the gate when the motorhome came to a halt and watched with a smirk as the side door of the vehicle was opened and a man fought with a blackthorn bush to exit the vehicle. 'Didn't you see the "Private Road, no entry" signs at the end of the lane then?' he began his practised admonishment.

The man who had exited the motorhome was using a jacket to push back the thorny branches and make his way toward the gate. 'Yah, but we lost!' came a heavily accented voice from behind the jacket.

'Well, you'd best un lose yourself and get reversing back the way you came chummy!' said Walter as he turned to walk away. He looked down at Monty and was wondering why he would be wagging his tail rather than barking at these unwelcome visitors when a voice he recognised spoke.

'Come on Walter, is that any way to greet your Godson?'

Walter turned to see a grinning JT at the gate stroking an excited Monty. 'Well now, you're a sight for sore eyes, Jonny, I'm guessing you'll be wanting tea?'

'Now that's a better welcome!' said JT, as he vaulted the gate. 'Can I bring some friends?'

'Friends of yours are friends of mine,' said a smiling Walter as he threw JT the padlock key.

A few minutes later they were sitting on the benches facing the River Rother. Across the river was the verdant expanse of the nature reserve and in the distance Camber Castle. JT had spent many happy summers here as a boy, playing in the river and learning survival skills from his Father's best friend. Walter had been a great teacher, a veteran of the Royal Marines he had been decorated for valour in the Falklands War and was legendary in the certain circles privileged to know of his exploits.

'So, you're still on the naughty step then?' said Walter.

'Sadly, yes,' replied JT

'Don't let the buggers grind you down Jonny, those pencil pushers wouldn't know one end of an enemy combatant from another.'

'Agreed! It'll all get sorted out eventually. There are lawyers making money out of it and politicians looking to make a name for themselves, but we did our jobs.'

'Sometimes it's doing your job they take umbrage with,' mused Walter.

'That's becoming increasingly clear,' said JT.

'So, how long are you boys here for? You're welcome as long as you like obviously.'

'Thanks Walter but we're actually on our way to France.'

'France? Why on earth would you want to go to France when England is available?' asked Walter incredulously.

'It's a long story, but I'm actually here to ask for your help.'

'Ask away, whatever you need,' said Walter meaning every word.

'Is the Peregrine ship-shape?'

'Bloody cheek, of course she is!' replied Walter with mock indignation. He gestured for JT to follow him and they walked toward the large boathouse. 'She's back just a month from de-fouling and the twin Perkins were replaced last year with a couple of Volvo diesel numbers, tad noisier but a fair trade-off for reliability.' He turned to the rest of the team, 'Come on you lot, come and meet a bit of history!' Walter opened up the door to the boathouse and gestured the men inside. They stood on a narrow wooden jetty and looked onto a beautiful and highly polished boat.

'Gents, meet The Peregrine,' said JT, who grinned at the sight of the Gentleman's Yacht he'd learned about the sea upon.

'This old girl is one of the few remaining Small Ships that helped evacuate our troops from Dunkirk,' said Walter as he stepped aboard.

'Permission to come aboard Captain?' asked JT, as he had done so many times before.

'Permission granted,' said Walter seriously, before continuing with a proud smile, 'bring your friends.'

The men dutifully climbed aboard and all marvelled at the condition of the vessel. The care and attention lavished upon her was plain for all to see. As was the pride of her Captain.

'A little run?' asked Walter.

'Yes please!' said a smiling JT and he went forward to cast off as he always had since the age of five. The deep throaty engines started first time with the touch of a button and The Peregrine glided effortlessly out into the smooth waters of the river.

Walter turned to port and downstream toward the sea. A mile or so downstream was Admiralty Jetty and a short distance beyond there Camber Beach and the English Channel. Thirty minutes later they were leaving the river estuary and headed out into the sea. It was early evening and several leisure craft were on the water. The locals were well used to seeing Walter and The Peregrine heading out on one of his fishing trips and they sounded horns of greeting while waving to him.

'Can you smell that?' Taff asked Cooky who was shielding his eyes from the sun. They were sitting on the deck near the bow.

'Smell what?' he replied.

'Freedom my friend, freedom,' said Taff, filling his lungs with the pristine sea air.

Back in the cockpit Walter turned to JT and asked, 'Care to take the wheel number 1?'

'Need you ask?' said JT, grinning he placed his hands on the wheel.

Walter stood beside him and despite the gentle rolling action of the waves, and his arthritic knee, he stood effortlessly straight and without holding on. 'Now, perhaps you should tell me what it is you need Jonny?'

CHAPTER TWENTY-ONE

Next morning at 0700 hrs Joe drove the motorhome up the ramp and onto the huge Ferry that plied its trade several times a day between Dover and Calais.

Whilst awaiting the instruction to embark the team had entered the passenger terminal to use the facilities and made sure they were visible to the numerous CCTV cameras.

Once onboard they asked a fellow passenger to take a group photo of them as the ship sailed and the famous White Cliffs were in the background. JT sent the photo of the six smiling men to Paddy back in Hereford with a "wish you were here" message. "Bonne fucking vacances! Don't get caught'" came the response. We'll try our best, thought JT.

Three hours later Joe was driving them down the ramp among the HGVs and fellow motorhomes.

The French Border Control officer looked bored and gave the passports a cursory look before stamping them and waving them forward to the Customs officers.

A Customs officer, with a broad droopy moustache that made him look like a caricature, stepped in front of the motorhome. He held up one open hand showing a palm in the universal sign language for stop.

'Halfway to a surrender monkey!' joked Joe, from the driver's seat.

'Play nice now,' muttered JT, from the adjacent passenger seat.

'Naturally,' said Joe, pressing the button to lower his window.

The Customs officer looked at the registration number then gave the faintest shake of his head as he changed course and walked to the right side of the vehicle to speak with the driver.

'You are English, yes?' he asked looking at his clipboard.

'Naw, I'm Scottish actually,' said Joe with a grin. The officer looked up from his clipboard, giving Joe a laconic look much favoured by French officials.

'I said play nice,' whispered JT.

'Just my wee joke there, officer, begging your pardon, we are mostly English and certainly that's what we speak.'

'What is your purpose in France?' the officer said, the last words like '*On Fronss*', his tone was one of professional boredom.

'Bit of a holiday, and some team building, with my colleagues here,' said Joe, maintaining his friendly and jocular tone, he gestured toward the rear of the motorhome.

'How many are you?' asked the officer.

'We are six,' said Joe, smiling.

'What do you carry in your vehicle?'

'Just us and our kit,' replied Joe, 'you can have a look if you like.'

'Yes, I can,' came the uninterested response. The officer looked at his clipboard and then beyond the rear of the motorhome at the long queue of traffic. He sighed and shrugged his shoulders before looking at Joe, 'Welcome to France, drive on the right.' Then he walked around the motorhome and approached the next vehicle in line.

'Merci beaucoup Monsieur surrender monkey,' said Joe under his breath, and he drove out of the holding lane and into a line of traffic leaving the port. 'Where first boss?' he asked JT as they got to the head of the queue.

'Straight to Paris, we'll use the toll roads, they'll log our number plate as we go.'

'*Paree* it is,' said Joe, following the road sign and carefully making his way around the roundabout.

'I reckon we'll be there in about 4 hours. Quick photo and we'll find an Aire to park up in. Then it's just a case of finding the right truck or trucks.'

#

Back in London, Easy was waiting anxiously for Maxwell to arrive. He had taken a train into the city and was standing outside Pret a Manger at Kings Cross. He was early and feeling self-conscious in his casual clothes as everyone around him seemed to be in suits.

A few minutes later Maxwell walked around the corner and walked past him gesturing for him to follow. They walked between the office blocks and across into the Coal Yard, a gentrified area of stylish shops and cafes by the canal. They bought coffee and found a bench made of thick reclaimed timbers to sit away from the crowds.

'Thank you for meeting with me,' began Easy.

'No problem kid, what's up?' asked Maxwell.

'I wanted to help, so I did some investigations,' replied Easy looking anxiously at Maxwell.

'What kind of investigations?'

'I wanted to help find my friend, she is still missing.'

'Yes, I know. We all want to find her and we're going to get some answers from those men,' said Maxwell, trying to sound confident.

'I just thought that maybe, you might have to kill the men, before they tell you,' Easy choked on the words.

'Shhh, don't go saying such things,' said Maxwell in a hushed voice, 'nobody is looking to kill anybody if they can help it.'

'They are moving the girls; we can save them,' Easy blurted out.

'What do you mean 'moving', and how do you know?' asked Maxwell.

'Do you know what a Hak 5 Pineapple is?'

'I know what a pineapple is,' said Maxwell, 'and I also know it doesn't belong on pizza.'

'Not that kind of pineapple, it is an electronic device that can penetrate wi-fi networks.' Easy looked for recognition from Maxwell before continuing, 'I used a pineapple to get access to their wi-fi at the bookies office.'

'Spare the tech geek stuff and get to the point Easy, what did you find out?'

'I read the messages between the Bad Men. They said the new 'stables' were ready and they had to move the girls.'

'Did they say where from and to?'

'Only that they are almost finished on the new place. That it would be open for business in 2 days. They said there's a truck ready to move them.'

'A truck?'

'Yes, there must be lots of them.'

Maxwell thought for a second and looked at his watch, 'I need to go finish something in the office kid, I'll meet you tonight.'

'I will eat with Uncle Samir and wait for you at the flat upstairs?'

'Perfect, it might be late.'

'I will tell my Aunty I am staying with a friend'

"Tell your Aunty", thought Maxwell to himself, I have to remember this is just a kid. 'Great, see you later,' he turned and walked quickly away.

CHAPTER TWENTY-TWO

The motorhome pulled up outside Parc de Princes the home of the French International Football and Rugby Teams. A quick photo taken in front of the iconic stadium sent to Paddy would give a time, date and location for the team. More importantly it would provide an alibi.

JT's phone rang as he was about to send the photo, he checked the caller ID and felt his pulse raise when he saw it was Maxwell calling. 'Hey Rory, hope this isn't your personal phone, it might be expensive as I'm in France with my team,' he answered.

Maxwell knew JT was confirming the line wasn't secure, 'Ah, then Bonjour vieil ami! Got some news for you,' he said.

'I'm listening.'

'Some of the unhappy guests we were talking about are leaving their lodgings and moving to pastures new.'

'Do we know where and when?'

'I'm told it was a management decision and the new accommodation will be ready tomorrow or the next day. Don't have an address.'

'Any way you can find them before they check out completely?'

'We're working on it.'

'We?'

'Yeah, got a young techy genius working on it, he's easy to work with.'

'Ok, good luck, keep me updated.'

'Will do. Enjoy France.'

JT hung up and ran through a revised plan in his head. He gathered the team around a map of Northern France and explained the update from Maxwell. 'Okay, I'll send this to Paddy and we're out of here. We need to get back to Calais soon as. Joe and Taff will park up here; at the Wissant Aire,' he said pointing it out on the map. 'Rest of us split into two teams. Cooky and Posty, you head East along the beaches, there's a wetland area and then decent dunes. The French put up drones, but if I were launching boats full of illegal immigrants that's a place I'd use. Rambo, you're with me, we'll go West toward Escalles. It's the same kind of terrain and 3 miles from Sangette, so hoping the people traffickers ply their trade close to the camps. Suffice to say we need something seaworthy, so no supermarket dinghies. Questions?'

'Rules of engagement Boss?' asked Taff.

'The people smugglers are bound to be a rough bunch; it wouldn't surprise me if they're armed. We don't want to attract attention to ourselves if at all possible.'

'So…?' replied Taff, leaning forward to make eye contact.

'So, we're in a foreign country, off book. If we get arrested, we're screwed.'

'I get that Boss, just checking what your thoughts were,' said Taff, sitting back in his seat.

'We do what we need to do, if someone needs put down, we put them down. The world won't weep for a dead people-smuggler. They won't weep for us either.'

5 hours later the sun had set as the motorhome slowed down to walking pace and the first team of Cooky and Posty jumped out of the side door and ran into the adjacent woods and headed North toward the beach.

Half a mile further on it was the turn of JT and Rambo, they jumped and took cover in a drainage ditch beside a field. When they were sure there were no vehicles approaching, they ran across the field and headed for the hedgerow on the far side. They reached the hedgerow and stopped as the increasing darkness made it appear an impenetrable wall. Skirting the hedgerow, they looked for a gap as a dog started barking in the distance. The still night made it difficult to estimate how close the dog was. The bobbing beam of a torchlight from the opposite direction meant it was easy to see someone was heading their way.

The open ground of the field would make them easy to spot and their only cover was the thick mass of the hedgerow. They crawled and inched their way into bushes, thorns and sharp branches scratching at their faces and hands. Once inside the hedge, the branches thinned out and thick older branches allowed them to climb up until they lay horizontally, off the ground. It was far from ideal but the thicker vegetation further up the outside of the hedge would offer some protection. As the torch beam came closer the men could hear the sound of tinny music being played through headphones. This good news was balanced against the fact that the torch light was illuminating the unmistakable outline of a double barrelled shotgun. Through the leaves JT could make out blue jeans and black and white Adidas trainers. Not a farmer then he guessed. In the same hand as the torch the man was also carrying a rough hemp sack. Poacher, decided JT. A poacher with a shotgun and they were in a hedge that quite likely contained his quarry.

As the poacher passed, JT slid down out of the hedge and out onto the path as he waited for Rambo to join him. He watched transfixed as the poacher nonchalantly swung his shotgun around, it was doubtless loaded. The poacher stumbled on a loose rock and as he did the torch fell from his grasp. The torch rolled in a semi-circle, the beam arcing over the ground until it settled on the crawling figure of Rambo emerging from the hedge.

The poacher stooped to pick up the torch but when he saw Rambo he stopped and raised the shotgun to his shoulder.

JT came at him from the dark and violently pulled the barrel of the shotgun downwards. The blast as the poacher pulled the trigger obliterated the torch and they were thrown into darkness. JT pulled the shotgun from the man's grip and clipped him to the side of the head with the butt. The man fell, unconscious before he hit the ground. As he landed his headphones fell out of his ears. Trashy europop whined louder than before and JT bent down and replaced the headphones in the man's ears. He checked the man was breathing and could smell the wine he'd consumed before heading out with his gun. Not smart, not smart at all, thought JT.

He was aware of, rather than saw, a movement to his left and had no time to react as the poacher's dog leapt at him grabbing his arm in its teeth. JT fell back with the impact of the dog then was surprised as it squealed and let him go.

He stood up and found Rambo holding the dog by its collar and tail at arms-length. He was spitting trying to get something out of his mouth.

'You okay boss?' he asked JT.

'Yeah, you?' JT replied, dusting himself off and feeling for blood on his arm.

'Dog hair,' replied Rambo between spits, 'I bit him to make him let go.'

'Well thanks,' said JT. 'Hang on a sec,' he reached down for the sack the poacher had been carrying and pulled it over the rear end of the dog. 'When I say go, you release the collar. Go!' He caught the dog in the sack and tied the top in a knot. He lay the sack beside the unconscious poacher and stepped back from the writhing, snarling sack.

'Think he got a good look at you?' he asked Rambo.

'Yeah, I reckon so, but I can smell the alcohol from him and let's face it, I look like a refugee from the camp, so he'll blame it on them.'

'Fair enough. Ok let's move,' he said as they started running, 'we've another mile to reach the beach.'

#

Cooky stopped and held up a hand, Posty stopped behind him and the two men crouched down. Ahead of them was the faintest outline of the sand dunes. Beyond them the beach. Hushed voices from the scrubby bushes and long coarse coastal grass were carrying on the night air.

'That's not French,' whispered Posty, 'sounds like Persian or something.'

Cooky stood up slowly and as he did was sniffing the air. He could smell petrol. The two men retreated back 100 yards away from the beach and circled round in the direction of the voices. As they approached, a group of people, mostly men from the size of their silhouettes stood up and started dragging an inflatable dinghy. The dinghy was 10 feet long and there were at least 14 people surrounding it. As the people crested the dune it was obvious that they were wearing orange life jackets but didn't appear to have any belongings beyond the clothes they were wearing.

The wind from the sea caught the dinghy and the group struggled to make progress. Two men started pushing them and kicking them toward the sea. One of the men carried a long stick and was beating the closest of the boat people.

Posty caught up to the man with the stick and slipped his arm around his neck in a choke hold dragging him back down the slope of the dune as he did. The man who had been taking the beating turned and saw Posty choking the man but said nothing and got back to the job of carrying the boat.

Cooky grabbed the second man but the soft sand caused him to lose balance and the two toppled down the dune into a thigh deep pool of brackish water. The man got to his feet and pulled a knife from his waistband. It glinted in pale moonlight, as did his teeth as he grinned at Cooky. He swiped the knife back and forth as he inched forward in a half crouch. Cooky backed away trying to feel for a solid footing and when he did, he stood his ground. The man came at him in a lunge that was telegraphed and from too far away. The water stopped the man moving quickly enough and Cooky half turned, allowing the outstretched arm of his attacker to straighten before he smashed his forearm against the man's wrist. The knife dropped from the man's hand as he gave a little yelp at the pain and surprise. Cooky followed up with a spinning elbow to the man's jaw as his trajectory had brought him into range. A satisfying crunch as elbow met jaw bone and teeth told Cooky he'd hit the spot.

The man fell sideways into the water, his head resting in some vegetation. Cooky looked around but no-one was coming to this man's assistance. Grabbing the man's feet Cooky pulled him into the deeper water and flipped him over face down. The man bucked and struggled, kicking out in despair. Cooky gripped the shoulders of the man's jacket and leaned into them so his weight pushed the man deeper into the black water. A last buck and the man went limp, Cooky held him there another 10 to 15 secs then stood up and dragged the lifeless body to the edge of the water.

Searching the man's pockets, he found a wad of wet Euro banknotes and a folding knife, he wore a watch and a wedding ring. In the back pocket of his trousers Cooky found a slim leather wallet. Inside was a plastic driver's licence. It was issued in Albania. Cooky briefly thought about the man's widow and where she might be, but the sound of Posty approaching soon rid him of that concern.

'Dead?' asked Posty.

'Affirmative,' replied Cooky without emotion, 'the other one?'

'Sleeping like a baby,' replied Posty. 'Should I finish him?'

'He'll only come back and brutalise some more of these poor bastards,' said Cooky by way of answer.

Posty turned to leave but stopped as two silhouettes appeared at the top of the dune. Their life jackets clearly identifying them as passengers rather than smugglers.

'Bon-jour?' one of them said in faltering French.

Posty turned to Cooky and said, 'Do we take their boat? It looks pretty shitty.'

Cooky walked to the top of the Dune and handed the first man the wad of Euros. He counted another 9 men standing holding the dinghy off the sand ready to launch into the sea. The wind was blowing stronger away from the protection of the dune and Cooky could hear the surf crashing against the concrete blocks that were remnants of anti-tank defences. These relics were a stark reminder of another time when the beach was fortified against invaders from England. Now they were a staging post going the other way.

Cooky approached the dinghy and the men closest tried to edge away from him. The dinghy was so under inflated it buckled as they moved. There was no way this boat could be put to sea; it would fold in two before clearing the breaking waves 50 metres from shore.

The dark faces of the men held a mix of fear and desperation and they dropped the dinghy as he tested the rubber hull with his hand. He shook his head and made a folding motion with his hands to tell them what would happen to the boat.

Posty approached, having dispatched the second people smuggler and he too felt the soft and soggy rubber of the dinghy. 'This things fucked,' he said to Cooky, 'we can't use this.'

'No,' said Cooky, 'and neither can they.'

'They're desperate enough to try, I should think,' said Posty looking at the men.

'We can't let them, it'd be suicide.'

'Agreed, but what do we do with them?'

Cooky thought for a moment as he formed a plan, 'Get two of their life vests.'

'We're not going out in this thing!' said Posty, surprised.

'No, we'll get the two bodies, put the life vests on them and send them out in this heap of shit. They'll wash up eventually and be just another couple of unlucky refugees. No-one will bother to work out how they died.'

'Good idea, but what about this lot?'

'Empty the guy's pockets, give these guys any valuables and they can find other smugglers to try again some other time.'

'We help?' said one of the refugees. He was a tall skinny North African of about 16 and had obviously been listening to the conversation.

'Yes, you help,' said Cooky, 'you can't go out in this boat, you'll be killed.'

'I said this, I told the man we need a better boat. He beat me with stick. He said I go in boat or he kill me.'

'How much did you pay him?' asked Posty.

'I do not pay. They make me work when I reach England.'

'I see,' said Cooky, 'go get the body with my friend here and bring it back,' he pointed to two of them and gestured for them to follow him.

When the two bodies were loaded aboard the group dragged the boat to the water. Posty jumped aboard and started up the meagre outboard engine. It spluttered to life and he lashed the throttle and steering handle to take the boat straight forward and out to sea. He jumped out into chest deep cold water and waded back to shore. The group watched as the dinghy cleared the first 2 or 3 waves before it hit the first breaker, it reared up and folded before toppling into the crashing water.

'You guys best get out of here,' said Cooky to the men, who nodded. Two or three shook his hand before they ran off over the dunes into the darkness.

'Look!' said Posty pointing along the beach. Two hundred metres away a group carrying a dinghy were sliding down the dune and heading for the sea. Cooky and Posty ran up and over the dune then sprinted along its landward side until they were behind the group. This time there were no smugglers. But this time there was a woman. And children.

They had reached the sea and the one man was passing the 4 kids one at a time to the woman in the boat. Without the engine running the boat was being pushed back to shore by the wind and waves.

As Cooky and Posty approached the man was pushing the dinghy into deeper water. The woman and children were all huddled inside as the man tried to haul himself out of the water and into the boat, as he did so the boat pivoted and the next wave crashed over them and swamped the boat. One of the children was washed overboard and Posty ran into the water then dived into the foaming maelstrom. Cooky lost sight of him for a full minute before he saw Posty as he fought to tow the child back to shore. Cooky waded in and took the child from him. The limp body bent backwards in his arms. He turned the child over, 'Come on kid,' he hissed and clapped his hand hard on the back of the tiny life vest. A gush of water came from the child's mouth and then the joyful sound of the child whimpering.

Cooky lay the child in the recovery position and went to help Posty pull the swamped boat to shore. The woman jumped from the boat and ran to scoop up the child into her arms. She sat and rocked the child as the other children and then the man ran to join her.

'Thank you, thank you,' said the man, 'you have saved my family.'

'What were you thinking going out in this weather?' asked Posty as he slumped down beside them.

'The men took our money. They said we had to go tonight or we must pay more money. I have no more to give them,' said the man sobbing. 'We have nothing left. I cannot even feed my family.'

'Where are the men now?' asked Cooky, scanning the top of the dunes.

'They went to another boat with lots of men.'

Posty looked at Cooky and took out the Euros that JT had shared between them earlier. 'Here,' he said to the man, 'get your kids some food.'

Cooky followed suit and handed over his share. 'Get out of here and go find somewhere to dry off. Get the little one to a hospital, she swallowed a lot of water.'

'Yes, we will try,' said the anxious father.

'If you go along the beach this way,' pointed Posty, 'there's a town. It's a fishing harbour, they'll know how to get you help. Now get moving, it's too cold to hang about.'

The family thanked them again then headed off along the beach. Cooky and Posty lifted one side of the dinghy and rocked it to displace enough water to allow them to invert it on the sand to empty it. It was a reasonably new dinghy and the wooden duck boards were intact in its hull. If they could get the engine to start, this might just do the trick.

A few pulls and an adjustment to the fuel intake, the engine fired into life. 'They must have paid extra for the VIP crossing,' said Posty, as he nodded approvingly at the boat.

'Let's see if it can get us past the break point, before we start celebrating,' said Cooky looking at the waves.

Cooky pushed them out from shore and climbed aboard into the bow of the dinghy. Posty revved the engine and wished for something more powerful but they were able to maintain a good pace into the waves.

As they approached the first breaker Cooky leaned back holding onto the bow line. The bow reared up and was almost vertical before he threw himself forward and they crested the wave. Three more times they fought the breakers as they headed out to sea, before they reached deeper water and deeper darkness.

Once they'd bailed enough water from the boat, they turned and headed along the coast toward their colleagues.

Cooky got his radio from his backpack and clicked the transmit button three times. He got 5 clicks in response which meant the other teams were ready, and in a position to receive a message. 'We have a boat, not perfect but serviceable,' he said into his handset.

'Good work, nothing doing our end. Can you pick us up?' replied JT.

'Bit of a struggle getting through the breakers, don't think we'd manage six up,' said Cooky.

'Shit, ok. We're running out of time and other than stealing a fishing boat, not sure how we do this,' replied JT.

'If you can swim past the breakers, we'll pick you up? It's easier going once we're past them.'

'Okay, needs must. Taff are you receiving?'

'Yes boss.'

'You and Joe come meet us on the beach. We'll RV about half a mile West of the harbour away from prying eyes.'

'Be there in 10 minutes. I've got the kit in waterproof bags; they'll provide a bit of buoyancy too,' replied Taff.

'Excellent, see you in 10. Cooky, let us know when you're past the harbour, we don't want to be hanging about waiting for you out there.'

'On our way.'

CHAPTER TWENTY-THREE

Ten minutes later the four men stood and stripped off all of their clothes before stuffing them into a dry bag. Naked they ran down to the water and gasped as it reached their thighs. Sticking together they waded until chest deep and then started swimming out to sea. Soon the towering waves were crashing around them and trying to rip their floating bags from their grasp. Time and again waves crashed over them as they fought the waves and the incoming tide. It took 15 minutes of strenuous effort to get past the breakers and now the cold was starting to affect them. Body heat is lost much faster in water than in air and the men knew they wouldn't survive much longer in the sea.

Above the noise of the waves and the wind they could hear the strained sound of an outboard motor approaching. They four men were holding onto a raft of dry bags to stay together and were all looking forward to climbing aboard when a deeper engine noise reached them. Leaving the harbour was a French Police launch and its big powerful engines meant the men could hear it even if they couldn't see it.

Posty and Cooky lay themselves flat inside the dinghy as the search-light on the bow of the launch was switched on and turned to scan the beach. The launch had slowed to walking pace and was further offshore than the dinghy or the team in the water and its searchlight would spot them easily.

The cold was making treading water difficult but the team knew if they stopped moving, they were dead. They also knew that if they were discovered it was game over.

Closer and closer the launch came, almost in slow motion, and they were within 50m of the searchlight spotting the dinghy, when the launch abruptly turned out to sea and throttled the engines hard before racing away in the opposite direction.

Posty revved the dinghy outboard hard and raced to the men in the water. He helped Cooky pull the men aboard, but before they could retrieve all of the dry bags the dinghy was lifted up and pushed back into the breakers. Posty grabbed the throttle and twisted hard as the dinghy was again lifted by a wave about to break. 'Lean!' he shouted to the team who threw themselves and their weight dragged the boat down the wave and out to sea.

'Shit, the clothes!' said JT and dived off the boat, back into the freezing water. The team watched as JT was thrown around in the breaking wave as he swam hard after the lost dry bag. He reached the bag and was rewarded with a huge dump of water hitting him in the face and pushing him back another10 yards.

Cooky grabbed the bow line and untied it. 'Get us closer!' he shouted to Posty.

'Much closer and we're all swimming,' shouted Posty, struggling to manoeuvre the boat.

Cooky took the almost empty spare petrol can and tied the rope to the handle then hurled it toward JT. JT kicked hard and got one hand to the petrol can before the next breaker dumped on him. His hands were so cold he struggled to keep a grip.

Rambo leapt into the water and went hand over hand down the rope to JT. Just as he reached him, JT lost his grip on the petrol can and Rambo grabbed his wrist. Rambo's' strong climbers fingers gripped vice like and he yelled 'pull!' as loud as he could.

Posty turned the throttle to full as the next breaker crashed over JT and Rambo. The boat lurched backwards on the taut rope as the sea tried to drag them to shore. Taff and Cooky hauled on the rope with all their might and gained enough rope for the others to grab and join in the tug of war against the waves.

The next breaker loomed high as JT and Rambo were pulled through the face of the wave and emerged through the other side as they were dragged slowly towards the boat and safety. Posty kept the boat heading further out to sea before killing the engine and the two men could be safely pulled aboard.

The men helped each other into dry clothes as the boat made its way out to sea and into one of the world's busiest and most dangerous shipping routes.

CHAPTER TWENTY-FOUR

Easy opened his laptop and after typing in a few commands showed Maxwell the screen. Six columns appeared, each containing a copy of the messages between different parties. Every second column was a translation into English. 'The Bad Men,' he said as Maxwell was reading the messages.

'Did you set up the translation?' asked Maxwell.

'Yes, it is a language app I have running in the background, it's not perfect, but better than Google translate,' said Easy

'It's Albanian then?'

'Yes, they use some words that are not recognised but I think they are maybe a local language.'

'A dialect?' said Maxwell as he passed the screen back to Easy. 'Can you bring up that image?' he asked pointing to a small photograph contained in one of the messages.

Easy clicked on the image and enlarged it. It showed a view from a window, rolling countryside and in the distance the sea. It appeared to be the view from a country house as the remnants of a formal garden were in the foreground and a large ornamental pond.

'Have they discussed where this is?'

'No,' said Easy, 'they have said this is the new place to take the girls. They call it Amazon.'

'Amazon, like the company or the rainforest?' asked Maxwell.

'I do not know,' Easy paused and then said, 'I have something else I can show you.' He tapped a few keys and the screen changed to a live image of the interior of a bookie shop.

'Is that where I think it is?' said Maxwell, his voice a little lower than usual.

'Yes, the man called Igor has started a direct link from the CCTV to his phone.'

'Has he indeed?' Maxwell purred, 'Can you control the cameras?'

'I could try, but it may alert him that someone else has access.'

'Good point.'

'When he is not inside the premises the camera image changes from outside the building, there are two cameras so they have two separate images, then the shop part and then the office. Each image lasts for 3 seconds on rotation.'

'So, he's on the premises just now?' Maxwell looked at his watch, it was almost midnight.

'I think so, there is a door at the back of the office, I think it must be the toilet or kitchen.'

'Can you look up planning permission from the council? That place used to be a bank, there should be public records of the design when they refurbed the place.'

'Yes, of course.'

'Meantime, I need to speak to a man about a pond.' Maxwell walked out of the flat and down to where his car was parked in the rear lane. He sat in the car in the dark and took a business card from his wallet. It was on good quality card but perfunctory in the extreme, it bore the name Hamilton and a mobile number. Maxwell dialled the number on his newly acquired burner phone and sat looking at the card as his call was diverted twice before it eventually rang. On the third ring it was answered.

'Yes?' came a voice that sounded as though he had been woken from sleep but that this was a regular and unsurprising occurrence.

'Hamilton?' asked Maxwell.

'What can I do for you Detective Inspector?' asked Hamilton.

Maxwell could hear him getting out of bed and walking out of the bedroom. Probably trying not to disturb his wife, Maxwell thought. 'You said I should call if I needed your assistance.'

'Yes indeed. I did rather mean during office hours, not,' he paused checking the time, 'at midnight.'

'Some of us are still working,' chuckled Maxwell.

'Hmm, and would that 'work' be official Metropolitan Police Service business?'

'It certainly should be,' replied Maxwell his chuckle gone.

'I see, then pray tell, how might I be of assistance?'

'I need you to find a garden for me.'

'A garden?' asked an incredulous Hamilton.

'I have an image of the garden taken from what appears to be a country house. It's the house I'm looking for.'

'Does this concern our Albanian friends?' asked Hamilton, sounding more interested.

'Yes, I think they are moving part of their operation there.'

'I see. Send the image over in the morning and I will have someone look into it.'

'No,' said Maxwell

'No?' repeated Hamilton.

'This is where they're taking their trafficked girls, I need you to move faster than tomorrow morning.'

'Indeed. Very well, send it over now and I'll see what I can do.'

'Great, thanks,' said Maxwell.

'Do you have an update on your military friends?'

'They're in France was the last I heard, if it's going to plan, they'll be on their way back.'

CHAPTER TWENTY-FIVE

The English Channel is busy with shipping traffic 24 hours a day, 365 days a year. Dover Strait is the narrowest stretch between mainland Europe and the United Kingdom. There are 40+ ferry journeys between Dover and Calais per day. Add to that the Dover to Dunkerque route and the dozen or so other routes across the channel makes it a constantly moving flotilla of ships. Every ferry leaving Dover has to navigate first the North Sea bound ships heading east up the channel and then the opposing shipping lane full of vessels heading West toward the Atlantic and Bay of Biscayne.

It was a Westbound ship that was heading toward them now. The fuel for the outboard motor had run out, and the replacement fuel tank containing a mix of petrol and salt water meant they were floating adrift in a tiny dinghy.

The LNG tanker New Dawn was sailing from Rotterdam to Cyprus and was steaming at 15 knots, 9 miles off the coast of France. She was also steaming straight for JT and the team. From the distance it was difficult to get the exact bearing of the ship but it was coming way too close for comfort. The port and starboard lights on her bow were now the only lights visible as the massive steel hull ploughed towards them. Without oars they were using their hands to try to paddle the dinghy away from a collision course that they would not survive.

'Harder! Faster!' yelled JT as they all frantically pulled at the water trying to find purchase and make the dinghy move faster. The dinghy was already sitting low in the water with the six men and kit aboard so it was cumbersome and difficult to make headway.

Now the bow of the ship was almost on top of them and kicking up a wave of frothing white water.

'Everybody on their knees and hold tight,' called Posty, 'we'll try to surf it.'

'Fucking 'surf it'?' shouted Joe.

'Just be ready to lean when I tell you, and hold the fuck on!' Posty shouted back.

The ship was right on top of them now and they were only just to the starboard side of the bow wake. As it hit them it lifted violently into the air.

'Lean right!' screamed Posty as they were pushed backwards and then upwards by the wave. The men on the right hand side of the dinghy could touch the metal hull and pushed with their hands to try to keep the two vessels apart. Their efforts were in vain as the rubber hull of the dinghy was ripped and instantly deflated. The effect was to catapult the men closest against the hull while the others clung to the side that remained inflated. JT, Cooky and then Joe surfaced from the churning wash alongside the ship's hull. They swam hard for the wrecked dinghy and the spilled dry bags which had been pushed out and away from the ship. JT counted heads in the water and confirmed all six were present. The high bridge of the ship was brightly illuminated and a pool of light showed they still had all of their kit bags but only one half of an inflatable dinghy.

'Injuries?' he asked his men as they all clung to the inflated side bladder.

'Just a bump or two Boss,' said Taff.

JT looked beyond the ship that had just rammed them and could see the position lamps of two more ships headed in their direction. The waves were at least 6 feet high and the wind was still blowing steadily from the north. They were being blown slowly but surely back toward France. The only problem was if the ships didn't get them, the cold certainly would.

'Quiet!' hissed Rambo as he tried to lift himself further out of the sea. He fixed his gaze looking north east and cupped his hand to his ear. 'There!' he pointed but as they were thrown around by the waves it was difficult to see anything at all.

'Yes, I hear it!' said Cooky.

The sound eventually carried to them all, the unmistakable sound of opera music. It could only be coming from a small craft as no ships were close enough. JT laughed as he took his torch out of his backpack and switched it on before holding it above his head and shining the light in the direction of the music. In response a searchlight on the boat flashed twice. The music was turned off and the noise of the engines increasing power was audible above the wind and waves.

They knew they were saved. They knew it was Walter and The Peregrine.

As the boat pulled up alongside a rope ladder was lowered and the six men eventually climbed on board. Walter sent them all below decks where he'd left a pile of towels and blankets waiting for them. 'There's a few old shirts and things in the lockers, help yourselves.'

A couple of minutes later the six men were half dressed, half clad in blankets. They all had enamel mugs full of piping hot cocoa and sat in silence coming to terms with their journey.

CHAPTER TWENTY-SIX

Maxwell returned to the flat to find Easy watching the CCTV feed from the bookies on his laptop. 'You ok kid? Can I get you anything, a can of coke or something?' asked Maxwell.

'No, thank you, but look at this,' Easy pointed to the screen where Igor was now stripped to his boxer shorts and lifting weights, he had a multi gym at the rear of the room and was positioning a full length mirror to watch himself as he worked out. The dual stack of weights on the multigym setup had a pull up bar stretched between them and the huge bulk of Igor was hanging there as he repeatedly lifted his straight legs directly in front of him until they were vertical.

'Jeez he loves himself huh?' said Maxwell as he watched Igor move closer to the mirror and flex his admittedly impressive six pack.

'He must lift weights every day to be so big,' said Easy, unable to hide the awe in his voice.

'That's not just weights kid,' laughed Maxwell, 'he'll have an arse like a pin cushion.' Easy's look of confusion made Maxwell explain, 'steroids kid, no-one looks like that without some chemical help. Human growth hormones, anabolic steroids, you name it, he'll be taking it.'

Maxwell's burner phone rang and he wasn't surprised to see the number calling was unknown. 'Hello?' he said after listening to three seconds of silence.

'It's me,' came JT's voice sounding a little hoarse.

'Good to hear from you, all go ok?'

'Swimmingly!' said JT with a forced laugh.

Maxwell could hear an engine running in the background, 'almost home?' he asked.

'I can see a windmill in the distance,' came the reply.

'How long until we see you again?'

'We need to sort ourselves out, it's been a bit wetter than we'd hoped. I'd say 5 hours.'

'Transport?'

'Bit of a squeeze but our Windmill friend will get us back to our own wheels.'

'Excellent, I have the info you asked for. Good target, should have all the kit you need.'

'Location?'

'Few miles East from here, semi-rural and they don't keep office hours so you should have plenty of time.'

'Ok, see you soon.'

Maxwell hung up and turned to Easy. 'Ok kid, I have another job for you,' he told him the address of an industrial unit near Tilbury docks. 'I need some decent maps of the area and do you think you can check for CCTV?'

'I can get maps for sure. CCTV is trickier, I would need to go there to search for Wi-Fi networks.'

'I just need to know where the cameras are if you can find them.'

'I'll see what I can do.'

Easy got to work and his typing speed earned an admiring nod from Maxwell. 30 minutes later Easy showed Maxwell the satellite images of the industrial unit. It was the last building standing in an area that had been demolished for a new brownfield housing development. The building had been saved as it was the only building beyond the freight railway line that ran into the Tilbury docks another two miles down the track.

The most recent satellite images were a month old and they showed no progress from the image that had been taken 2 months earlier. The housing development appeared to be delayed. That meant there were piles of rubble strewn across the site and would provide excellent cover on the approach. The other side of the building faced onto the Thames and there was a jetty which the latest satellite image showed a small freighter moored against. It didn't appear in the earlier image.

'Someone is working off that jetty,' said Maxwell, pointing to the boat.

'What kind of work do they do?' asked Easy.

'Import and export I guess you would say,' replied Maxwell as he ran his finger along the path of the only access road on the screen.

'What do they import?'

'Drugs mostly, but a little birdy tells me they also deal in weapons.' He wondered how Hamilton might feel about being called "little birdy" and not for the first time wondered how Hamilton had such intel but it wasn't shared with the Police.

'Why are we interested in these people? Are they the Bad Men?' asked Easy as he wiped clean his screen.

'They certainly are Bad Men kid, but not the Kosanians. There are lots of Bad Men out there sadly. We are interested in these particular bad men as, with a bit of luck, the good guys are going to relieve them of their guns.'

'I see,' said Easy, 'I am afraid I cannot see if there is CCTV and where it's located. The building has electricity as the security light was on in the last images.'

'Ok, then grab your stuff, we're going for a drive.'

CHAPTER TWENTY-SEVEN

JT tied the bow line after Walter had skilfully reversed the Peregrine back into the boatshed. The team disembarked and made their way to the windmill where they dressed in navy blue coveralls. They were a far cry from their usual tactical clothing but they would do the job. They would also tie in with their cover as builders back in London.

Walter went to his gun cabinet and removed a rifle which he handed to JT, JT in turn handed it to Rambo who inspected the weapon. 'It's old and American but still serviceable,' said Walter, 'that scope is newer and pretty good. I've taken the occasional fox with it from upstairs. Buggers like to steal the eggs of the birds across in the wetland reserve.'

'This'll do nicely,' said Rambo examining the lever action.

Walter handed Rambo a box of ammunition, 'I make these myself, .32 and they'll take down a deer at 500 yds. The 30-30 packs more punch but I've never had the need,' he said as he turned back to the gun cabinet. He removed two cloth bundles and placed them on the writing bureau. Unwrapping them he said, 'Spoils of war.' He handed JT one of the pair of High Power Browning semi-automatic pistols, '9mm parabellum, these unfortunately are my last box of 9mm ammunition,' he said reaching in once again and lifting out the small cardboard box, '30 rounds is all I can offer I'm afraid.'

'That should be more than enough, we aren't looking to have a fire fight with anyone,' said JT.

Walter then lifted out a steel box painted green and with an Argentinian flag painted on the side beside some stencilled numbers. 'These,' he said, 'were a gift from an Argentinian chap I met in the Falklands,' he unclipped the metal fastener and swung open the lid to reveal three hand grenades. Lifting one out he threw it to Taff who caught it cleanly.

'Christ, are these things still safe?' said Taff looking slightly alarmed.

'It's a grenade, it's not meant to be safe!' chuckled Walter.

'But it must be at least 40 years old,' exclaimed Taff.

'Yes, I suppose, it is,' smiled Walter as he carefully lifted the fuses from the bottom of the box. 'I removed the fuses on board the Canberra as she brought us home. Not the easiest of tasks in the South Atlantic, it was pretty rough all the way up to doldrums.'

'They're deactivated?'

'Yes, but they can be reactivated by screwing one of these fuses back in. Then again, sometimes a big lie is as useful as the truth to misquote Hemmingway.'

#

It was tight as they all squeezed into Walter's Mercedes G Wagen. Spotlessly clean inside and out, the black leather in the rear seats had never seen a passenger's bum joked Walter. Rambo and Joe were tucked up in the cargo area alongside the kit bags as Taff and Cooky filled the middle row of seats.

Two cramped hours later they pulled into a car park alongside a scruffy van with Southend Building Services liveried on the sides.

Joe laughed as he read the company name on the van 'SBS! After the amount of time we've just spent in the sea, we could well be Shaky Boats!' The others laughed at the nickname the SAS used for colleagues of the sister regiment, the Special Boat Service.

'We ain't got webbed feet just yet,' laughed Taff.

'I don't think Easy will have understood the relevance when he bought the van for us,' said JT.

'Just how did the kid manage that anyway, he can't even drive,' said Taff, giving the exterior of the vehicle a check over.

'He's a kid of many talents, and it's amazing what you can get - if you can afford to pay for it,' said JT

'I'm definitely going to get him to sort out my pension!' replied Taff, giving a thumbs up as he completed his inspection.

After locating the key where it had been hidden by arrangement the men loaded their kit and themselves into the van. Cooky took the driver's seat and started the van, it turned over first time and sounded healthy for a 5 year old transit van with 80,000 miles on the clock.

'Thanks again Walter,' said JT shaking his Godfather's hand.

'No problem at all. I've quite enjoyed being back in the game,' he smiled at JT, 'I'll have Peregrine fuelled and ready to go whenever you're ready. If at all possible, I'd like my guns back too, one of them nearly did for me at Goose Green.'

'I'll do my best,' said JT and turned to climb into the passenger seat. As the van drove out of the car park Cooky handed JT a dust mask and they both put them on and pulled baseball caps low over their eyes. If this plan was to work out, they needed to make sure they couldn't be identified. And survive.

CHAPTER TWENTY-EIGHT

Maxwell and Easy drove to the farthest edge of the demolished industrial site. After driving a loop of the entire site, they drove to an area that had been re-greened alongside the river. From here they could see the freighter tied up at the jetty beside the target building. There were lights on in the wheelhouse superstructure and across the deck. The jetty itself was in darkness as was the industrial building.

'There'll be PIR sensors for the security lights,' said Maxwell.

'We are too far for my phone to pick up any wi-fi signal,' replied Easy.

Maxwell scanned the building with his binoculars and wished they were more powerful. He also wished his eyesight was as perfect as it once was. He thought for a moment then handed the binoculars to Easy. 'See if you can spot any cameras on the building,' he told him.

Easy took the binoculars and turned the dial to refocus them. Slowly he moved his head as he took in first the building and then the surroundings. 'There at the top corner nearest the road,' he said pointing with his free hand, 'there is a dome camera, the little light blinks every few seconds.'

'Makes sense. Anything on the riverside end?' asked Maxwell.

'Not that I can see. Something is strange with this building though. If they deal in drugs and guns, they should have a fence or something, no? Anyone could drive up to the building.'

'Hidden in plain sight I guess,' replied Maxwell, and *if the intel I've been given is correct* he thought to himself. He considered calling Hamilton but movement on the freighter caught his attention. A man stood on the deck near the bow and lit a cigarette. Taking the binoculars from Easy he quickly refocused them on the freighter. The man stood looking at the building and casually smoking. Another man appeared beside him and the first man used a match to light his companions' cigarettes. This confirmed a few things for Maxwell, they were both light skinned Europeans, neither of them were concerned about a sniper and more importantly, both were carrying Heckler and Koch MP7 submachine guns.

Maxwell tapped Easy on the shoulder and gestured for him to move. They kept low behind the shrubbery and made their way back towards their car. 'This is definitely the right place,' he said as he started the car, 'let's go meet the team and tell them the good news.

#

They drove to the rendezvous point and waited for the team to arrive. Easy continued his work trying to get as much detail about the target as possible. 'This could be important,' he said, 'I was checking the planning permission for the residential development. They have removed the electricity substation and need to replace it as part of their permission.'

Maxwell looked confused, 'What does that mean?' he asked.

'It means they must have a generator, and it must be on the far side of the building. There was a yellow rectangle on the satellite images, I thought it was maybe a storage container or one of those waste compactors,' he said as he expanded the image and pointed at his laptop, 'Here.'

'The tree line along the river bank leads to right behind it. I wonder if the freighter is connected to it too, I didn't see any exhaust from its engines,' replied Maxwell looking at his watch. 'Two hours to sun up, if the guys are going to go in the dark, they better hurry up.'

On cue the builders van drove around the corner and parked in the street light shadow cast by a big tree. Maxwell drove the car up alongside the van and rolled down the window, 'Jump in, Easy and I will brief you en route, the guys can follow us,' he said to JT.

JT jumped into the passenger seat and was joined by Taff from the rear of the van. Maxwell drove off followed by the van. 'Tell me about the target,' he said to Maxwell.

'It's an industrial unit down by the river about 2 miles from here.' Easy held up the laptop so the men in the back seat could see the images. Maxwell continued, 'The intel came from Hamilton, it was never on the Police radar. They are drug dealers who branched out into weapons, is what I'm told.'

'What kind of weapons?' asked JT.

'No details but the two goons on the freighter were sporting MP7s.'

'Freighter?' asked JT appearing unconcerned by the news of the submachine guns.

'There's a coastal freighter moored at the jetty adjacent to the building.'

'Ok, what else?'

Easy clicked his laptop and brought up an image of the building, 'There is a CCTV camera at this corner, we couldn't see if there are any more. There is no perimeter fence and one road in that runs alongside the railway line. The road is about 400m long leading off the public road. There are no gates.'

'Hidden in plain sight,' said Maxwell.

'How many operators?' asked JT.

'Again, no intel sadly, other than the two on the freighter, we saw no-one,' replied Maxwell.

'There is also this,' said Easy, 'I believe it is a generator, the mains electricity has been disconnected.'

'Useful,' said JT, his mind racing to formulate the bones of a plan.

'Sun up at 0617 hrs,' said Taff through the speaker phone, 'we have less than 2 hours of dark.'

'Any high ground?' asked JT looking at the satellite images.

'Nothing obvious that's close. There's a crane in the building site but not sure what kind of sight lines it would have. You'll see it as we drive past.'

'Ok, slow down when we get close.'

'This is the entrance we're passing now,' said Maxwell pointing to an unmarked roadway. 'No sentries and no CCTV that we could see,' he pointed ahead through the windscreen, 'and there's the crane.'

JT could see the red air traffic warning light on top of the crane and realised it was a tall fixed crane with a long horizontal boom, 'Ok pull in up ahead, dark spot if you can.'

Maxwell pulled into a bus layby under a broken street light.

JT got out of the car and went to the rear of the van carrying Easy's laptop, 'Rambo, this is the target building, CCTV here,' he pointed at the spot on the screen. 'Two operatives seen aboard this tub moored here. They're smokers. There's a crane across the road, take the rifle and see if you can get a position to provide cover.'

Rambo grabbed the rifle and slung it over his shoulder. Checking there was no traffic he sprinted across the road and leapt at the hoarding, getting his feet halfway up the board and his hands onto the top. He vaulted himself up and briefly onto the top of the hoarding then jumped down on the other side. The loose rubble slowed his progress slightly in the dark but he was quickly stood at the bottom of the crane. There was steel shuttering up the first 10 feet of the crane structure. It was designed to prevent kids climbing up the crane but for now it was an obstacle to be overcome. The bolts and padlock securing the shuttering provided just enough purchase for Rambo to defeat the security measure and reach the purpose built climbing frame. Here he was in his element and he paused after 5 metres of climbing to get his bearings. The boom of the crane stretched 25 metres in the wrong direction. The counterweight boom was only 10m long, but crucially was pointed toward the target building. He scaled the rest of the crane and made his way along the footplate to the end of the boom. 'Cover in position.' He said into his covert mic.

'Sit rep,' replied JT.

'Have visual of the north and east sides of the building, I have limited sight of the boat, bow to wheelhouse is clear. No movement.'

'What's the cover like from the treeline to the yellow generator?'

'Less than 10 metres. There's a forklift there too.'

'Live updates please Rambo. We're parking up.'

Maxwell led JT and the team to the vantage point they'd used earlier. JT had the benefit of a night vision monocular telescope and was able to see the building clearly. The building was of metal sheeting construction so would have a steel infrastructure. There were no windows and one large roller-door with a pedestrian access or fire door adjacent to it. Rambo reported a forklift on the reverse side of the building which likely meant another roller door or loading bay. He scanned again noting the position of the CCTV camera. Its design encased in a darkened glass dome made it impossible to tell where the camera was pointed.

'Listen up. Taff you'll take the van back up the road and drop Cooky and Posty upstream and they can make their way back to the freighter. We'll jump out and come East through the tree line to get to the generator. Once you've dropped them off, they'll have 5 minutes to reach the boat then I want you to drive along the road and up to the north side of the building. Just make a slow three point turn and then make your way back out. If there's someone monitoring the CCTV, I want their eyes on you. We have to assume there's another camera on the South West corner but we can't escape that. Hopefully there's only one set of eyes on the camera screens. When we're in position and we know the score with the boat we'll cut the power. Then we'll breach the building. If there's not a door on our side then you can bring the van back around and take out the roller door. You boys take one of the Brownings. Neutralise the guys on the deck and if possible secure the boat. Rory, you take the car and make sure no-one else comes down that road. Rambo will provide high cover but let's try to keep this quiet. Apologies for the sketchy planning but we've no time to do it properly. Questions?'

'What do I do?' asked Easy.

'You are going to provide our distraction.,' said JT taking down the life preserver from its stand. He fished in the litter bin and came out with a plastic water bottle and a sealable plastic sandwich bag. He handed it to Joe and told him to soak it in petrol from the can in the back of the van. JT lashed the rope attached to the life preserver back and forth around the ring to create a makeshift webbing. He put the half full bottle of petrol into the bag and stuffed the petrol soaked rug in around it. He closed the Ziploc leaving a corner of the rag exposed.

'When I give you the order, I want you to light the rag and throw the preserver out into the river. It doesn't have to go far out, just has to stay this way up. Once you've thrown it, get yourself back up to the road and wait for us at the bus stop but stay out of sight. Understood?'

'Yes,' said Easy grinning and glad to be part of the plan.

'If we don't make it back, get yourself the hell out of here and if anyone asks, we never met,' JT told him seriously. Easy nodded, his grin gone.

#

'Still two on deck,' said Rambo from his vantage point, 'both armed.'

'Easy, go!' said JT into his phone as he made his way with Joe through the trees toward the west side of the target. He was hating the lack of planning but focused as always on getting the job done. He knew plans never lasted beyond first contact but that didn't make the rigours of planning any less valuable.

Easy lit the petrol soaked rag and frisbeed the life preserver ring out into the river. It floated with the tide in the direction of the freighter. The flames burned under the plastic bottle which duly melted and a steady stream of petrol poured out and erupted with a roar of flames.

The operatives on the deck ran to the side of the freighter to see what had caused the explosion. At the same time Posty stuck his head out from the side of the wheelhouse and threw a grenade.

'Grenade!' he mock shouted as it clattered against the metal decking and rolled towards the operatives. They watched terrified as the grenade rolled in their direction, then instinctively threw themselves overboard and into the river. The weight of their weapons and Kevlar body-armour dragging them beneath the surface to their deaths.

Posty chuckled as he ran to retrieve the deactivated grenade and checked overboard to see if the operatives had made it. A steel bulk-head door squealed as it opened and Posty spun round to see an operative take aim at him. In a blur a big black hand appeared as Cooky stabbed the man in the throat with the folding knife he'd taken from the people smuggler the night before. A torrent of blood poured down the man's front as he dropped his weapon and tried in vain to stem the bleeding. Cooky pulled him backwards dropping him to the floor then stepping over him to pick up the MP5SD, he checked the magazine and cleared the chamber before reloading and resetting the magazine.

'Cheers Cooky, that's some Gucci shit these boys have, suppressed too, are they sponsored by H and K or something?' asked Posty.

'Pass, but this thing is brand new. I've cleared the wheelhouse and accommodation but need to do below decks. You go check the accommodation again, see if there's any more H and K goodies we can borrow. Meet you back here,' he checked his watch, 'lights out in 3 minutes, let's move.'

The bleeding man groaned from the floor almost dead. Cooky shot him in the face to help speed up the process. It also allowed him to confirm the weapon worked properly.

Two minutes later Posty emerged onto the deck with an MP7 in hand and a MP5SD slung across his body.

Cooky looked at his watch. 45 seconds to lights out. 'Freighter cleared, 3 down and we have secured three SMGs, all suppressed,' he said into his mic.

'Nice work. Taff, you are a go,' said JT, 'Think you can take out the south west CCTV camera Cooky?'

'Standby...' said Cooky then resting the barrel of his MP5 on the rung of a steel ladder he selected single shot. He depressed the trigger and instantaneously the glass dome shattered.

The suppressed noise of the MP5 was loud enough to startle a heron roosting in a tree above JT and as it took off so did JT and Joe. They could hear Taff driving the van and as he reached the building the painfully bright security lights were activated. They sprinted to the generator and ripped open the cover on the control, a master breaker switch was in the form of a big red button. JT checked his watch then nodded to Joe who slapped the button. The lights on the freighter went out and only pale emergency lights above doorways illuminated the dark building.

A door opened in the loading bay and a voice echoed from the building. 'Fix that fucking generator will you, I'm trying to work here.' The accent was unmistakably Irish.

The man who had opened the door replied, 'Keep your hair on, it'll have tripped is all.' This accent was nasal East Coast American, possibly Boston, thought JT. The American appeared and walked toward the generator, he switched on a penlight torch and froze when the beam shone on the open control panel. He went to his waist band and drew a pistol then stopped as JT placed the barrel of the Browning against the back of his neck.

'Quiet now friend. How many are inside the building?' he asked him.

'You've fucked up big time here you know,' came the American's reply.

'How do you figure that when I have the gun to your head?' asked JT.

'You don't fuck with the I...R...A and get away with it.'

'You're the IRA?' asked JT wondering what the hell they'd walked into.

'That we are and you're a dead man if you don't get the fuck out-' JT didn't let the American finish his sentence and clubbed him across the head with the grip of the Browning knocking him unconscious.

'Hurry up!' came a shout from the Irish accented man inside the building.

JT had an idea, 'Let me get to the door of the loading bay then turn the lights back on.'

Joe nodded and picked up the handgun dropped by the American. He moved into position by the control panel and when JT reached the door, he switched the lights back on.

'Hurry up and shut the bloody door!' shouted the Irish voice.

A wall of sandbags stood eight feet high beside the door and prevented JT seeing into the rest of the building. He took a piece of cardboard from the floor and folded it twice then pulled the door shut using the cardboard to wedge the locking mechanism. He crouched down at the end of the wall and used his phone camera to film what was on the other side. He saw that the wall of sandbags was matched on the other side and it appeared an entire bunker had been constructed of sandbags.

JT stepped out holding the Browning ready and looked at the rest of the building. Wooden packing cases took up most of the available space and he recognised the H and K branding on two of the cases. Others had Russian military symbols and one appeared to have Israeli markings. There was one table with several packages of what appeared to be light brown powder. 'Heroin' thought JT, he'd seen plenty of it in Afghanistan and Pakistan.

Joe opened the door and entered which brought a shout from the Irishman, 'Where the fuck are you going now O'Neill?' A second later he appeared through the doorway of the sandbag bunker. He was a tall skinny man with thick round glasses and thin grey hair swept back off his face. He wore a brown leather apron on top of the white paper suit that covered his clothes.

'Who the fuck might you be?' he asked JT.

'I'm the one asking the questions,' said JT calmly.

'Do you know who you're messing with, Mr...?' asked the Irishman

'Like I said, I'm the one asking the questions.'

Cooky's voice came in JT's ear, 'You want us in there, boss?'

'Yes Cooky,' JT replied.

'Cooky? I've not been called that in a long time,' said the Irishman, surprised.

JT showed no emotion and replied, 'So what do you get called now?'

'Now, well many things I suppose behind my back, but to my face most call me Mr Forrest,' he eyed JT and then continued, 'and what do they call you, officer?'

'Like I said, I'm asking the questions. Once more and I'll put a round in your knee.'

'Steady on there now. I see now you're not Police...' he was about to go on, but when JT pointed the Browning at his knee, he stopped himself.

JT pointed to a chair at the table with the drug packages. 'Take a seat.'

Forrest took a seat.

'Turn it to face this way.' JT instructed.

Forrest stood and spun the chair round and sat back down. As he did his hand slid under his leather apron.

JT pointed the Browning at his head and said, 'Hand out, slowly.'

Forrest withdrew his hand and in it was a pouch of tobacco. He offered it to JT who declined the gesture.

'Go ahead,' said JT, 'but those things will kill you.'

'Ach, I'm older than I ever thought I'd be. Besides, I get the feeling that's why you're here.'

'I have no interest in killing you, as long as my questions get answers.'

'Fair enough,' said Forrest as he rolled his cigarette.

'What is this place?' asked JT.

'You mean you don't know? Sorry, that wee question was an accident!' he said quickly, holding up his hands and smiling. 'What this place is, should be pretty self-evident but the real question you should be asking is, who does this place belong to.'

'Don't tell me, the IRA,' said JT.

'Aye, that's right, the IR fuckin' A. The self-same IRA that will hunt you down and hunt your family down too,' said Forrest as he eyed JT for a reaction but getting none.

'Okay so we've established ownership. What's your role here?'

'My role here, is the same as it is, everywhere. I am a master craftsman. A Cook if you prefer. I make the most delicious surprises.'

JT looked at the sandbag bunker and it all became clear, 'You're a bombmaker for the IRA?'

Forrest chuckled, 'I'm not just "a bombmaker", I am *The* bombmaker. I am also not exclusively employed by the IRA. There are plenty of customers willing to pay for my services. Talking of which, if you look in those two holdalls over there, you will see my latest payment for services rendered. Two million pounds in a mix of Euros, Swiss Francs and US Dollars. Naturally, it's yours, if we can come to some sort of an arrangement.' Seeing JT was unimpressed he went on, 'I am paid handsomely for my skills and have been saving for my retirement. My pension pot would be a small price to pay, should I be allowed to walk out of here. There is a little over ten million in a numbered Swiss account. It's yours once I leave here.'

JT thought for a second, 'Joe, take a look in there,' he said nodding toward the bunker.

Joe stepped back out of the bunker, 'It's a cross between a clock makers and a chemist's lab in there.'

'I hope you didn't touch anything,' chuckled Forrest.

Joe ignored him and looked in the holdalls. They were full of stacks of banknotes as Forrest had described. Joe tipped it toward JT to show him, 'Two million you say?' asked Joe.

'I haven't counted it but yes that's what'll be there.'

Cooky and Posty arrived through the docking bay door, 'What do you want us to do with the guy outside boss?' asked Cooky.

'Best bring him in here and tie him up,' then as an afterthought JT added, 'and gag him too, he sounds like Ben Affleck with a broken nose.' Into his mic JT said, 'Taff bring the van down.' He received a click of transmission in acknowledgement. 'Rory, you're going to want to see this but go fetch the kid and bring him down here too, tell him to bring in his laptop.' Rory clicked acknowledgement and set off.

Cooky and Posty carried in the unconscious American and found cable ties to truss him up and some packing tape to cover his mouth.

'Who is this guy?' JT asked Forrest.

'His name is O'Neill, American obviously. Hails from Boston where his Daddy and Granddaddy were major fundraisers for their "brothers across the sea". Young O'Neill has the fire in his belly to be a bit more hands on in the glorious struggle, and that brought him here.'

'Why here?'

'The drugs I suppose. He handles the drugs between here and Libya. That little ship of his out there has half a ton of heroin aboard. It's shipped here from Rotterdam. Some gets sold here and some arrives state side via Canada. The US Dollars then go back to Libya in exchange for the weapons. Some of the weapons are kept for 'the struggle' and others are sold on to whichever warlord or gangster can pay the price.'

'You don't seem to be much of a believer in "the struggle", said JT.

'Ach, I got disillusioned long ago. The dream of ridding Ireland of the British and reuniting the Island of Ireland has long been forgotten. Now it's just about who can make the most cash out of it. They do the odd bit of paramilitary action to keep the cogs turning but they're glorified gangsters now.'

'You didn't just pack it in and retire.'

'Oh, I'd love to retire, but as I said my skills are in demand and I can be pimped out accordingly, so my retirement will come when my eyes finally give up on me, or they decide I'm no longer useful.'

'Do you think they'll let you live?' asked JT, 'You must know enough to put them all away'.

'I can only hope that I can slip off, with enough cash to be able to hide well enough that it takes them a long time to find me, or they get bored looking.'

'But you've offered me the money in your bank account,' said JT.

'There may just be another bank account, a smaller one mind, but enough to get by.'

Taff walked in after reversing the van into the loading bay, 'Well, what have we here then?' he said, eyeing up the packing crates.

'Open these up and let's take anything we can use,' said JT.

Taff, Cooky and Posty set about opening the crates. They removed 8 H and K suppressed MP5SD, 8 MP7s and several cases of ammunition. Inside one of the cases they found two rifle cases containing Russian made SVLK-14s *Twilight* sniper rifles capable of destroying a vehicle at a distance of 2000m. 'Fuck me, it's like bloody Christmas,' said Taff as he eyed their haul.

'Let's ask Santa for these too,' said Posty as he pulled a Tavor TS12 Semi-automatic shotgun out of its straw packing. 'The Israelis do make a good shotgun. Not sure how they feel about Christmas though!'

Maxwell and Easy arrived and stood wide eyed as they surveyed the scene.

'Get your laptop set up,' JT told Easy. 'Mr Forrest here is about to give you access to a Swiss bank account.'

'Okay, which bank?' asked Easy.

Forrest gave him the details from memory including the 24 word password to access and service the account. JT gave Easy details of an offshore account in Grand Cayman to transfer the money to. Once it was complete, he told Maxwell to take Easy back to London.

As Easy packed up his laptop he looked around the building, 'Where's the monitors?' he asked JT.

'Monitors?' replied JT

'There are CCTV cameras, there has to be somewhere to monitor them.'

'Fuck!' said JT, 'Rambo how's it looking?'

'All clear from up here boss. Oh standby, vehicle approaching along the main road at high speed, looks like a Range Rover.'

JT turned to Maxwell, 'We expecting company?'

'Not that I'm aware of,' he replied and checked his phone. He'd received no messages.

'Get in the car and get out of here, move, we'll RV later!' he said to Maxwell, who sprinted with Easy and jumped in the car.

'ETA Rambo?'

'They're a fair way out, maybe 1 minute.'

CHAPTER TWENTY-NINE

Maxwell floored it without using headlights and screamed up the 400m of track before he hit the main road, he pulled a handbrake turn and then drove fast to the bus layby they'd been in earlier he mounted the kerb and parked the car behind the bus stop and killed his headlights. 'We're out', he said into his mic.

'15 seconds until the track. Want me to slow them down,' asked Rambo.

'Yes, we'll get set up here.'

Taff and Cooky finished loading the weapons into the van. All 5 team members were now in possession of suppressed MP5s, a weapon they had trained with for years. The unmistakable sound of a rifle shot was followed shortly thereafter by the sound of a vehicle crashing at high speed. Unfortunately, the rifle was not as accurate as Rambo would have liked and his round had smashed into the engine compartment before ricocheting up and through the windscreen. The Range Rover careered off the road into the trees and came to a rest 20 yards off the road. The 4 occupants jumped out and one of them opened fire at the crane. A round hit the metal structure 6 feet away from Rambo and he realised the shooter was aiming blind. Rambo took aim and adjusted the sight allowing for the minor discrepancy in his previous shot. He steadied his breath and took the tension of the trigger half way then in the space between breaths he squeezed the trigger and watched the shooter slump by the car. 'One down 3 heading your way through the trees to the East. I have no visual, repeat no visual.'

'Stay put and watch for any other traffic,' replied JT. Rambo clicked his acknowledgement.

Taff drove the van around the West side of the building then jumped out and ran to join Cooky on the freighter to give them the high ground and a view of the rear yard. JT and Posty pushed over some of the sandbags and took up a firing position in front of the door. Joe stood guard over the prisoners and bound Forrest to his chair.

The first rounds came through the door from somewhere among the trees. The firing was indiscriminate as the sandbag wall prevented anyone seeing anything beyond the doorway.

'This is covering fire,' said JT, 'they'll be trying to get around the building.'

'I've got the East side covered, no movement,' said Taff from the bow of the freighter.

'Rambo?' said JT into his mic.

'No movement, I can't get visual through the trees,' he replied in his usual calm and measured voice.

'Keep overwatch of the East side and the road Rambo,' said JT, 'Taff, you and Cooky be ready to engage when they break the treeline. Posty and I will loop round into the trees from the North. We'll flush them out or we're stuck here.' A series of clicks confirmed his message was received and understood. He turned to Joe, 'tuck yourself in and stay away from that bunker, I get the feeling there's a bloody big bang in the making in there.'

Forrest laughed, 'Now didn't I tell you the IRA would hunt you down, there'll be more on the way and you lot will be dead shortly. Your families however, they'll die slow and painf –' he didn't finish the sentence as JT shot him in the face, the back of his head exploding and the chair falling backwards.

JT found himself thinking of the woman in Afghanistan, she had been wearing a bomb vest made by someone just like Forrest – a technician without a care about who, or how many innocents, their creations killed. He could see every feature of her terrified face. She knew she was going to die and had tried to warn him. He had shot her, without blinking.

'Boss?' said Joe looking at him.

'Sorry Joe, what is it?'

Joe pointed at the American who was trussed up and lay on the floor wide eyed, 'Him too?'

JT thought for a split second as he looked at the American, 'Leave him be for now Joe, he might come in useful, but if he gets in the way, do what you have to.'

Posty was waiting at the fire exit door ready to push it open, 'West clear Rambo? We're coming out.'

'Clear,' came the reply.

The number of incoming rounds through the door had lessened with 15 seconds or so between fire. 'I think they're conserving ammo,' said Taff, 'They've not come prepared for the long haul. They'll try to rush the building soon.'

'We're entering the trees now,' replied JT, 'We'll flush them towards you.' He and Posty moved stealthily through the trees and gave themselves a wide arc to get behind the attackers. They could see the

Range Rover where it had crashed and one headlight cast long straight shadows between the trees.

Suddenly gunfire erupted from the car and rounds thudded into the trees beside them. JT heard Posty grunt and fall behind a tree. Whoever was shooting at them was low down beside the car and the dazzling light of the headlight was making it difficult to see the shooter. 'Rambo!' began JT but he was stopped by the report of a rifle. The shooting from the Range Rover stopped instantly.

'Neutralised,' said Rambo, as JT ran to find Posty. He was sitting up but dazed and had sharp splinters of wood stuck in his face and one long shard of wood sticking in his shoulder.

'You ok?' asked JT, crouching beside him peering out into the trees.

'Never...' he grunted as he pulled the splintered wood out of his shoulder, '...better,' said Posty, getting to his knees.

More shots came at them, this time from the trees ahead of them. They crawled to the crater left by the roots of a fallen tree. More rounds were fired and the muzzle flash moved as the shooter ran toward them. JT waited and let the man come before double tapping him to the chest. The man crashed to the ground and then there was silence. 'Two down,' said JT into his mic. That left two more, somewhere in the trees.

JT tapped Posty on the shoulder and pointed for him to go left while JT went right.

The attackers would know they had been outflanked and would either run or turn and fight. JT hoped they would fight, he wanted to get this over and done with. He moved from tree to tree stopping to scan the area and wishing he had night vision goggles. His eyes were accustomed now to the dark but there were deep shadows still with an hour to go before dawn. A movement stopped him in his tracks. A darker shade moving across a shadow. Confident he hadn't been seen he waited poised to take his shot. A burst of fire from his left lit up the trees. Three controlled bursts told JC that it was Posty who had fired.

'Three down,' came the confirmation in JT's ear.

The shadow had ducked down when Posty fired and been enveloped in the greater dark of the undergrowth. JT moved carefully forward, aware that the twigs and leaves underfoot could give his position away. He stopped and picked up a stick then threw it into the shadow. The last attacker jumped out of cover and ran. JT fired but the mass of trees absorbed the rounds he fired. The attacker ran straight toward the building seeking cover and he'd gotten no more than two steps clear of the treeline when he was knocked off his feet by a volley of fire from Taff and Cooky.

'Four down,' said Cooky.

'Good work lads, let's get packed up and get the hell out of here.'

JT and Posty emerged from the trees and ran to the building where they found Taff and Cooky waiting for them.

'What do we do with him?' asked Taff pointing at the American.

'He can identify us,' said Cooky looking at JT for the inevitable order to neutralise the threat.

Before JT could answer, Rambo said, 'Two vehicles travelling west at speed.'

Police, thought JT, 'Blue Lights?' he asked.

'No, looks like one SUV and one car.'

'Okay,' said JT to Taff, 'You and Cooky get the van and try to get it out of here with the kit. If you can get it out onto the main road somewhere safe then head back on foot. We'll get set up here for whoever is coming next.'

'ETA 1 minute. These guys aren't sparing the horses,' said Rambo.

'Go, now!' said JT.

Taff and Cooky ran to the van and gunned the engine as they wheel-spun out of the loading bay. They rounded the building and headed up the track.

'Not going to get clear guys. 15 seconds,' Rambo told them.

Taff drove the van onto the verge opposite where the Range Rover had crashed. They opened the driver and passenger doors and pushed them wide open before climbing into the back of the van taking cover behind the front seats.

A few seconds later they heard the two vehicles coming along the track. They slowed to a stop and two men got out the rear vehicle before the cars carried on in the direction of the building. The vehicles continued cautiously as they saw the Range Rover and their dead colleague.

'Two coming your way Taff,' said Rambo, lining up his rifle on the first vehicle.

The two men had drawn their sidearms and approached the van from both sides. They appeared simultaneously and were shot at close range as they peered into the van.

Taff said, 'Two down,' as he climbed back into the driver's seat.

'We'll retreat through the trees, we've been here too long as it is,' said JT and moved toward the loading bay door.

'Gimme a sec, I have an idea,' said Joe. He ran to one of the packing cases and lifted out a pair of anti-personnel mines. He grabbed the American dragging him toward the bunker and placed the mines on the man's chest. He lifted a sandbag on top of it then pulled the priming tab to make it live. 'Don't you move now,' He said as he gently slapped the terrified man's face. Joe sprinted to join the others in the tree line. 'We might want to move a bit further,' he said and led the team further into the trees.

'They've parked on the East side,' reported Rambo. 'six of them, four are heading into the building, one sentry by the cars and one heading for the freighter.'

'We'll give you a shout when we get clear and RV back at the bus stop,' replied JT.

#

Rambo watched as the four men entered the building. They gave each other cover as they'd seen on TV but he knew they weren't professionals. They'd deployed all wrong for a start. The sentry that stood by the cars was watching his colleagues enter the building rather than looking outward for threats. The sixth man took his time to climb the gang plank, obviously not keen to board the freighter alone.

Inside the building Michael McConnel, the head of IRA security in London, was apoplectic with rage as he saw Forrest lying on the floor in a pool of blood. He surveyed the scene taking in the broken packing cases and the table which still had intact packages of heroin on it. He pulled his phone out of his pocket and pressed the speed dial, 'We've been hit.'

'Who the fuck by?' came the reply in a broad Liverpudlian accent.

'I don't know yet.'

'Forrest?'

'Dead. Someone shot him in the head.'

'Execution?'

'Maybe.'

'This one's still alive!' shouted one of the men.

McConnel had never liked the American and saw that he was gagged. He could see tears in the American's eyes and it looked like he'd pissed himself. 'Hang on a second, the Yank is alive, he'll tell us who did this.' He held the phone away from his mouth and turned to the men nearest the American, 'get him up and talking.'

McConnel took a step toward the bunker as one of the men lifted the sandbag off the American's chest. As the mine detonated the explosion sent thousands of steel ball bearings through the air ripping apart flesh and bone and destroying everything in a 360 degree radius. Hearing the explosion, the sentry ran toward the door just as a secondary explosion ripped through the building. Pieces of metal siding ripped from the building shredding the sentry.

Rambo watched as the man on the gangplank ran up and onto the freighter, turning his head left and right, while rooted to the spot through panic and indecision. Rambo made his mind up for him and shot him with a round that entered his gut and lodged in his pelvis. The man slumped holding his belly in shock for a second before he toppled forward and rolled off the gangplank crashing into the water below.

'Six down,' said Rambo, already up and making his way to the ladder inside the crane structure. He slid down using his gloved hands and feet on the outside of the ladder. 10 seconds later he was running across the rubble and back to the hoarding where he waited until the van appeared in the bus stop layby.

Maxwell and Easy had watched the explosion from the car and were shocked to feel the force of the blast rock the car.

As they waited for the team to arrive Maxwell's phone rang. It was Hamilton. 'Excellent work chaps.'

'Pardon?' said Maxwell.

'Excellent work, I hope the team got what they were looking for?'

'There's been an explosion,' said Maxwell, almost apologetically.

'Yes, I know. Probably best that you don't hang around,' suggested Hamilton.

'We're about to leave,' he paused a second before going on, 'How did you know?'

'I make it my business to know.'

'I'm guessing we just did some of your dirty work for you?'

'All present, and correct?' said Hamilton, ignoring the question.

'Yeah, the team are all out of there. More than I can say for the other guys.'

'An occupational hazard. They won't be missed by anyone decent.'

'Yeah, if you say so.'

'Oh I know so old chap. I have something for you.'

'Go on,' said Maxwell regathering his focus.

'Your garden. Palmerston House, it's a health spa and retreat near Haywards Heath. I understand the previous owners had an equine stud farm and the extensive stable blocks were being renovated into luxury accommodation.'

'It's a front then?'

'I am told it is terribly exclusive and people fly into Gatwick from around the world to visit. I am also researching the possibility that some notable figures from here in the UK might also be patrons.'

'Ok thanks.'

'I'll be in touch,' said Hamilton and hung up.

JT got out of the van and Rambo jumped into the vacant passenger seat. JT went to Maxwell's car and climbed in the back seat. 'Let's get out of here,' he said to Maxwell who drove the car out from behind the bus stop and onto the road.

'Where to?' asked Maxwell.

'Back to the flat, we need to regroup and Posty needs fixing up.'

'He's hurt?' asked Easy.

'A few cuts, nothing serious hopefully.'

'I'll go the long way,' said Maxwell turning the car away from London, 'the Met will have everybody and their granny headed this way in a few minutes.'

The car and van headed East toward Basildon and were passed by several emergency vehicles going the other way.

'We know where the girls are going!' blurted Easy suddenly.

'What do you mean?' asked JT.

'Hamilton called,' said Maxwell, 'the photo of the garden the kid found, it's a health retreat or something. Haywards Heath.'

'When do they move?' asked JT stifling a yawn,

'Tomorrow,' said Easy

'Ok. You can do your computer magic and show me later.'

#

They pulled over near a farm and Easy used a black marker pen to alter a couple of the numbers and letters on the car registration plates. It wouldn't pass close scrutiny but might just confuse the roadside cameras.

In the back of the van Rambo used the pliers from a multi-tool to extract the shards of wood from Posty's face. Stitches would have to wait. Eventually they turned back toward London and had the sun rising behind them. They pulled into the lines of city bound commuter traffic and those that could, got some sleep.

JT curled up on the backseat of the car as much to keep his face hidden as to get comfortable. He drifted off to sleep and found himself in a familiar dream. A new face joined the characters, Forrest as he shot him in the face, blending with the Afghan woman and Esmé on their wedding day. This time the wedding day images had Esmé opening her wedding dress to reveal a bomb vest. The dream turned to the sea and JT watched a huge ship coming toward him. The white foam of the bow wave growing bigger he could see Esmé in her wedding dress laughing as she tumbled through the wave. JT was transfixed, unable to swim as the white water engulfed him.

He woke up with a start as the car wash brushes rolled down the side of the car. Sitting up he found himself gasping for air as he processed the dream. 'Where are we?' he asked Maxwell.

'Ten minutes from the flat, thought we'd wash away any evidence. I'll give it a proper clean later but this will have to do for now.'

'Good thinking. The others behind us?'

'They've gone on to the flat, they wanted to patch up Posty.'

'Yeah okay. I could murder a brew,' said JT rubbing at his beard, 'and I'd love a hot shower.'

'No hot water at the flat I'm afraid,' said Maxwell looking at his friend in the rear view mirror. 'I could take you round to mine and you use the facilities then bring you back?'

'No, thanks all the same, but if the team can't get a hot shower, no way I can.'

'You were dreaming,' said Maxwell gently.

'Yeah, me and Phoebe from Friends were having a chicken pathia on a roundabout in Milton Keynes. Funny how I dream about food when I'm starving,' answered JT without meeting Maxwell's eyes in the mirror.

'I always liked Monica myself,' said Maxwell going along with the pretence, 'Rachel was hotter but a bit obvious. Monica just had a bit of secret dirtiness about her!' he laughed as he completed the sentence.

JT gave a bit of a guffaw but the atmosphere changed when Easy asked, 'Who is Esmé? You were saying her name as you slept.'

His question stung JT and made Maxwell shift in his seat. After an awkward silence JT cleared his throat and said, 'Esmé is my, no sorry, Esmé was, my wife.'

'I am so sorry to hear that,' said Easy turning to face JT, 'How did she die?'

'Easy!' exclaimed Maxwell.

JT put a hand on his shoulder and said, 'It's alright Rory, kid means no harm.' He took a breath before continuing, 'She's not dead kid, she just didn't like me being in the army, so she left me.'

Easy thought about this for a moment then said, 'Perhaps she will be happy that you are now rich and come home?'

'Now that I'm rich?' replied JT.

'I transferred ten million pounds to your account, remember? You are a rich man!'

'That's not my money kid,' said JT remembering the details.

'Then whose money is it? That man is dead, he cannot want it back.'

'Well, that's a good question kid, a bloody good question,' replied JT as they drove out of the car wash. It was too much for JT to think through properly in his exhausted state. He needed to sleep and he needed time to process the last 48 hours.

Pulling on his surgical mask JT sat upright in the back of the car as they drove out of the car wash. He watched the people go by in cars and buses and on foot. Their faces washed through his vision, none of them in focus, none of them registering. Then he saw the little boy. Instant recognition of those eyes, full of uncomprehending hurt and shock. He was holding his mother's hand. She had him close to her, like he was literally attached to her hip.

He saw the bandaged hand that the kid held slightly away and in front of his body, trying to keep it from touching anything. It would still be too painful, thought JT. Almost unwillingly he lifted his gaze to the face of the young woman. She looked tired beyond her young years, her hair unwashed and unbrushed. Her cheap clothes made her look unkempt. He had heard of sexual assault victims trying to make themselves unattractive in an effort to avoid the attention of men. It didn't work of course, rapists and the sort of men who like to hurt women don't care what they look like. It's about power not attraction.

He felt it in his stomach first. The disgust at the memory of what he'd seen on that video made him feel nauseous, but that quickly evaporated as it was replaced with something else. That something else was growing and getting hotter until it boiled in his gut. He could taste it now. It was rage.

The woman and her son crossed the road and he watched them go. I will make him suffer for what he did to you he silently promised them. Him and all of his kind.

#

When they arrived back at the flat the team were getting cleaned up and Rambo was stitching the wound on Posty's shoulder. Posty winced as Rambo pulled the thread to close the skin. 'Jesus, you'll make it scar like a cat's arsehole if you pull it any tighter,' he said through gritted teeth.

When the patch up job was complete, they all sat around the room waiting for the debrief. JT sipped at his tea and savoured the refreshing hot liquid in his mouth before swallowing it. It did nothing to extinguish the burning anger but he fought to get it under control. Anger was good if it gave you energy and determination but it was a hindrance to clear thinking and planning. 'We've crossed the Rubicon now guys,' he began, 'we've broken so many laws even Rory here has lost count!' He tried to smile as he said it but the joke fell flat. His team, as well as his friend and a young kid he barely knew, all looked at him. They wanted leadership, information and to know what they were going to do next. For the first time since he took command of the team JT felt like an impostor. He didn't know what to say.

Maxwell's phone rang and he looked at the screen. Another un-known number. He looked to JT who nodded that he should answer it. 'Yes?'

'Good morning, Detective Inspector.' came a cheery voice.

'Mr Hamilton, I, or rather we, are in a meeting. Can this wait?'

'No, I think not. Perhaps you could do me an obligement and open the front door?'

Maxwell hung up and turned to JT, 'He's here.'

CHAPTER THIRTY

Maxwell opened the front door to find Hamilton with a bottle of Irish whiskey in one hand and a briefcase in the other. 'Aren't you going to invite me in?' he asked with the usual eyebrow raise. Maxwell took a step back and held the door as Hamilton entered. 'Good morning, Gentlemen,' he said as he walked into the room and looked at the slightly bedraggled looking men. His gaze fell upon Easy, 'Ah, you must be Ezekiel.' He handed the whiskey to Taff and then offered a hand for Easy to shake.

'My friends call me Easy,' replied Easy with a handshake not nearly as firm as Hamilton's.

'Then I do hope we will be friends,' said Hamilton, already moving on to face JT. 'Captain St-John Templeman,' he said with a suitably firm handshake.

'And you are?' asked JT.

'Hamilton.' The accompanying smile didn't quite reach his eyes as he appeared to take measure of JT. He turned and looked at the weapons and holdalls stacked in the corner. 'A good result then?' he asked over his shoulder as he looked inside one of the holdalls.

'Depends on who you ask,' said JT looking to Maxwell for some clarity on what was happening.

'Indeed,' said Hamilton, turning back to him. 'I would suggest that the IRA just suffered one of their biggest losses in decades. They are now seriously diminished because of it. We on the other hand have been rather handsomely rewarded,' he gestured toward the holdalls and weapons.

'Is that why you sent us there, for 2 million pounds.'

'Oh please, nothing so vulgar!' said Hamilton with mock indignation, 'Were you not listening when I said you delivered a serious blow to the IRA? At the same time, you also put a dent in the illegal arms and drug trade that has blighted Europe, and our own dear Blighty, for years. You served in Northern Ireland, I'd have thought you relished the opportunity to hit back, with the gloves off so to speak?'

'You already had the intel, why did MI6 not take them out yourselves?' asked JT.

'There are wider ramifications of action, and indeed inaction, as, I believe, you gentlemen are only too aware.'

'So, you sent us to do your dirty work instead?'

'You seem to have the wrong of the stick here dear boy. The timing of your intervention last night has ruined years of work that went into identifying and infiltrating organisations from Ireland to North Africa and further afield.'

'Then why?' asked JT.

'Because I understood that you urgently required some seriously specialist equipment. There are very limited opportunities to obtain such equipment without borrowing some from Her Majesty's Armed Forces. I also understood that your proposed actions involving these

"Kosanians" are neither sanctioned by your Regiment nor would they be legal.'

'Why would you want to help us?' asked JT, feeling like he was on the back foot.

'Why indeed?' said Hamilton. 'I could tell you that I am disgusted by these people traffickers and abusers, that I want to see you rescue those being abused. I could tell you that I know your service in Afghanistan was exemplary and that you are victims of grave injustice? I could tell you that there is a Political motive to your suspension and that I believe they will not rest until you are made an example of?'

'But none of those are the real reason, are they?' It was Maxwell who joined the conversation.

'None of them? All of them happen to be true, and each would be a fitting reason for my assistance. There is, however, another reason, one that brings me here this morning.' He looked around the room before continuing. 'We live in a world where our Political classes are saturated with idealists at the expense of realists. We no longer have leaders with a stomach for direct action and who believe they can 'negotiate' with tyrants and terrorists. I happen to understand that there are occasions when only the most direct action is apposite. My understanding is allied with the knowledge that there are very few people with the skills and fortitude to carry out the required direct action.' He turned on the spot making deliberate eye contact with each of them in turn before settling in front of JT. 'I believe that you and your team, along with your allies here, are a formidable force that, with my direction, can make the world a safer place.'

'Rory is still a Police Officer, Easy is a kid, and we,' JT gestured at his team. 'are all soldiers of the British Army. None of us are exactly in a position to help you make the world safer.'

'Yes, of course, but I believe circumstances change. Some changes are made through choice, others are forced upon us. I happen to know there is a plot to make your team the poster boys for British military war crimes. They intend to ruin you and your reputation.'

'Why?' asked JT.

'And Who?' added Maxwell.

'We have a Foreign Secretary who is weak and not fit for purpose. She does not understand war or soldiering. Instead, she believes we as a country should self-flagellate and spend our tax payers hard earned money paying reparations to the grifter descendants of our colonial subjects. She, as you may know, has ambitions toward the top job and she believes that her anti-war stance will persuade the electorate to give her that honour. That would spell disaster for our country as she would decimate our Defence budget and destroy our standing on the world stage. It is therefore imperative that we are able to function, at times, beyond the purview of our elected officials.'

'So, you expect us to run missions on your behalf when we're on leave?' asked JT.

'My dear chap, may I call you JT?' JT nodded. 'You do not, I fear, understand the lengths they are willing to go to. They have built a case against you that will at best see you discharged from the Army and at worst see you spend many years behind bars.'

'We did nothing wrong, we followed orders and the Boss had no option but to shoot that woman. We'd all be dead if he hadn't.' said Taff.

'Yes, I know,' said Hamilton, 'I saw the bodycam images before they were 'accidentally erased'. As I have attempted to explain, you are being offered as a sacrifice and they will stop at nothing to have their pound of flesh.'

'Is there nothing you can do?' asked Maxwell, 'you've seen the images, you can testify on their behalf.'

'That is not how this game is destined to play out. I would not be permitted to testify and indeed could never disclose how I came to view the images.'

'So we're fucked then!' said Taff.

'Not quite, Sergeant. I am offering you the opportunity to continue fighting the good fight. The shackles would be removed but the same could be said of the back-up. You are all decorated warriors and understandably proud of your service and your connection to the Regiment. That connection will soon be severed through no fault of your own. You face the prospect of prison, and/or a civilian life, or perhaps an unsatisfying role as overqualified security contractors in former war zones.'

'Who would pay the bills?' asked JT thinking out loud as he tried to compute what was being suggested.

'You all became millionaires tonight. With the skills of young Easy here, you could live comfortably for the rest of your days. You would perhaps have to live abroad or HMRC would be asking questions about your windfall. I get the feeling JT that you were not alluding to salaries? I believe you are asking who would issue orders?' He gave JT the eyebrow treatment.

'Yes, how would it work?' asked JT as his mind raced.

'Well, I would be selecting targets and be positioned to provide intelligence. Detective Inspector Maxwell would be our inside man in the Police Service – although I believe he may consider his position, when I share some intelligence I received on the way here.' He looked at Maxwell then continued, 'more on that later. Young Ezekiel has already equipped himself admirably in the IT department, I can arrange for him to develop his skills with our very best in that field. Together, we would make quite a team, a force to be reckoned with.'

'We won't be much of a team if they court martial us and send us to prison!' said JT.

'I believe that scenario can be avoided completely. As I have said, you are to be a sacrifice. If you resign your commissions and accept a discharge, they will have their pound of flesh but you will live to fight another day. The grounds of such a discharge could be medical or administrative if you prefer. You would keep your pensions for what they are worth.'

'I would be willing to join the team,' said Easy earnestly.

'Yes my boy, regardless of the outcome here, I have a place for someone with your skillset.'

'Thank you but I would want to work with this team,' said Easy, looking around the room.

'Indeed, I sincerely hope that will be possible.'

'When do we need to make a decision?' asked JT.

'Soon; your detractors are moving quickly to set the grounds for a court martial. I would think it could happen as soon as next week.'

'A week?' sighed JT rubbing hard at his scalp with his fingertips, he couldn't quite believe how this was panning out. He thought about what he'd given up for his career in the military, for The Regiment. The sacrifices he'd made for his country and this was how they planned to repay him. He could hear Esmé's words from the night she'd left – "you have no room in your life for me, you're married to the Army!"

'Perhaps we should take a moment to let all this sink in.' said Hamilton, 'I know it will have come as a shock to you all. Might I suggest we open the whiskey and toast last night's success? You'll see I brought Jameson's as it seemed quite fitting. In truth I prefer Scotch but those murderous bastards of the IRA deserve toasted in their own tipple.'

Taff, who was still holding the bottle, looked at JT who nodded his approval. Taff unscrewed the lid and took a swig straight from the bottle. He handed it to Joe who took a long slug letting out a satisfied 'aaah' as he looked at the label before passing it on. Easy was next and looked unsure but with everyone watching he took a sip of the burning liquid and made a face that made the others laugh. The bottle moved around the room until it reached JT who handed it straight to Hamilton. Hamilton nodded and took a slug before handing it back to JT. He looked around the room and back to make eye contact with Hamilton as he took a drink from the bottle. He savoured the heat in his mouth and his throat. His anger was still burning in his gut and the whiskey added to the flames.

JT held out a hand and Taff threw him the lid. He screwed it back in place and set the bottle down before saying, 'Gents, you all need to get some kip. Easy, you need to go home before your Aunt starts worrying. Rory, can you give him a lift please?'

'No, it's ok, I have my bike, my Aunt would wonder where it was if I didn't ride it home.'

'Perfect, can you be back here for,' he looked at his watch, '1600 hrs?'

'Yes, my Aunty goes to her bridge club on Friday's so she won't expect me for dinner.' Easy gathered his things then said, 'Do you need my laptop? I think you will be doing planning while I am gone.'

Hamilton lifted his briefcase and said, 'I can provide everything required for now I believe.'

They waited until Easy left then moved to the kitchen with Maxwell so the team could get some sleep.

'You should be resting too,' said Maxwell concerned at his friend's red rimmed eyes.

'I will do, but first,' he nodded to Hamilton, 'I need to know what's in that briefcase.'

Hamilton opened his briefcase and handed both men military grade tablet computers. Their toughened rubber casing made them feel clumsy to hold at first until they utilised the hand strap on the rear. Next, he placed an envelope on the worktop. 'These,' he explained, are SIM cards you can use in your current mobile phones. Your tablets are also fitted with them.'

'What are they for?' asked JT.

'They are for secure communications. Each of these SIMs create a signal that dances and bounces between other nearby communication devices to scramble and encrypt messages. They are impossible to intercept as the message is dissected then reassembled at the recipient's device. I have also had my friends at GCHQ create a blackhole.'

'A blackhole?' asked Maxwell.

'As you know GCHQ intercepts and scans all communications here in the UK. You possibly know that their reach is in fact global and their computers monitor every text message, email and voice message sent. Even the Israelis don't realise their every word is analysed by supercomputers and flagged to the GCHQ boffin analysts. I had them develop the black hole for the private communications of Her Majesty The Queen. Once they built the system, I commandeered it, and now we can make use of it. I have access to a similar system with the Automatic Number Plate Recognition System, you can use the vehicles freely, the system diverts any queries to numbers of the same age and models of cars.'

'Does Her Majesty know?' asked JT thinking he already knew the answer.

'Good heavens no, all of her messages are read by at least a dozen departments.'

Hamilton unfolded a large schematic drawing of Palmerston House and its stables development. He spread it over the trestle table and flattened out the creases. 'The house was originally built for Lord Coullane, he was a banker of some description and used the place for him and his friends to escape London at weekends. It's a grand old pile with some 32 bedrooms, a ballroom and its own spring that's said to have rejuvenating powers.'

'Hence the health spa.' Said Maxwell.

'Indeed, the place was turned into a hotel in the 1970s but then bought over 2 years ago by a consortium.'

'Consortium?' asked JT.

'Yes, unnamed foreign investors through offshore banks.'

'I thought that was illegal nowadays?' said Maxwell.

'Indeed it is, but the consortium has a British face too. The news I received on the way here were the names of the Directors of the UK listed company fronting for the Consortium.'

'Let me guess, Viktor Liriazi?' asked Maxwell.

'Yes and no, he might well be the person behind the name but it is another name; a name you already know; Ella Misu.'

'Shit!' said Maxwell.

'Who else?' asked JT sensing there was more to come.

'There is another name on the list of Directors. Ursula Harper – wife of a certain Chief Superintendent Steven Harper.'

'Hang on, a Police Officer and another's wife are directors of a dodgy hotel and no-one in professional standards picked up on it?' asked Maxwell.

'Apparently so. It seems the hotel and spa have made a reasonable profit since opening but that profit has been reinvested in the re-development of the stables.'

'The gardens in the photo I sent you were a bit overgrown, is it currently operating as a spa?'

'That photo was taken from The Lady's House. It seems his Lordship didn't particularly like his wife being around when he was entertaining and he built her a miniature version of the main house in the grounds half a mile away. It's apparently used as staff quarters now.'

'Are you married?' JT asked Hamilton the question coming out of the blue so that JT himself wasn't sure he'd asked it.

Hamilton looked at him and then looked away, 'I was, I am a widower.' he said.

'I'm sorry to hear that.' said JT sincerely and a little embarrassed that he'd asked the question.

Hamilton stood upright and seemed to pull his shoulders back. 'My wife was a wonderful woman. She was a primary school teacher. I was working in Northern Ireland and rarely home so she went off to Oman to teach girls there during her summer break. I was, to say the least, unpopular with the IRA as I had developed something of a reputation in Belfast. They made three attempts on my life but couldn't get to me. So, they decided to go after an easier target. The girls found her with her throat cut in the classroom when they arrived for lessons one morning. Her killer had left a note with the words 'Brits out'. It took me 9 years to find the man who killed her and a week of torturing him to discover who had sent him. I killed them both.'

JT put his hand on Hamilton's shoulder. Hamilton looked at him and nodded then tapped his hand on the building plans, 'So, what are you thinking?'.

'I'm thinking, we go rescue those girls, and we kill any of the bastards who get in our way.'

CHAPTER THIRTY-ONE

Four hours later JT woke as Taff roused him with a cup of tea. 'Sorry boss, no bacon rolls, we're on biscuits again.'

JT swung his legs round to sit up and yawned as he took the tea from Taff, 'Cheers Taff.' He took a sip of his tea then said, 'maybe Uncle Samir could rustle up some grub for us?'

'It's Friday boss, he's away to Mosque, won't be open for another hour.'

'Ok, in that case let's get our planning done before we eat,' said JT standing up. 'Just let me get a wash.' He took a cold shower and let it shock the tiredness from his mind and body. The previous couple of days were a whirlwind he'd yet to process but all he could think about was Hamilton's words from earlier. Was his time in The Regiment truly coming to an end? Were they to be sacrificed as Hamilton had said? He rubbed hard at his face with his hands using the bar of soap on his skin and beard. The hard London water meant it barely lathered and as he rinsed himself, he still didn't feel clean. He thought of Esmé and her ritual of washing him in the shower when he came home on leave. A knock at the bathroom door brought him back to the present.

'Hurry up Boss,' said Cooky, 'or I'll have to piss in the kitchen sink!'

JT wrapped a towel around his waist and gathered up his clothes. He looked at himself in the mirror and the dog tags he had rehung around his neck this morning. Maybe it was time to move on, he thought. He opened the door and Cooky rushed past him, he smiled as he heard the blast of piss hit the water before he'd pulled the door shut on his way out.

Getting dressed he watched Rambo and Joe dismantling, checking and rebuilding the weapons they'd taken the night before. Rambo looked especially happy with the sniper rifles. Posty sat loading magazines while listening to music through his headphones. He'd had several stitches in his face and shoulder. His right cheek was darkening as the bruise developed, but he was happily lost in his task and the music.

Cooky came back in, drying his hands on his trousers and went to help load ammunition. Posty took out one of his earphones and gave it to Cooky who put it one ear as they sat down shoulder to shoulder.

JT looked at them, this was his team, no, more than that, this was his family. He walked into the kitchen and joined Taff at the table where they pored over the building plans and aerial photos of their next target.

CHAPTER THIRTY-TWO

Maxwell sat in his car having used the showers at his office and changed into his spare shirt and suit. He called the Metropolitan Police Switchboard and asked to be put through to Chief Superintendent Harper. The phone rang three times before it was picked up.

'Chief Superintendent Harper's office.' said a female voice.

'I'd like to speak to Mr Harper please.'

'I'm sorry he is unavailable, he is leaving shortly for the weekend, he'll be back on Monday morning. I can put you through to Superintendent Bilal if you wish?'

'No, thank you, it's Mr Harper I need to speak to, it's regarding his wife.'

'His wife? Is everything ok?'

'I really need to speak to him.'

'One moment please,' said the female and Maxwell was treated to some awful saxophone music for a few seconds.

'Harper here, who is this?'

'DI Maxwell, Counter Terrorism Branch here Mr Harper. I need to speak with you urgently.'

'What about? Cheryl said it's about my wife,' he sounded concerned which pleased Maxwell.

'Yes, but this is not a conversation for over the phone.'

'What do you mean, what's this about DI Maxwell?' he was sounding angrier now and more than a little on edge.

'Let's meet and I'll be able to explain it all,' said Maxwell.

'I'm going to my place in the country for the weekend, I have no time for this.'

'Are you driving? I can meet you somewhere enroute? Where are you headed?'

'Sussex if you must know.'

'Oh lovely, I'll take as little of your time as possible but I really do need to speak with you urgently.'

'Very well, I'll be picking up my clubs from Royal Blackheath at New Eltham, do you know it?' said Harper after a few seconds of thinking time.

'I can find it,' said Maxwell already typing the name into his sat nav.

'I'll be there at 4.15, if you are not there to meet me, I will not wait and whatever you want to talk to me about will have to wait until Monday. Four fifteen!' he said and hung up.

Maxwell set off, he knew the traffic would be busy on a Friday afternoon and he wanted to make sure he found the right spot. Enroute, he called JT, 'I'm on my way to meet Harper,' he told him.

'On your own?' asked JT.

'Yes, on my own. I'm meeting him at his golf club.'

'What's your plan?'

Maxwell thought for a second, he was winging this but the details he'd heard this morning made him want to see this man face to face.

'I'm going to tell him I'm investigating links between one of his cops and terrorists and see what he says. He's bent as hell and I want to look him in the eye.'

'Ok, keep me informed,' said JT, 'we're doing some planning just now, so come meet us after you're done and we'll fill you in.'

'Will do,' said Maxwell and disconnected. Next, he phoned Hamilton and told him of his upcoming meeting with Harper.

'Perhaps you might leave the line open and let me listen in to your conversation?' suggested Hamilton.

'Why?' asked Maxwell, surprised.

'I would like to get a feel for the man,' said Hamilton, 'I much prefer to meet someone face to face but, in this circumstance, it's unlikely I will meet his acquaintance.'

'Ok, I can do that,' said Maxwell.

'I am assuming they have something on him that has made him turn to the dark side. Blackmail is a deliciously powerful weapon. The poor fools who fall for it never realise that the little bit of info they are made to secure is a mere appetiser, until it's too late and they can't find a way out. Suicide used to be the gentleman's escape, but alas nowadays they just hide their heads in the sand and hope they won't get caught.'

'It might not be blackmail, he obviously has expensive taste, his golf club fees are £20k per year. A Chief Super can only earn £150k and if he's not taking any profits from the spa then maybe it's old fashioned greed and he gets paid for his troubles,' said Maxwell.

'Indeed. Greed, like fear, is a great motivator,' agreed Hamilton.

A silver BMW 7 series pulled into the car park. The rear windows were tinted but Maxwell could see Harper driving. He was wearing a roll neck sweater over a tweed jacket and looking every bit the country gent. After parking the car in a committee member space, Harper trotted into the clubhouse then returned a few minutes later carrying a set of golf clubs. As he put them into the boot, he looked around the car, then looked at his watch looking impatient.

Maxwell climbed out of his car and crossed the car park. As he approached Harper opened the driver's door and indicated to Maxwell to get in the passenger side. Maxwell looked around the car park and at the clubhouse, there was no-one around as he climbed into the passenger seat. Before he could speak, he felt the barrel of a gun pressed against the back of his head.

A female voice came from behind him, 'DI Maxwell I presume?'

Maxwell instinctively knew the voice would belong to Ella Misu and cursed himself for not thinking to check the rear seat. He sat without speaking but turned his head enough to see Harper's face. Harper looked scared, he was pale and sweat was forming on his forehead.

'You seem keen to stick your nose in where it doesn't belong, DI Maxwell,' said Harper.

'Whereas, you had yours in the trough? You're a disgrace Harper.'

'I'll ask the questions!' said Misu from the rear and jammed the gun hard into his head.

'I'm not going to answer any of your questions Chief Inspector Misu, or may I call you Ella?'

'Who knows you're here?' she asked slightly taken aback that he knew her name.

'The Counter Terrorism Unit knows I'm here. Who do you think?'

She poked him again in the back of the head, 'I think I'm the one asking the questions. I also think you're full of shit. There's no way you'd be here alone if this was an official investigation. So, I'll ask again, who else knows you're here?'

'You're going to kill me anyway, so I don't think I'll be answering any questions.'

A car drove into the car park and parked two rows back from the clubhouse. Two middle aged men in pastel pullovers climbed out of the vehicle and started walking toward the clubhouse.

Maxwell smiled at Harper as he saw the rising panic in his eyes but the smile faded when he felt the needle enter his neck. He felt himself falling backwards and then the lights went out.

'Is he dead?' asked Harper as he sat gripping the steering wheel with shaking hands.

'Calm down, Steven, of course he's not dead, we need to know what he knows, and who else knows.'

'We open tomorrow, Ella, the Sheikh and 20 VIPs are coming for Christ's sake. We need to get rid of him, and quickly.'

'You're not thinking clearly Steven. We can take him with us, there's plenty of room and we can keep him quiet until our guests have all gone. Now, I suggest you drive.' Misu reached down the side of Maxwell's seat and reclined him back out of view. As the seat moved, Maxwell's phone slid from his pocket and fell down the side of the seat coming to rest underneath it.

On the other end of the phone was Hamilton who had listened with interest to the entire exchange.

CHAPTER THIRTY-THREE

Taff was marking spots on the building plans for entry and exit points as Rambo was looking for potential overwatch positions. The range of his new Russian rifle was more than a mile but without being able to test and zero the weapon he would look for easier shots.

JT was examining access roads wondering they could intercept the truck that would be delivering the girls. He was considering how long the police response might be and if the police helicopter based at Gatwick airport would be scrambled. Those were questions for Rory when he got here. As ever any plan they made before arrival on the plot would be updated with what they found in front of them. That updated plan would go to shit with the first contact but each plan was made in layers. The enemy were gangster thugs and would offer no real challenge to the fully armed team. The real challenge was how they got in and out without being identified and without getting caught.

They had agreed among themselves that they would not speak about Hamilton's offer or their future in The Regiment until this mission was complete. JT, just like the rest of them, was trying to push that thought to the back of their minds, and failing.

The vibrating phone in his pocket brought JT's thoughts back to the present. He looked at the screen and saw the number was withheld. He pressed the speaker button then placed the phone on the table.

'They have Maxwell,' said Hamilton.

'Who has Maxwell?'

'Steven Harper and Ella Misu.'

'Where are they?'

'They're headed South out of London. I believe they are enroute to Palmerston House.'

'What do we know?'

'Maxwell went to meet Harper to confront him. It seems he was taken by surprise by Misu. I believe they incapacitated him, probably with an injection of some sort. They plan to interrogate him.'

'Shit!' said JT slamming his fist on the table, 'we need to move now!'

'Actually, I believe we have more time than you realise,' said Hamilton, with his usual calm demeanour. 'Maxwell left his mobile phone line open to me and I overheard the entire conversation. The stables at Palmerston House are having a VIP opening tomorrow with a Sheik and 20 VIP guests attending. As you know 'Sheik's' are ten a penny, so I have people tracking down which of them will be in the UK tomorrow. I fear London is awash with them at any given time so we may need to just narrow it down.'

'Never mind the bloody Sheik, what about Rory?' demanded JT.

'Yes, yes, let me explain. They spoke about keeping Maxwell until they could interrogate him but only after the Sheik's departure on Sunday. You can still work to your original deadline of tomorrow.'

'What else?' asked JT, sensing there was more.

'They also spoke about the delivery of the girls. Their arrival has been brought forward to tonight so that they can be prepared ahead of the guests' arrival tomorrow.'

'What did they mean 'prepared'?'

'I could hazard a guess that they will be cleaned up and doubtless drugged to make them submissive, although...' he tailed off.

'Although?' asked JT.

'Although, I have heard that some of these establishments offer young girls who are not stupefied.'

'What are you saying?'

'I am saying that some of these animals desire the whole 'rape' experience. They want the girl to fight back. Misu used the name Amazon, I remembered young Ezekiel mentioning it. I believe I finally worked out what it meant; they will deliver anything their customers want.'

'Fucking hell,' said JT.

'Indeed, I suggest you carry on with your planning but you should assume there will be many more visitors and staff than anticipated. I will get back to you soonest with whatever else I can find out. If not beforehand, then I will see you at 2030 hrs. I have the tactical clothing you requested.'

'We need to put these fuckers down Boss, and put them down hard,' said Taff. 'You remember that war lord in Chaman?'

'How could I forget that evil old bastard?' said JT, with a steel to his voice.

'Who was this?' asked Rambo.

'Before your time Rambo,' began Taff, 'we were working up the North West Frontier. The border is a bit debatable up in the mountains and we were officially in Pakistan when we were dealing with this old war lord. His domain straddled into Afghan territory and the

CIA had turned him so he would provide intel on who, and what, was crossing the border. We were hunting Mubashir Hassan and knew he was using the pass controlled by our friendly war lord. We spent two weeks living in the war lords compound. He had three wives, and they had their own area. A little boy used to take messages between the women and the men folk, so they didn't ever have to mix. Boy's name was Ayaan – it means 'God's gift' - and he was 9 years old. The old war lord used to rape the lad every Friday after prayers. Since the kid was 6 the dirty old bastard had raped him. The kid tried to run away a few times but they would always find him and drag him back. The other men in the compound seemed to think it was funny. The more often the kid ran away the worse the beatings were when he was brought back until eventually, they chopped off one of his toes. The kid still tried to run away until they took off all 5 of his toes. So, the kid limped back and forward between the men and women and every week without fail the old bastard raped him.'

'What did you do?' asked Rambo.

'We had the CIA guy with us and we were told in no uncertain terms not to interfere.'

'You left him there?'

'No, we stayed until the Friday. Then we got the news Hassan had been killed in a drone attack. The CIA guy sloped off to go hand a suitcase of cash to some other war lord. We were left with the old guy in his compound until dark before we were due to head back into the mountains.'

'Come on, tell me you helped the kid,' said Rambo impatiently.

'Yeah, we helped the kid.'

'And the old man? What happened to him?'

'He took a fall from the roof of the compound, broke his neck.'

'I'll bet the CIA weren't happy,' laughed Rambo.

'They were fucking furious, seemed to think it was something to do with us,' said Taff as he shrugged.

'And did it?'

'We don't like rapists,' said Taff and he went back to his map work.

CHAPTER THIRTY-FOUR

Walter was testing the second hand RIB he'd picked up from the boatyard when his phone rang. The number was unknown and he half expected some sort of sales call or scam when he answered.

'It's me,' said the familiar voice of JT.

'Hello you,' replied Walter.

'All good with you.'

'Ship shape thank you, how is it at your end?'

'Complicated, but we're going to try to reach a resolution tomorrow.'

'Tomorrow?'

'Yes, hoping to be packed up before dark.'

'Are we meeting at the same place?'

'Work is taking us further West, maybe we could meet on the riviera?'

'Tell me where and when and I'll be there.'

'Thank you; for everything.'

'Don't mention it, just stay safe.'

'I will.' JT hung up and was about to put his phone in his pocket when it rang. 'Hello?' he answered.

'I have an update,' said Hamilton.

'I'm listening.'

'It seems that our Sheik is one Hamad bin Rashid al Mhartoum. He is a lower ranking member of the House of Mhartoum. He is also an obscenely wealthy man. It appears he is also a man of unusual tastes, which has seen him in self-imposed exile. He is based in Istanbul and has amassed a fortune in trading with Russia. He is something of a Mr Fixit apparently. He keeps business under the radar and the Turkish authorities turn a blind eye to his criminal activity and to his questionable tastes.'

'Ok, so who are the other 20?'

'As far as we can tell, Al Mhartoum runs a bit of a club for very rich perverts. He has a harem of women back in Istanbul but he has a preference for younger girls and occasionally boys. The 20 VIPs are arriving on his private jet into Gatwick first thing tomorrow morning. He, the Sheikh, however is already here in the UK. He has been staying at Claridge's but checked out late this afternoon. I should think he will be on his way to Palmerston House. They also spoke about 'Matriarku'.'

'Who is Matriarku?' asked JT.

'I don't yet know, but the name means Matriarch in Albanian.'

'Maybe the chess Queen you've been looking for?'

'The thought had crossed my mind.'

'Security?'

'The Sheikh always travels with eight bodyguards. They will doubtless be armed but I'm afraid I have no further details.'

'Ok, good to know. Any update on Rory?'

'No, his phone has been tracked to Palmerston House but I don't know if it was still in his possession.'

'Well, if he's there, we'll find him and get him out.'

'I have another piece of news.'

'Yes?'

'I have a plan to direct attention well away from these shores when they look for those responsible for what will unfold at Palmerston House.'

'I have it in hand, we'll be back in France by Sunday morning.'

'That may provide something of an alibi but to make sure we require someone else to be in the picture. As discussed previously, the Kosanians were chased from Istanbul by the Russian Bratvas. There remains a lot of bad blood there and it appears the Kosanians have used their connection with Sheik Al Mhartoum to hit back. He has been playing both sides for quite some time.'

'How does that help us?'

'I'll be heading over shortly, and all will become obvious. I have a gift for you in the boot of the car,' said Hamilton sounding quite pleased with himself.

#

At 2030 hrs Hamilton arrived and called to say he was at the door of the flat. JT opened the door and found Hamilton wearing black combat trousers and a dark green Mil-Tec jacket.

Hamilton smiled at him and stepped past him into the hallway.

'Fancy dress?' asked JT.

'Very droll,' said Hamilton without looking back. He made his way into the lounge and spoke to Joe and Cooky. 'There are some boxes in the rear of my vehicle downstairs, be good chaps and bring them up, would you? There's ski masks for each of you too.' He handed Joe the keys.

Joe and Cooky went to the door and a couple of seconds later Joe returned, 'Which vehicle?' Joe asked Hamilton.

'The Range Rover,' he replied unfazed by the question.

'You brought more than one vehicle?' asked JT.

'Yes, it was a bugger to tow but I thought it might come in handy.'

'Care to explain?' asked JT and not for the first time he realised that he couldn't get a read on Hamilton.

'The second vehicle belongs to a certain Konstantin Kusnetz Kalganov, aka KKK.'

'Who?' asked JT.

'KKK is the name of a Russian hitman who works for the Russian Mafia, and pretty much anyone who would pay him enough. His real allegiance, however, was always to a man named Alexei Vassiliev, ex KGB and the head of the Soltnsevsya Bratva.'

'So where is he now, and how come you have his car?'

Hamilton smiled, 'He is in the boot.'

'He's what?' said a shocked JT, wishing he had a better grip on what was going on.

'As I told you earlier, it will be beneficial to have someone else to blame for the mess you're going to create at Palmerston House. Mr Kalganov will provide an alternative direction for the finger of blame to point as it were.'

'Hang on, you brought us a dead body to leave at the scene?'

'Oh, he's quite alive I assure you.'

'Where did you find him?'

'Mr Kalganov, and his associate who we have been unable to identify – he is also in the boot by the way,' Hamilton spoke as if this was the most natural thing in the world, 'were here in London, it appears, to apply some pressure to a Belarusian Diplomat over a business venture they feel he can assist with. They have been trailing the Diplomat and his family for two weeks now. Fortunately for the Belarusian, he has been persuaded to work for us, and, we have taken steps to ensure his safety.'

'So, there are two guys trussed up in the boot of the car down there, and we've got to take them with us to Palmerston House?'

'Not exactly,' said Hamilton. 'Kalganov is alive and suitably restrained but his companion didn't require restraining as he is dead. Is there a possibility of some tea? I'm a little parched.'

JT knew this was an attempt to bring the conversation to a close but ignored it, 'Dead, how exactly?'

'He seems to have had a weak heart; bit of a surprise, considering his line of work.'

'He just keeled over with a heart attack, just like that?'

'If you must know all of the minutiae,' said Hamilton with just a touch of irritation, 'his heart attack was brought on by shock.'

'Taser?' asked JT.

'No, old fashioned trauma induced shock, you see I was cutting off his arm,' Hamilton's voice didn't show any emotion at all and JT was aware he was being examined as Hamilton looked for a reaction.

'You cut off his arm?' JT couldn't keep the surprise from his voice, 'Why?'

'I saw an opportunity to tie him to last night's events at Tilbury, it was too good an opportunity to waste. His arm is heavily tattooed, in the fashion of the Bratva and Russian prisons. His arm will be found when they dredge the Thames and find the other bodies there. Quite an elegant solution, if I do say so myself.'

'Won't the Police wonder how he managed to get from Tilbury to Sussex after losing an arm?'

'If we were unable to identify him, then the local Constabulary most certainly will not be able to.'

'But a one armed man? Bit of a coincidence don't you think. The plods are a bit thick at times but they're not that stupid,' said JT, thinking he'd found a flaw in Hamilton's plan.

'That brings us neatly to the gift I have for you. One of the boxes on the backseat of Kalganov's car contains 2 M183 demolition charge assemblies. The other box contains 6 of the claymore anti-tank mines that miraculously survived the blast at Tilbury. The sandbag wall had been buttressed in front of their box apparently. I think there may be more than one arm lost in the explosion, don't you?'

'You seem to have thought of everything,' said JT impressed.

'That's my job,' smiled Hamilton.

'You haven't explained why you're wearing tactical gear.'

'I know the 6 of you are very capable, but you will be facing an unknown force. I figured another pair of hands might be required. I assure you, I am quite proficient with a weapon JT. I was not always behind a desk you know.'

CHAPTER THIRTY-FIVE

Palmerston House was a frenzy of activity as catering and house-keeping staff battled to get ready before the deadline. They were being paid extra to get the job done and be gone by the time tonight's guests arrived. They had already seen some strange goings on but knew better than to ask questions. They packed up their vans and drove off with a sizable amount of cash for their troubles with the promise of more highly paid work to come.

As the vans left and set off south down the 3 miles of service road toward Haywards Heath, a Mercedes people carrier turned through the electric security gates and into the main drive toward the hotel. The drive was almost half a mile long and wound its way through the silver birch copse that shielded the building from the road and onto the beautiful sandstone bridge that spanned the land-form installation and pond designed by Charles Jencks. Submerged lights illuminated the bridge from the water and shadows were cast over the undulating grassed slopes of the spiralled hills on either side. It was one of Jencks largest works and had been seen by comparatively few people here in the very private grounds.

The people carrier stopped and two armed men took up positions at the gate. Then it stopped again at the bridge depositing two more armed men. They took up a position at either end of the bridge.

The vehicle came to a halt just beyond the main house and 4 more armed men stepped out and took up positions. Two flanked the hotel entrance door and two made their way to the far edge of the ornate garden beyond the drive.

Two more vehicles then entered through the gates, the sentries stood almost to attention as the vehicles passed. The first vehicle was a sleek grey Mercedes S Class. All of the windows had mirrored privacy glass except the windscreen but even that was tinted. The engine of the S Class was almost silent as it purred along the drive followed by another Mercedes people carrier. The vehicles stopped outside the main entrance to the hotel. Eight more armed men stepped out of the people carrier and formed a protective ring around the S Class.

Steven Harper watched from the window of the drawing room and waited. He knew who was in the car and it terrified him. He lifted the crystal tumbler of scotch to his lips but his shaking hand made it too difficult to drink so he put it down on the table beside him.

A minute passed and then another with no sign of movement from the car. The faint cloud of exhaust was the only clue that the vehicle's engine was still running.

Harper looked at the armed men. They were all tough looking and wearing the same dark suits and open necked white shirts. Each of them had a Sig Sauer MCX Rattler submachine gun. The short barrel at 5.5 inches and folding stocks made them an ideal discrete weapon to conceal, but these guys were a show of force. Some held them across their chests and others by their sides with the stock folded away.

He heard it before he saw, the pulsing thrum of the helicopter came from the North and it's landing lights washed the front of the hotel and the gathering in the driveway before the pilot swivelled the Bell 525 and took it out over the gardens to land on the helipad. The helicopter was designed to carry up to 16 passengers but this luxury model had just 6 comfortable leather seats. The door opened and out stepped two muscular men in jeans and tight fitting t-shirts. They each wore pistols in shoulder holsters. One of the men held out a hand and assisted a man wearing a black suit down the step to the ground. Harper knew who the man was. Viktor Liriazi had a fearsome reputation for ruthless violence but he was not what scared Harper. Liriazi and his men ducked as they started toward the hotel and the helicopter lifted off and headed back in the direction from which it had arrived.

They walked through the ornamental garden crunching on the gravel as they went. As they approached the S Class they stopped at the ring of armed guards. The uniformed driver of the S Class got out and put on his hat before he placed his hand on the handle of the rear door. At the same time the opposite rear door opened and a man exited. His brown leather blouson jacket marked him out as different from the armed men encircling the car. He stood for a second and assessed his surroundings before he nodded his permission for the driver to open the rear door. The driver opened the door fully then stepped forward and offered his arm, holding onto his arm, out stepped what would appear to the uninitiated, a little old lady.

Harper watched the driver escort the lady two steps forward then he retrieved her walking cane and presented it to her before closing the door. The man in the leather jacket was instantly by her side and his gaze continually swept left and right.

Liriazi stepped forward with a grin and held out his arms as if about to embrace the old lady. As he reached her the old lady struck him hard across the face with such force that Harper thought he heard the slap.

One of Liriazi's men instinctively reached for his gun but before he could remove it from its holster the man in the leather jacket had drawn his pistol and shot him in the chest. The man clutched at his chest as the blood spread across his t-shirt and he fell to his knees. His partner moved to help him and then thought better of it and took a step away from him.

Liriazi recovered from the blow and stood up straight, his smile was gone.

'Please, Matriarku,' he said and held his hands in a mock prayer fashion.

'You kept me waiting for almost ten minutes. You forget yourself, little brother,' said the old lady and then turned and made her way to the front door of the hotel where Ella Misu stood waiting to greet her.

'Welcome Matriarku,' she said, bowing her head slightly.

'Come child, give Grandmother a hug,' she held out her arms and took Misu in a tight grip. She sniffed at Misu's hair and then stood back from her. 'Are you still smoking?'

Misu reddened but smiled, 'No Matriarku, I travelled here in the car with Steven Harper. He smokes a lot when he is nervous.'

'Nervous? Is he not supposed to be a big strong Policeman?'

'He is nervous as we have had someone nosing around,' explained Misu.

'Who is this someone? Have they been silenced?' asked Matriarku as she moved into the drawing room.

Harper stood when the two women entered the room.

Misu waited until Matriarku had taken a seat by the fireplace before she replied. 'A Detective from Counter Terrorism contacted Steven today and said he wanted to talk about his wife.'

'His wife? Why does that concern us?' asked Matriarku not deigning to look at Harper.

'When we had to produce a list of Directors for this place, we needed UK citizens. We used Steven's wife Ursula.'

'This Detective, he has linked this place to Mrs Harper, and to us?'

'We-'started Misu.

'We don't know that yet,' interrupted Harper, 'he hasn't actually said that!'

Matriarku looked at him with black eyes, 'If you interrupt my Ermonella again, I will cut out your tongue, do you understand?' she said through bared teeth.

'Yes, yes, I am sorry. Forgive me Matriarku,' said Harper his voice panicked.

'Go on child,' said Matriarku to Misu, her voice back to its measured tone.

'We have not yet had time to question him.'

'We can send Princ to locate him and question him. Princ can always get answers, can't you Princ.'

Princ stood in the doorway removing his leather jacket. 'Of course, Matriarku, whatever you desire,' he said, staring at Harper.

'Right now, I desire Mr Harper to go fetch me a drink,' said Matriarku taking a small silver pill case out of her bag and sitting it in the lap of her plain black dress.

Harper stood to attention desperate for an excuse to leave the room and avoid the staring Princ, 'What can I bring for you Matriarku?'

'I would like Vodka with apple juice,' she told him.

'Yes of course, right away. I'll be right back,' said Harper as he scurried out of the room and headed to the bar.

'Bring me his glass,' Matriarku told Misu.

Misu handed her the tumbler that was still almost half full of Scotch. Matriarku removed a tiny white pill from her silver pill box and dropped it into Harper's glass. Misu replaced it on the table and took a seat next to her.

Harper returned a moment later carrying a glass containing vodka and a small crystal jug of apple juice. 'Forgive me Matriarku, I wasn't sure how much apple juice you would like,' his hands shook as he held the jug ready to pour.

'You are shaking so much you will spill it! Set it here, I shall pour it for myself.'

Harper set the glass and jug before her and the old lady deftly poured apple juice into the glass.

'For pity's sake, come sit with me here, get your drink, it will calm your nerves. Come sit and you can tell me about this Detective and your lovely wife,' she gestured to the seat opposite hers.

Harper felt the relief wash over him; it was going to be alright. He could explain everything he knew and the old woman would have her men fix it. He collected his glass and sat down facing her.

'Your health,' she said, lifting her glass in a toast to him then taking a long sip of her drink.

Harper willed his hands to stop shaking as he lifted his glass and drained it of the scotch.

'Now, who have you been speaking to Mr Harper?' she asked him.

'No-one,' he said, confused by the line of questioning. 'DI Maxwell called my office this afternoon and said he wanted to talk to me concerning my wife. I told Ella right away, no-one else. We met with him and brought him here. We will question him once the Sheik has gone.'

'You brought him here? Alive?' asked Matriarku.

Harper heard the question but it sounded as if it came from far away. He blinked hard as he tried to focus on her face, it kept moving and he was feeling light headed. He could feel his heart pounding in his chest, he couldn't understand what was happening as his throat started to close and it became difficult to breathe. Then he knew it, he looked at the empty glass in his hand as his vision began to swim. He tried to say something but couldn't formulate a word. The glass slipped from his hand and landed intact on the soft plush carpet at his feet.

'Have someone get rid of his body Princ, have them do it now, the Sheik will be arriving shortly,' said Matriarku, without emotion.

CHAPTER THIRTY-SIX

The team drove in a loose convoy south out of London and into Surrey. Cooky drove the builders van with Posty and Easy. JT and Rambo drove with Hamilton in his Range Rover and Taff and Joe were driving the Subaru Forester with two Russian hitmen in the boot. Taff had checked that *KKK* was still alive before setting off. The man looked up at him impassively from the boot with his dead, and partially dismembered, friend lying on top of him.

The journey to the RV point south of Palmerston House would take less than 90 minutes. Hamilton and JT would take a slightly longer route to drop Rambo off at the Royal Botanical Gardens. From there he would travel on foot for two miles to reach the Eastern edge of the Palmerston House estate. The Eastern boundary was marked by a small escarpment which, despite being only 20 feet high, was the highest ground available that gave a view of the House and stables. The distance was just over half a mile but with his new Russian sniper rifle that would not be an issue.

On the A22 outside Croydon, Hamilton overtook an Amazon delivery HGV. JT found himself looking at the lorry on the way past. Something stirred in his memory but he couldn't quite put his finger on it as his mind was on the mission.

'Are you sure bringing Easy along was a good idea?' JT asked Hamilton.

'The kid has technical skills that could come in very handy,' he replied, 'the drone I have given him is state of the art and he can provide an eye in the sky from a safe distance.'

'I sure hope so. Civilians don't belong in conflict zones.'

'Indeed, but needs must, and I will be there to help keep him safe,' said Hamilton.

'If this all goes south you have to get him out of there,' said JT.

'Yes of course, my intention is to see that we all get out of there,' Hamilton glanced at him before returning his eyes to the road, 'and in one piece. I have a lot invested in this group's future.'

'We haven't said yes to your offer yet.' JT shot back at him.

'Indeed,' said Hamilton, 'not yet.'

'You're rather sure of yourself Hamilton,' said JT.

'The only thing I am sure of, is you and your team doing the right thing, old chap.' He stole another glance at JT then continued, 'The Botanical Gardens are up ahead another mile. Let me know when you want me to stop Rambo.'

'Anywhere beyond the gates will do me fine. I'll be in the OP in 30 minutes.'

'Once we're in, you can come up to the wife's house if possible Rambo. Overwatch from there until we are at the EV point. We can cover you back to join us.'

'Understood Boss,' said Rambo, as he smeared camouflage cream across his face and passed the tin to JT.

Hamilton pulled into a field entrance and Rambo climbed out of the car and strapped his rifle case across his back. As the car pulled away, he stood against the hedgerow and listened. When he heard nothing but the sound of nocturnal nature, he took a bearing and started jogging across the field towards the OP.

#

A couple of miles away a three car convoy was heading for Palmerston House. Two Jaguar XF saloons flanked a gold coloured Rolls Royce Ghost. The driver of the Rolls Royce glanced in the rear view mirror and watched the Sheik snort a line of cocaine from the glass topped armrest table. He quickly looked away and kept his attention on the road as he knew it was healthier for him to mind his own business. He did not like the Sheik but his father had driven for the man's father and the job paid well. It was a pity that he had to be around these men and their disgusting behaviour but it was the job and he tried to put it out of his mind.

'How long?' asked the Sheik.

'We should be there in 20 more minutes, Highness.'

'Good, tell Mustapha to drive faster, I need to take a piss.'

Chapter Thirty-Seven

Rambo crawled into a gap between gorse bushes and laid his poncho over the prickly branches that lay on the ground. His Night Vision Goggles made everything around him appear in various shades of green light but he soon found he didn't need them to see the target. The House itself was a large old stately home with a sweep of steps up to the main entrance. The windows to the front of the building were huge and each was illuminated from within. The building had been extended at the rear and the modern extension had attempted to copy the style of the original building. Again, every window seemed lit. The stables sat 200m to the East of the main building and looked as grand and solidly built as the original house. An ornate archway led into what Rambo knew from satellite images was a courtyard. The rooms above the archway would have been accommodation for the livery staff. Then there was the little house which had been for the wife of the original owner. Little was not the right word for it as it was a sizable property in its own right. Again, all of the lights were on and there was movement there. Eight men were unloading kit bags from two people carriers. They all wore suits and Rambo could see they were all carrying sub machine guns.

'Overwatch in position,' he said via his throat mic.

'Report,' came the answer from JT.

'I'm seeing eight, repeat eight, heavies with SMGs loading gear into the smaller house.'

'The Sheik's guys?'

'Can't confirm, they're all wearing suits and the kit bags look like overnight bags rather than kit,' said Rambo, 'standby, I have 2 more suits with SMGs at the front door of the main house. I can also see a suit at the bridge between the Teletubby hills. He has his back to me but he looks like he's holding too.'

'Confirm eleven suits,' said JT.

'Affirm- standby, make that thirteen, repeat thirteen, there are two by the statue at the end of the rose garden. They've just lit up a smoke or I might have missed them due to the statue.'

'Confirming thirteen. Any more good news?'

'The two houses are lit up like Christmas Trees but the stables are in darkness. Maybe the girls aren't on site yet.'

'Fingers crossed,' said JT and meant it.

#

Misu unlocked the door to the basement in the smaller house, and pushed it open. Princ led the way with a pistol in his hand. It was his preferred FN 5.7, it was lightweight even with a full 20 round magazine, mostly though he liked it because it was reliable and extremely accurate. The basement was warm as it housed the boiler and a utility area with an industrial washer and dryer. On seeing Maxwell attached to a steel support pillar in the middle of the room, Princ holstered his gun and crouched down beside him.

'Detective,' he said and prodded Maxwell in the shoulder.

Maxwell stirred and squinted as the bright overhead lights were blinding him. He was groggy recovering from the propofol injection he'd been given.

'Detective Inspector Rory Maxwell, yes?' said Princ, as he lifted Maxwell's face to meet his.

'Where am I?' asked Maxwell, slurring the words.

'Where you are is not important,' said Princ, 'what is important, is why you are here?'

'Ok, why am I here?' asked Rory as he caught sight of Misu on the stairs.

'You are here to answer questions, and to die, Detective,' said Princ. 'How you answer the questions will decide the speed with which you die and how much you suffer before your death.'

'I'm telling you nothing,' said Maxwell quietly.

'Excellent!' said Princ, 'I was so hoping you would say this.' He slipped off his leather jacket and hung it on the back of a chair. 'Too many people now are so keen to spill their guts, they are too afraid of a little pain. But you, I think you, Detective, will allow me some sport this evening.'

A voice from the top of the stairs called down, 'The Sheik is two minutes out. Matriarku wants you back at the main house.'

'A reprieve for now,' said Princ to Maxwell as he turned and reached for his jacket, 'if you will excuse me, I shall return later to continue our pleasant little chat.'

'I'll look forward to it,' said Maxwell without too much conviction.

Princ left the basement and Misu spoke to Maxwell from the stairs, 'Tell him what he wants to know, don't try to be clever and he will make it quick; put a bullet in your brain. You will feel nothing.'

'And if I want to be clever?' asked Maxwell.

'Then you will die in a world of pain,' said Misu, making her way up the stairs.

Maxwell heard the bolt being slid on the door as it was locked. It was a tinny sound rather than the thud of a heavy lock; it gave him the tiniest glimmer of hope.

#

The guards on the electric gate stood back as it swung inwards and the three cars made their way through. One of the guards spoke to the driver of the first car then waved them through.

Rambo watched as Princ and Misu left the smaller building and walked back to the hotel. 'Movement, a man just put on a brown leather jacket and a woman in a black coat just left the smaller house heading for the main house. Male has a sidearm in a shoulder holster. Female looks to be the Police woman Misu.'

'Any sign of Maxwell?' asked JT.

'Negative. Standby, vehicle lights past the Teletubbies. I have two, no three vehicles approaching, 2 black Jags and a Gold Roller.'

'That's got to be the Sheik,' Hamilton said to JT.

A few seconds later Rambo continued, 'Counting eight more security exiting the escort vehicles. All carrying. I'm seeing two teams of four, two per team carrying assault rifles. The others all have sidearms. This lot look a bit more professional than the black suits, definitely ex-military. These guys are all in grey suits and wearing ties for Christ's sake, it's like Saville row down there.'

'Confirming eight more security?'

'Affirmative, I've counted 21 suits so far and there must be at least 2 at the gate. Add in Mr leather jacket and we're at 24 for the bad guys team. They also have home game advantage.'

'I hear you Rambo. We'll get the drone up shortly and check the gate situation.'

'Here comes the Sheik out of the Roller now, his driver appears unarmed and the Sheik is wearing his gleaming white Thawb and head gear. He's heading into the hotel and it looks like there's a little old lady coming out to meet him.'

'Description of the old lady?' said Hamilton.

'She's the quintessential little old lady, looks to be around 70, white hair in a bun, wearing a black dress, like one of those cheap woollen dresses all the old girls wear in the Balkans. She has a walking stick. The Sheik just bowed his head to her so I'm guessing she's high status.'

'The Matriarku?' JT asked Hamilton.

'Yes, it seems likely, and maybe, just maybe our missing Queen.'

CHAPTER THIRTY-EIGHT

Maxwell shifted his position and tried his strength against whatever was securing his wrists.

The restraint bit into his flesh and the sharp edge made him think it was plasti-cuffs or cable ties they had used. He looked around the room and saw several canvas bags full of bed linen and towels. He found the answer to what was securing him when he spotted the bag of long cable ties hung on the wall. They would be used to secure the bags of laundry for transporting them. He looked at the cable ties and looked around for the safety cutter that would go with them. Knowing it would be a sharp blade within a slotted plastic handle he searched with his eyes. It would be near, or with the cable ties he guessed but there was no sign of it in the plastic bag on the wall. Pushing himself back against the metal pole he pulled his feet toward him and slowly, painfully pushed himself upward until he was standing. The effort was making him sweat and he tried to wipe the sweat away from his eyes on the shoulders of his shirt. He'd caused the skin on his wrists to tear and as the numbness of his fingers subsided, he felt the trickle of warm blood make its way down his thumb.

Now that he was on his feet, he could see the top of the industrial washer and dryer. No sign of a cutter beside the neatly folded towels. He worked his way 360 degrees around the pole. He had known he was in the basement but this was bigger than a domestic house. Palmerston House, he thought to himself, I'm under the hotel. The realisation at once filled him with dread as he was a long way from where anyone knew he had been last; the golf club, meeting Harper. 'I can't wait to see you get what's coming to you Stevie boy,' he muttered to himself.

There were shelves of cleaning materials against the far wall. Commercial sized bottles of detergent and bleach sat beside boxes of miniature soaps and shampoo bottles. Something about them looked a bit cheap for the upmarket health spa this place was meant to be. This caused him to doubt his first theory of this being Palmerston House until he remembered the smaller house built for the wife and now used as staff quarters. Of course, it made sense that they wouldn't keep him in the main hotel where guests might see or overhear something they shouldn't. So, he was under the staff quarters. What did that mean for him?

It meant that Ella and the man who was going to kill him were busy in another building, and that meant he had some time.

He looked back at the bag of cable ties. They looked pretty robust but not exactly industrial. He did another 360 of the pole and he felt his trousers snag on a piece of peeling paint. Standing on his tiptoes he moved his hands to find the cause of the snag. A jagged piece of paint had peeled off the metal. Feeling with his fingertips it was obvious the paint was thick after layers and layers had been added over the decades. Working his thumbnail into the edge he tried to pick the paint. It felt solid and in no mood to budge, but it did have a serrated edge.

CHAPTER THIRTY-NINE

The Sheik sat in the chair that had less than an hour before been occupied by the dying Steven Harper. Matriarku sat opposite him looking into the fire as Misu poured tea.

'What time are we expecting delivery?' he asked as he took the cup of tea from Misu. His fingertips touched her hand and she felt her skin crawl as his eyes swept her. She stepped back and pulled her hand away quickly in a way that caught Matriarku's attention.

Misu placed a tea cup in front of her and she received a rare smile in return. 'This child is most precious to me,' she began. 'Her mother was a stupid woman and a liability, but this one is very smart and one day will lead my family.'

'You have a son; does he not stand to inherit?' asked the Sheik.

'My son is a man,' she said, fixing him with her black eyes, 'and like all men he is weak. Weak because he cannot control his flesh, his base needs.'

'It is a man's right to satisfy his needs however he can afford is it not?' smiled the Sheik.

'A man has his rights, but when he tries to assert those rights over a woman, he better be sure she is one of the weak ones or else he can never sleep.'

'You are an unusual woman Matriarku,' said the Sheik

'I am not so unusual,' she said returning her gaze to the fire, 'all women have it in themselves to get out from under weak men, sometimes they cannot find the strength easily, but it is there nonetheless.'

Silence followed and the Sheik sipped at his tea while his gaze moved from the old woman to Misu and then found himself being stared at by Princ. The man had the audacity to stare at him and to try to intimidate him. As soon as this business is complete, I will have Amar kill him he thought to himself. He looked up to see Amar stood close at hand as always. Amar had also noticed Princ's stare and was watching him closely.

The tension was broken when a man entered the room. 'Excuse me Matriarku, I thought you would want to know, the delivery is almost here.'

The old woman nodded without looking away from the fire.

'Excellent,' said the Sheik, 'I will want to inspect them,' he looked directly at Misu and continued, 'perhaps I will test some of the merchandise tonight before my guests arrive tomorrow.' The smile formed on his lips but disappeared as he licked them.

Misu fought the urge to look away but instead looked him in the eye, 'The merchandise is not yet yours to test Sheik Hamad. When the deal is done you can do with them as you wish,' she took a step toward him causing Amar to stiffen, 'Until then you may look but not touch, unless Matriarku says so.'

The Sheikh laughed, 'So feisty, young 'Ella',' he said her name with a long soft aahhh, 'I see now you have your Matriarku's fire. Tomorrow, I have 20 guests arriving, each will be pledging one million pounds as an annual membership fee for this,' he waved his around, 'this 'club' we have created. The merchandise arriving tonight will be used within the next 6 months and will require to be replenished. That will require you and I to have a 'working' relationship, at the very least. You will continue to provide the goods and I will continue to pay you extremely well for your efforts.' He smiled at her, that same lecherous smile, 'However, please don't assume that you are the only supplier available,' he stood and brushed past her followed by Amar who put himself between the Sheikh and Princ.

When he had left the room Misu turned to Matriarku, 'That animal makes me sick to my stomach.'

Matriarku turned on her, 'This is business child, your stomach should not be involved, only your brain! He is a disgusting excuse for a human being but that is not our concern. Tomorrow we will be 20 million pounds richer and we can move on to the next location.'

'Where do we go next?' asked Misu.

'Next we go to Budapest, we have a small set up there but we will build it up as we have here and the Sheikh and his child raping friends will pay for another club they can visit.'

'What about London?'

'London can run itself, even that idiot son of mine can't make a mess of things now.'

'I thought maybe I would stay here and run things now Matriarku,' said Misu, failing to hide her disappointment.

'There are bigger and better things waiting for you child. You will no longer have to degrade yourself with that stupid Police uniform, no, you will be where you belong, at my side until it is time for you to take over.'

CHAPTER FORTY

The guard at the gate recognised the driver of the Amazon truck and gave him the thumbs up as the HGV carefully negotiated its way through the electric gates and slowly drove toward the bridge.

'We have a vehicle entering,' said Rambo from his OP, 'looks like a big bugger too, maybe a truck.'

Something occurred to JT, something from earlier suddenly clicked into place. 'Amazon,' he said.

'Good guess!' said Rambo as he read the name on the front of the HGV entering the driveway in front of the main building. He watched as one of the guards instructed the truck driver to park in front of the stables. 'The truck won't fit through the archway into the stable courtyard so they'll be unloading the cargo outside.'

'The drone is ready to fly, we'll get an eye in the sky shortly,' replied JT.

Easy finished his practice run and was satisfied he had mastered the controls. The infra-red camera sent clear images to the monitor in front of him but he also had an electronic receiver Hamilton had provided him with that he intended to drop as near to the building as possible.

'Send it,' said JT and he watched as the drone took off vertically then shot off in the direction of the target. 'What's the total flying time for that thing?'

'About 50 minutes tops, depends on wind conditions etc obviously,' answered Hamilton.

'If I can set it down somewhere safely that has a view of things the camera will last for up to 16 hours in low res,' said Easy without taking his eyes off the screen in front of him. The drone buzzed through the air and it was sent at full speed, Easy knew it was almost silent at low speeds or in hover mode but time was of the essence. He followed the service road and saw two farmers style wooden gates closed and padlocked over cattle grids. Whatever animals they were designed to keep in had long gone. There was a different breed of animal inside the gates now.

'Soon as we've had a visual, we can move in,' JT said to the team who stood patiently around the rear of the Range Rover. 'Remember we get the girls out, point them toward the Botanical Gardens and then we exfil back here and get down to the coast before daylight. There's a lot of firepower up there so let's avoid a firefight.' He turned to Hamilton, 'Hamilton, are you sure you want to take the Subaru up that road?'

'Yes, I don't see a viable alternative. I can take the service road up and round the back of the stables. The helpful thing about places like this is that the owners never wanted to have to see any of the staff. The road is cut down 4 or 5 feet and there are trees and bushes planted as cover, so I should hopefully make it undetected.'

'If they spot you?'

'Then the explosive charges will look like KKK and his chum had a little accident. I can make my way to join up with Rambo and we can ex-fil together.'

'I'm coming up to the helipad now,' said Easy

'Take it higher Easy, the two goons are still there and one of them is looking up at the sky,' said Rambo from his overwatch position.

Easy pulled back on the joystick to gain altitude but at the same time slowed the drone down to be quieter, he took it to 450 feet which was around where radar might be able to detect it. The proximity to Gatwick Airport meant there might be increased radar vigilance to protect aircraft. 'I see them,' said Easy as the two guards came into view, 'they've gone back to chatting.' He flew in a wide circle giving a view of the hotel and of the truck parked outside the stable block.

'I'm sending you screenshots,' said Hamilton and pointed at the computer tablet JT was holding.

JT studied the images and counted. 'Two at the gate and two on the bridge. I'm counting that as 24 suits plus the leather jacket guy. If this goes sideways there'll be a lot of lead heading our way.'

'Just as well we're bulletproof!' chortled Taff, as he patted his body armour.

'Let's just get in and out quietly so we don't have to find out,' said JT, seriously. He knew Taff was just being his usual upbeat self and trying to calm any nerves in the team but this wasn't any ordinary mission. They were operating off book, with a 16 year old kid and a MI6 agent he didn't know if he could fully trust.

CHAPTER FORTY-ONE

Easy took the drone over the roof of the main building and set it down next to the communications mast at the rear. He checked the signal before releasing the electronic device next to the control box and then took off again heading for the stable block with the staff quarters above the archway. It was a still night and he gently lowered the drone on top of a chimney stack. The stack had no chimney pots as they had been replaced with metal cowling caps. He guessed this would camouflage the drone well if anyone should happen to look up.

'Sheikh on the move,' said Rambo.

Easy turned the camera and switched on the sound as he followed the Sheikh and Amar as they went to the back of the truck. The driver was standing smoking at the rear of the truck. The Sheikh was pointing at the back of the truck and gesturing for the driver to open. The driver refused and Amar the bodyguard grabbed him and threw him out of the way.

'What do you think you are doing?' asked Misu as she and Princ approached the truck.

'I am about to inspect the merchandise, as is my right,' said the Sheikh. 'I may not sample one tonight but I wish to confirm they are, how shall I put it, they are of the required desirability for my guests.'

'Why don't you give me half an hour to get them into their rooms and then we can inspect them together?' suggested Misu.

'Let's not be too late, Ella, my guests will be here at 8am for breakfast and I wish to take a bath before bed.'

'Very well, 20 minutes and I'll give you the guided tour,' Misu waved and eight men came out of the staff building.

'Movement,' said Rambo, '8 suits headed for the truck.'

From the bottom of Easy's screen the eight men appeared and headed to the truck where the driver was swinging open the back doors over the tail lift. Two of the suited men climbed into the back of the truck and appeared pushing small figures with pillow cases over their heads. Six of these figures were lowered on the tail lift and they were grabbed by the six waiting suits. One of the figures kicked out and thrashed despite her hands being taped behind her back. The suit punched her in the stomach and she crumpled to her knees gasping.

'How delightful!' squealed the Sheikh, 'The unbroken ones are a personal favourite.'

'She is our newest acquisition,' said Misu, 'appears to be 'intact' too.'

'Ah a virgin no less, I will enjoy her after breakfast,' the Sheikh purred.

'Once the deal is done, you can enjoy her whenever you like,' said Misu. 'There are 3 more who have not been used yet. There is a special surprise I have for you, but you may have to make me an offer as this one is extra,' she looked at him and watched him stand straighter and lick his lips.

'Money is not an issue for the right merchandise, as you well know, Ella,' said the Sheik, getting aroused and fidgety.

Another 4 loads of six little humans were taken out of the truck and away into the stables.

'30 as agreed. All excellent quality,' said Misu.

'You mentioned a special surprise?' said the Sheikh, unable to hide his avarice.

'Bring them out,' Misu said to the men in the truck.

They led out a woman in her early 20s, she was unhooded and looked terrified. On her hip she carried a toddler no more than two years old and stood beside her, clinging to her leg was a little boy of about four. He was sobbing and burying his face into his mother's leg.

'Fucking hell,' said Rambo as he watched through his rifle scope. 'Permission to take these fuckers out right now Boss?'

'Standby Rambo, we've got to get them all out before any shooting starts.'

'Perhaps it is time to re-evaluate our plan,' said Hamilton.

'Let's hear it,' said JT, though he was pretty sure he knew what was being suggested. He was also pretty sure he'd agree to it.

'We have the opportunity to rid the world of some sick people, and in doing so make sure there are no more women and kids that require saving,' said Hamilton.

'I'm not sure you understand what's at stake here,' replied JT. 'You have a get out of free jail card thanks to MI6, my men on the other hand will risk their lives and if they survive face the possibility of court martial or civvy prosecution and life behind bars.'

'Of course, I do understand but this is an opportunity we will never get again. We will dismantle the Kosanians and take out the Sheikh and his paedophile ring at the same time. Remember we have KKK and his friend here waiting to be held responsible. Your boat to France can still get you there and keep your alibi intact.'

'Let me think,' said JT.

'Boss,' said Taff and JT turned to look at him. 'As Mr Hamilton says, it's a chance to rid the world of these bastards. I was with you when you pushed that war lord off the roof for raping that wee boy in Pakistan, this is the same sort of thing. We'll get in deep shit if we get caught but it's the right thing to do.'

'I know Taff, it's the right thing to do but if this goes south up there, no-one is coming to rescue us. There's no cavalry.'

'Boss, we've been in worse places. It'll be worth it just to put these bastards down.'

'I'm with Taff Boss,' said Joe. The other men all nodded their agreement.

'Rambo are you hearing all this?' asked JT.

'I'm in Boss, just say the word,' came the expected reply.

'Easy, you get a vote too kid, no-one will think badly of you if you want to sit this one out,' said JT to the back of Easy's head.

'I do whatever the team does,' he said without turning around, 'and some good news, our signal hacker has found its way in, I've got access to the CCTV from the stables and the two buildings, they're connected by microwave link.'

'Show me,' said JT moving to Easy's shoulder.

Easy brought up a screen full of thumbnail images on his laptop, 'There's 30 cameras in total.'

'They are keen on hotel security then,' said JT

'Not so much,' said Easy, 'these cameras here, 24 of them are in the stables,' as he pointed, he clicked on some of the thumbnails. The images were of rooms without windows. Into each room was being pushed a person, sometimes 2 people and in one room a mother and two young children. What they had in common was that they were all prisoners and they all looked terrified. The rooms had different set ups, some like monastic cells with just a bed and some were bigger with furnishings set up like a studio flat. In all but one room the occupants sat on beds as far from the door as possible, others stood in a corner, tensed and anxious. The one room where the image stood out was where a young girl paced back and forward. She was angry and looked ready for a fight. She had little hearts on her shoes.

'Show me the external cameras,' said JT, not wanting to look at the wretched prisoners a second longer.

Easy brought up 5 cameras simultaneously onto the screen, 'There's a camera in the intercom at the gate, one overlooking the helipad, two looked down at the driveway in front of the main building – their angle suggested they were positioned at roof level on opposite corners of the building. Another camera looked down at the door of the smaller building, watching who entered and left the building.

JT took in the scope of the cameras and traced them in his mind, 'That's a lot of blind spots. They're obviously confident no-one is coming knocking at their door.'

'They are more interested in what happens in the stables it seems,' said Hamilton, 'They'll be looking for insurance that none of the guests go blabbing about what goes on here, there'll always be incriminating evidence.'

'Easy, you said 30, where's the last camera?'

'It's internal and of a big hotel room.'

'Like a function room?'

'No,' said Easy clicking on the image, 'like a suite. The camera is different, I think maybe it's hidden like a spy camera.'

'Judging by the Louis Vuitton luggage, I would hazard a guess that this is the Sheikh's suite, they are spying on him,' suggested Hamilton.

'Probably,' agreed JT, 'no honour among thieves after all. Easy, can you access the recorded images?'

'Yes, I can, but I don't know how far back it goes.'

'I just want to know if Rory is here,' said JT. 'Hamilton, what time did they leave the golf club?'

'About 1615 hrs, if they drove straight here and were lucky with traffic, they might have made it by 1800. I doubt they'd have been here any sooner.'

'You said Rory's phone tracked to here, what time did it arrive?'

'1820 I believe.'

'Easy, check the cameras from 1815-1825, see if any vehicles arrived.'

'Give me a minute, it's a digital system, I'll download a copy of that timeframe and send it to your tablet. Then I can download the rest of it onto my spare hard-drive.'

'Good lad,' said JT, then as an after-thought added, 'and thanks.'

Easy smiled to himself enjoying the appreciation and feeling like a valuable part of the team.

JT motioned to Hamilton to join him with the rest of the troopers, 'If we are going to do this it means we have to go in and use the cover of darkness to try to secure the place and neutralise their security teams before the VIPs arrive, all while not alerting the authorities. Then we wait up and take out the VIPs when they get here.' He rubbed his scalp hard with his fingertips.

'Or the alternative?' asked Hamilton.

'We get ourselves in a position to try and take out the whole bloody lot of them at once.' said JT, already regretting the lack of planning time.

'And that means a daylight strike,' said Hamilton thoughtfully.

'Exactly, our chances of surprising them will be negligible as they'll be getting ready for the VIP's arrival. It's scheduled early enough that the nightshift sentries will still be up. They'll be tired so that's one thing in our favour. The others? Who knows how well trained they are, or how well equipped they are.'

'I would expect the Sheikh's men to be ex-military, perhaps even Saudi Special Forces. The Albanians tend to be hired thugs with guns but the Matriarku might have some better security. We should probably add Harper and Misu into the mix too, they've a lot to lose so I'd expect them to come out fighting.'

'Count Harper out,' said Easy, 'looks like he's dead, they carried him out and threw his body in the boot of the BMW.

'A pity, I was rather hoping to have a little chat with Mr Harper,' said Hamilton.

'Any sign of Rory?' asked JT

'Yes, it's on your tablet. They carried him into the staff building.'

'Alive?'

'Couldn't tell but Harper and Misu carried him not dragged him so maybe that says something,' said Easy, typing furiously at this keyboard.

'Ok, see if Rory leaves that building, and who else goes in there.'

Chapter Forty-Two

Maxwell grimaced as he rubbed his bindings against the rough paintwork of the metal pole. His hands felt sticky with blood and his shirt was wet with sweat. The occasional jerk as the plastic of the cable tie was notched gave him encouragement to carry on through the pain. He could no longer feel his fingers properly and rested a moment to wiggle and clench them trying to get the blood flowing properly.

He felt sure he was making progress and pulled hard using his back against the pole, he felt the plastic stretch as it bit into his wrists and he pulled with all his might, the plastic stretched another few millimetres then stopped. He grunted with the effort and the pain in his wrists.

The plastic didn't snap but it had stretched and he now had more movement in his hands and wrists. Moving them back and forward trying to rotate them did nothing other than to open the cuts further. There was a steady drip of blood onto the floor behind him and it occurred to him that if they left him here long enough, he might just bleed to death. He thought about Siobhan, and how many times she said his job would be the death of him, as he slid down the pole to his knees. They'd stayed 'friends' after the divorce, but that had changed when she'd met that accountant guy. He may be boring but he's reliable, she had told him. The guy used zip ties to keep his briefcase attached to his electric scooter for Christ's sake.

'Zip ties, bloody zip ties!' he muttered to himself. He knew some of them had a little release tag so you could adjust or remove them without cutting them. He looked at the bag on the wall and then at the zip tie that had fallen to the floor. There it was, the little tag of the release mechanism.

Getting back to his feet he rotated his left arm to open the mechanism up to the fingers of his right hand. The stretched plastic gave him just enough room to curl his fingers and reach the little tag. He worked at it with his middle finger but couldn't get enough purchase to pull it back and release it. Again and again, he tried using different fingers and trying to get his fingernail to grip the tab. After 5 painful minutes he gave up and slumped to the floor. In frustration he banged his head back against the pole and a few hairs snagged on the chipped paint-work. He quickly felt around on the ground behind the pole until he found a sturdy paint chip and tried to push it into the mechanism. He dropped the paint chip as his fingers were numb and clumsy. He cried out in frustration and as he scrabbled to find the dropped paint chip, he heard the basement door being unlocked.

Slow tentative footsteps came down the steps toward him. A man in a black suit appeared holding a gun. He looked at Maxwell and then around the room. The man said something in what Maxwell guessed was Albanian. Rory looked at him without answering.

'Who the fuck are you?' the man asked him in heavily accented English.

'I'm nobody,' said Maxwell, thinking that this guy probably hated the Police.

'Then shut the fuck up Mr Nobody, people are sleeping,' said the man as he turned to go back up the stairs.

'Wait!' said Maxwell, 'Can you get me some water?'

The man looked at him then shrugged and went upstairs before returning with a glass of water.

'Thank you, thank you so much,' said Maxwell and lifted up his face with his mouth open ready to take a drink.

The man stopped and then chuckled to himself, he placed the glass between Maxwell's legs and said, 'You want drink, help yourself!' He grinned as he walked away and climbed the stairs locking the door behind him.

Maxwell waited a few seconds before he clasped the glass with his feet and dragged it toward himself. The water spilled over the floor but that wasn't what he wanted. Getting back to his feet he used his foot to drag the glass against the pole. He placed his heel on the glass and gradually exerted more pressure on it until it smashed. Sitting back down he grabbed a shard of glass and forced it into the mechanism then wriggled his wrist to work the cable tie looser and looser until eventually he was able to free his hand.

He sat for a moment letting the elation he felt settle and the feeling in his hands and shoulders get back to something approaching normal.

Grabbing a towel from on top of the washer he wiped away the blood and checked the cuts. Nothing too serious he decided and he made fists with his hands to check they were functioning properly. He dropped the towel and grabbing the biggest shard of glass he made his way up the stairs. Stopping to listen at the door, he pressed his ear against the wood and tried to settle his breathing. He couldn't hear anyone moving about so turned the handle slowly and pushed gently on the door. The door barely moved before the bolt did its job. He considered shouldering the door open but he had no idea who or what lay on the other side.

Needing time to consider his options he returned down the stairs and looked around for a weapon. There were no knives or other tools in the basement but there were chemicals and that gave him an idea. First, he needed to look after the cuts to his wrists. Using a piece of glass, he cut into a clean pillowcase and tore long strips to use as bandages. After strapping up his wrists he took stock of the chemical assortment. The bleach was in 5 litre tubs and too unwieldy for his purposes, so, grabbing half a dozen small empty shampoo bottles he made his way to the washing machine. Next, he carefully poured bleach into each of the shampoo bottles and secured the lids. Flicking open one of the lids he squirted bleach into the washing machine to test the distance it could be propelled.

Satisfied, he took the base of the broken glass and wrapped it carefully with a facecloth so that a hard and sharp chunk of glass protruded.

After looking around and failing to find anything else he could fashion into a weapon, he sat down and did the only thing he could - waited.

CHAPTER FORTY-THREE

At 0430 hrs JT and the team stood to and despite having done so several times already, checked their weapons and comms.

'Gents, from what we've seen the security detail here is somewhere between shit and amateur. We can't vouch for the Sheikh's men but anticipate that they are well trained and highly motivated. We have 30 friendlies plus Rory in there to get out. Taff and Cooky once you are finished at the staff building, get yourselves to the stables. There are two guards but Easy should locate them for you through CCTV. Joe and I will take out the two garden sentries and the front door guards at the hotel unless Rambo can get the shot. Then it's all about the grand entrance from Posty and Hamilton. All clear?'

He received nods and 'Ayes' from the troops.

'Overwatch sitrep Rambo,' said JT into his throat mic.

'Still the same set up, this is the best position so staying put. I have total of 5 targets, repeat 5 targets. Two at the main building front door, two in the ornamental garden and one on the bridge. I also have a

Gucci piece of Russian sniper rifle complete with suppressor and 30 rounds looking for a home.'

'Received. No movement from the staff building?'

'No movement, counted 8 black suits in, zero have reappeared.'

'Received. Stables?'

'No movement and a much better line of sight since the truck has gone.'

'It's your direction we'll be sending the captives, as soon as they get to the Botanical Gardens, join Hamilton at the service road. We'll all exfil together,' he turned to the team, 'Everyone knows their tasks, any questions?'

'Will we have the eye in the sky operating when we strike?' asked Joe.

'Easy reckons he'll have 30 minutes tops flying time so we'll need to move quickly. He'll have to wait for some activity to cover the take-off noise too.'

He spoke to Easy, 'Anything from CCTV?'

'Nothing, it looks like everyone sleeps.'

'Are you a Pavarotti fan too?' he asked.

'Pava who?' asked Easy, bemused.

'Nessun Dorma!' seeing no recognition, 'oh never mind!'

'I saw Luciano do an evening of Puccini in Bergamot a few years ago, simply breath-taking!' said Hamilton.

'I reckon the Boss likes that in his tea!' said Taff, finding his own joke hilarious.

JT turned and looked at Hamilton who was pulling on leather gloves, 'Cold Hamilton?'

'Not at all, but I wouldn't want to get my hands too dirty!' he said, with a grin.

'Okay let's get this done and then get the hell out of here,' said JT.

Hamilton and Posty climbed into the Subaru and wound the windows down.

'Is he still alive back there in the boot?' Joe asked Hamilton.

'He's like a cockroach, Mr KKK, it'll take a lot to kill him.'

Joe looked at the explosive packages in the rear seat, 'This lot should be just the job then.' He said with a satisfied nod.

Hamilton drove the car down the road away from the RV point and away from Palmerston House. Instead, they headed for Gatwick Airport.

CHAPTER FORTY-FOUR

JT and Joe started through the rough pasture land toward the helipad. There was a pond between them and their first objective that they had to get around, or if all else failed, through. Their first objective was to reach the entrance of the old ice house which was built into the slope between the helipad and ornamental garden. They would have to cover the last 50m over the lawn, and without cover, undetected. Otherwise, they were sitting ducks for the two sentries who would hold the higher ground. They moved slowly and silently from bush to bush and tussock to tussock.

Cooky and Taff set off to the east of the others and used the service road to move up toward their objective which was the vehicles parked close to the front of the staff building. 15 minutes later they reached a small bridge that crossed a tiny stream.

'How are we looking Rambo?' asked Taff, 'We're out of cover for a bit.'

Rambo scanned the area from his vantage point, 'All clear,'.

The two men moved on and made quick progress over the bridge and to the next dip in the road. They knew Rambo had them covered but it paid to be careful. Making their way through the last of the trees they reached the lawn bordering the parking area. They moved slowly on their stomachs across the damp grass. They knew they'd be leaving a trail in the grass but it couldn't be helped.

Once in position they made themselves comfy in their firing positions and worked out where and how they would move forward or backwards as required.

JT and Joe were cursing their luck as they found the area around the pond was effectively a bog. Moving through the sucking mud was difficult, moving quickly or silently was impossible. They were saved by the incessant chatter of the two sentries up the slope ahead of them. They were happily smoking and sharing war stories and the tales of female conquests as is the norm when men get together doing a boring job.

As the ground started to firm JT signalled to Joe and they completed the last 50m in a combat crawl. When they finally reached the entry to the ice house they found the stone floor and walls were immaculate but the grass surrounding it had been allowed to grow long. It would make the perfect firing position, if only it were 20 feet up the slope and facing the other direction, thought JT.

Now that they were in position, he pressed the transmit button three times. He got the same three clicks from Cooky and Taff. They were all in position, now it was down to Hamilton and Posty.

'Movement,' said Rambo, 'Leather jacket guy leaving main building. He's heading for the staff building.'

Cooky clicked acknowledgement, he and Taff were nicely concealed by the lavender hedge behind the parked BMW and then the two Mercedes People Carriers were between them and the building.

They watched the man in the Leather jacket walk purposefully into the building, whistling to himself. Cooky recognised the tune; *I shot the Sheriff* by Bob Marley. Not if I get you first matey, he thought to himself.

CHAPTER FORTY-FIVE

Maxwell heard the bolt on the door being slid open and he tensed. There was nowhere he could wait in ambush and he was certain they wanted to question him or else he'd already be dead. He crouched by the pole with his hands reaching round behind him as if he was still tied up. Then thinking back to how he'd been positioned when Princ and Misu left earlier he slid his feet out from under him and sat on the floor. In one hand he had the glass wrapped in the towel and in the other a shampoo bottle full of bleach.

Princ descended the stairs and Maxwell saw that this time he didn't have his gun in his hand. So far so good, he thought to himself. Maxwell tried to look terrified but it didn't take too much acting when he saw the murderous look in Princ's eyes.

'Now Detective, you and I are going to have a little chat.'

'What about?'

'You're going to tell me everything you know and everything you have told to anyone else.'

'Go fuck yourself,' said Maxwell, bracing himself for what he knew would be coming. He tucked his chin down to his chest as he expected to be kicked or punched in the face. Instead, the kick came to his gut and it was all Maxwell could do not take his hands out from behind the pole.

Maxwell had tears in his eyes as Princ crouched down and grabbed his hair to lift his head. He heard the flick knife click open in Princ's hand before he saw it and cringed. Princ drew his face closer to Maxwell's but suddenly stopped when he saw broken glass on the floor. He looked over at the washing machine and saw the bloodied towel lying there and as he turned back Maxwell squirted the bleach into his face and eyes. At the same time Maxwell swung his hand holding the glass and raked it across Princ's neck. Princ swung blindly with his knife and caught Maxwell, slicing his tri-cep as he rolled out of the way.

Maxwell gasped and dropped the shampoo bottle. Grabbing his bleeding arm, he stumbled to the pile of towels and made a poor attempt at a tourniquet with a towel. Realising it wasn't going to stem the flow of blood he wrapped the towel around his arm and used one of the cable ties to secure it in place.

Princ was writhing on the floor holding his hands to his face and Maxwell took the opportunity to kick him in the head. Princ went still and lay motionless on the floor.

Maxwell grabbed the knife and made his way up stairs. The door was slightly ajar and he could see it led into a kitchen. He pushed the door open and stepped up into the kitchen then turned and slid the bolt on the door into place. There were two more doors, one leading to the hallway the other to a set of plain stone stairs. Servants stairs he thought when he saw them.

He made his way to the door into the hallway and then stepped back quickly when he heard voices approaching. They were speaking what sounded like the same language as the guy who'd brought the water, more Albanians he thought to himself.

Stepping as quietly as he could he made his way through the other door and up the stairs. He stopped to look out of the window and could see what had once been an ornamental garden. Now he knew for sure he was at Palmerston House.

Following the stairs up he tried the door on the first floor but it was locked. Hearing voices in the kitchen below him he climbed the next flight of stairs. The door on this last level was locked too. He looked around trying to fight the growing panic he felt.

A set of ladders led to a skylight and obviously onto the roof. Maxwell climbed the ladder and pushed open the skylight. The roof was flat and covered in lead that was slippery with morning dew. He made his way on hands and knees to the edge of the roof and looked over. He could see the stables and across them lay the hotel. He carefully made his way to the opposite side of the building looking for an escape route.

Chapter Forty-Six

'Movement,' said Rambo, 'there's an entourage counting 7 coming out of the hotel. Sheikh plus four men, Old lady with Misu. All heading for the stables.'

'Shit,' said Taff, 'we're moving.' When they heard the crunch of numerous feet on the gravel, they took the opportunity to crawl through the hedge and under the closest of the parked people carriers. It was light now and the cover was poor. They readied their weapons, Taff facing the group walking to the stables and Cooky covering the door of the staff building.

Easy also used the noisy gravel to mask the sound of the drone taking off. He skirted the roofline across the building and away from the approaching group then took the drone high, and in a loop, so he could get in position to hover.

'I love the smell of lavender,' said the Sheikh, 'it reminds me of Provence.'

Taff silently cursed as he realised, they had disturbed the hedge and caused the scent to float into the air.

'It's unusually strong,' said Matriarku looking over at the hedge, 'I will cut some to take home when I leave, with your permission of course, Sheikh Mhartoum, by the time I leave, all of this will be yours.' She smiled at the Sheikh who failed to notice the lack of warmth.

'But of course, my dear Matriarku, you shall have all that you desire,' he stopped and gestured gallantly with his hand as he allowed Matriarku to walk through the archway and into the stables courtyard first.

'They've entered the stables courtyard,' reported Rambo, 'you guys are clear.'

'I can see them now,' said Easy, 'they've gone into the stable building.'

'Moving,' said Taff, crawling out from under the vehicle. He looked around to see if there was a position which provided adequate cover but there was none available so he tried the sliding door on the people carrier. It was unlocked and he climbed in sliding the door shut behind him. Cooky followed suit and climbed aboard the other people carrier. 'Thank god for tinted windows,' muttered Taff.

CHAPTER FORTY-SEVEN

Hamilton and Posty had picked up the Executive Coach on its way south from Gatwick Airport, the journey would take approximately 30 minutes. They followed it discreetly for 25 of those minutes, its size meaning they could sit a distance back, that, and they knew its destination.

'5 minutes out,' reported Posty.

'Received,' said JT, 'Easy, have you got eyes on the gate?'

'Yes, two men at the gate and two men now at the far end of the bridge.'

'Excellent,' said Hamilton with a smile, 'looks like we'll arrive bang on time.'

Posty rolled his eyes then laughed.

'Movement,' said Rambo, 'on the roof of the staff building. Couldn't see who it was, they've ducked down again before I got a visual.'

'Let me see,' said Easy, he spun the drone before zooming in the camera. 'It's Mr Maxwell! He's on the roof!' he said excitedly. 'He's bleeding, looks like his arm is soaked with blood.'

'Does he have a way down?' asked JT.

'I can't see anything obvious, but the skylight is open, that must be how he got to the roof.'

'Ok, keep an eye on him, it's almost show time.'

Maxwell looked over the edge of the roof and saw a cast iron drain pipe led from the outflow of the flat roof and down to ground level. It also passed close to two rear windows. He decided he would wait until he heard movement out front before attempting his descent, figuring that staff would likely head for the hotel to start work.

Beneath him, down in the basement Princ was trying desperately to wipe his eyes clean with towels, the bleach had burned his skin raw across his face and his eyes wept tears that stung. His vision was completely blurred in his left eye but his right eye still functioned. He staggered up the stairs and hammered on the door.

One of the men inside the building came into the kitchen and opened the door for him. Princ fell to his knees and demanded the man get the eye rinse from the first aid kit.

When the man handed it to him, he lay on his back and squirted the liquid into his eyes. The stinging made it difficult to keep his eyes open but he forced them until the liquid was finished.

The man handed him a towel soaked in cold water and Princ held it against his face and then gently wiped at his skin until the anger in him made him rub his face vigorously and roar into the towel. He threw the towel to the floor and that's when he saw the drops of blood leading to the servants stairs. He drew his gun and headed for the stairs. The other man did the same.

'Go do your job,' growled Princ, 'this one is mine and mine alone.'

The man backed off and Princ headed up the stairs. His eyes still burned and with only one fully functioning eye he swivelled his head back and forth scanning for tell-tale blood spots. He tried the first door and then headed up to the top floor. The door was locked but he had already spotted the open sky light and ladder. He started to climb tentatively.

Maxwell heard the sound of the ladder creaking and decided it was now or never, he stood up to climb over the parapet wall and lower himself down the drainpipe.

'Movement' said Rambo 'I think that's Maxwell going to climb down from the roof but I haven't got a visual. Easy, can you see him?'

'I'll need to move the drone, gimme a sec.'

'Movement,' said Rambo again, 'Leather jacket guy just appeared on the roof, he's armed.'

Rambo watched as the man looked from the roof down to the front of the building, then moved to the side. If Taff and Cooky hadn't used the vehicles for cover he might have spotted them, Rambo realised. 'He's heading toward the rear where Maxwell went over, I don't have a shot and I can't see Maxwell.'

Easy flew the drone and pointed the camera at the roof. He could see the man walk up to the parapet and lean over. He had obviously spotted Maxwell and was climbing up onto the parapet. He stood upright and pointed his gun. Before he could fire, he heard a loud buzzing noise and turned to look just as Easy flew the drone into his face. Princ fell backwards and passed Maxwell who was clinging to the drainpipe, landing with a dull thump.

Maxwell reached the bottom and found Princ lying across a cast iron bench with a broken neck. He picked up the gun and crouched down while he tried to work out where to go next.

'Drone is down,' said Easy but before he could explain what had happened, Rambo interrupted.

'Chopper approaching from my 2 o'clock. Coming in low, must be heading for the helipad.'

'Shit,' said JT, their position could be compromised as they tried to get up the slope.

He watched as the helicopter rotated and dropped gently onto the helipad. The rotors eventually came to a halt and the doors opened. Out stepped the pilot and three heavies. Despite the rotors being stopped the heavies all stooped as they made their way from under the blades. The four men walked across the ornamental bridge that spanned the pond and up the path past the ice house entrance up the slope toward the ornamental garden.

'Hey fellas,' called the pilot, 'we're here to collect Mr Liriazi.'

'He's not going to be ready for a while, come up and get some breakfast,' replied one of the sentries.

'What's that?' asked one of the heavies pointing at the ice house.

'It'll be an ice house,' said the Pilot, 'they used them as olden day freezers before electricity. It's like a big cave they filled with ice off the pond in winter.'

'Sounds cool, I'll take a look,' said the heavy as he took a step onto the grass.

JT and Joe readied themselves to shoot their way out of their position as the heavy approached. They watched as he stopped to look back at the distance from the pond to the ice house. Joe took aim at his head.

'No time for sightseeing,' called the sentry, 'the VIP bus is about to arrive, you need to get out of the way.'

The heavy shrugged his big shoulders and trotted over to catch up with others.

JT and Joe exchanged a look that said, 'that was close.' A moment later they heard the message they had been waiting for.

'The bus is coming through the gate now,' said Posty as he readied his MP5SD at the window. Hamilton had his weapon ready and he accelerated the Subaru then turned it into the still open gate.

The two gate sentries had been watching the bus make its way toward the hotel when Posty shot them both from behind. They fell where they stood and one was dragged a few feet by the electric gate as it started to close and then jammed. 'Two down,' he reported.

Hamilton accelerated until the Subaru was just feet from the rear of the bus. As the bus approached the bridge, he stopped the car and he and Posty leaned out of their windows and shot the two sentries as the bus passed them.

'Four down,' said Posty as he jumped out of the car grabbing a bag from the rear seat.

Hamilton drove forward until he was on the bridge then jumped out and grabbed a gun from the dead sentries. He used the butt of the weapon to scrape two holes into the gravel of the drive where it met the bridge. Posty opened the bag and took out two of the anti-tank mines they'd stolen from the raid on the IRA at Tilbury. He primed them and carefully laid the rifle across the two pressure pads then pushed gravel gently back over the mines until they were almost covered.

'Bus stopped at the main door,' reported Rambo, 'passengers alighting.'

The passengers were all in high spirits as they stood around admiring the view and waiting for the Sheikh to come and welcome them. The bus driver pulled his bus forward and went to park in front of the staff building.

'Movement, the Sheik's group are leaving the stables,' said Rambo.

Hamilton finished setting the Subaru up and pushed the accelerator to the floor, wedging it with the sentry's gun. The Subaru shot off toward the hotel and he said, 'Fire in the hole!' as he ran to join Posty up the slope of the landform hill.

That was the signal for JT and Joe who ran out of cover and up the slope taking out the sentries with three round bursts from their suppressed MP5s.

The crowd of VIPs and the four from the helicopter were all transfixed as the driverless Subaru careered across the driveway and hit the front steps of the hotel where it exploded with frightening force. The VIPS and the two door sentries were literally shredded by the blast from the combination of plastic explosives and claymore mines that Posty had surrounded with bags of nails.

One of the heavies was fatally injured and fell to the ground but the pilot and the others turned to run for the helicopter just as JT and Joe crested the slope and shot them. Rounds started hitting the ground at JTs feet and he took aim at the upper window of the main building just in time to see the shooter's head explode as a round fired by Rambo from a mile away found its target.

Amar, the Sheik's body guard Amar grabbed his boss and dragged him behind the bus which was now stationary as the driver lay flat on the floor. The rear window was smashed, but the bus didn't appear too damaged. 'Stay here Highness, we will clear the way,' he said and called his men forward.

The Saudi security team formed up around the Sheik and tried to make their way to the staff building.

'Come out you cowards!' shouted Amar to the Albanian security guys, who he knew were in the building.

A few seconds later the eight Albanians, all in black suits, ran out weapons drawn. They turned to face JT and Joe in the ornamental garden when the doors of the people carriers slid open. Taff and Cooky opened up on them with a hail of fire. All eight were put down before they'd fired their weapons.

JT and Joe were now taking more fire from the main building as the three remaining Saudis within tried to shoot their way out. They threw themselves behind the bodies of the fallen heavies and felt incoming rounds thud into the dead bodies. Returning fire blind in the Saudis direction as they picked their way through the slick mass of body parts at the front door. As they stepped out into the open focusing on JT and Joe's position, they were cut down by Posty and Hamilton.

Now it was the turn of the Sheikh's remaining guards. Two stepped out from behind the bus and ran toward JT and Joe's position laying down a hail of fire as they went.

The first guard collapsed like a rag doll as Rambo took him out with another long range shot. His colleague stopped momentarily, a fatal error, as JT rolled out of cover and put two rounds in his chest.

Amar ordered the last two guards to engage the vehicles where Taff and Cooky were positioned. They fired at the vehicles and windows shattered as Taff and Cooky rolled out of the vehicles and sprinted for the staff building. The Saudi's took up positions behind the people carriers and while one laid down cover fire at the building the other fired at JT and Joe.

Amar tried to take the Sheikh back toward the Stables but stopped as he saw one of the Albanian security emerge from the archway only to be struck by a sniper round from Rambo. The round had hit the man as he moved and left a bloody stump where his arm had been, the man fell screaming until, after a few seconds, he was dead.

Matriarku and Misu stood stunned and unsure of where to go until Amar started shouting.

'The bus Highness, we cannot stay here!' he cried, and shoved the stunned Sheik around the bus and on through the door.

Misu pulled Matriarku to Harper's BMW and they climbed in and hid in the back seat.

Amar jumped aboard the bus, 'Drive!' he screamed at the driver who was still lying on the floor.

'No way!' said the man, who scrambled to his feet and ran down the steps of the bus.

Amar shot him in the back of the head and then climbed into the driver's seat. 'Ahmed,' he shouted to one of the guards, 'stay here and give us cover. Bilal, you come on the bus you can shoot these infidels as we move.'

Bilal jumped aboard and wedged himself in the doorway ready to fire as Amar gunned the engine and spun the bus round. Bilal fired at JT and Joe until a round from Rambo ripped through the bodywork of the bus and knocked him off his feet. He fell forward and landed in the drive where Joe double tapped him to the head to make sure he was dead.

Posty started firing at the bus and the windscreen shattered as his rounds hit, before Hamilton put his hand on Posty's weapon and said, 'Let them go.'

The bus was still accelerating as it drove through the landform hills and past Hamilton and Posty.

'We are saved Amar, we are saved!' shouted the Sheikh, as the bus drove over the anti-tank mines and was ripped apart in a huge fireball.

Ahmed, the last remaining Saudi, stood transfixed by the sight of the explosion and knew the Sheik must be dead. He took a second to consider surrendering, before a round from Cooky smashed into his throat, and made the decision for him.

The shooting had stopped and Maxwell, who had remained in cover behind a vehicle, came out to survey the carnage. As he came around the building he was joined by Taff and Cooky.

'You made it then,' said Cooky and slapped him on the shoulder.

'Ouch!' said Maxwell, then smiled when he saw Cooky grin at him.

'JT is over there, you best stay here,' said Taff, 'we've got a job to finish.'

CHAPTER FORTY-EIGHT

Taff and Cooky reached the stables and moved slowly into the courtyard.

'I've got no line of sight for you in there, boys,' said Rambo.

'No worries, by my count there's one suit left,' replied Taff.

'Sounds right to me, happy hunting.'

There were two doors into the building. One led up to the staff quarters and Taff took that door while Cooky covered the other door. All of the windows and the stall doors that had faced the courtyard had been bricked up. Some had been painted with frescoes of children's playgrounds.

Taff quickly cleared the staff quarters, then joined Cooky, 'Easy, you got eyes on the internals here at the stables?' asked Taff.

'Yes, they're all still in their rooms.'

'Good, can you get a fix on the suit?'

'The cameras in the corridors have gone off line. I only have the rooms.'

'Shit,' said Taff, 'we'll need to flush him out and time's getting on.'

'JT, you clear at the main building?'

'Four of us just about to enter. We need to get this done and get the hell out of here, we're already late,' replied JT.

'We're going into the stables now.'

They edged carefully into the semi dark corridor. The walls had been covered in a crimson fabric that moved gently with the airflow from the open door. A heady perfume, sweet and pungent filled the air. As they moved forward, they found and cleared two executive shower rooms that had equipment befitting a grand hotel. Two more rooms contained 4 poster beds and a large flat screen TV on the wall. There was music playing in one of the rooms and in the other a porn film was playing complete with grunts and moans. Cooky ripped the power cable from the TV and the fake pleasure noises were silenced.

Then they found an austere tiled and steel shower-block that looked like it had been modelled on a prison. Taff took up position at a corner to cover the next corridor as the building turned 90 degrees around the courtyard. This was where the rooms lined up next to each other on either side of the corridor. Cooky moved forward around the corner then crouched beside the wall. They leapfrogged each other to move constantly covering the corridor ahead.

Cooky used the back of his hand on the first door handle, their training had taught them to anticipate a door handle could be wired to the mains. Using the back of hands would prevent a reflexive grab of the handle and a fatal shock. The door handle felt safe and he leaned back as he twisted it to avoid any rounds fired through the door. No shock and no rounds came as he pushed the door open and was surprised to find that it had been unlocked. Taff jumped through the open door swinging his MP5 left and right as he looked for threats. Instead, he found a terrified young woman, making herself as small as possible in the corner. She held up a scrawny hand as an instinctive defence.

Taff moved to her as Cooky lifted the bed pointing the muzzle of his gun underneath as he did so. 'It's all right lass,' began Taff and reached for her hand. The hand was snatched away and tucked inside the human ball she was creating in a painfully tight foetal position.

'It's alright lass, we're here to save you,' he said gently.

Very slowly she uncurled her head from her chest and looked up at him still cowering.

Taff crouched before her and gave her his friendliest smile, 'We're the good guys love, we'll get you out of here.'

He went to stand up but a hand shot out and grabbed his arm, 'Don't leave me,' she whimpered.

Taff put his hand on hers and patted it gently. 'Don't worry lass, we'll be right back. There's one of those bad guys in here somewhere and once we've taken care of him, we'll get you out, we'll get all of you out.' He gently uncurled her fingers to persuade her to let go, then stood up and looked at Cooky, 'let's get this bastard.'

#

At the door of the main building JT and Joe lined up to the side of what was left of the front entrance, Posty and Hamilton were on the other side.

'You guys take left then sweep the down stairs; we'll go right then up the stairs.'

'Shouldn't we stay together?' asked Hamilton.

'No time,' said JT adjusting his ski mask, 'the tide is out at 1117 hours and we need to be on that boat.' He moved forward with Joe close behind him and stepped carefully through the debris. The grand staircase was directly in front of them and it split in two from the central landing in semi circles to the top floor. Once they were halfway up the main section the debris they had been scrambling over stopped and they could make better progress. At the landing he gestured for Joe to move left and he moved right. Keeping their backs against the curved walls they pushed themselves up the stairs always anticipating an ambush while here in the most exposed of positions. They reached the top of the stairs without coming under any fire and found the two massive rooms that made up the front of the house empty. JT saw shattered bay windows had thrown millions of pieces of glass across the polished floor and the enormous dining table that had been set for a grand breakfast. He wondered where the staff were who would be serving breakfast and in the next room he found out. As he swung open the door 6 scared looking men and women in white waiting staff jackets were huddled at the rear of the kitchen. A dead man lay slumped against the commercial fridge with a large kitchen knife in his belly. His white shirt soaked with recently spilled blood.

'You staff?' JT asked

They nodded in unison.

'How long have you worked here?'

'We were brought here yesterday from Turkey,' said a middle aged man, 'we came yesterday and were due to leave tomorrow after serving lunch.'

'What happened to him?' he asked.

No-one spoke, they all just looked at their feet.

'You all need to stay in here. Keep out of the way and you'll be safe,' he turned to leave and then it struck him. The guy on the floor was wearing the same uniform trousers as the rest of them, the same sensible polished black shoes, he raised his MP5SD and turned back into the room. The staff shrank back further into the corner. 'You at the back, step forward.'

No-one moved but as JT took a step forward the crowd started to part and he saw them. Crocodile skin boots. The man wearing them still had his head bowed and not showing his face.

'You at the back, I won't tell you again. Step forward or I'll shoot you where you stand. The man looked up and JT recognised him, 'Step forward Mr Liriazi.'

Liriazi looked at him with a sneer which twitched to a smile as he looked to JT's right. A roar came as the pantry door flew open and the last of Liriazi's men charged at him with a pistol in his hand. JT instinctively batted the pistol away and dropped his MP5 to free his hands as the big ape barrelled into him smashing him into the fridge door.

The big man had his forearm over JT's throat and his bulk had trapped JT's arm between them so he couldn't reach for his sidearm. JT tried to roll the guy off of him but he was jammed between the fridge and the dead guy on the floor. Unable to breathe he tried to turn his body to ease the pressure on his throat but the guy was too strong, and too heavy, to shift. JT reached for his combat knife but the guy saw his movement and knocked the knife out of JT's hand. The big man grinned as JT flailed in a last attempt to get free. His arm slapped across the dead body as he flailed and bucked. He felt for the knife that had killed the man until his fingers located the hilt. With a twist and a tug, the kitchen knife came free and JT drove it into the side of the big Albanian who yelped in pain, and took his arm from JT's throat. Desperately gasping in some air, JT wrenched the knife from between the big man's ribs and stabbed it into his neck. The Albanian fell back, a thin jet of blood spurting from between his fingers as he choked and spasmed until he died.

JT tried to get to his feet but the floor was now slippery with blood and Liriazi took his opportunity as he picked up the fallen pistol. JT got to his feet and Liriazi pointed the gun at him.

'Who are you? Did the Russians send you?' he asked.

JT didn't get a chance to answer before the middle aged man in staff uniform hit Liriazi with a cast iron skillet and knocked him off balance. JT threw himself at Liriazi and wrestled the gun from him. Liriazi leaned back against the sink and looked defeated.

'Thanks,' said JT to the to the middle aged man, 'that was brave of you.'

'He killed my nephew,' the man replied and looked at the body on the floor. 'Now you should kill him,' he said pointing at Liriazi.

'No, wait, I have money, lots of money, it's in my room you can have it all,' he pleaded as Joe came into the room.

'You heard the man,' said JT to the staff, 'go find his room and take his money, then get the hell out of here.'

The people hesitated and then filed out of the room.

'We've got Liriazi,' said JT into his throat mic. 'He's the last one. There's 5 staff all in white coats going to be coming out of the main building shortly, they're friendlies. Posty point them in the direction of the Botanics and get them out of here.'

'Ask him about Matriarku,' said Hamilton, 'she and Misu are un-accounted for.'

'Standby,' replied JT, 'where is Matriarku?'

Liriazi laughed, 'I don't know and if I did, I would not tell you.'

'In that case you're no good to me,' said JT, then put two rounds in his chest.

#

Easy was scanning the CCTV images from the stables when he saw it. The woman with the young kids. She was no longer sat on the bed holding her children. She had backed herself into the corner and was using her body to shield the kids. 'I think I might have found him,' he said.

'Where?' answered Taff.

'I think he's in the room with the mother and kids. I can't see him but I think he's under the bed.'

'Which room are they in?' asked Taff.

'I don't know, but the first room you went in was Camera 1, their room is camera 20 so it is probably the last room,' said Easy.

Taff and Cooky made their way down the corridor to the last door. There was a plaque attached to the door that read "Family Room" with a picture of a happy family playing a board game together. 'I think we've found it,' said Taff. 'What else is in there? I don't want any stray rounds hitting the kids.'

'Just a bed and a table with little chairs,' replied Easy, 'the only hiding place is under the bed. It's on the left as you enter, the family is huddled on the right.'

'Okay,' said Taff, visualising the room.

Cooky took hold of the door handle and when Taff nodded, he twisted the handle and threw the door open. Taff fired two quick bursts into the bed, then Cooky ran in and lifted it to reveal the suited man bleeding out from several wounds. Cooky dropped the bed and left him to die.

CHAPTER FORTY-NINE

They gathered all of the prisoners in the courtyard. They looked terrified and cowed. None of them wanted to move, they were too scared.

Taff had carried the little boy and stood beside the mother who was cradling her daughter. He had an idea, he looked for the girl with the hearts on her shoes, the angry girl. She stood and looked back at him whereas the others all looked at their feet. 'What's your name, little girl?' said Taff in his best disarming voice.

'I'm not a fucking little girl,' she hissed, 'I'm 16!'

'Ah right, sorry miss, I'm getting on a bit myself and it's not easy to tell nowadays,' he said, smiling at her from behind his ski mask.

'Stacey.'

'Ah, well pleased to meet you, Stacey. You seem like a smart girl, I mean a smart young woman, so I need you to look after these people for me.'

'How?' said Stacey, looking at the rest of the group.

'It's obviously not safe here Stacey, but just through the woods and on a bit, in that direction there's a big Botanical Garden. If you go there the staff will help you. Do you understand?'

'Yeah, I understand.'

'Good, now I need you to lead these people over there, can you do that?'

'Yeah,' her face fixed with a steely determination as she looked at the group. Then she turned to Taff and held out her skinny arms to take the little boy from him. 'It was that Felix and them scooter boys, you know, what done this. They gave me to that woman.'

Taff handed her the little boy, 'They'll get what's coming to them Stacey.'

With a few shouts and a bit of cajoling Stacey got them all moving and they headed into the woods and toward safety.

Taff watched them go then joined the rest of the team forming up in front of the hotel as Rambo came jogging in.

'You left the rifle?' asked JT.

'Yes, a fine piece of Russian kit for the plods to find,' he replied. He patted his backpack, 'brought the ammo with me though, wouldn't want someone playing with it.'

'Good move.'

'What about Matriarku and Misu?' asked Hamilton.

'I didn't get eyes on them, either they were on that bus with the Sheikh or they're in the wind,' said Rambo.

Hamilton looked disappointed, 'I'd have enjoyed questioning those ladies.'

'What's the plan boss?' asked Taff looking at JT, 'we're not going to catch that tide.'

'Actually, I have an idea,' said Hamilton and he turned to look at the helicopter.

'None of us can fly that thing,' said JT.

'No, but I can.'

'Christ, you're a man full of surprises Hamilton,' said JT. 'We need to get Rory here, and Easy out of here too.'

'And my car,' said Hamilton.

'I can take Harper's car to get back down to Easy, then swap to your car and we can RV somewhere away from here?' offered Maxwell.

'Good idea,' said Hamilton.

'You need to torch the van too,' said JT, 'preferably without our kit, if you've time to collect it up.'

'Okay, I'll sort it. Now you guys have a boat to catch, get going.'

CHAPTER FIFTY

The troopers and Hamilton ran across the ornamental garden and crossed the bridge to the helipad.

Maxwell stood for a moment and took it all in before he ran over toward the staff building. He heard the whine of the helicopter engine starting as he reached the car parking area. Then something occurred to him. The man with the leather jacket had been with Misu when he first spoke to him in the basement. He was dead but he might have a phone or something useful. He went round the back of the building and watched the helicopter take off and fly low south away from the house.

Searching the body, he found a phone in the inside pocket of the man's jacket. He tried to switch it on but it was password protected. He placed the dead man's thumb against the phone just in case it might work but he'd been dead too long to fool the security.

Oh well, worth a try he thought, I'm sure Hamilton or Easy will be able to get into it. He put the phone in his own pocket and remembered he had the man's gun stuck in his waist band in the small of his back. What the hell have I become he thought as he made his way back round to the front of the building.

Movement made him jolt, and then the engine of Harper's BMW fired into life. There in the driver's seat was Ella Misu. He ran forward and she saw him. For a moment neither of them moved and then Misu floored the accelerator and the BMW shot forward with a hail of gravel from the rear tyres. She drove straight at Maxwell who threw himself to the side and rolled over drawing the gun from his waistband. Misu braked hard then put the car into reverse and tried to run him down. This time he was ready for her and took three quick steps to the side and shot her through the side window. The car came to a stop against one of the people carriers.

Maxwell opened the door and Misu fell sideways out onto the gravel with blood leaking from the wound that entered her shoulder and left via her chest. Her once beautiful face twisted as she coughed blood then ruined her perfect make up. Looking into the car he was shocked to see a little old lady curled up in the footwell of the passenger seat. He pulled Misu the rest of the way out of the car and climbed into the driver seat.

'Matriarku, I presume? I know a man who is very keen to speak with you.' He pulled the car door shut and reached down to slide the seat back.

'I don't think so,' said Matriarku and emptied the contents of a small silver pill box into her mouth. She looked at Maxwell and smiled. Her eyes went wide and rolled back in their sockets; she was dead.

'Shit! You crafty old bugger,' said Maxwell, then reached over to open the door and pushed her lifeless body out.

Two minutes later the BMW smashed through the farmers gates on the way down the road and Maxwell screeched to halt beside Hamilton's Range Rover. Easy was waiting for him stood beside a pile of equipment bags as he threw a lit rag into the rear of the builders van. Flames erupted with a whoosh as Easy threw the bags into the back of the Range Rover and climbed into the passenger seat.

'Got everything kid?' asked Hamilton, taking up the driver's position.

'Yes thanks,' he replied, clicking his seat belt on.

Maxwell drove hard down the road, but slowed down as he passed through the outskirts of Haywards Heath. Two fire engines and a Police car roared out of town in the direction of Palmerston House. Maxwell pulled the car over like everyone else to let them pass.

CHAPTER FIFTY-ONE

'I'll get you as close to the harbour as I can then I'll go dump this thing,' Hamilton shouted to JT, who replied with a thumbs up.

The team had dumped their weapons and body armour back at Palmerston house and now sat wearing a variety of coloured t-shirts they'd worn under their battle dress. JT looked at his watch and sent a text message to Walter; "Ten minutes."

A few seconds later a message came back, 'Too late, missed the tide. Fishing off Normans Bay instead. BBQ later RIBs on the beach.'

JT brought up a map on his phone and showed it to Hamilton, he pointed in the general direction as he worked out the precise course.

'Find me a field to set you down in, don't want people seeing us on the beach,' shouted Hamilton.

Scanning the map JT pointed to a field half a mile from the shore. Hamilton nodded and kept the helicopter low to the ground headed in that direction. Ten minutes later the wheels barely touched the ground before the team leapt from the helicopter and it took off again.

They ran hard for the beach and then walked across the sand trying to look as nonchalant as possible. Further along the beach they saw the RIB waiting for them. Dragging the boat into the sea they jumped aboard. Cooky started the engine and steered them out to sea and toward the waiting Peregrine which was anchored a few hundred metres offshore.

Walter waited on deck for them and caught the bow line to pull them alongside. The men climbed aboard and went below into the cabin. They sat down and for the first time in what felt like days they relaxed. Walter secured the RIB to the rear of the Peregrine then pulled the anchor aboard. He started the engine and took them out into the Channel.

CHAPTER FIFTY-TWO

Hamilton banked the helicopter and scanned the countryside around him. Somewhere near his position was an abandoned large scale quarry but without gaining height it wasn't easy to locate. Finally, he spotted the waste heap over to his right and he flew over it and dropped down into the quarry. It was a wide expanse and he was able to locate a bit of flat ground bedside the flooded belly of the quarry.

He landed gently to test the ground and satisfied it was solid enough he killed the engines and climbed down from the cockpit. An old portacabin sat at the edge of the quarry and he ran over to look inside. In an old locker was a dirty grey sweatshirt that smelled of damp. He took off his Mil-Tec top and pulled on the sweatshirt. The smell was awful and caught in his throat. Back outside he grabbed a few rocks and shoved them into the pockets of his Mil-Tec and threw it into the body of water where it splashed and sank.

Running to the top of the quarry decline he climbed to the highest ground and plotted his path away from the quarry and to somewhere away from people. He ran regularly to maintain his fitness but was feeling the effects of the come down after combat as he jogged down the road and then across the fields.

Two hours later he was sitting behind a billboard in a layby near Robertsbridge on the road from Hastings to Tunbridge Wells or Royal Tunbridge Wells as he liked to call it. As Maxwell pulled into the lay-by, he ripped off the sweatshirt and stuffed it into the litter bin then climbed into the rear seat of his car.

'Jesus, what's the smell?' asked Maxwell as they drove off.

'Don't ask,' said Hamilton, and got himself comfy for a long drive.

CHAPTER FIFTY-THREE

'There's been a bit of a storm in the Bay of Biscayne,' said Walter by way of explanation as the rough sea tossed the Peregrine around. 'I reckon it's going to be running hard for the next 8-10 hours through the Dover Strait.'

'Can you get us across Walter?' asked JT, coming up to join him in the wheelhouse.

'This old girl has seen worse but it's not that you have to worry about. That RIB isn't designed for these sorts of seas and those French beaches will take a right old bashing in this.'

'We need to get on that Ferry out of Calais at 0630 tomorrow morning,' said JT, gripping the back of Walter's chair to steady himself.

'How long will you need to get yourself to the port from where you're parked up?'

'It's only a 90 minute or so drive but the security checks can take ages so they tell everyone to arrive at least 2 hours before sailing time.'

'Then you need to be at your motorhome by 0300 hrs at the latest.'

'The very latest Walter, if we're to keep this cover and give ourselves a rock solid alibi we need to be on the French side ASAP.'

'I hear you Jonny but your alibi won't be worth much to you if you're face down in the Channel. Here's what we're going to do, we'll sit this out for a bit and let her blow herself out. I'm also mindful of what happened to you lot on the way out, and you should be too. Those big ships will plough right through this stuff, and through you too,' he looked at JT with a look of genuine concern, 'I'll get you to the beach by midnight and you can have a glass of rouge before your ferry. How does that sound?'

'We definitely can't go now?'

As if by way of answer a big rolling wave pushed the Peregrine sideways and at a precarious angle before Walter could fight the wheel to right herself, 'Definitely!'

CHAPTER FIFTY-FOUR

They pulled the Range Rover into the carpark of the Asda supermarket and Easy went off into the shop. It was 6pm so the shoppers had started to thin out but there were still queues at the tills. It took him three attempts to feed £20 notes into the self-service machine and he heard tutting from the queue behind him. He returned 40 minutes later with two bags and placed them on the back seat beside Hamilton before he climbed in.

'Not a lot of choice I'm afraid,' he said, making eye contact with Hamilton.

Hamilton fished out a navy hoodie with "Surf's Up" emblazoned across the back and a pair of beige chinos. Last came a pair of trainers that were as light as they had been cheap. 'Thank you, I think you may put my tailor out of business,' said Hamilton, as he stripped off his t-shirt.

'There's wipes and some deodorant in there too,' said Easy then turned to Maxwell. 'There's a Jumper in there for you and some bandages and stuff for your arm and wrists.'

'Good lad, thanks,' said Maxwell, and drove out of the car park to find somewhere less public to dress his wounds. After driving out of town he looked at Easy as he sat looking sullenly out of the window, 'You ok Easy? You've barely spoken for a while.'

'I'm fine,' he said unconvincingly.

'Killing a man is not an easy thing to do but you shouldn't feel bad about it, he was going to kill me, you saved my life!'

Easy just looked at his hands and sighed.

Maxwell looked at him and placed his hand on his shoulder, 'Look today has been a lot to deal with. You've seen some horrible things they're bound to have an impact.'

'No, it's not that,' Easy realised that maybe he was supposed to feel something, remorse, shame, maybe even pride, but instead he hadn't given killing the man another thought.

'So, what's up then kid? You shouldn't keep things bottled up and we can't help if we don't know what's bothering you.'

'It's Dionne. She wasn't there. I thought she must be with them and that we were rescuing her, but she wasn't there.'

'Ah I see,' said Maxwell, understanding Easy's demeanour. 'Well once we're back in London, we'll just have to find her then, won't we?'

'I think she is probably dead,' said Easy, with a quiver in his voice trying to hold back tears.

'We don't know that, and if she's alive then we'll find her,' said Hamilton from the back seat.

Easy looked at Maxwell and then Hamilton, 'Promise?'

'Promise,' said Maxwell and prayed it was a promise he wouldn't have to break.

Hamilton tried to lighten the mood. 'Shall I drive now Rory, while you sort out your bandages? I will treat you both to supper at The Three Tuns in Sittingbourne. I have a standing reservation.'

'In Sittingbourne? Long way from London to go for supper?'

'I keep a place down there by Faversham. We can stay there tonight. I dare say we may even find some less 'street' attire!'

'I need to tell my Aunty I won't be home,' said Easy.

'Will that be a problem?' asked Maxwell.

'I don't think she'll be happy as I didn't tell her beforehand, but it'll be ok.'

'Ok, then Sittingbourne for supper it is!'

CHAPTER FIFTY-FIVE

Walter sailed The Peregrine around Dungeness seeking some shelter from the rough seas. When anchored close to New Romney, he went below and made a meal of pasta with smoked sausage and jars of pre-made pasta sauce.

'Sorry lads, not my best work but it'll fill a hole, there's a loaf of bread there too, so get stuck in.'

They all thanked him as they devoured the pasta and wiped the plates with slices of bread.

'Thanks for this Walter, and thanks again for everything,' said JT.

'We're not finished yet Jonny, there'll be time for thanks when this is all over.'

'True enough.'

'Have you worked out your longer term plans yet? I should think you've been a bit busy to give it serious thought.'

'To be honest, Walter, when I try to think about it, I get tied up in knots. It's like I need more information but at the same time it's too much to pull it all together.'

'I know what you mean,' he studied JT for a moment before he continued, 'here's what I can tell you from my own experience. Life has a way of kicking you when you least expect it but it also gives you opportunities. We all make a choice when we're knocked down to either stay down or get up and get back in the fight. Like you, I made my life in the service, it gave me a purpose, adventure and a family that was as close as any blood ties. It also cost me my wife, at times my sanity and the freedom to make the choices I knew to be the noble ones. You, from what you've told me, have the opportunity to have the best of both worlds, you can keep your family – those men down there - together, you can save your sanity by not having the interfering Politicos breathing down your neck and you can make your own decisions about what's right and wrong. It seems money won't be an issue so when you decide to hang up your boots it will be on your terms and when you choose.'

'You make it sound like a pretty simple choice,' said JT.

'Another thing, although you may not want to hear it of course, is that if you leave the Regiment, you are solving the problem that made your beautiful Esmé leave,' he looked at JT waiting for a reaction, 'Who knows there may even be a possibility of reconciliation at some point down the line?'.

'Reconciliation? I think that ship has sailed Walter!' said JT shaking his head.

'Hmmm?'

'I don't even know where she lives?' he said, turning back to face Walter.

'Ah yes, well perhaps now you'll have the time to find out?

CHAPTER FIFTY-SIX

The Three Tuns sat beside what was once a quiet road four miles from Sittingbourne in rural Kent. A quintessential English pub replete with thatched roof and windows of old fashioned imperfect glasses. The inglenook fireplace held a roaring fire and the subdued lighting made it the ultimate in cosy.

The barman gave Hamilton a second look as they walked in. He saw the man, who he had always seen smartly dressed and rarely without a tie, wearing a hoodie and trainers.

'Good evening, Anthony,' said Hamilton, 'I have a couple of companions with me this evening, allow me to introduce Rory and Ezekiel.'

'Good evening, Mr Hamilton, and welcome gents,' said Anthony, still mesmerised by Hamilton's clothing.

'As you can see, we have had a spot of bother and got covered in mud when changing a tyre. These were the best we could find at short notice,' he gestured down himself at his outfit, 'and we are famished so thought we'd call in before heading to the house.'

'Then I'll send Tabby straight over to take your order.'

'Wonderful, many thanks,' smiled Hamilton, heading off to his table by the fire.

'I can recommend everything on the menu,' he said, as they took their seats. 'Ezekiel, if there is anything on the menu you don't recognise just "holler",' he used his eyebrow to enquire whether he had used the term correctly, 'and if Rory or I don't know what it is, we can ask Tabitha.'

Easy knew what Hamilton had done to avert the possibility of him being embarrassed, and felt both gratitude and a new affection for the man.

'I think I'll have the roast beef,' announced Hamilton.

'Me too, that sounds good,' said Easy, pushing his menu away.

The conversation was stilted and shifted to life in London and the places they had all lived. No-one would mention the days' events within earshot of outsiders and they were all feeling sleep deprived and sleepy due to the heat of the fire.

After their meal Hamilton settled up the bill and they headed back out to the car.

'Well sated chaps?' asked Hamilton as they climbed into the Range Rover.

'Best roast beef I've had in a while,' said Maxwell.

'Yes, thanks,' said Easy.

'Excellent, we'll be back at the house shortly but first we need to stash the weapons and kit.'

'Got somewhere in mind?' asked Maxwell.

'Yes, I have a little woodland a couple of miles from here. We can bury them there,' he said, starting the engine before adding, 'for future use.'

'Future use?' asked Maxwell.

'Assuming the team make it back in one piece, I am confident that they will see their future with The SAS is over, and that we can form a team between ourselves. A team that can do a lot of good in the world.'

'You mean they become MI6? I can't see how that would work,' said Maxwell.

'Two things,' said Hamilton as he drove out of the pub car park, 'firstly, I am referring to all eight of you as the team, and I include myself, although in practical terms my role would be less *hands on,* than the rest of you.'

'Secondly?' asked Maxwell.

'I am not, strictly speaking, MI6.'

'Not 6? Then who are you?'

'It's complicated.'

'Complicated?'

'My role does encompass MI6 but I also have,' Hamilton paused for a second, 'a broader remit.'

Maxwell laughed, 'So exactly what kind of spy are you? Who do you report to?'

'I report to the Prime Minister on some matters. On other matters the PM is, not in the loop, as it were.'

'Jesus, you're autonomous?'

'You could say that. As we have proven today, there are times when due process has to be circumvented as the ultimate form of prevention.'

'What about oversight? Who decides what's worth breaking the law for?'

'I understand this is difficult for you to comprehend as a Police Officer, however, you are also witness to the innumerable, and to my mind unforgivable, failings of the judicial system to protect the people we serve.'

'So, you're forming a team of vigilantes?'

'If that's the terminology you are comfortable with.'

'I am far from comfortable with it.'

'As you wish. You are of course welcome to resolve it in your mind as you see fit.'

'I want to help,' said Easy from the rear seat.

'Glad to hear it, Ezekiel,' said Hamilton, smiling at him in the rear view mirror.

'You need to think it through properly,' said Maxwell, swivelling in the seat to make eye contact with Easy.

'I have thought about this since before I went to find help from the SAS. I can't trust the Police.'

'Thanks very much,' said Maxwell feigning hurt.

'You know what I mean,' said Easy flatly.

'Sadly, I do,' said Maxwell, looking out of the window.

They drove on in silence until Hamilton turned into an unmarked dirt road and then turned again into a thickly wooded area. 'Welcome to Briar Wood gentlemen.' He stopped the car and unlocked a gate before driving on through deeper into the woods.

The headlights swept across trees as the car climbed a rounded incline then dropped down into a clearing. A log cabin sat in the middle of the clearing and Hamilton pulled up outside, 'This is Briar Wood Lodge, my office away from London.'

CHAPTER FIFTY-SEVEN

It was dark before the sea finally started to ease up but the Peregrine was still being rocked as she sailed out into the channel. They had crossed the first of the shipping lanes closest to the English coast heading north east up the no-man's land between the lanes. The waves were being pushed up behind them out here in the middle of the channel but Walter explained they were less likely to come to the attention of either country's authorities while on this course.

'I've booked a berth at Boulogne-Sur-Mer,' said Walter, 'I'll be looking to catch the turn of the tide at 0100 hrs so you can take the RIB in from about 3 miles out. It'll be rough as you get broadsided by the swell, but I've given you a 35 horse power Yamaha, that'll get you ashore soon enough.'

'3 miles will be less 30, I'm sure we'll be fine. We'll pay you back for the RIB and outboard Walter,' said JT, 'you've been a life saver.'

'Don't worry about that, you've got bigger fish to fry,' Walter kept his eye on the brass compass that had been fitted when Peregrine was built in 1934. 'I turned off the transponder so we'll be invisible to ships unless their radar finds us among the waves; doubt it though.'

'How do the little migrant boats get picked up?' asked Joe, handing Walter a mug of coffee.

'They're looking to get picked up once they reach the British Territorial Waters, I reckon they shine torches at any passing boats, I'm told they even phone '999' once they have mobile phone signal to say 'come and get us!' Walter laughed. 'Poor buggers don't realise how risky the crossing is, they'd be safer staying in France but the smugglers push them out in all weathers. There's also the Border Force and RNLI patrols that go out looking for them.'

'Doesn't seem right the RNLI going out to bring illegal immigrants ashore, the RNLI are all volunteers,' said Joe.

'Don't get me started on the RNLI,' said Walter, 'bloody heroes, the lot of them, and it's a bloody charity. Makes no sense. They should be paid for risking their lives.'

'That's the dishes done and stowed,' Cooky announced as he came up into the wheelhouse. 'The guys are just packing up the dry bags.'

'Excellent. It's time for us to steer south, we're across the Dover-Calais ferry route and I can see the Dunkerque ferry out there to starboard. I can't see anyone looking for migrant boats on a night like this, this far North. JT, check those tow-lines on the RIB, don't want to lose her to the waves.'

'She's tied fast,' called JT from the stern deck.

'Right Gents, standby we're coming about and it's going to get a bit rough!' shouted Walter. The waves grabbed at the stern of the Peregrine and pushed at the RIB which was tossed around. Walter looked back with concern lining his face. 'The RIB could do with some ballast to be on the safe side, she's getting thrown about back there, bit risky.'

'Will it be safer with all six of us aboard or will a couple do?' asked JT.

'More the merrier Jonny,' said Walter, 'she'll be safe enough under tow if you're all aboard.'

'Okay, guys bring the drybags up and get your life vests on, they are automatic if you end up overboard.' Said JT as he turned to start pulling on one of the securing lines attached to the RIB. 'Gimme a hand here Cooky, we'll bring her leeward.'

'*Whatward* boss?' said Cooky, grabbing the second rope.

'Leeward, opposite side from the wind and waves,' said JT, 'we'll make a sailor of you yet.'

'No thanks boss, I've had my fill of boats and the sea this last couple of days!' laughed Cooky.

With the RIB alongside, Taff timed his jump aboard but still ended up in a heap. He sat up and got ready to help the others. One by one they jumped until they were all aboard and their bodies steadied the RIB which now rode the waves better.

30 minutes later Walter steered the Peregrine to starboard and turned into the wind. Instantly the nauseating corkscrewing motion eased for the men in the RIB and Walter was rewarded with thumbs up when he looked back to check on them. They were past half way now. In an hour he would cast them loose and let them make their own way to the shore.

JT looked out at the dark sea with just the occasional light from a ship visible in the distance. He looked back to where he knew the French coast lay and then he saw it. The red and green position lights said the boat was still a long way off, but it was definitely coming toward them.

'Walter!' he shouted at the top of his voice, and pointed off to the port side.

Walter looked back at JT and then grabbed his binoculars. 'Shit, it's Border Force,' he shouted, 'they're coming to check us out!' He turned The Peregrine to head toward the Border Force vessel trying to hide the RIB to her stern.

'How long until they reach us?' shouted JT.

'3 minutes tops,' replied Walter, 'they might decide to board me if they think I'm suspicious. There's no way we can outrun them, those cutters can do 30 knots.'

'Any suggestions?' JT asked the team in the RIB.

'Who Dares Swims!' said Taff, 'we can't let them see us and we can't outrun them. We have to swim for it. Walter can come back for us when they've gone.'

'Are you serious?' asked Rambo, looking at the cold dark water.

'Deadly,' said Taff, picking up his dry bag. 'We need to go now and let Walter put some distance between us.

'He's right,' said JT. He shouted to Walter, 'we're going in, get rid of them and come find us!'

'You're bloody mad you lot!' shouted Walter. 'Flash a light and I'll find you! If they're going to take too long, I'll just have to come clean, you won't survive long in there!' he turned back to the wheel and set a course to meet the Border Force Cutter.

'Grab your gear and we go on three,' said JT and sat up onto the hull with his feet in the water. 'Ready, 1,2,3!' he called and they all slid into the black and turbulent sea. The cold hit him and took his breath away despite him knowing it would. He looked left and right until he counted 5 heads in the water beside him.

'Raft up!' called Taff, and they all swam into a circle using their drybags as extra buoyancy.

They could only watch as Walter and the Peregrine sailed away from them and left them to fight the cold sea to survive.

'By fuck it's cold,' said Joe, his teeth chattering.

'We've been in the water 3 minutes, at this temperature we'll be in trouble in 15,' said Taff.

'Ok, we've got to keep moving. We'll give it 8 minutes then we'll light ourselves up. Let's just hope Walter can get rid of them. I can see they're alongside now.'

#

Walter shielded his eyes from the spotlight as the Border Force Cutter approached and slowed to pull alongside. They used a loud hailer to call to him. 'This is Her Majesty's Cutter Valiant. You aboard Peregrine, please show yourself and prepare to come alongside.'

Walter waved from the wheelhouse then went on deck to throw a line to the larger vessel. 'Good evening officers, to what do I owe the pleasure?' he said to the three uniformed men looking down at him.

'We tried to hail you by radio, do you have comms issues?'

'Actually yes. My radio is acting up, I stupidly don't have a spare fuse aboard,' said Walter.

'What do you need?' asked the older of the officers.

'A 5 amp fuse, it blew before, there's obviously an issue and my repair guy thought he'd fixed it,' said Walter, shrugging his shoulders.

'Standby, I'll grab you one of our spares,' said the older officer.

'Very kind.'

'You're sailing solo? Where are you off to tonight sir?' asked the younger officer craning his head to look through Peregrine's cabin portholes.

'I'm heading for Boulogne,' said Walter cheerfully, 'I have a date for petit dejeuner with a rather lovely French lady.'

'You're out of Dover?'

'No, Rye. I came this far North to tack back down rather than run straight across these seas. Like me, this old girl prefers a more comfortable journey,' said Walter with a smile.

'It's been rough, right enough. What's with the RIB?' said the officer shining the search light over the empty boat.

'She's a replacement tender, I picked her up this afternoon and brought her in case I missed the tides.'

'You're obviously keen to get to France,' the older officer said.

'If you had met my Jocelyn, you would understand. She is a lady without equal on our side of Le Manche.'

'Want me to take a look at your radio?' asked the older officer holding a pack with a fuse inside.

'It's a simple enough job, I can manage, if that fuse is for me?' said Walter, 'You're welcome to come aboard if you wish, I assume you guys are looking for something?'

'We had a report of a vessel towing a dinghy. Naturally we thought it might be some illegal immigrants trying to make the crossing, or maybe they'd been rescued. We couldn't reach you by radio, so we headed over.'

'I see, oh well sorry to have caused you the unnecessary journey. Personally, I think you should be dropping these people back off in France, it's not right they rock up in England and sponge off the taxpayers. If you've any aboard I'll happily deliver them for you,' said Walter, doing his best Little Englander impression.

'That won't be necessary, but thanks for the offer. There's nobody stupid enough to try to cross illegally tonight so no rescues required. Sorry to have troubled you.'

'No worries, have a good night gents and thank you for your service!' said Walter and turned for the wheelhouse.

'You forgetting something?' came a shout from behind him.

Walter stopped dead, before turning slowly, expecting the worst.

'Your fuse,' said the officer and tossed it to him.

'Thanks again, I'll get fitting it right away.'

'Nine minutes,' said JT, looking at his watch, 'how is everyone doing?'. The cold was hurting now and gripping his drybag was becoming difficult.

'Hanging in here boss,' and similar acknowledgements came from the dark silhouetted faces around him.

'Just another minute to see if Walter can do it, if not we light up and activate the beacons,' said JT. He had been in many life threatening situations but this was different. The idea of drowning at sea rather than in battle just seemed too bizarre to consider.

'They're leaving!' said Taff as he watched the Cutter get under way, 'come on Walter, get a shift on now!'

Walter swung the Peregrine around and headed in the direction he'd last seen the team in the water. He knew the wind and waves would push them North so he looked in that direction. After what seemed like an eternity, he saw the single flash of a torchlight. Racing to that point he turned the Peregrine round in a pirouette to let the RIB drift into the team in the water.

They gratefully grabbed onto the RIB and after struggling with ice cold limbs, they pulled themselves aboard. Walter had put the kettle on to boil some hot water then filled his two thermos flasks, he threw them to the team who were all now suffering from the effects of the cold.

Pushing the throttle forward as much as he dared, he watched anxiously as his wash buffeted the RIB. He knew the team needed to get ashore urgently, not just to catch the ferry but to avoid hypothermia.

French lights were clearly visible at 1 mile out, Walter had brought them closer than he'd planned but he'd had to push things further, 'Good luck guys, see you on the other side,' he called as he cast off the towing line, and the RIB took off under its own steam.

JT gave a cold and tired wave as they bounced away out of sight and toward the beach. He looked at his team as they huddled in the little boat, they were in shit state, he thought. Out of the cold water but still soaked and without the opportunity to move around to warm themselves this was dangerous. They would be on the beach shortly and then they'd be running, quite literally for their lives. Cooky drove the RIB hard and fast with the engine on full throttle.

'Shortest route to the sand Cooky!' shouted JT over the noise of the engine. 'We need to get everybody moving'

'Tide's well in,' said Cooky, 'we won't have too much sand to cover.'

'There are obstructions in the water, remember!' called Taff, as he strained to see ahead of them.

'It's a risk we'll need to take Taff, just get us on the beach please Cooky. Everyone get a grip of your drybags, we have 45 minutes to get to the motorhome and we need to be on that ferry.'

CHAPTER FIFTY-EIGHT

The men all picked up their drybags and clutched them to their chests. They changed positions so that they were on one knee, heads down and leaning against each other in pairs for stability. They were ready to leap out of the boat and get running.

'Two hundred metres,' called Taff, 'One hundr - ' His words were cut short as the boat struck a big concrete anti-tank block that had been invisible among the waves but sat just under the surface. The force of the impact ripped the underside of the RIB apart and violently catapulted the men through the air in a writhing mass of limbs.

JT was thrown around in the rolling tumult of water and sand. He had no concept of which way was up and knew he had to let the wave do its thing with him before he could find the surface. Eventually the wave let him go and he felt the pull of his life vest lifting him. His head broke the water as another wave crashed into him and pushed him further towards the shore. This time he was able to push off the bottom and surface to take a full breath. He looked around and saw figures moving and wading the last few metres through the surf. Gaining his feet at last, he found his drybag and dragged himself ashore. Counting three figures sat on the sand trying to find their breaths, he turned and saw Cooky pulling a body through the surf. JT ran to help and could see it was Rambo he was pulling.

'He's unconscious!' shouted Cooky, 'I think my knee caught him in the head when we hit the water.'

JT hooked his fingers through Rambo's life vest and checked for a pulse with his free hand. 'He's still with us,' said JT. 'Joe!' he shouted, 'get going, bring the motorhome closer.'

Joe, who was the fastest runner in the team, ripped off his life vest and jacket and sprinted off across the sand and onto the road beyond.

After checking Rambo over the team created a makeshift stretcher from life vests and jackets.

'We don't have anything to use as a neck brace so we'll just have to pray he's not suffered any spinal damage. We need to get moving, now.' said JT.

They picked him up and started running up the beach.

CHAPTER FIFTY-NINE

'Some office!' said Easy, looking around the inside of the log cabin taking in the spartan furnishings. He looked at the large wooden farmhouse style table, two dining chairs sat either side. A pair of old easy chairs sat in front of the fireplace which held a wood burner stove. A few utensils hung from the fireplace and a pot and kettle sat on top of the stove. A bed platform was in the corner with a sleeping bag and pillow. 'You sleep here too?' he asked Hamilton.

'It has been known,' said Hamilton.

'I don't mean to be rude, but it's a bit...basic,' said Easy, still looking around.

'This place has everything I need,' said Hamilton with a smile, placing the car keys on the table. He walked over to the bed, undid a catch and dragged it away from the wall. The platform sliding on well-oiled runners.

Easy stood wide eyed as electric light came up from the now visible staircase.

'Follow me,' said Hamilton, as he started down the stairs.

Easy looked at Maxwell who shrugged and gestured for Easy to go first.

At the bottom of the stairs there was a metal door which Hamilton opened using a keypad.

'What is this place?' asked Maxwell, when he reached the bottom of the stairs.

'As I said, this is my office,' said Hamilton, 'a better question might be, what *was* this place?' He looked at his companions before continuing, 'this was until relatively recently one of a number of bunkers which were built during the cold war.'

'I've heard of them' said Easy, 'they're museums and stuff now, right?'

'Yes, some have been opened up to the public,' said Hamilton, 'this bunker was one of three that were built separate to the chain of the better known bunkers.'

'Separate?' asked Maxwell.

'The cold war was a difficult time, both sides had spies operating within each other's intelligence community and military. In short, we never knew who we could 100% trust. I have no doubt the Russians knew the location of all of the bunkers, apart, that is, from this and its sisters.'

'How do you build something like this and keep it a secret?' asked Maxwell, checking the thickness of the steel door.

'We used mine and construction workers that we brought from India and from South Africa. The workers were brought in covered vehicles from a camp so they never knew where they were. Once they had completed their bit of work, they were flown back home and paid handsomely for their troubles. Add in some clever subterfuge to give them the idea that they were working at a specific site of one of the main bunkers and this is the result.'

'Very clever,' said Maxwell.

'Yes indeed,' said Hamilton, 'which is why I secured it for my, or should I say for 'our' use.' He pulled on a power lever and the low sound of fans starting up filled the stairwell. 'I will show you downstairs in a moment but for now I think we should bring the weapons and equipment down here.' He opened another metal door and revealed a walk-in armoury with racks of rifles, sub machine guns and a plethora of military grade equipment.

'You're ready for a war!' said Easy, staring at the weapons.

'Or preventing one,' said Hamilton, and turned to climb the stairs.

CHAPTER SIXTY

Joe drove the motorhome out of the aire, and headed along the coast road. He had run hard for 20 minutes and sweat had formed on his head as his body went from cold to hot. As he drove, he stripped off his wet top and was now bare chested. He was still in his wet trousers and had put a plastic bag on the driver's seat which squelched as he leaned into a corner he was taking as fast as he dared.

Three miles down the road he saw them in his headlights, running in tight formation and carrying Rambo between them. He stopped and helped lift Rambo aboard then tended to him on one of the rear bunks as the others stripped and changed.

'I'll look after him now,' said Posty, and started stripping off Rambo's wet clothes as Taff took over driving and did a seven point turn using both verges.

'Floor it Taff,' said JT, as he pulled a sweater over his head.

Joe sat on the bunk beside Rambo and felt the bump that was now obvious over his eye. 'You caught him a good one Cooky,' he said, 'but at least it was his skull and not his eye socket big man. Sure, he'll have had worse butting heads with one of his mountain goats.'

With everyone getting dressed into dry clothes and the heating on full blast they headed for the Port at Calais.

'We're going to be late,' said Taff, for once his jolly demeanour deserting him.

'Keep going, we have to try,' said JT.

'Phone the port and tell them there's a bomb on the boat or something, that'll make them delay it,' suggested Posty, 'they did that regular like, back home.'

'No need,' said JT looking at his phone, 'there's a one hour delay due to the weather. We're going to make it guys, barring another bloody disaster we're going to bloody make it!'

'What about Rambo?' asked Joe, 'he'll have to get through immigration and they won't accept him sleeping in bed.'

'We'll deal with that when we get there,' said JT, 'right now we just have to make sure we get there.'

Forty-five minutes later they followed the ferry signs through Calais and came to a stop at a traffic light beside a hotel. JT had an idea and told Taff to pull over. He jumped out of the motorhome and ran into the hotel reception.

'Excuse me, do you speak English?' he asked the startled receptionist.

'Yes, of course. What can I do for you Monsieur?'

'I need some Pastis,' said JT, pulling a 50 euro note from his pocket. I promised my wife some and I've just read on the ferry website that it's out of stock on board. Can you help me please?'

The young woman looked at him and then at the 50 euro note. 'We are not supposed to sell by the bottle Monsieur.'

JT pushed the money into her hand, 'Please no one will know, you can buy some from the supermarket tomorrow and replace it, no one will miss it before then.'

She looked at him and then nodded and walked out from behind her desk to the bar. She returned with the bottle wrapped in a bar towel and handed it to him.

'Merci beaucoup!' called JT over his shoulder, as he ran back out to the motorhome.

Back aboard the motorhome he splashed some of the strong smelling aniseed pastis on Rambo's sweater and in his hair. Then passing it around the team he told them to take a drink or rinse their mouths out. Taff didn't have any as he was driving.

'We'll tell them we've been on a stag doo and Rambo's pissed,' he explained, 'anyone actually like this stuff?'

'I used to drink Pernod with blackcurrant until I made myself sick with it when I was 15 or something,' said Joe, 'smell of it still makes me a bit queasy.'

'It's meant to be drunk with water but it's still pretty rank,' said JT, 'importantly though, it stinks, so hopefully it will convince the border guards. There's British as well as French guards so it has to work twice.'

Taff drove them into the dock where they were ushered through the customs and passport control lines beside the lorries and trucks. As they approached, they moved Rambo from his bunk to one of the passenger seats and fastened his seatbelt.

Joe sat in the adjacent seat and placed a pillow between them with Rambo's head resting on it. He was glad when Rambo groaned, it was the first sound he'd made since he was in the water and Joe took it as a good sign.

As the vehicle in front of them completed its checks and was waved through, Posty started singing 'Fields of Athenry', Joe joined in and they did their best to sound a bit drunk.

The French official took the six passports and scanned each of them in turn.

'My colleague will check your vehicle; do you have any other passengers on board?'

'No, just us six,' said Taff, smiling at the man, but getting no friendliness in return.

'Open all external lockers please,' said a young French woman in a uniform and fluorescent raincoat.

Taff got out of the vehicle and walked round, opening each of the several doors and hatches in turn.

'Now I look inside,' she said.

'Help yourself ma'am,' said Taff, opening the side door for her.

She stepped up into the motorhome and her colleague stepped onto the first step so as to block the doorway. 'Your friend, he is ok?' she asked looking at Rambo.

'He's fine darlin', just a bit bevvied, you know, drunk.' said Joe using his hand to mimic drinking from a glass.

'He has an injury?' she said pointing to her head, 'Does he need a Doctor?'

'Naw he's fine, he fell out the door when he was going for a piss and bumped his head. He's fine though, and we'll keep an eye on him until we get him home to his boyfriend.'

'D'accord,' she said, and looked in the toilet and under the beds. 'You have a safe journey home gentlemen.' She stepped out of the motorhome and Taff climbed in, closing the door behind him.

Taff got into the driver's seat, waved to the officials and drove off toward the holding area where he was directed into a lane behind a removal truck.

'Boyfriend?' asked Cooky.

'Ach, you know how we're all modern men and all,' laughed Joe, 'besides, gay men are perceived as less threatening, so it was to put her at ease, if you know what I mean?'

'If you say so.' Said Cooky, 'have you ever met that boxer in the Marines, the gay guy. He's a monster and I doubt there's many who wouldn't find him threatening!'

'Aye, very true, I saw him leather the American Navy heavyweight champion guy in an exhibition match in Gibraltar a couple of years back,' said Posty.

'What do you call him again?' asked Taff, joining in the conversation.

'Anything he fucking wants!' said Posty, and they all laughed until they were stopped by a groan from Rambo.

'You alright there Rambo?' said Joe, looking at his friend.

'What the hell happened, my head feels like I landed on it!' he opened one eye and screwed up his face in pain.

'It was Cooky that landed on it, or at least his big bloody knee did,' said Joe, winking at Cooky.

'I just remember the RIB hitting something and getting thrown through the air.'

'That about sums it up, your head met Cooky's knee and you've been out cold since.'

'Then thanks whoever saved me, I owe you one.'

'You've saved all of us often enough Rambo, nobody is keeping score, but Cooky pulled you to shore,' said JT, relieved to see him conscious. 'We'll get the medical staff on the ferry to do a concussion check on you, it'll be good to have it recorded. Shit, I almost forgot, let's get a quick photo with the Calais sign, so I can send it to Paddy!'

Chapter Sixty-One

'This was the communications room,' said Hamilton proudly showing his guests around his bunker, 'I've had the system updated and it links me directly to GCHQ, the Ministry and all of the Secret Service Departments.' He looked at Maxwell, 'Obviously the Police systems are available too. Because it is part of the internal system it doesn't show up on external threat tests and my pet boffin has several "back doors and cul-de-sacs" in play should anyone come fishing.'

'This is some set up,' said Easy, admiring the hardware in the room.

'Thank you, I had a feeling you might approve Ezekiel. This could be our operations room for future missions but I would think we might benefit from a forward operating vehicle too. That is something you might wish to assist in the development of? Ferdinand, my afore-mentioned pet boffin, would build it but he doesn't work front line duties. That, I think, is a role you are well suited for.'

'You said about learning about hacking?'

'Yes, I can have you trained by GCHQ's best, they are pretty amazing and give the North Korean's a run for their money.'

'I'd like that,' said Easy, as he sat down in a swivel chair and pushed himself in a circle.

'Where does the budget come from for all of this?' asked Maxwell.

'It is a self-funded project you could say, although the taxpayers made an initial contribution.'

'Self-funded how?'

'Much like the money the team just secured, we have seized funds from criminal enterprises and even from unfriendly Governments, all of which has been used to facilitate our operations,' explained Hamilton.

'That's the first time you've used the term *we*, who else apart from your boffin is involved?'

'We are a very small group of like-minded individuals with overlapping spheres of influence. Our efforts have until now, largely been surveillance and electronic disruption based. Now, we have the opportunity to operate in the physical world and to take the fight to those who would do harm.'

'You've had this all planned for a while then?'

'This is the work of years. We have hired in help from time to time when timeous interventions have been required, but our own elite team, ready to deploy both here at home and to wherever they can make a difference, that has been something I have imagined and coveted for a long time.'

'Assassinations?'

'Serious threats have been neutralised, yes, but only when necessary to protect others.

CHAPTER SIXTY-TWO

The nurse aboard the ferry finished checking over Rambo. She said he possibly had a mild concussion and should go to hospital when back in the UK for tests. After promising he would go to hospital as soon as possible Rambo joined the others in the lounge and ordered coffee.

'Get the all clear?' asked Cooky.

'She said my head looked like I'd been hit by a car. I told her you were more of a truck!'

'Just glad you're okay man,' said Cooky.

'I'm fine, will just have a headache for the next couple of weeks,' Rambo smiled and enjoyed the smell of the coffee, especially as it masked the smell of the alcohol from his sweater.

JT read them the reply from Paddy after he'd sent him the team photo taken at the ferry port in Calais; "Welcome back to blighty. Give me a call tomorrow, there's legal trouble at Home".

'What's the plan when we land then boss?' asked Taff.

'We need to drop the motorhome back off and we can get the 4x4s, then we need to go see Hamilton and Rory. We need to know none of the last couple of days can be linked back to us. Once we've established that then I think it's time we headed back to Barking. We have some gear back at the flat to collect. After that we're going Home.'

'I thought the Brass said we had to stay away?' said Taff.

'It's time to force their hand Taff, they either court martial us with their non-existent evidence or we get back to work.'

'What about the third option?' said Taff, 'Mr Hamilton made a good case for going off-book.'

'We all know guys making lots of cash as PMCs,' said JT, referring to Private Military Contractors – ex services, often ex special forces – who worked as private security or to augment US troops in deployments, 'but I'm not sure Hamilton's plans involve babysitting engineers and executives in Baghdad.'

'There's also the question of 12 million quid,' said Taff.

'Yeah, I don't know what we're going to do with that.'

'I've been thinking about those kids we rescued, will Rory or Hamilton be able to find out what happens to them?'

'I would think so, Hamilton seems to have access to everything and everyone.'

'That woman with the two little kids, I reckon we should give her some money to help her out, get back on her feet, someplace decent like.'

'Good idea, we'll work it out Taff, there's plenty to help them all out.' JT sat back and reclined his seat then closed his eyes. After every mission he played back a film reel of events in his head. Preparation, Intel, Planning, Execution, he called it his PIPE dream. He ran through the last couple of days in his head, considering what had gone right, what had gone wrong and what they could have done better.

This willingness to critique his own and his team's performance kept them alive.

It was 0630 when the motorhome rolled off the ferry and joined the long line of vehicles making their way out of Dover Port.

'Boss, are we stopping at Sally's?' asked Posty.

'Of course, wouldn't want to miss out on a full English.'

Twenty minutes later they found a parking place for the motorhome and trudged wearily into Sally's cafe. At 0700 the place would be quiet enough they'd all get a seat. By 0800 there'd be a queue outside.

'Jesus, look what the cat dragged in!' said the effervescent Sally, stepping out from behind the counter as they walked in, 'Haven't seen you boys in months, been deployed then?' Sally was the mother of a trooper who had been killed in Iraq, and the team made an effort to stop by whenever they could.

'Hi Sally, we're just back from training in France so thought we'd come see you,' said JT giving her a hug, 'how've you been?'

'Run off my bloody feet as usual but can't complain, business is good and it keeps me busy, you know.' She looked over the team assessing them and her gaze fell on Rambo's swollen and freshly bruised head, 'What the hell happened to you?' she asked him.

'I was hit by a truck!' said Rambo, pointing at Cooky with a grin.

'It was an accident!' exclaimed Cooky.

'Well take a seat, I'll bring you tea and coffee and something for that head.'

The team pulled two tables together and sat down. A moment later Sally appeared with a dish towel filled with ice, 'get that on there, kid.' and she placed two paracetamol in front of him. 'You know the drill, headaches or nausea you get to the hospital, and no mucking about, that truck caught you a good one.'

'It was an accident!' exclaimed Cooky, with a big toothy smile.

'What about you Posty, Cooky been scratching your face?' asked Sally, as she looked him over more closely.

'I had a fight with an angry cat Sal, apparently it thought I had mice living in my beard,' said Posty with a grin.

'Who sewed you up?' she asked inspecting the stitches.

'All my own work, wouldn't let any of this lot near me with a cotton bud never mind a needle,' he told her with a wink.

'Well, you've done a sterling job. Next time you're down this way you can knock me up some curtains for my caravan!' she returned his wink.

Terry the cook came out of the kitchen, and shook everyone's hands, 'Good to see you lads, you should've called ahead I'd have had it on the table waiting for you.' Terry was a veteran of Iraq and lost half his leg to an IED. His cheerful smile never wavered and his prosthetic leg was no hindrance to a man who had run several marathons wearing it.

'Good to see you Terry,' said Taff, 'How's the family?'

'All good thanks Taff mate. Mabel is walking now and getting into everything, I'd show you a photo but she's still an ugly wee brute,' he laughed even as Sally clipped him round the ear.

'My god-daughter is not ugly!' she said, and pushed him back toward the kitchen, 'Six breakfasts, with extra black pudding for my Joe, and hop to it!' They all laughed at the well-worn and much loved joke.

Sally produced a tray with two tea pots and a big cafetiere of steaming hot coffee. 'Help yourselves,' she said, 'you're all having orange juice and no arguments, you look as if you need it. Jonny, sorry I don't have none of your silly tea, you'll have to slum it.' She bustled off and into the kitchen to fetch the orange juice.

'Good old Sally, she takes better care of me than my Ma,' said Posty, as Cooky handed him a mug of tea.

'Your Ma always takes good care of me when I'm over,' said Joe.

'Probably because she actually likes you, unlike me, who she just tolerates!' laughed Posty.

JT watched with satisfaction as the team fell into their usual banter, despite their physical and mental exhaustion from the last few days, they were in good spirits.

A couple of workmen came in and ordered take away filled rolls and cast an eye over the team but quickly looked away when Taff and Cooky made eye contact with them. They were a formidable looking bunch and all needed a shave and a good wash. JT rubbed at his beard as he took them all in, a few cuts and bruises but otherwise they had gotten through the last couple of days unscathed.

They had fought and eliminated two groups in off-book situations, despite their best efforts to conceal their involvement he couldn't ignore the nagging feeling that it would come back to haunt them some day. Maybe someday soon.

CHAPTER SIXTY-THREE

Hamilton lifted the whistling kettle from the Aga in his kitchen, half a mile from the village of Faversham. He had been in the kitchen for a couple of hours as he let his guests sleep. Removing the loaf tin from the proving drawer he checked that his bread dough had risen sufficiently then, opened the top oven door and placed it inside before quickly nudging the door closed with his hip.

He sat down at the breakfast bar and poured himself a cup of tea, before switching on the radio. Listening to Classic FM he tapped his fingers along with the piano as if he was playing along with Ludovico Einaudi.

The kitchen window overlooked the rear garden, he watched the Robin land on top of a headstone, bouncing as it eagerly chirped, to all who would listen, that this was his domain. Hamilton reached and opened the window pushing it open by a few inches. Damp grass and clean country air mingled with the smell of bread from the oven. This was his heaven.

The kitchen door opened tentatively and Maxwell stood in the doorway as if waiting for permission to enter.

'Come on in Detective Inspector, I see you found the shirt I left for you, take a seat and I'll fix you some tea. Or no, you are a coffee man, aren't you?'

'Good morning, if you have coffee, I'd love some thanks.'

'Coming right up. Is young Ezekiel still sleeping?'

'I heard him on the phone to his Aunty, he'll be down shortly I should think.'

'Did you sleep well?'

'Like a log,' said Maxwell, 'it's so quiet here, it makes me realise how noisy London is but you become immune to it.'

'Yes, I love it here, it certainly is very peaceful.'

The Robin landed on the windowsill and hopped onto the breakfast bar where it started pecking at a little pile of seeds Hamilton had left for him. Seeing Maxwell notice he said, 'Robin is my friend and neighbour, he keeps an eye on the place when I'm not around.'

Maxwell watched intrigued as the little wild bird stood proudly and without fear. The kitchen door opened behind him and the little bird flew out of the window as Easy came in.

'Good morning, Ezekiel,' said a smiling Hamilton, 'can I offer you some tea or coffee?'

'Eh, no thanks, do you have any juice?'

'I have some apple juice or tomato juice in the fridge.'

'Apple please. I can't believe I've just slept in a church.'

'You slept well?'

'I've never slept in a double bed on my own before, it was lovely. Not like when I shared with my little cousin Adintayo when we were on holiday. I'm definitely getting a double bed when I get my own place.'

'You smoothed things over with your Aunty then?' asked Maxwell.

'Yes, she was a bit angry at first but she just worries about me. I told her I've stayed at Danny's working on a computer project while we look after his Gran. As long as I'm back for school tomorrow it'll be ok,' he looked at Maxwell and then at Hamilton, 'I will be back at school tomorrow, right?'

'Yeah kid, we'll get you back for school,' said Maxwell.

'Ezekiel, I wonder if you might like to come fetch some eggs? Come and I'll introduce you to Sofia and Florence the hens.' Hamilton opened the rear door and walked out followed by Easy.

Maxwell sipped his coffee and watched them walk out into the garden. A few seconds later the Robin returned and hopped in through the open door to stand in the threshold. It looked at Maxwell and chirped at him. 'I bet you're wondering who I am and what I'm doing here, little guy.' The Robin held his gaze, 'well to be honest, right now I'm not sure who I am or what I'm doing here either.'

Maxwell's phone rang and he recognised the number as JT, 'Hey, how was your holiday in France?' he asked.

'Oh, you know, pretty uneventful, rude waiters and a bit wetter than we'd hoped.'

'Il peut de cordes?' asked Maxwell.

'If that means 'it's raining ropes' then no not quite, we were literally swimming, and more than once.'

'Shit, everyone ok?'

'Yeah, we're all sorted now. Where are you guys?' asked JT.

'We're at Hamilton's place, and he's out collecting eggs with Easy for breakfast.'

'Collecting?'

'Yep, long story. How about you guys head for Donnington, it's just off the M2, we're half an hour from there.'

'The traffic is pretty bad, so I'll call when we're getting closer.'

'Pity you can't come here; Hamilton has baked homemade bread and his place is amazing.'

'We've just had breakfast at Sally's, best fry up in Kent. Our Hamilton is just full of surprises, isn't he?'

'He certainly is, there's more than you know. I'll fill you in when we meet,' said Maxwell and clicked off his phone.

'JT?' asked Hamilton, as he walked back into the kitchen.

'Yes, they're on their way up from Dover, I suggested we'll meet them at Donnington. I figured you wouldn't want them coming here.'

'Probably for the best, a motorhome would certainly be noticed but the locals are all very friendly, and none too nosy,' said Hamilton.

'We've got 6 eggs!' said Easy excitedly, looking like a child discovering something new, 'One of them is still warm!'

'Excellent,' said Maxwell, his concern for Easy stealing any emotion from his voice.

'Bread will be ready in 5 minutes, and I'll scramble these up so we can get on our way to meet our Team,' said Hamilton, as he busied himself with a big frying pan.

Maxwell noted the use of "our Team". He knew Hamilton was attempting to use Psychology to persuade him to become part of this "Team". He just couldn't quite work out what it would actually mean.

As they sat down to breakfast, Easy buttered himself a slice of the bread he thought made the kitchen smell like a slice of heaven. 'So, how come you live in a church?' he asked.

'This place was the family business a few years ago. I've inherited it, you might say,' said Hamilton, pushing the sliced bread into the middle of the table.

'You mean it was a holiday let?'

'Not quite, my Grandfather was the minister here back in the day. Like so many rural parishes there aren't enough worshippers to sustain congregations, so the Church of England sold the building. I was lucky enough to be able to buy it. I also own the vicarage and I do rent that out as a holiday let in the village. It employs one of the local ladies as a housekeeper, and the visitors help keep the village pub viable.'

'Don't you get scared being around the old graves and stuff?'

'No, not at all, some of them are my family so it's like a reunion of sorts whenever I'm here.'

'Nice way of thinking about it,' said Maxwell.

'As you know only too well, it is always difficult, in our line of work, to maintain family relationships. This place gives me a link to my family.'

'Our line of work? What is that line of work exactly?' asked Maxwell, still grappling with the realities of the situation.

'We are in the business of keeping people safe, from those who wish to do them harm. Or am I misinterpreting the role of a Police Officer.'

'You can't trust the Police,' said Easy, as he finished chewing some bread and butter, 'I know you're maybe different Mr Maxwell, but there's too many who are corrupt. You can't tell which are the good ones.'

'No offence taken kid. They're poorly paid and overworked so they're vulnerable to corruption, but most are honest and hard working. The majority are good people and want to do the right thing but they're too busy chasing targets and doing paperwork.'

'Which is where we come in,' said Hamilton. 'Without the encumbrance of red tape and a woeful justice system, we can remove the biggest threats and let the Police get back on top of things.'

'So, definitely vigilantes then?' asked Maxwell.

'The word "vigilante", comes from the Latin 'Vigilare' meaning literally 'to keep awake'. The earliest Police Constables were little more than watchmen. Their job was to alert their fellow villagers or townsfolk that there were miscreants about. It was the villagers who meted out punishment. The modern interpretation is one who takes the law into their own hands, or as the movies would have it, *judge and executioner*. I make no apologies for the judgement and execution of monsters.'

'But where does it stop?' asked Maxwell.

'That is a matter of conscience,' said Hamilton, as he stood up from the table and picked up a tablet from its stand. 'Perhaps you might be persuaded by some visual evidence?' He placed the screen on the table and pressed play on a video. 'This is a compilation of images, taken from CCTV and some found on computers after the event. This man is named Nathaniel M'bumba, he was sentenced to 5 years in prison at the third attempt after two mistrials. M'bumba was a drug dealer who took over a patch in Liverpool and took to torturing his rivals, by attaching electrodes to them. When that didn't work to his satisfaction, he turned his attention to their children. The next image you will see is of 3 year Chantelle Sommers, M'bumba as you are about to see, branded her by heating his knife on the hob until it was red hot then pressed it onto her face.'

'Oh for fuck's sake!' said Maxwell.

'Is the little girl ok?' asked Easy, concern written over his face.

'She survived, if that is what you mean, but her life will never be the same. Her little brother Conner was not so fortunate. M'bumba started enjoying himself and used the hot knife repeatedly on Conner's little body. The video shows him scream the first time and then he goes quiet, as his little brain tries to make sense of what is happening to him, mercifully perhaps, his little heart could not cope and he died before the rest of the injuries were inflicted upon him post mortem. The father of the children, it turns out, owed M'bumba £50.'

'He's in prison now?' asked Easy.

'Yes, he is currently enjoying 5 years of his life and infamy in Walton Gaol, or Liverpool Prison as it is now known.'

'5 years for killing a child and maiming another, how?' asked Maxwell.

'His conviction is for being found in possession of Class A drugs for the third time. The Police couldn't find any witnesses willing to testify against him. Even the parents refused to testify. Young Chantelle is now in care.'

'But you have the videos.'

'Yes, we obtained the videos but they can never be used in evidence as we obtained them without warrant and through channels we cannot disclose publicly – for obvious reasons.'

'Animals like him should be put down,' said Easy.

'I quite agree Ezekiel, I quite agree.'

'I take it there's more?' said Maxwell.

Hamilton went on, 'This next man is Steven Shepherd. Shepherd is or rather was a member of a splinter group from the Ulster Volunteer Force called The Red Hand Brigade. Shepherd's speciality was explosives, improvised car bombs to be precise. One of his targets was the Head Teacher of a Catholic Primary School in Coleraine. Shepherd decided that it would be better to detonate the bomb remotely rather than the usual tilt switch. He sat and watched the Head Teacher walk a group of pupils past his car on the way to the waiting school bus. He later bragged that he had killed "14 little Fenians" along with 2 teachers.' He looked at Maxwell as the images of the bomb scene came up on the screen.

'I remember that incident,' said Maxwell, staring at the screen.

'The reason I am showing you this, rather than one of the hundreds of other terrorist atrocities, is that Shepherd was under surveillance. The Police and MI5 were well aware of him but were trying to compile evidence that would stand up in court. The children and the teachers died because they were failed by our judicial system.'

'I remember Shepherd, it was after my time working in Belfast, but I remember the case. He committed suicide before he could be arrested.'

'It was not suicide. We were too late to prevent the bombing in Coleraine but we made sure it was his last.'

'You killed him?' asked Easy.

'Yes, we did. We found plans for another two bombs targeting school teachers. Those teachers and probably some children, were saved because we made sure he couldn't harm anyone else.'

'I swore an oath to uphold the law, I can't just ignore that,' said Maxwell.

'Did you know how inept the system is at times before you took that oath?'

'No, but that's not really the point, is it?'

'I have something else to show you,' said Hamilton, pressing play on another video, 'This man is Murad Yousef Al Kharmin, do you recognise him?'

Maxwell shook his head, 'No, I don't think so.'

'This next man and woman are Syed and Fatima Hossein. They are a husband and wife team who work for Al Kharmin. You don't recognise them either, I see.'

'No, I don't,' said Maxwell.

'The next person you will definitely recognise.'

'What the hell is this?' shouted Maxwell, getting angry.

'And this house?' asked Hamilton, maintaining his same level tone.

'It's my Mother and that is her house. Now what the fuck is going on Hamilton?'

'Bear with me here please. All will become clear. When we met the other day, I had some background run on you, as you would expect.

Something that hadn't come across my desk previously was brought to my attention. Al Kharmin is better known as *Jihadi Joe* and he is the leader of Al Tawbah.'

'Okay, now I know who you're talking about. What has this to do with my Mother?'

'You have been investigating Al Tawbah and their infiltration of the Masjids in North London for some time now, haven't you?'

'Yes, but I never identified Al Kharmin, hence *Jihadi Joe*.'

'Al Kharmin on the other hand was able to identify you, and at least 2 of your colleagues. He has very recently managed to identify your Mother and her house too. Which brings us to the Hosseins. They are the Al Tawbah hit team, thought to have been responsible for several murders in Yemen and Syria. We tracked them down to Brussels and then they showed up in London 5 days ago.'

'Why doesn't my Department know about this, and what does this have to do with my Mother.'

'If your Department knew, then our hands would be tied.'

'We could arrest them.'

'You would have to compile evidence before you could arrest them. The locus of the murders they are suspected of are in Countries with whom we do not have extradition treaties or intelligence sharing protocols. They appear to have followed you to your Mother's. I assume your anti-surveillance techniques have kept your own address secure.'

'Your people are looking after my Mother, I take it?'

'MI5 are plotted up there but they, like everyone else, are thin on the ground.'

'This feels like an almighty coincidence and you are telling me this so that I join the team and we take them out?'

'I am telling you this as I thought you should know,' said Hamilton, he stood up and moved the tablet. 'We can discuss the situation with JT and the Team when we meet. Perhaps you should call your Mother?'

'To say what, there's some mad Islamists following you to get to me? Or take a look outside your window, there's a man watching your house?'

'Detective Inspector, simply, if it was my Mother, I would want to call to check on her. Meantime I can access the live feed from those with eyes on the Hosseins, I can see from the GPS pin that they are currently in Winchester Road. Your Mother lives at number 31, I understand.'

'Let me see that!' said Maxwell, snatching the tablet. The screen was split in four with an image of a grey Ford Mondeo parked in the street and a Middle Eastern couple sat in the car. The next image was of the rear of the car and a wider street view, he recognised his Mother's house and her car parked outside. There was an image of the rear of his Mother's house with the camera partially obstructed by the leaves of a tree, it looked as if the camera had been placed in a hurry and gave a less than optimal view. The last image was from a camera looking directly into the front room and he caught his breath as he saw his Mother sitting in her favourite chair by the fire reading a newspaper. She would be doing the crossword or sudoku, he knew. 'There's no way they can be arrested then?' he said finally.

'You would know better than I, but as yet they have not committed a crime. Merely sitting in a car is not an offence. We could manufacture a reason for uniform officers to be in the street to chase them off, but we always run the risk of losing them. That could of course lead to all sorts of problems.'

Maxwell put his elbows on the table and held his face in his hands. After a few seconds he said, 'Okay, okay, I'm in this whether I like it or not already. I shot and killed a woman yesterday. It was in self-defence but that doesn't hold water since I just left the scene of the crime and didn't report it. I'm not comfortable with this by any means, but I understand why you're doing what you're doing.'

'What *we* are doing, Detective Inspector. We will be a team, and despite your reservations I assure you we will always be the good guys.'

'First up, you can go back to calling me Rory or Maxwell if you prefer, my Police rank isn't appropriate in the circumstances.'

'Very well Rory it is,' smiled Hamilton.

'Second, I'll want safeguards put in place to protect Easy here. He's still a kid.'

'I'm 16,' said Easy indignantly, 'I'm not a kid anymore. Yesterday I killed a man, and I'd have killed more if I had to. I'm not a kid.'

'Perhaps the apposite nomenclature would be *young man*?' offered Hamilton, 'Rory is quite correct to be concerned for your welfare and I,' he looked at Maxwell, 'and the team, will ensure you are looked after. As I mentioned previously, I will see to it that you receive training and equipment that will allow you to make full use of your skills. Your role will however, be as far removed from the front line as possible.'

CHAPTER SIXTY-FOUR

As the motorhome drove into the village hall car park, JT spotted the Range Rover parked behind the row of recycling bins and a bottle bank. He pulled in beside them and nodded to Maxwell who he could see was not happy.

They all alighted from the vehicles and after hellos and hand-shakes, they walked across the football pitch beside the village hall and made their way to the picnic tables beside the stream.

'There are no cameras in the village, and only 12 houses so we're unlikely to be disturbed,' said Hamilton as he saw JT and the team looking around.

'Good choice,' said JT as he took a seat. 'What's happened?' he asked Maxwell.

'Someone is sitting outside my Mother's house looking for me.'

'Who?' asked JT.

'A couple – literally a couple - of Islamists. It seems I've been getting too close and they either plan to take me out or scare me off. The former being the more likely.'

'Are your guys going to arrest them?'

Maxwell glanced at Hamilton and shook his head, 'Sadly not, until they've committed a crime, they can't be arrested.'

'Okay, so what's the plan?' asked JT.

Maxwell looked again at Hamilton, 'That's what we have to discuss.'

'You're thinking we go in and take them out?' asked JT, 'In London?'

'I don't know yet,' said Maxwell with a sigh, 'I just need to make sure my Mother is safe.'

'And you,' said JT.

Hamilton took his opportunity to steer the conversation, 'Perhaps it's time we decided on how we intend to proceed more generally first. We said we would convene when you chaps came back from France. I take it you've had time to discuss the matter fully whilst travelling?'

'We need to know what's happening with the case against us. We are still soldiers and part of the Regiment. I had a message telling me there's 'legal trouble' waiting for us and we really need to clear our names.'

'Ah yes, I have some more information on that. My understanding is that they intend to Court Martial you all on charges of Murder of civilians in Afghanistan. They claim to have witnesses to testify against you but the witnesses are insisting on being given asylum here in the UK. The alternative would be for you to resign your commissions, which I understand your Commanding Officers would reluctantly accept.'

'But we did nothing wrong!' said Joe, banging his fist on the table.

'I believe you, sincerely I do,' said Hamilton holding up a placatory hand, 'you are, however, something of a political tool. The Governments both here and in Washington are rather weak and their shambolic handling of the withdrawal from Afghanistan is being used to weaken them further. It would be politically expedient for them to point the finger at yourselves as part of the reason to withdraw. It's nonsense of course, but they are feeding you to the media and the bloodsucking Human Rights Lawyers for their own ends.'

'What do you suggest?' asked JT stony faced.

'That is not for me to decide, nor advise. You must make your own decisions in this matter. I can only share with you what I know. There is of course a question of honour, for you as individuals as well as your Regiment, but there is also the practical consideration of what would happen should there be a trial by Court Martial.'

'The truth would have to come out in a Court Martial,' said JT although he already had doubts that this was true.

'The facts would come out, but only certain facts are supported by evidence and they hold the keys to the evidence.'

'So, you think we should resign?' asked Taff.

'As I said, only you can decide,' said Hamilton and looked at his phone. He looked at Maxwell and said, 'They're out of the car, apparently, they've done a walk through reconnaissance of your Mother's house.'

'Shit!' said Maxwell, 'I need to get over there. It's me they're looking for.'

'Then we need to come up with a plan,' said Hamilton.

'We can sort out our situation later,' said JT, 'right now, let's focus on Rory's mum.'

CHAPTER SIXTY-FIVE

Four hours later, and with the MI5 agents stood down, Cooky rode a bike up Winchester Road as Taff drove a 4x4 in the opposite direction. They timed their progress to meet when they were just in front of Hossein's Ford Mondeo. As planned Cooky made his bike wobble and he fell in front of the 4x4 immediately adjacent to the Mondeo. Taff jumped from the vehicle and went to see to Cooky.

The Hosseins watched from their car and while their attention was diverted Posty opened the rear door and pointed a pistol at the startled couple. At the same time, JT Got out of the rear of the 4x4 and climbed into the rear passenger side of the Mondeo.

Cooky got up and rode away on the bike while Taff got back into the 4x4.

'Follow that car.' said JT as he pressed the barrel of his browning into the back of the female driver's neck, 'both hands on the wheel.'

Posty had his gun poking the male in the passenger seat in the ribs, 'put your hands behind your head and grab the headrest.' When the man did so Posty slipped handcuffs courtesy of Maxwell on the man's wrists securing him to the headrest.

The female started the car and tried to alter her position to see JT in the rear view mirror. He poked her hard in the head with his Browning. 'Eyes front and get driving Fatima.' He saw her flinch at the mention of her name.

'Who are you?' said the male from the passenger seat.

'Mouth shut!' said Posty, jamming his gun further into the man's ribs.

They drove on in silence and followed the 4x4 until it eventually turned into a car park. The Hosseins were transferred to the motorhome and searched before they were bound and gagged. They were trussed up with their hands and feet behind them and laid on the bottom bunk, with Joe detailed to watch over them, as the motorhome started up and drove out of the car park. Posty fixed false number plates to the Mondeo and they drove off in a convoy.

Hamilton directed them to meet him at a car tyre depot in Lewisham and was waiting with the big roller doors open as the vehicles drove into the building and the rollers doors closed behind them.

'All went smoothly, I take it?' asked Hamilton.

'Exactly as planned,' said JT.

'Where are they?' asked Maxwell keen to see the people who were targeting him.

'Gimme a sec,' said JT. He went into the motorhome and after adjusting the restraints, dragged the male from the motorhome and sat him on the depot floor.

The man sat blinking as Maxwell ripped the tape off his eyes. He didn't react when his wife was un-ceremoniously dumped down beside him.

'What is your name?' asked Maxwell.

The man gave him a dismissive look then looked around at his surroundings as best he could. 'You know who I am.' He said in a strange Americanised accent.

'Do you know who I am?' asked Maxwell.

'I want a lawyer,' said the man.

'I asked you a question, do you know who I am?' Maxwell moved closer to him as he asked. Hossein did not flinch.

'You are a policeman, and a police man who will be a good boy and call me a lawyer.' He looked Maxwell in the eye and tilted his head as he gave a faint hint of a smile.

'So, you know who I am, that's good. Why were you on Winchester Road?'

'It's a free country, we can go where we please.'

'I'll ask you one more time, why were you on Winchester Road?'

'Fuck you, you Infidel pig, I will not answer your questions. Now get me a fucking lawyer. It's my rights!' Hossein stared hard at Maxwell so was taken by surprise as Joe clamped a red jump-lead cable to his ear. The serrated metal teeth of the clamp drew blood as the delicate skin of the ear tore.

'We'll see about that!' said Joe in his ear as he passed the black cable in front of Hossein's face to make sure he knew what was happening.

Hossein laughed a forced laugh and said, 'You think you can frighten me? Assad's boys tried to torture me for weeks but I told them nothing.'

Maxwell nodded to Joe who attached the black cable to the opposite ear.

'You are bluffing!' said Hossein with less confidence than he tried to portray.

'Last chance,' said Maxwell, 'What were you doing in Winchester Road?'

'Fuck you!' said Hossein, puffing out his chest and trying to make himself appear bigger.

'Go ahead,' said Maxwell to Joe.

A flick of a switch sent the current racing through Hossein who jolted violently and curled up into a ball until Joe turned the power back off.

'Is that the best you've got? You know this will cost you your job, right?' he said grinning as he sat himself back up.

Maxwell nodded to Joe who sent Hossein into a series of spasms until a clamp came loose from his ear. The smell of burning flesh filled the area as part of an earlobe sizzled in the clamp.

Hossein took longer to recover this time and was drooling as he tried to sit back up. He composed himself as he looked at his wet trousers where he'd involuntarily wet himself.

'More?' asked Maxwell.

'You cannot torture me to make me tell you anything, you are weak but my faith makes me strong!' Hossein tried again to puff out his chest, his head was sweating and his cheeks flushed red with adrenalin.

'Do you know what? I think I believe you,' said Maxwell. 'But I think deep inside you want to tell me, don't you? You want to tell me why you were outside my Mother's house.'

Hossein laughed, 'Ah yes, your Mother. I look forward to raping the whore who made you, her bastard son. I will laugh when she begs me to stop.' He looked at Maxwell for a response, expecting a kick or punch to come his way.

Instead, Maxwell bent over toward him and unclamped the jump lead. 'Yes, you do like hurting women, don't you? All of those Yazidi women who you and your friends raped repeatedly. Some of them died from their injuries, but they were the lucky ones, weren't they?'

'God provides us with these infidel women, they are all whores, it is not rape when they are not real Muslim women!' Hossein hissed.

'What about Fatima here, is she a real Muslim woman?' asked Maxwell as he attached the jump lead to her ear. Her squeal of pain was muffled as she was still gagged. Maxwell ripped the tape away from her eyes and could see tears forming.

'Don't touch her! She will tell you nothing!' blurted Hossein.

Maxwell picked up the other lead and gestured to Posty to switch on. He brought the clamp to meet its partner attached to Fatima's ear. The sparks flew and she yelped in pain.

Hossein tried to throw himself at Maxwell but his efforts were futile against his restraints. 'Leave her! I will kill you! By Allah I will kill you and your family! I will kill all of your families!' he screamed.

Hamilton stepped out of his Range Rover from where he had been watching the proceedings. 'Syed, my dear chap, please excuse my friends and their treatment of your lovely wife.'

'Who are you?' asked Hossein, his voice still rasping but without the anger.

'I am your ticket to freedom, yours and Fatima's, of course,' said Hamilton smiling.

'What do you want?' asked Hossein, suspicion in his eyes.

'I just want you to confirm something for me,' Hamilton took out his phone and turned it to show Hossein a man's picture. 'Can you just confirm to me that this man is Murad Al Kharmin?'

Hossein looked at the picture and after the briefest of hesitation he nodded, 'Yes, yes that is Al Kharmin,' he said eagerly.

'Wonderful,' said Hamilton, he swiped the screen of his phone then turned it to show another photo. The surprise and recognition in Hossein's face was enough for Hamilton. 'Oh, now, it appears your little attempt at subterfuge didn't quite work out, did it Syed?'

'What do you want, why are we here?' said a dejected looking Hossein.

'Actually, your purpose was to confirm the identity of a man we have been seeking for a number of years. Your friend Murad has killed, and caused to be killed, hundreds of people, including some of the colleagues of my friends here.'

'So now you let us go?' asked Hossein.

'Oh no, now my dear chap, now you die.'

Joe took one of the cables and wrapped it around Hossein's neck. Fatima stared wide eyed as Joe tightened the cables until her husband's head lolled and he lost consciousness.

'You've got him then?' Maxwell asked Hamilton.

'He was picked up outside Finsbury Park Mosque half an hour ago. The triangulation work on this pair's phones led us to him. He came quietly, apparently content that he couldn't be properly identified.'

'What happens to him now?' asked JT.

'He is going to join this lovely couple when their homemade bomb, that they planned to detonate somewhere in London, explodes in their car before they can plant it.' said Hamilton as he walked to his car. 'If you are happy enough to wait here, I will go collect him.' He climbed into the driver's seat and closed the door then wound down the window. 'I was thinking I might bring back fish and chips for everyone, what do you think?'

Chapter Sixty-Six

Posty put the finishing touches to his explosive creation. It was in effect an incendiary device using the three gas canisters from the tyre depot along with an acetylene welding rig, with some gunpowder and plastic bag of syphoned petrol. Using Fatima Hossein's mobile phone as a dummy detonation trigger and instead using a burning candle under a shoelace trigger, he set the candle in place and lit the wick.

He had parked the Mondeo outside but not too close to a former Territorial Army building which was due for demolition. The site had been Hamilton's idea and Joe was happy to see that no-one was likely to be anywhere near it, especially kids.

He was back in the 4x4 driving away before the candle started to melt and the flame grew enough to reach the shoelace. The shoe lace started to melt and stretch as the nylon turned black and shrank away from the flame. After a minute or so the integrity of the lace gave way. The tension released from the shoelace and the candle tilted into the torn rags that sat in the lap of the unconscious Murad Al Kharmin. The flames spread to the rags which had been splashed with methylated spirits as an accelerant. In turn the flaming rags reached the plastic bag filled with petrol and when the bag ruptured the petrol hit the flame and the car was a fireball. The three terrorists inside the car were almost dead by now, the fumes from the gas mixture slowly leaking from the acetylene tank mixing with the butane from the gas canisters would have seen to that. The gunpowder was a belt and braces feature in case the slightly open car windows didn't allow the correct mixture of air and gas. The explosion could be heard from several miles away and Posty silently congratulated himself on a job well done. He knew the forensic guys would sift through the remains and that they would work out it was a crude but effective device. The three bodies, or what was left of them would get identified and logical conclusion would be that they were carrying a Vehicle Borne Improvised Explosive Device and they had become unwitting suicide bombers.

'Good job lad,' said Taff.

'Yeah, the air mix situation was a bit of guesswork but it did the job.'

'There'll be little bits of Jihadi kebab all over that car park.'

'Too right!' said Posty, 'Never feels quite right when it's a woman though.'

'No, I know what you mean, but your lass Fatima was an evil murdering cow.'

'Yeah, I won't lose any sleep over it, just saying.'

'Glad to hear it.'

'I wonder what she'll get now she's a martyr?'

'How'd you mean?' asked Taff looking at him quizzically.

'Well, her hubby and that Al what's his name, they'll get a load of virgins and stuff. I just wondered what women get.'

'Bloody good question lad,' laughed Taff, 'I reckon they'll all be wandering around in Burkas having to clean up after their husbands while they're shagging virgins.'

The two men were laughing as the first sound of sirens reached them.

'Tell you what Taff, those fish and chips Hamilton brought were bloody good.'

'I enjoyed mine too, just needed a pint of something cold to wash it down.'

'I reckon there's some of that Pastis stuff left in the motorhome,' joked Joe.

'You should have used that shit in your bomb lad!' laughed Taff.

CHAPTER SIXTY-SEVEN

In the rear of the motorhome JT was on a call with Paddy. 'Gimme a second, I'm on my way outside, too many ears in here.' said Paddy. JT listened to the sound of footsteps and doors opening and closing. 'Still there JT?'

'I'm here Paddy.'

'How's the Team, all ok?'

'Yeah, we're all fine thanks.'

'You guys have fun in France?'

'You know how it is, cheap wine, lots of cheese, it was a bit wet for my liking though.'

'Well, I have some news that you're not going to like, JT.'

'Give it to me, Paddy.'

'The brass are gunning for you for sure. I've been hearing they're bringing in some hot shot lawyer to get a Court Martial going asap.'

'Yeah, I'd heard something like that.'

'I also heard they've got 3 civilian witnesses, all Afghans who are getting Asylum for testifying.'

'That'll take months Paddy, they must have something else if they're trying to push for it asap.'

'That's the thing, these alleged witnesses are being flown in next week. One of the Colonel's staff told me he was ordered to arrange the flights.'

'Shit, they really are going for it then.'

'I don't get it JT, I saw your debrief reports, it was a good kill, she left you with no choice.'

'Some politicians think there's no such thing as a 'good kill'!'

'Look, I didn't see your bodycam images but the staff at the base must have done at the time you submitted your reports. If they hadn't matched up, you'd have been asked to explain at the time. It's bullshit that the images were 'lost', an entire hard drive just disappeared, my arse!'

'Paddy, we have to drop off this motorhome and then we have some shit to sort out before we come in. We've got the kit to return and I intend bringing it back in person. I'm going to see Colonel Dalgleish and sort this shit out once and for all.' He was referring to Colonel Harry Dalgleish, the highly decorated and well respected Senior Officer in charge at Hereford.

'Glad to hear it, I'll come in with you if you like?'

'Thanks Paddy, might be a good idea in case I lose the plot.'

'That settles it then. When can we expect you?'

'3 days ought to be enough, I'll see you Thursday.'

JT hung up and called Taff, 'Taff, we'll be at the motorhome depot in about 2 hours. Can you and Joe grab the other 4x4 and meet us down there? We can head back to my place and get a decent kip and clean ourselves up.'

'If you throw in a couple of beers, you've got a deal,' said Taff.

'Grab some on the way, I could do with some myself.'

CHAPTER SIXTY-EIGHT

Hamilton and Maxwell dropped Easy back near the edge of his estate.

'You've got to get to school tomorrow and your Aunty will want to know about your weekend. Have you thought about what you're going to tell her?' asked Maxwell.

'Yes, I will start using technical phrases about coding and GPU's. She'll soon glaze over and go back to watching TV until it's time for her to go to church. Maybe I will go with her,' replied Easy.

'Are you religious Ezekiel?' asked Hamilton from the driver's seat.

'Not really, but my Aunty is quite devout, I like the gospel singing, oh and the food.'

'Then enjoy, kid, remember you have my number if you need anything or if you want to talk,' said Maxwell and shook his hand.

'Mr Maxwell,' he began.

'Call me Rory,' said Maxwell.

'Ok, Mr Ma...I mean Rory, but tomorrow you will start looking for Dionne yes? You too, Mr Hamilton?' he said looking back into the car.

'We're already working on it kid,' said Maxwell as he got back into the passenger seat and glanced at Hamilton then back to Easy. 'We'll speak tomorrow, ok?'

'Ok, what time?'

'Whenever we get the chance, kid, don't worry I'll call you tomorrow after school.'

'Ok, bye,' Easy stood and watched the Range Rover drive away then walked around the corner before he started jogging. He cut through the garages and saw Crew B standing smoking beside their mopeds parked outside old Mrs Roberts house. He was still amazed that Mrs Roberts refused to leave there after what had happened to her. He never saw her outside anymore but sometimes he would see a community nurse or social worker going in to see her. Hers was the only house in that row of 4 still occupied and the Crew B were always hanging around there. He stopped for a second and looked at them, then looked at the houses. Something itched in his mind that he couldn't quite grasp.

'What the fuck are you looking at?' the shout startled him and he didn't bother to look to see which of the Crew B had said it.

He set off jogging again and saw Michelle with her little boy. She was holding his hand and carrying a bag of shopping. Her boy's other hand was still bandaged. He felt the colour rise in his cheeks as the anger filled his chest. There was unfinished business here and he knew the Team were the only people who could finish it. He watched as Michelle saw the Crew B guys and abruptly did an about turn walking the long way round rather than have to pass them.

One of the Crew B saw her and gave a wolf whistle, then shouted some obscenities about fucking her.

This had to stop, thought Easy. Maybe now the crooked Police officers were dead, the new ones might make things better. He quickly dismissed the idea and remembered that he couldn't trust the Police. Well maybe Rory, he seemed like one of the good guys but it remained to be seen whether he was true to his word and found Dionne.

Once he'd gone around the ugly concrete and brick block of Pretoria Court, Easy slowed down and walked the last few hundred yards. He was making sure he didn't arrive home to his Aunty out of breath, as she'd worry that he'd been chased.

As he walked through the front door, he heard her singing in the kitchen and could smell that she was cooking spicy jollof rice which was her staple recipe. Thankfully Easy loved it too as he'd already eaten fish and chips. 'Hello Aunty!' he called.

'Come here Ezekiel, let me look at you!' she called back.

He took off his shoes and jacket and walked through into the kitchen. 'Smells good Aunty.' he said.

'Of course, it smells good boy, since when did I make food that doesn't smell good?' she said as she looked him up and down. 'You look different Ezekiel,' she said knotting her brow.

'Really Aunty, in what way?'

'You look older now,' she said, shaking her head slowly, 'I swear you left me the other day a boy, and you've come back a man!'

Easy could see the worry in her face so decided to move the conversation on. 'I thought I might come to church with you tonight, Aunty.'

'Church? You mean to say you don't have homework to pretend you're doing when you're up there playing on your computer?' she asked, giving him a lopsided smile.

'No, I did all of my homework with Danny. We were working on this amazing code, it's pretty cool, we can create a game - '

'Steady on boy, you know I don't understand none of your computer bitcoin stuff. It gives me a sore head trying to keep up,' she smiled at him while pretending to massage her temples. 'Now go and get cleaned up, I can have the Jollof ready for when you come back down. Oh, and wear that nice blue shirt I bought you, if you are coming to church, I want them all to see what a handsome young man I have.'

Easy went upstairs, undressed and turned on the shower. After brushing his teeth properly for what felt like the first time in days, he stepped into the shower and enjoyed the feel of the hot water. He stood for a few minutes just thinking and running through the events of the last few days. There was a link between Dionne going missing, Crew B and the Bad Men, and he was determined to find out what it was. He had been shocked when she wasn't among all of those people they had rescued. It just didn't feel right that she'd vanished without a trace. He could feel it in his blood that she was alive, somewhere, and that she needed his help.

#

Easy hadn't prayed for a long time but when the pastor spoke about seeking forgiveness, he found himself thinking about the man he'd knocked from the roof and killed. He replayed the images he had watched on the screen. The camera on the drone allowing him to fly it with pin point accuracy. The man was standing at the very edge of the roof. He was pointing his gun. He was about to shoot Rory Maxwell. The image getting bigger and bigger. The man turning right at the last moment. Confusion mixed with terror on his face before he flailed his arms, and then tumbled backwards. The drone had crashed onto the grass below, but the camera still worked for a few seconds before it died. It surprised Easy that he cared more about the drone than he did about the man he'd killed, but then he wasn't a man, he was a Bad Man.

CHAPTER SIXTY-NINE

The 4x4s were parked up in their usual spot away from Mayfair and the six men made their way to JT's flat in 1s and 2s via different routes. JT had arrived first after being dropped off closest and was opening his mail. Most of his bills were paid by Direct Debit and statements etc were paperless but there was always an occasional invitation or something in between the junk mail.

He recognised the handwriting straight away. It was hers. It had been such a long time ago that he would receive postcards and letters from Esmé when they first met and had their tentative long distance relationship.

Using his father's silver letter opener, he slit open the envelope and removed the single sheet of writing paper. It was more of a note than a letter, and he was disappointed when he sniffed at the paper that there was no trace of her perfume. Looking at the note he immediately went to the signature. There was no 'xxx' as there always had been. No 'Love always'. Just the flowing curves of her stylised writing. He touched the ink but felt only the dry paper.

Giving himself a shake, he read the note; 'Dear Jonny, Walter tells me you're in a bit of trouble with the Army. I won't say I told you so (but I did!). Anyway, I know you'll be doing your usual thing of bottling it up inside, but, if you need someone to talk to, then you can call me. I don't mean any drunken, love sick 3am calls, but if you want to talk, properly talk, then I'm ready to listen. Esmé.'

There was no return address and maddeningly no telephone number. Did she want him to search for her? Maybe she assumed he had her contact details and that he'd just chosen not to instigate contact? His head hurt as he tried to figure it out. He'd be having words with Walter.

He read it again, and then a third time, trying to decipher what the note was saying. Not the words themselves, the bit between the lines and the meaning woven between the words.

'Hi, honey I'm home!' came Rambo's cheery voice as he walked in the front door.

JT put the note into the desk drawer with the other correspondence to be dealt with another day and slid the drawer closed. He stood up from the desk, then hesitated before he re-opened the drawer and retrieved the note. He scanned it for a last time then folded it and slipped it inside his wallet.

'Boss?' said Rambo after getting no reply.

'I'm in the study Rambo, be right there,' he called, and straightened himself, as he walked out of the study and back to reality.

'I picked up some beers,' said a smiling Rambo, brandishing a box of Thai Singha beer, 'They didn't have original strength so I got this one.'

'Lovely stuff,' said JT, taking it from him, 'how's the head?'

'Ok as long as I don't touch it,' said Rambo, gently fingering the bump.

'Any nausea or headaches?'

'No, all fine Boss, it'll take more than Cooky to finish me off – but don't tell him I said that!' said Rambo with a wink.

'Your secret is safe with me Rambo!' laughed JT as he took the beer into the kitchen and decanted them into the fridge. He came back with two cold bottles of Peroni and handed one to Rambo then the two of them sat in the lounge waiting for the others to arrive.

Half an hour later Taff was the last to arrive and swallowed the first beer he was handed down in one. He let out a satisfied 'Ahhh!' then picked up his second beer while taking a seat on the sofa beside Joe. 'Iechyd da!' he said as he clinked bottles with Joe.

'Slainte Mhath!' replied Joe, with the Scots version of Taff's Welsh.

The others lifted their bottles to toast and everyone took a welcome slug of their beer.

CHAPTER SEVENTY

Hamilton was as good as his word and as soon as he was back at his place in Kensington, he made some calls to get the ball rolling on finding Easy's friend Dionne.

In 20 minutes, he was showered, changed and pouring himself a decent measure of 21 year old Macallan, his favourite whisky.

Ready to relax for the first time in days he switched on his B&O turntable and lifted the stylus on to an album, the static crackles gave him the same warm feeling they always did as the needle found its way and the first piano notes filled the room. He closed his eyes and felt the last few days wash from him as he congratulated himself on a job well done. He knew he almost had the buy-in from all of the team, if he could bring them together, they would be a potent force and make a real difference in the world. They already had.

His phone buzzed and he turned down the volume before answering. 'Yes?' he said, taking a sip of whisky.

'Sir, I have checked the hospitals, morgues and Police custody records as you asked. No record of anyone of that name. There are 3 Jane Does but none match the description of a 16 year old girl.'

'Ok, thank you.'

'There's more sir, I checked to see if there was a passport issued in that name to see if she'd left the country, but there's no record of one. In fact, there's no record of a Dionne Samuels anywhere other than her school.'

'How very interesting,' said Hamilton, intrigued. 'Thank you for your diligent efforts.' He hung up and turned the volume back up and sang along with Nina Simone as she sang 'Ne Me Quitte Pas.' When the track finished, he sat at his desk and switched on his computer, he had some work to do.

That Dionne existed he was of no doubt, her real identity however was a mystery and the solving of that mystery might just help to track her down. He had thought her most likely dead but the possibility of her simply assuming another identity made him reconsider that thesis.

\#

Across London, Maxwell climbed out of his basement pool. He stood dripping onto the poolside as he watched the water jets throwing bubbles and turbulent water out into the pool. He had used his 30 minutes of freestyle to work the tension out of his shoulders and now he felt able to think without the burning anger in his gut.

He had called his Mother and was met with her usual cheery disposition as she was blissfully unaware of the threat she had faced. It was a threat he had brought to her door. Just for doing his job. 25 years he had given blood, sweat and tears to the job. He'd always said he was living the dream. He'd wanted to be a cop since he was a little boy watching The Sweeney with his Grandad. His parents wouldn't have approved but it was his Grandad's favourite, so it became his too.

They'd also loved The Professionals and he'd fantasised about being Bodie or Doyle with their cool clothes and Ford Capri. He wondered whether Hamilton had watched it and thought of himself as a George Cowley figure, the hard but fair boss with a ruthless streak.

What was it about Hamilton that bothered him so much? He knew it was that he couldn't get a proper handle on the man. He was too elusive, too ethereal at times. Having worked with MI5 and MI6 agents in the past he knew that it was how they were trained to be. They were at once present and real and yet not there as they swapped identities like other people changed their socks. Was that who he was thinking of becoming? Was the team that Hamilton was trying to create going to mean a life in the shadows? What would it mean to his identity, what would it mean to who he saw himself as? For so long he was first and foremost a Policeman. Never off duty and everyone who knew him saw him as solid and reliable, the person you turned to when you needed something.

He looked at his phone and saw a message from JT checking he'd gotten home ok. This was what it would be like he realised, always having each other's backs. JT and the guys were trained to a level he could only dream of, what would that mean in practical terms, what would his role be?

So many questions were running through his head that it took him a second to register that his phone was buzzing with an incoming call. 'Hello?' he said, towelling his hair.

'Rory,' said Hamilton, 'we have a problem.'

CHAPTER SEVENTY-ONE

'Please take a seat Detective Inspector, Mrs Wilson will be right with you,' said the friendly school secretary as she reached to answer the phone.

A middle-aged woman bustled into the secretary's office shrugging off her coat and hanging it on a hook behind the door. 'Good morning,' she said, appraising Maxwell and extending her hand. 'Sorry to have kept you. I like to welcome all of the children at the gate on a Monday morning. I believe meeting the Headmistress sets the tone for the week.'

'Good morning, and please don't apologise, it's good of you to see me at such short notice.'

'Not at all, as the Mayor likes to say, we are all one big team when it comes to looking after children,' she gave him a playful look and went on, 'Can't stand the man myself but he talks a good game!' she winked, and guided him to a chair by a low coffee table. 'Coffee?'

'That would be lovely, thank you.'

'I'm slightly addicted myself, so I brought in this old machine from home, the instant stuff they have in the staff room is simply awful.'

'We sing from the same song sheet,' said Maxwell, thinking he already liked this woman. He watched her carry the two mugs of steaming coffee and place one gently on a ceramic coaster on the coffee table in front of him.

Arranging herself in her seat she lifted her coffee and took a sip. Then she changed and her demeanour was all business, 'Now, what can I do for you Detective Inspector Maxwell?'

'Please, call me Rory,' said Maxwell.

'You are in a school Rory; don't you know it's the law that you must address everyone as Mr or Mrs Whoever?'

Rory took a second to realise she was teasing him. She smiled at him pleased with her own little joke, 'then, Rory, you may call me Eleanor, it is after all my name, out in the real world.'

'Thank you, Eleanor. I am here inquiring about one of your pupils.'

'At least it's not one of the staff then, which child?'

'Dionne Samuels.' he said, watching for a reaction.

'Ah yes, Dionne, I remember her, nice girl, not particularly academic as I recall, but sporty.'

'Do you know where she is now?'

'No, she stopped attending school a couple of weeks ago. I can check her attendance record to get an actual date for you.'

'She just stopped attending?'

'Yes, it's not uncommon in our school or many other urban schools. We have a catchment area that means almost all of our children come from a background of poverty, broken homes and crime. Among them are obviously lots of wonderful children and some of them are even keen to get an education. We lose several children a month at times and they are replaced by whichever family moves into the area next.'

'Do they tell you that they are leaving?'

'Usually, yes. There are a number of children who wait until their 16th birthday and then just never come back.'

'Do you tell Social Work that these kids have dropped out?'

'Rory, this school alone submits at least 25 Social Work Referrals every week, sometimes as many as 50. We take our Safeguarding duties extremely seriously. Alas the Social Workers are swamped and only ever action the most serious cases. I doubt very much our referrals, about children of school leaving age no longer attending school, go anywhere other than in the bottom of a filing cabinet.'

'Yes, I can imagine, now you put it like that.'

'May I ask what is your interest in Dionne?'

'I'm afraid I'm not at liberty to say,' said Maxwell.

'Oh, you could tell me but you'd have to kill me?' she said and laughed but the serious look on Maxwell's face cut her laugh short. 'Shit, she's in trouble?'

'Honestly, I don't know, but I'd like to find her so I can find out.'

'Yes, of course.'

'Would you have records of who was in her friend groups, clubs, that sort of thing?'

'Her form teacher might know. Mrs Khan, I can ask her.'

'I'd be very grateful.'

Mrs Wilson got up and went to her desk and after checking a list of numbers, dialled from her phone. A few seconds later she said, 'No reply, I can nip along there and see her in her classroom. I'll be as quick as I can.' She walked out the door and called back over her shoulder, 'help yourself to coffee!'

Rory took out his phone and sent a message to Hamilton. 'She's not been in school for two weeks, obtaining some background now.'

Then he went to the coffee machine and poured himself another coffee. He was tempted to take a biscuit from the glass jar but he hadn't been offered one and he wasn't a thief. He was, among many other things, now a killer, but he wasn't a thief.

10 minutes later Mrs Wilson returned with another woman and a tall skinny young girl with skin so dark it was like coal. 'Detective Inspector Maxwell, this is Mrs Khan who was Dionne's Form Teacher and this is Sha'maa who played Netball with Dionne.'

'Hello, as Mrs Wilson has obviously explained I am trying to track down Dionne Samuels, so anything you can tell me about her will assist me.'

'She wasn't a bad child,' said Mrs Khan, 'not one for school work, more interested in sports, make-up and boys I would say.'

'She had a boyfriend?'

'Not anyone in school I don't think, but I heard her tell one of the other girls that she was with an older boy.'

'Do you remember his name?' asked Maxwell.

'No, sorry, I just put in my notes that there was an older boy, just in case, well, you know?'

'Is she in trouble?' asked Sha'maa.

'What makes you think that?' Maxwell asked, turning to her.

'You're Police for one thing.'

'The other thing?' he asked gently.

'She was with them boys with the scooters.'

'Which boys?'

'They call themselves Crew B, she liked one of them, she said his name was Felix or something.'

'Any idea where Felix lives?'

'All of them Crew B hang about on the Gascoigne. Don't tell no-one I said nothing but they deal drugs and stuff.'

'Stuff?'

'I heard they like robbed people and stuff. They're always trying to get girls to go with them.'

'And do they?'

'Only the stupid ones, or the ones that want drugs.'

'Was Dionne stupid or into drugs?'

'I never saw her with drugs and don't think so. She was real serious about Netball, said she would play for England one day.'

'But was she stupid enough to go with Crew B?'

'All I know is she was really excited about this Felix guy. Then she missed practice and didn't come back.'

'Did you try to contact her?'

'Yeah, she didn't answer her phone. I went round to her house and her cousin said she must have left. She wasn't bothered, she's got another 4 or 5 kids or something.'

'Did Dionne ever call herself anything else?'

'Like what?'

'I don't know, maybe a nickname or something?'

'No, not that I know of.'

'Did she ever talk about her birth parents?'

'Only once, she said her Mum and Dad had been killed in a car crash. She said they'd had loads of money so she got sent to England but her Grandma didn't want her so she ended up in Foster care. I didn't believe her; just thought she'd made up a story because her parents had abandoned her or something.'

'Ok, I understand, thank you very much, you've been most helpful.'

'When you find her, and if she's still alive, tell her I said hello.'

'Why 'If ' she's still alive?'

'She's not the first girl to disappear around here, some of them never come back.'

#

When it was just Mrs Wilson and him left in the office Maxwell said to her, 'can you confirm her last address for me please?'

'You don't have her address?' asked Mrs Wilson, with a quizzical look.

'I have an address for her, but there was no reply at the door, from what Sha'maa said I would have expected someone to be home.'

'I see, let me get it for you.'

A few minutes later he left with an address on a piece of paper and as he got into his car, he called Hamilton. 'The school thought she was an orphan living with a cousin.'

'You don't think so?' asked Hamilton.

'I'm on my way to find out.'

#

Easy was walking between classes when he heard that Sha'maa had been sent to the Head Teacher's office and had spoken to a Policeman about Dionne. He found her outside the gym hall and pulled her aside anxious to know what had been said.

'Why do you want to know?' she asked him.

'She's my friend too and I want to know she's ok,' Easy told her.

'I knew you were sweet on her,' said Sha'maa, blowing a bubble with her chewing gum, 'I saw you waiting for her after Netball.'

'We were just friends, that's all. We walked home together and I helped her sometimes with her homework.'

'Yeah, you're too geek for her, no wonder she preferred Felix.' She looked at him with a mix of ridicule and anticipation of him reacting.

'Felix who?' he asked.

'You know, Felix from Crew B. You must know who Felix is?' she said.

'One of the guys who hangs around on a moped?' asked Easy although he already knew what the answer would be.

'Yeah, that's him. He's the well fit one, always wears designer gear.'

'You think Dionne is with him?'

'I don't know if she is still with him, but I do know she was. Like I told the Detective guy, I saw them together the last day she came to school.'

'Do you know where he lives?' Easy asked her.

'You don't want to go near him or his Crew, I heard they've got guns and everything.' she said, leaning toward him conspiratorially.

'Where would guys like them get guns?' Easy asked her thinking she might be making this bit up to scare him off.

'They're tight with the Kosanians, I've seen them in and out of the bookies, and, my cousin was there when they robbed some bloke up the Broadway. They car jacked him and everything.' She looked past Easy and pointed, 'there he is now, ask him if you don't believe me. Jamal!' she called and waved him over.

'Hey Sham, you alright, heard the cops were here?'

'Yeah, all good, wasn't about me. You know Easy, right?' she pointed to Easy as he stood beside her.

'Yeah, I seen you around, what's up?' said Jamal looking at Easy.

'Tell him about the Crew B having guns when they robbed that guy.' Sha'maa instructed him and she walked away into the changing rooms.

'Not much to tell really, them 'proppa gangsta' now. They was robbing folk just grabbing bags and stuff, but then they got guns. I heard they robbed a jewellers up West, I thought it was bollocks but a few weeks back we was playing football up the park. There was a geezer in an Audi A5, real nice, smart alloys and tints, he was watching his kid play football and they jacked him. He wasn't for handing over the keys but that one they call Felix and another kid pulled guns on him. He just gave them the keys and they drove away in his car.'

'Definitely the Felix guy?' asked Easy, trying not to sound too eager.

'Yeah, but that's like not his real name, right?'

'What do you mean?' Easy asked.

'His real name is like Treyvon or something, but he gets called Felix.'

'Why Felix then?'

'Like Felix the Cat, you know like the movie? He says he's the black cat that attracts all the pussy,' said Jamal rolling his eyes. 'Dude loves himself big time!'

'Do you know where he lives?'

'I heard he used to live in Havana Rise with his Mum but she kicked him out when he was 16 or something. I don't know where he lives now but he's always in the Gascoigne. Him and his mates deal for the Kosanians and their patch is the Gascoigne.'

'What is it they're dealing?'

'Usual shit, Coke, Ketamine, Crack, Spice, you name it they can get it. You looking to score?'

'No thanks. What about girls, do they deal in girls too?' asked Easy.

'You mean like Pimps? Nah, I don't think so, I ain't never seen no prostitutes around them.'

'Have you seen them with any girls?'

'They're always out sharkin' you know? I heard they like the young ones, I've seen them hang about outside school. There's always like some little girls getting fags off them and stuff.' He looked at his watch, 'listen man need to go. If you like really want to find Felix and his crew then check down at the garages or where that old lady's house was torched, they're always around there.' With that he gave Easy a fist pump and took off toward his next class.

#

Maxwell parked his car more than throwing distance from the block of flats. He'd learned the hard way that police cars were fair game to the many inhabitants of high flats that don't like cops. A vivid memory surfaced of an old fridge embedded in the roof of a patrol car from his days in uniform. He wouldn't make that mistake again. He was about to walk into an unknown situation alone, another mistake he'd sworn not to make again, but needs must, he told himself.

He reached into the glovebox of his car and took out a folded sheet of A4 paper. It was a photocopy of a Metropolitan Police Letter used to let people know about burglaries or vehicle crime marches in their neighbourhood. A few minutes later he walked along the open balcony servicing all of the 5th floor flats. He'd checked the lifts which seemed to be working but stank of stale urine so he opted for the stairs. He walked along the corridor and found the 3rd door along was number 53, the address he'd been given by the school. The noise of mopeds below in the street made him look over the balcony to see 4 mopeds riding along, each two up and nobody wearing a helmet. Proof, if any was needed that the rule of law had deserted this place.

Maxwell knocked on the door and as habit dictated stood to the side. A few seconds later he saw the lens of the peephole darken as someone looked out. Holding up his warrant card in front of the lens he said, 'Police, can I have a word please?'

'What do you want?' asked an anxious female voice from behind the door.

'I just want to ask you a couple of questions about a missing girl.'

There was a pause as the woman behind the door hesitated and then said, 'I don't know nothing about no missing girl.'

'As I said, I just want to ask you some questions, it won't take long. You can answer them here, or,' he took his phone bill from his pocket and briefly waved it in front of the peephole, 'or, I have a warrant to search your place and can force entry to do so. The council won't just give you a new door, so you'll be charged £500 too.'

After another brief hesitation, the door was unlocked and opened. A small, round woman with hair bleached yellow blonde stood with her back to the wall to let him past. 'You on your own?' she asked him when no-one else came through the door.

'Yep, it only takes one of me to ask some questions. Who else is at home?'

'Just me, the kids are at school.'

'What's your name?'

'Cassandra.'

Maxwell moved around the flat opening doors and looking in each room. He counted three bedrooms.

'Dad?'

'Which one? All four were useless pricks, and didn't want to stay around and play families.'

'You have 4 kids?'

'Yeah, 5, 6, 8 and 12. That's them in that photo.' She said pointing to a blown up version of a family photo.

'You don't consider Dionne as your child then?'

She looked at him with a mix of suspicion and fear. 'What do you want?' she asked as she reached for an inhaler from the coffee table.

'First of all, I want you to answer my questions. Take a seat,' he nodded his head toward the garish red leather sofa. Like her it was past its best and looked battered by life. Both she and the sofa groaned as she sat down heavily.

'Is she dead?' she asked with a face full of genuine concern.

Maxwell wondered whether the concern was for the missing girl or for herself. Either way this was something he could use. 'Is who dead?'

'Dionne, obviously, that's why you're here innit?'

'I honestly don't know yet if she's dead, but it's a possibility, yes. Tell me about her.'

'She was a good girl really, I always made sure she went to school. She was good at sport, wanted to play netball, said she was going to be professional and be on telly like.'

'When did you last see her?'

'About 2 weeks ago, she didn't come back from school.'

'You reported her missing?'

The woman stared at her hands and shook her head.

'Why not?' he asked.

She looked up at him with tears forming in her eyes. 'Look you obviously know everything or else you wouldn't be here, you know why!' she sniffed and wiped her nose on her sleeve before Maxwell could offer her his handkerchief.

'As you say, I know everything, but it's important I hear it from you, that way I can verify things and know if you're holding anything back. So, start at the beginning.'

'The beginning? That was 12 years ago. You want all that too?' she sobbed.

'Yes, how about you make us a cup of tea and then you can tell me, from the start.' He asked, trying to settle her.

'Don't have no tea,' she said without embarrassment, 'it's not my day for the food bank until tomorrow. Besides I use all my vouchers on food for the kids. I've not had anything to eat since Saturday.' She suddenly looked indignant, 'my kids don't go hungry though, and neither did Dionne!' Tears came freely now and they rolled down her face as she closed her eyes and looked to the ceiling.

Maxwell watched her for a second then stood up and walked into the kitchen, he looked in the fridge which was empty apart from an almost empty bottle of ketchup. Opening the cupboards, he found them empty. The kitchen was clean and he saw stacks of 6 bowls, 6 plates and six multicoloured plastic cups. One of the walls had pictures drawn by young kids stuck with blu-tack. The middle picture was of a family group of stick people. All of the stick people had round heads with smiling faces. The blonde hair of the person in the middle was obviously the mother with 4 little people around her and one much taller stick person; Dionne.

'What time are the kids due back from school?' he asked from the kitchen.

'I pick them up at 4.45 from after school club on a Monday, they get their tea there, cos I've nothing left for them after the weekend.'

'Get your coat on,' said Maxwell walking back into the living room.

'You can't arrest me!' she said panicking, 'I've not done nuffink wrong. Please, I need to be here for my kids.'

'I'm not arresting you.'

She caught her breath and then took a puff on her inhaler. 'Then where are you taking me?' she wheezed.

'First up, we're going to find a café that does a decent breakfast and then we're going shopping.'

'Breakfast? Shopping? What are you on about?' she gasped, her confusion adding to her breathlessness.

'Look, I'm going to buy you breakfast and you can answer my questions. If you answer my questions then I'll take you to the supermarket and buy you some supplies. How does that sound?'

'Why would you do that?' she asked.

'Because you need some help, and I'm in a position to help.'

Thirty minutes later he was watching her devour a full English in a local cafe. It was quiet enough that they could sit in a booth at the back without being disturbed. He had left his suit jacket and tie in the car but his attempts not to stand out didn't prevent him receiving curious looks.

His heart filled when she took two slices of bread and placed the sausages from her plate on them. She cut the sandwich carefully into 4 pieces and wrapped them in a napkin. 'For the kids breakfast tomorrow.' she said looking at him.

'I said I'd take you shopping,' he replied.

'No offence Mr Maxwell, but I've been lied to and cheated on by every man I've ever met.'

'Ok, fair point, but here,' he took out his wallet and placed £40 in front of her. 'I'll still take you shopping but if I don't, then you can buy some food with that, deal?'

She looked at the money and then looked at him before slipping the cash off the table and into her pocket. 'You're not a normal copper, are you?' she asked him.

'From what I've heard about the cops around here, no I don't suppose I am. We're not all bad guys you know.'

She took a gulp of tea before lifting the teapot. Maxwell watched as she topped up his mug before refreshing her own.

'It was Malcolm who brought her to me.' she began.

'Malcolm?'

'Junior's dad,' she saw the question in Maxwell's face and went on, 'Junior is my eldest. I was 17 and pregnant to Malcolm. The council gave me the flat when I told them I was expecting. She was 3 when he brought her to me, he said her Mum had died from an overdose and her Dad was getting deported back to Jamaica or somewhere. I knew she was really his though, but I thought we could be a family like, you know?'

Maxwell nodded and waited for her to go on.

'Malcolm didn't come around much, just every now and again, when he wanted something. He called her Kaleisha but said we had to give her a new name so no-one could find her. I named her Dionne; after my Nan's favourite singer Dionne Warwick. When I was too pregnant for him to be interested anymore, he just stopped coming. I was 8 months pregnant and had a 3 year old to look after. I didn't know what to do. Mrs Koslowski was my next door neighbour and she took Dionne for me when I went to the hospital. I had to stay in for 5 days, because I tore a bit, you know?'

He nodded again but wasn't entirely sure he understood the mechanics of it all.

'I came out and Mrs Dobson looked after me. I was just a kid and didn't have a clue what to do with a new baby.'

'What about your own parents?'

'They wanted bugger all to do with me. As soon as they knew I was pregnant and the Dad was a black fella they threw me out. Never spoke to them again. My mum sent me some baby stuff but said my Dad couldn't find out. Then nuffink, I was on my own.'

'Did you tell Social Services you had Dionne to look after?'

'No, Malcolm said they would put her in a Children's home or something. All I could think about was all those kids that get abused in them places, so I decided to keep her safe.'

'You've never had financial support to look after her?'

'No, I get my benefits for the other four and I just have to make do. None of their Dads ever helped out. Only Giselle ever met her Dad and then he got himself killed about a month later. She was a baby so don't remember him.' She looked at him and narrowed her eyes.

'You're thinking I'm just some stupid slag that keeps getting knocked up and can't keep a man, aren't you?'

Maxwell looked at her, 'Not at all Cassandra, I'm thinking you are quite a remarkable woman.'

'Yeah right!' she snorted.

'You single-handedly brought up 5 kids, one of which wasn't your own, and kept her despite it making your life considerably harder. That is quite something.'

She blushed as he spoke and had to take a sip of tea to steady herself. 'No-one's ever said nuffink nice to me like that before.'

'Well, it's true. I couldn't have done what you've done. You obviously love your kids and do your best for them.'

'I still can't put food on the table for them every day though. The council says I should get a job and they cut back my benefits. I've tried, I have, but there's no jobs around here, unless it's selling drugs. Look at the nick of me, I couldn't even sell myself if I wanted to.' She looked him in the eye, 'Not that I would do that anyway, I'm not no whore.'

Maxwell held up his hands in submission, 'It never crossed my mind,' he said honestly. 'Tell me about Dionne, any idea where she's gone?'

'No. I was really worried and called the school but they said she'd just left. We'd had an argument the day before because she'd been late back. She said she'd met some boy. He sounded like a gang kid to me so I said she couldn't see him. You know what young girls are like, she said she was 17 and could see who she wanted. I told her that while she lived with us then she had to do what I told her. She said some horrible things and stormed out. I was really hurt, you know? I looked for her, and a couple of her friends came looking for her but no-one knew where she was.'

'Did she mention who the boy was?'

'No, but she had a name written on her hand when she came back from school one day. It said 'Felix' and she'd drawn a love heart around it.'

#

After carrying the bags of shopping up the stairs to her flat Maxwell said goodbye to Cassandra.

'If you find her,' she said, taking hold of his hand, 'tell her to come home, tell her this will always be her home.'

'I will, I promise,' said Maxwell.

'And thank you again for all this,' she pointed to the bags of shopping. 'I still can't believe it!'

'Least I can do,' said Maxwell and opened the front door to leave.

'Any time you want to come back, I'll have some tea for you,' she said and smiled at him.

'I might just take you up on that,' he said and pulled the door closed behind him. As he drove away from the flats, he could hear the whine of multiple mopeds from an adjacent street, he couldn't see them but he heard them. He knew they were out there, and he knew they were the key to finding Dionne.

CHAPTER SEVENTY-TWO

Hamilton arrived at the flat above Uncle Samir's 5 minutes after JT and the team.

'What's the plan?' asked JT.

'I don't yet know, I'm afraid,' said Hamilton unbuttoning his jacket, 'Rory called us together but I see he is not yet here.'

'He's picking up Easy, should be here shortly,' said JT. 'Any blow back from Ilford or Palmerston House?'

'Nothing that can't be handled,' said Hamilton. 'Those investigating have been suitably directed by the evidence we left. There is lots of talk of an internecine conflict between Albanian and Russian crime groups.'

'And the IRA?' asked JT.

'There are long standing links between both groups and the IRA. They have been dealing in drugs and weapons with anyone who would do business with them for many years. I should think those groups will start seeking retribution from each other before long and hopefully do some damage to each other in the process.'

'Nothing is going to come back to us then?' pressed JT.

'I had one of my people do some clean-up work at both sites, there will be nothing to link to you or the team, I guarantee that.'

'What sort of clean-up?'

'We left behind a sophisticated drone and hacking device which I felt prudent to be recovered, we also ensured that any areas where Maxwell had been captive were suitably sanitised. The rest of us wore gloves and there is so much DNA spread over the site they'll never be able to identify anything we might have left behind.'

'What about the women and kids?' asked Taff.

'They're all being well cared for. Most had already suffered some horrendous trauma and some were about to find out what their future held.'

'They heard our voices; they'll know we're British.' said Taff.

'Most of them weren't British nationals themselves. I doubt some of them could speak English. Thanks to the ski masks it's unlikely any of them saw our faces. It would also be likely that any group operating in the UK would have local operatives working for them. No, I don't consider there to be any risk of our being identified.'

'Glad to hear it,' said JT. 'What about the hotel staff?'

'They've disappeared and are most likely heading back home with enough cash to set them up nicely. When do you intend to go back to Hereford?' asked Hamilton.

'I've told them I'm going Home on Thursday morning.'

'What do you plan to do when you get there?'

'I'm going to get some answers. This court martial stuff is political bullshit and I've had enough of being kept in the dark.'

'Have you considered what I said about resigning?'

'Why are you so keen for us to resign?' asked JT, annoyed.

'I am keen for you to avoid prison. It would be an incredible injustice and also a wasted opportunity. As I have explained, I believe the Army is being pushed into a corner by Politicians and do-gooders outside, and within, their own hierarchy. You are being fed to the wolves as it serves their purpose.'

'But you have your own reasons for wanting us,' said Maxwell.

'Of course I do, and I won't deny a selfish interest. Your situation has given me the opportunity to do something I've wanted to do for some time. The same Politicians and do-gooders who are seeking your scalps, have made my job and that of the Service next to impossible. We are charged with keeping the nation safe but expect us to heed whatever fashion or cause celebres they have the media pushing. We have already made a significant impact and saved numerous people from death or a fate much worse.'

'I know, I know,' said JT, 'but when it comes down to it, we are still soldiers of the British Army.'

'That will most certainly not be the case if they take you to Court Martial.'

'You know it's all nonsense so why do you think we wouldn't be exonerated?'

Hamilton fixed him with a serious look, 'Because the verdict has already been reached.'

Just then, Maxwell and Easy came into the flat and immediately sensed the tension in the atmosphere.

'What's happened?' Maxwell asked Hamilton.

'Bit of a reality check, I'm afraid.'

'You ok?' Maxwell asked JT.

'Not really no, but as Hamilton says, it's reality.'

'What do you have for us Rory?' asked Hamilton, keen to change the conversation.

'Easy's friend Dionne, her real name may be Kaleisha. Seems she was given to a 17 year old to look after when she was just 3. Her adoptive mum has 4 kids of her own but has raised Dionne like she's her own daughter. Poor as dirt, but she's given everything to her kids. I was there today and she had no food in the house at all. She gets to use a food bank once a week but goes without herself so she can feed her kids. Meanwhile, Dionne has turned into a hormonal teenager. She's been seeing a kid called Felix who is part of Crew B. He is the worm they dangle to attract young girls, then I think, it's likely they sell them on to the Kosanians.'

'She wasn't at Palmerston House though,' said Easy

'No, she wasn't. Did you notice that all of the girls and kids in Palmerston House were white? Dionne is black or mixed race, so I think maybe there's somewhere else for different clientele.'

'Did they ever mention another place in their group chat Easy?' asked JT.

'No, not that I ever saw.'

'The only one left, that we know of, is Igor across in the bookies. He most likely knows by now that his boss is dead,' said Hamilton.

'Maybe we should go ask him?' said JT.

'I have another idea,' said Maxwell, 'this Crew B is the heart of a lot of what goes on around here. The foot soldiers might just get the idea that they can take over from the Kosanians. I suggest we make sure that doesn't happen, and they can tell us where Dionne is, if she's still alive.'

Easy looked uncomfortable, 'I know she's still alive,' he said, 'I can feel it.'

'Well, let's hope so,' said JT. 'What's your plan Rory?'

'They hang around on the estate but it's a bit too open and too many eyes there. We need somewhere we can grab them and have a chat.'

'I know just the place.' said JT, 'There's an old disused warehouse across the road in the street parallel to this one. They park their mopeds in the goods yard when they come to the bookies. We know they rock up at the same time each day so we can be ready for them.'

'Excellent,' said Maxwell, 'do we get them before or after they've been to the bookies?'

'I think after,' said JT, 'no point in alerting Igor that they're not around. That would give us 24 hours with them before he knows there's anything wrong.'

'He's been messaging looking for the others,' said Easy. 'I saw his messages. He has asked someone for some more men. They said they would send him some by the weekend.'

'Who said?' asked Hamilton.

'I don't know who they are, but the number he dialled is from Albania.'

'I am looking forward to making Igor pay for what he did to that woman and her boy,' said Cooky.

'We all are,' said JT.

'Me too,' said Easy. 'I saw her yesterday, she looked scared and turned around when she saw the guys on their mopeds.'

'They're not much more than kids themselves, no more than 21 but I am told they have guns,' said Maxwell.

'They're a cancer,' said Hamilton, 'and the best way to deal with cancer is to cut it out.'

CHAPTER SEVENTY-THREE

'4 mopeds, 7 up. All hoods and scarves, no helmets. 30 seconds out,' said Rambo from his overwatch position on the roof.

Stood in position on the fire escape of the disused warehouse, JT watched the 4 mopeds drive through the goods entrance and into the yard. There were 7 of the B Crew and one was detailed to stand guard over the mopeds.

'Be 10 minutes Dazza,' said the apparent leader while he and the others swaggered toward the alley and away to their appointment at the bookies.

JT could see that 'Dazza' was the guy from the fishing Lake a few days before. He had a plaster cast from where Taff had broken his arm.

As soon as they were clear of the alley Cooky staggered into the goods yard holding an empty vodka bottle and pretending he was drunk.

'Oi, fuck off out of here man!' shouted Dazza.

'Ah'm a just gonna take a piss,' slurred Cooky, still staggering in the direction of the parked bikes.

'I told you to fuck off already!' said the youth as he pulled an old fashioned snub nosed revolver from his waistband. He lifted the weapon until his hand was above shoulder height and tilted it sideways in the fashion of so many big screen gangsters.

Cooky raised his hands and mumbled as he turned on the spot as if about to walk away.

'Yeah! Good move before I pop a cap in yo' ass!' sneered the cock-sure youth.

Posty clubbed Dazza's wrist before he was aware that someone had sneaked up behind him. The revolver bounced off the moped seat and into a pile of litter. The youth spun to look at Posty who punched him in the throat with a Leopard Strike. He crumpled to the floor grasping his throat and rasping as he tried to force air into his lungs.

Cooky picked up the gun then grabbed the back of the youths collar and dragged him over to the goods entrance of the building which was being opened by Joe.

Posty and Taff pushed the mopeds up the ramp and inside before pushing the roller shutter back down until it was 18 inches from being fully closed.

Ten minutes later the 6 other members of Crew B came back into the goods yard. They were all jumpy and excitable after the snort of coke they'd enjoyed courtesy of Igor.

'What the Fuck?' said the one who appeared to be the leader.

'Felix, check this out bro,' said one of them pointing at the mopeds through the partially open roller door, 'our bikes are in there.'

'What's the dickhead put the bikes in there for? Ain't even raining,' said Felix who was obviously the leader. 'Dazza!' he shouted, 'we're splittin' man, what the fuck you playin' at bro?' His shout was met by silence and the group all looked to Felix for what to do next.

'Fucking idiot be takin' a shit or something!' he said and made his way to the roller door. He tried to lift it but found it was locked off in position. 'Need to do it inside,' he said to his crew and got down on the ground then rolled himself under the shutter followed by the others.

They stood up and froze when they saw the reason they couldn't open the roller shutter; their friend Dazza was hanging with the chain wrapped around his neck. They were too busy staring at Dazza, and at his piss soaked joggers dripping onto the floor, that they didn't notice the 4 men wearing ski masks enter through the door behind them.

'Hands in the air,' said Cooky pointing the revolver at them.

They spun around, their shock and fear obvious. They all held up their hands. All except one, Felix.

'You know who the fuck you messin' with bro?' he snarled.

'I ain't fucking messing,' said Cooky, 'now lift your hands.'

'We connected bro,' said Felix, 'you boys've proper fucked up!'

The youth closest to the door threw himself to the floor and tried to roll out and escape. Taff stepped forward and kicked him full force in the head. The blow knocked the youth unconscious and Taff dragged him away from the door as his friends watched on open mouthed. Sitting the semi-conscious body up he wrapped the roller shutter chain around his neck. Stepping back, he pulled down hard on the chain which hoisted the body off the floor and closed the shutter. The youths legs kicked and thrashed for a few seconds then after a final violent buck, went still.

Posty walked forward and searched the youths where they stood. He found several knives, but no more guns until he reached Felix. He removed a Sig Sauer P320 from his waistband. 'Ooft, nice hardware kiddo, where'd a wee shite bag like you get a fucking Sig from?'

'From the guys that's gonna fuck you up!' snorted Felix trying to up his bravado.

'And who might they be?' asked JT from the gantry above.

Felix looked up at him, 'We're with the Kosanians and they'll kill all you fuckers nice and slow, if you don't let us go now.'

'Oh dear, we're terrified, I'm sure. Tell you what, you answer a few questions and we'll get you out of here,' said JT, with a smile that didn't reach his eyes.

'I'm telling you fuck all!' snarled Felix.

'Oh, well that's a pity. I'm sure one of your friends will answer though.'

'My Crew won't be saying jack shit,' said Felix, looking around at his remaining friends with implied threat.

'We'll see about that,' said JT. 'Carry on Taff.'

Taff walked over to a manhole cover and lifted it. 15 feet below where they stood a fast flowing sewer was taking the last couple of days of rain and sewage away. Taff walked over to the smallest of the group and swept his feet away from under him before dragging him across the floor dropping him screaming into the sewer with a splash followed by silence.

He walked toward the next closest one who backed away and shouted, 'No stop, I'll tell you anything! Anything!'

'Shut it, Hoskins!' hissed Felix.

'Where is Dionne?' asked JT.

'I don't know any Dionne,' said Hoskins cowering.

'Wrong answer,' said Taff and punched him in the solar plexus bending him in half. Hoskins was too winded to scream but his face was scarlet in terror as Taff threw him down into the sewer. 'Anyone else want to try telling me lies?' said Taff.

'I can take you to her,' said Felix trying desperately to process the situation and stall for time.

'Just tell me where she is,' said JT

'Who the fuck are you, and what you want with the bitch anyways?' said Felix.

Cooky stepped forward and slapped him open-palmed across the face, hard enough to knock him to the ground. 'That's no way to talk about a lady,' he said quietly.

Felix wiped his mouth and spat blood from his split lip on the floor. 'That bitch ain't no lady, me and my boys, we been making sure of that,' he said it with an insolent pride that took Cooky aback for a second.

A second later Cooky's size 14 boot crashed down on Felix's hand and he squealed like a wounded animal. He rolled around for a few seconds clutching his hand before his squeals were replaced by sobs and groans.

'I know where she is,' said one of the two remaining Crew looking up at JT.

'Where?'

'We got a place, an empty 'ouse like, we keep her there.'

'What's your name?' asked JT

'They call me Blade.'

'Well Blade, where is this house? I want an exact address and my colleagues will be going to check it, so make sure you get it right,' said JT.

'I don't know the address,' he stepped back when he saw Cooky look at him, 'but I can tell you where it is!' he blurted out.

'Ok, go ahead but I'll need plenty of detail.'

'There's an 'ouse, it's a row, there's 4 'ouses. Up Gascoigne. Where the old woman's 'ouse got burnt.'

'Which old woman?'

'Dunno her name, boys torched her 'ouse 'cos she tried to grass us up.'

JT lifted his phone to his ear, 'You getting all this Rory?'

'Yes. Easy says he knows the houses. We can be there in 5 minutes.'

'Okay, you go check, we'll keep these guys until we hear back from you.'

'Can we go then?' asked Blade.

'We're verifying the address and if Dionne is there, and alive, then you'll be leaving here. Meantime you can answer some more questions. What's the deal with you lot and Igor at the bookies?'

'We do jobs for him and he pays us,' said Blade with some reticence.

'What kind of jobs?'

'Like run errands an' shit.'

'Dealing drugs?'

'A bit yeah, but mostly we deliver them to the dealers.'

'What else?'

'We get him jewellery and stuff.'

'Get it how?'

'We rob folk, we done a jeweller as well but just the once.'

'Girls?'

Blade shifted uneasily; he knew what was coming but thought better of lying. 'Yeah, we found him some girls.'

'What do you mean, found?'

'Shut the fuck up man!' hissed Felix from the floor, which earned him a kick in the ribs from Cooky.

'What do you mean, found?' repeated JT.

'We would get them girls, take them back to the house and give them some drink and some drugs, then the Kosanians would come and choose which ones they wanted.'

'Go on,' said JT.

'They took away the ones they wanted.'

'The others?'

'Depends, sometimes they would fuck 'em and leave 'em for us, sometimes they just said we could have them.'

'I see, and what happened with Dionne?'

'They don't like the black girls, them's a bit racist, you know?'

JT looked at Blade who was obviously mixed race himself and wondered why he wasn't more offended, or maybe money was just more important to him.

'If you knew they don't take black girls, why take Dionne?'

'She was just a Crew bitch. We just kept her for us to use.'

'What exactly do you mean 'Crew bitch'?'

'She's our bitch, we're supposed get shots each like, when Felix is finished wiv her, but I never touched her, not once, you can ask her, I'm not no rapist man, she'll tell you!'

'The others?' asked JT.

'Yeah man, or I think so, maybe,' Blade turned to look at his one remaining standing companion who had not spoken at all. 'You fucked her right Waxy?'

'No, no, never touched her man, it was Felix man, him and the other boys, not me!' his voice got progressively higher and louder as he spoke.

JT held up a hand to silence them and answered his phone which buzzed in his hand.

'We've got her,' said Maxwell, 'she's in a mess, we found her handcuffed to a bed.'

'She's alive that's the main thing,' said JT, 'anything else there?'

'They'd turned it into a sort of clubhouse with a couple of locked rooms and the windows boarded up. There's a hole knocked through the wall leading to the adjoining house. I just had a look, there's 3 maybe 4 bodies in the bathtub. They've tried to dispose of them with chemicals but not got it right. At least one of them was a little kid.'

'Fuck sake,' said JT gripping the metal handrail. 'What are you doing with the girl?'

'I'm going to drop her off at the hospital, Easy will stay with her until I can take Cassandra over there. What's your plan?'

'I'm going to finish cutting out the cancer,' said JT and hung up.

'I told you, didn't I?' said Blade, virtually bouncing on the spot. 'Ask her if Blade raped her. I never touched her, like I said Man.'

'Don't worry I believe you,' said JT, 'But before we get you out of here, I want you to help tidy up a bit.'

'Yeah man, no problem. What do you want me to do?' asked Blade, suddenly excited.

'You and your pal Waxy there, need to get those two down from the chains and put the bodies down the sewer. Think you can manage that?'

'No problem,' said Blade and pushed the stunned Waxy over to the first chain. 'Grab his legs and lift him up a bit so I can get the chain,' he told him.

After some huffing and puffing they got the first and then the second body down.

'Down here,' said Taff over by the sewer.

They dragged the bodies over and pushed them one at a time, head first, down into the filthy torrent below.

'We can go now, yeah?' asked Waxy.

'Not you, no.' said Taff and grabbed him in a headlock then threw him headfirst into the mouth of the manhole. Waxy spread his arms as he fought to stop himself falling to his death but a heavy kick sent him tumbling forward with a short truncated scream.

'You said we could get out of here!' shouted a panicking Blade, as he backed away from Taff.

'And you will,' said JT, 'or at least, one of you will.'

Blade and Felix stared up at him desperately trying to work out what was going to happen next.

'Gents, bolt that door, then come and join me up here please,' said JT, to the team.

Cooky bolted the doors and a moment later, they were all standing on the gantry with JT. 'Chuck them each a knife,' he told Posty.

'Catch!' said Posty and dropped two of the vicious looking knives he'd confiscated earlier.

Felix struggled to his feet and stared up at the team assembled on the gantry. He had worked out what was coming next while Blade was still waiting bemused.

'Only one of you will be allowed to leave here alive, you can decide between yourselves who that will be,' said JT, and rested his arms on the guardrail ready to spectate.

'Think you're fucking Caesar or something?' said Felix sarcastically as he picked up the knife in his good hand and turned to face Blade.

Blade had finally caught up with what was happening and snatched up the other knife.

'You should have kept your fucking mouth shut Blade,' said Felix as he moved forward and slashed sideways with the knife.

Blade threw up his arm to protect himself and winced as the slash cut into his forearm. Blood ran down his arm as he kept it up as a guard. He took up a fighting crouch ready for the next attack.

Felix faked a thrust and drew Blade into a block while he kicked out and caught his shin. Blade staggered and gasped as Felix lunged and stabbed him in the thigh.

Blade punched out and caught Felix across the shoulder. The knife sliced deep into the flesh as their opposing momentum ran the length of steel into the muscle.

Felix yelped as his already injured arm was soaked with his blood. Blade danced round Felix's unprotected side and drove his knife deep into his ribs. Felix arched back and trapped the blade as he spun round, as he fell, he plunged his own knife into Blade's stomach.

They both hit the ground and lay still for a few seconds assessing their wounds. Blade moved first rolling slowly onto his side, then onto his knees while clutching the wound in his belly. He was bleeding heavily and it seeped through his fingers. He looked up at the gantry where the team watched on impassively.

Beside him Felix moaned as he tried in vain to remove the knife stuck in his side. Blade staggered, then with some difficulty bent forward to pick up the knife from the ground. He fell to his knees next to Felix and examined the knife in his hand before looking up at the audience.

JT held out a hand with his thumb horizontal until he met Blade's eyes. He held his gaze and when he turned the thumb downwards, Blade drove the knife into Felix's chest.

Blade fell back and lay on the ground blinking hard.

'Put him down the sewer and then you're free to go,' said JT.

Blade struggled slowly to his feet and looked at the 2 metres to the manhole. He reached down and taking hold of Felix's hood started dragging his dying friend. Twice he fell and each time it took him longer to regain his feet. Sweat dripped from his chin and he was breathless as he knelt down and finally pushed Felix over the manhole. He pushed the feet in first and slid the torso forward. He roared in pain as he lifted the shoulders to fold the body into the opening and as Felix's body disappeared, he slumped forward and teetered, before he too fell head first into the void.

'Looks like the cancer destroyed itself,' said JT, as he turned to the other men on the gantry, 'that just leaves one more disease that needs eradicating.'

CHAPTER SEVENTY-FOUR

The 4x4s stopped at the guard post, JT wound down his window as a trooper approached.

'Good morning, JT,' said the trooper. 'Paddy is expecting you.'

'Thanks, Smudger' he said as he wound his window back up and drove under the raised barrier then into a space behind the guard room.

JT got out of the car and walked to the boot which he opened and lifted out a box which he tucked under his arm as he walked to the guardroom. He stopped and looked around him. This place had been Home for nearly 12 years. Today, a bit of him felt like he was a visitor.

'Hey JT, how's it going?' asked the Sergeant behind the desk.

'Pretty good Falk, how's things with you?

'Still here mate, still here.'

'Is he in his office?'

'Yes, go on through.'

'Thanks,' said JT and he walked along the corridor to the door at the end. As he approached the door opened and Paddy stood holding the door to allow him in.

'Welcome Home,' said Paddy and shook his hand as he pushed the door closed behind him.

'Cheers Paddy, wish I could say it felt good to be back.'

Paddy looked at him with concern in his eyes and nodded as he took a seat.

'Here, I brought you back a gift from France,' said JT.

Paddy opened the box, 'Guiberteau Saumur Blanc,' he said reading the label, 'fantastic – merci!'

'I'll confess now, I bought it on the ferry back.'

'Seriously? No time for shopping then?'

'We got a bit carried away with our training,' said JT, with a grin.

'No worries, I'll save this for next time you come for dinner,' said Paddy.

'I've got the kit to return in the back of the car too.'

'Gimme your keys, I'll get Falk to sort it out with the QM.' Paddy took the keys and left the office.

JT looked around the room. Regimental pennants and plaques lined the walls alongside some of the few photos that existed of the entire regiment in one place at one time. The photos were all at least 40 years old. There were always teams deployed across the world and JT knew he could easily go a year without seeing some of his colleagues.

Paddy came back in, 'We've got 30 minutes before we see Colonel Dalgleish, time for a brew, or are you getting into uniform?'

'Yeah, cheers Paddy, why not? I'm going in as I am, they can't suspend me and expect me in uniform!'

'Come on, we'll grab one in the officer's mess on the way over.'

As they walked around the parade square, JT found himself reminiscing about some of the beastings he'd both received and delivered there. He couldn't help but feel like a naughty schoolboy on his way to see the Headmaster. The feeling made him angry and he was glad to have Paddy by his side as a calming influence.

At the officer's mess several men came to shake JT's hand and welcome him Home. It still felt different to him, not like before and unlikely to be the same again.

Paddy handed him a cup of tea, 'It's not up to your usual standards but it's not a bad cuppa. Besides, word will get upstairs that you're relaxing downstairs and that'll shut a few gossips up.'

'Thanks again for doing this Paddy,' said JT.

'Don't mention it, just wish there was more I could do.'

The door to the mess opened and a uniformed man not of the Regiment walked in. He saw JT and Paddy and walked straight to them.

'Good morning, Paddy,' he said without looking at him and instead focusing on JT. 'You must be Captain St-John Templeman,' he held out a hand to shake.

JT thought the handshake felt strangely weak after Paddy's earlier.

'Allow me to introduce myself, Major Cliff Symmons, I'm currently attached to the legal office of the Deputy Chief of the General Staff, Lieutenant Gen-'

'I know who she is, and I know who you are, Major,' interrupted JT.

'Ah then you are better informed than I was led to believe,' he gave a supercilious smile that made JT consider punching him.

'We're having a brew Symmons and as I don't recall inviting you in here to the Regimental Officers mess, I will ask you to take your leave and go shove your head back up someone's arse upstairs.' He smiled at

Symmons and stepped closer to him then said quietly, 'Another thing, if you ever address me without looking me in the eye again, I will take it as an invitation to punch your shiny little face. Do I make myself clear?'

'Perfectly old bean.' He turned on his heels and as he walked away gave a cheery, 'Toodle pip, see you both upstairs.'

When he had left JT turned to Paddy, 'Thanks Paddy but you need to be careful my friend, fuckers like him only exist to climb the ranks and don't give a shit who they tread on to get there.'

'Fuck him,' said Paddy, 'him and his ilk make me sick. Fucking desk jockeys who've never seen combat and never will. He's a bloody administrator, not a soldier.'

'Amen to that my friend, but these guys are dangerous when they have the ear of top brass,' said JT taking over the role of calming influence.

'I know, I know but the little prick just came in here to wind you up.'

'Well, it almost worked, but he forgot one important thing. I've got you on my side.'

#

They were shown into Colonel Dalgleish's office by an adjutant and found Major Symmons was sitting in a chair at the back of the room. He gave a little smile as JT and Paddy entered the room and then stood to attention in front of the Colonel's desk.

'At ease Gentlemen,' he said and stood up to walk round his desk and shake JT's hand. 'Bloody awful business all this JT, I've tried to make HQ see sense over it all but sadly to no avail,' said Dalgleish

'Thank you, sir,' said JT.

'You well? How's the team?'

'All well sir, we've been training so match fit should the call come.'

'Yes, bloody ridiculous isn't it, I'm forced to suspend 6 of my best men and ban you from Home, but if the shit hits the fan, you're expected to drop everything and go fight for Queen and Country. How was France?'

'Bit wet sir, but we did what we set out to do,' said JT.

'Good stuff, good stuff. Gentlemen, please sit down. I have some bad news to share.' Colonel Dalgleish walked back round to his seat and sat down with his straight back and steely gaze. JT and Paddy took the two seats in front of the desk before the Colonel went on. 'Before we begin, I want you to know that all of this is coming from on high. Bloody Politicians are baying for blood as they try to cover their own arses after making a series of fuck ups. The bloody puppets over in HQ-'

Symmons cleared his throat from the back of the room.

The Colonel's face visibly reddened, 'Those bloody puppets over in HQ don't have the backbone to stand up to our Political masters and tell them to fuck off.'

'Begging your pardon sir,' began Symmons, before the Colonel slammed his fist onto his desk.

Colonel Dalgleish stood up and shouted at Symmons over the heads of JT and Paddy, 'I don't know how things work in whichever part of bloody Whitehall you come from, but in my regiment a Major does not interrupt a Colonel. I allowed you here as a courtesy Symmons, but you have outstayed your welcome. Now get the fuck out of my office!'

'Sir!' said an ashen faced Symmons standing to attention then walking out.

'Fucking leach,' said the Colonel when his office door closed. His manner changed instantly and he spoke as if nothing had happened. 'JT, I'm sorry about this lad, it's all fucked up. I don't know how you came to be in their crosshairs and it's probably just bloody bad luck, but they fully intend to make an example of you.'

'So I've heard sir. I take it the body camera footage is still lost?' asked JT.

'Yes, someone wiped the drives. The IT guys say they can't work out how it happened, that it must have been a faulty drive,' said the Colonel.

'That's just nonsense, Sir,' said JT.

'I know it bloody is, I've had three sets of techies look at it, but they all say they can't explain how it was deleted other than someone has done it deliberately and covered their trail.'

'They claim to have witnesses too Sir?'

'Yes, I'm told three civilians just turned up, out of the blue, claiming to have seen you murder a woman and then blow up a building to hide any evidence. It's just so obviously a set up, but the Foreign Office are working overtime to get the asylum in exchange for their testimony.'

'Do we have any options Colonel?' asked Paddy.

'If you mean the Regiment Paddy, then no, I've tried everything. I even called in my biggest favour but I got nothing other than the option for the team to resign.'

'Then that's what we'll have to do then,' said JT, 'We can't let them ruin the name of the Regiment.'

'Not so fast JT. It's true some of the powers that be would rather we didn't exist. They seem to think they can resolve conflict through diplomacy and a computer virus. But the real powers know they need us to do the jobs no-one else can. The Regiment will survive no matter what they throw at us. Meantime, even if you were to resign, they can and likely will pursue you through Court Martial or Civilian Courts. They are that determined, and also that confident, of getting a result.'

'I still think it might be best if we walk away Sir, they'll throw enough mud that some will stick and that would damage the reputation of the Regiment.'

'What would you do? There's lots of PMC agencies crying out for men with your training but they're unlikely to employ you with the threat of arrest over your heads.'

'We'd sort something out Colonel. We've got a bit of rainy day cash tucked away and I'll look after the guys.'

'I can't say it makes me happy but it sounds like you've given this a lot of thought.'

'It's been pretty much all we've thought about since our suspension, Sir.'

'Well, it may just be that your resignation would satisfy some of the blood lust and who knows, maybe they'll get their act together and have someone who knows what they're doing discredit these so-called witnesses?'

'I think it's for the best, Sir.'

'Okay, if that's your decision, I'll have the paperwork drawn up and see what can be done about pensions etc. You all had psych evaluations when you came back, I'll get the Doc to have a look and see if we can get medical discharges. We all have PTSD in some form or another after all.'

#

JT drove away from Hereford and thought that the next time he came here would be his last. He called Hamilton from the car.

'How did it go?' asked Hamilton.

'As expected,' said JT, 'the Colonel confirmed everything you said.'

'Well, for what it's worth, I'm sorry your career had to end this way,' said Hamilton.

'I'm coming more and more to realise that there's a whole world out there outside the Army. I also think you're right about fighting with the gloves off.'

'Glad to hear it. It took me a while to come to the same conclusion. We can't just let the bad guys do whatever they want while we tie ourselves up with laws and political rules of engagement.'

'I'll be back in London tonight and tomorrow we will finish the job in Barking.'

'Igor?' asked Hamilton.

'Igor.'

CHAPTER SEVENTY-FIVE

'Easy, can you go see if Uncle Samir is back from prayers? If so, ask him to come up here,' said JT.

'Here?' said, looking at the weapons and kit on the table.

'Yes, I reckon the old man knows more about what we've been doing than you'd think. Besides, he's going to enjoy the task we're going to give him.'

A few minutes later, Easy returned with Uncle Samir. The old man was carrying a bag filled with foil takeaway dishes. 'As-salaam u alaikum,' he said with a smile and slight bow of the head, as he looked into the faces of the men in the room.

'Wa alaikum as-salaam,' said JT as he stepped forward and shook his hand. 'Thank you for coming up.'

'No problem,' said Samir, as he placed the carrier bag on the table between two handguns. 'I have brought for you some pilaf from the Masjid. We are celebrating the birth of a grandson to the Muezzin.'

'Shukran,' said JT, 'very kind of you.'

'The most loved food of Allah is that which is shared by many hands.'

'Then please, come sit with us and eat. We have a proposition we wish to discuss with you,' said JT.

They all ate some of the aromatic rice with little chunks of lamb in silence until Samir sat back from the table with his legs crossed. 'You are soldiers, yes?' he asked JT.

'Yes, we are soldiers Uncle,' said JT, not surprised by the old man's power of deduction.

'And my boy Ezekiel here?' he asked.

'No, Ezekiel is not a soldier, but he has been helping us.'

'Helping you to do what?'

'I have been helping them to get rid of the Bad Men Uncle,' said Easy.

'Ah, then Bis-millah, it is God's work you have been doing,' he said, nodding his head as he considered this information.

'We need your help too Uncle,' said JT.

'What help I can give is yours for the asking.'

'Are you due to make a payment at the bookies today?'

'Yes, I must go to pay them money shortly.'

'Ok, then there's something I'd like you to do when you're there.'

#

JT watched as Samir crossed the road and returned the 'hellos' and waves of locals as he went. In his left hand he held the £100 in cash he would be paying to the Kosanians and in his right hand he held a note.

After stopping briefly to speak with a smiling woman walking past with her children he carried on up the steps and into the bookies shop. The girl behind the counter looked bored as usual and took the money and counted it before him. Samir looked at her taking in the tired baggy eyes and the cheap rings on her fingers. 'What is your name child?' he asked her.

She looked up, surprised at the question. None of the people who came in to pay their money spoke to her usually. She'd initially been told they were all paying back loans the Kosanians had given them, but she knew better than that. They all had the same look, scared and a little ashamed. Not that she'd blame them, Igor was a horrible person and bloody scary. 'It's Charmaine,' she told him.

'How long have you worked here child?' he asked.

'Errm, nearly a year now.'

'Do you like it?'

She looked over her shoulder to the door to the office behind her. 'Not particularly, but I don't have much choice,' she said quietly.

'Today, you do,' said Samir, then passed her the note.

She read it, then read the words again, 'At 3 o'clock there will be a power cut. Take all of the money you have collected today and do not come back. Find a better job.' She looked at Samir who simply smiled and said, 'Do as it says child, do exactly, as it says,' then he left with the same smile he'd had when he entered.

The time on her phone said it was almost 3 o'clock, it would be time for the Crew to come in. She hated those cocky little shits with their smart-ass remarks and treating her like dirt. Making up her mind, she started packing up her things and putting them in her bag. Her hands were shaking so much she dropped her hairbrush onto the floor beneath her desk. She was bending forward to retrieve the brush when the office door opened behind her and out stepped Igor.

'What the fuck are you doing?' he growled, seeing her bag.

'Just tidying up, thought I'd clean the desk up a bit,' said Charmaine, not looking at him.

Igor stepped up behind her and was reaching for her ass when the lights went out. 'What the fuck?' he said, heading back into the office.

Charmaine stuffed all of the cash from the desk drawer into her bag then stepped up onto her chair and vaulted over the counter. As she walked out the front door she turned and looked back at the dark office. She spat on the floor and walked out.

Charmaine ran down the street to the crossing. She glanced back and saw two big men walk into the bookies and the external doors were pushed shut.

CHAPTER SEVENTY-SIX

Igor fumbled with the torch on his phone as he looked at the fuse box. The master switch had tripped and when he flipped it back on the lights came on and he could hear the fridge where he kept his vials of growth hormone hum back into life. He heard footsteps upstairs and shouted, 'Don't panic Charmaine, I fixed it.'

As he emerged from the basement, he found a big black man sitting in his seat. 'Remember me?' said Cooky as he swung his feet up onto the desk.

Igor took half a stride forward but stopped when he saw Taff had a gun pointed at him. 'Do you know who I am?' he hissed at them, 'you are fucking dead men if you think you can come in here to steal from us.'

Cooky looked around the room, 'I don't see anyone else here but you.'

'We are the Kosanians, you are going to die for this, your families will die.'

'Now, now, don't go making threats you can't keep,' said Taff as he stepped forward and used the butt of the Sig Sauer to deliver a blow to the back of his head. Igor stumbled and went down on one knee. 'Hard headed bastard, eh?' said Taff as he hit him again harder, knocking him out cold.

Cooky went to the rear fire exit and opened it to let the rest of the team in.

'All secured?' asked JT.

'Sleeping like a baby boss,' said Cooky.

'Some size of a bairn!' said Joe as they walked into the office.

Taff was stripping the clothes off Igor, 'Gimme a hand lad, the big oaf weighs a ton.'

Between then they stripped Igor naked, then with Cooky's help lifted him into his big leather office chair. They wheeled him over to the multigym and started preparing phase 2 of the plan.

'The bloody safe is open!' reported Posty from a side room, 'and it's massive.'

'It'll be the original safe from when this was a bank,' said JT as he walked over to join him.

'There's a shit ton of money in here, drugs and a whole load of paperwork too.'

'Ok, let's bag it up and take it with us. Leave the drugs. On second thoughts, go flush them down the toilet, don't want anyone else finding them.'

They found a holdall and a briefcase in a cupboard. The briefcase was full of jewellery.

'This'll be from Crew B guys, there must be a couple of hundred grand worth in there.'

'Do we take it, boss?' asked Posty.

'Yeah, we'll give it to Rory, maybe he can get it back to the rightful owners.'

'What about all this cash?'

'I've got a plan for that too, for now, let's just take it back to the flat.'

When Igor came to, he found himself naked in his office chair. His head hurt and it was only when he tried to move his hand he realised his arms were outstretched and his hands were secured as if he was being crucified. His eyes began to focus and he saw the black man from earlier sitting on his desk watching him.

'You remember me now?' Cooky asked him.

Igor's head hurt too much to think, but slowly a memory formed in his mind and he knew where he had seen this man before. 'I remember you Blackie,' he spat the last word out as he stared at Cooky who in return laughed at him.

'Stand up Igor,' Cooky told him.

'Fuck you!' roared Igor, but almost immediately he cried out in pain and looked at his crotch. A thin cheese wire was wrapped around his genitals like a noose and Taff had just given it a tug.

'My friend told you to stand Igor, I suggest you do before I pull a bit harder on this wire,' Taff told him, in an almost amicable voice.

Igor got slowly and carefully to his feet and felt the slight tension in his arms. He realised his hands were each tied to a pulley grip in opposite directions. Cooky took the chair out of the way and laughed again as he looked down at Igor's genitals. Igor followed his gaze and looked down this time following both ends of the wire to where they were attached to the big stacks of weights. Each stack was held up off the floor by a stick wedged under it. Tears pricked in his eyes as he saw a piece of rope was attached to each stick and led back to the desk where Cooky had sat back down and was holding the ropes in each hand.

'Now then Igor,' said Cooky, 'now that you are fully acquainted with your circumstances, I have a little job for you.'

'Who are you and what the fuck do you want?' he said sounding more defeated than he'd wanted to.

'We represent some Russian friends, friends who you and your Kosanians have cost a lot of money.'

'You are not Russian,' said Igor.

'No, we are not, but we are currently employed on their behalf.'

'What do you want, I have money, I have papers in the safe. There are deeds for properties, here in England and even an Island, you can take it all.'

'An Island?' asked Cooky.

'Yes, it is in Scotland, it has a castle, my boss bought it a few months ago.'

'Interesting,' said Cooky, 'but what I want right now is for you to make a call.'

'A call, to who?' asked Igor.

'To Albania. I want you to call whoever is sending you reinforcements. I want you to tell him the Bratva are coming for him.'

'What, why would I tell him that?'

'Because if you don't you can say goodbye to your dick and balls.'

Taff held the phone to Igor's mouth and pressed redial for the Albanian number. 'Make it good lad, and in English.' He said tapping the wire and making Igor wince.

'Alo? Igor?' came the voice on the phone.

'Shefi, the Ruset Bratva, they are coming for you.'

'Çfarrë? What are you saying Igor?'

'They are here Shefi, they told me to tell you they are coming for you.'

Taff ended the call, 'Good job Igor, good job lad.' Then he stepped back and took a photograph of the cruciform Igor and sent it to the same Albanian number before dropping the phone and stamping on it.

'They will be waiting for you now, the Shefi has an army that will kill every Bratva they can find.'

'That's the idea lad, that's the idea!' said Taff.

#

Easy stood at the front door and rang the bell. He saw the net curtain move in the kitchen window and then Michelle opened the door with the security chain in place.

'Ezekiel?' she said.

'Yes, Michelle, may I speak with you?' he said.

Michelle undid the chain and opened the door. 'What is it?', she asked, as she looked to see if anyone else was around.

'May I come in?'

Michelle hesitated before she opened the door further and invited him in. 'What's going on?' she asked.

'Is your son here?'

'Ryan? He's upstairs, why?'

'Is there someone who could look after him for a while?'

'Why? You're scaring me now Ezekiel, what the hell is going on?'

'I want you to come with me,' said Easy.

'Why would I want to come with you?'

Easy lifted his phone and showed her the photo of Igor. 'Because of this.' Michelle stared open mouthed at the photo. 'My friends have him and asked if you want to come.'

'Why?' she croaked past the lump in her throat.

'We know what he did to you, and to Ryan,' said Easy, looking at his feet.

After a moment Michelle went upstairs leaving Easy in the hallway. She returned carrying Ryan and Easy saw his little bandaged hand.

'Hello Ryan,' he said, 'I am Ezekiel but my friends call me Easy.'

'Am I your friend?' asked Ryan.

'Yes, I hope so,' said Easy, smiling at him.

'A bad man hurt my hand and hurt my Mummy' said Ryan showing Easy his bandages.

'Yes, I know,' said Easy, 'but that man will never hurt you or your Mummy again.'

'Promise?'

'Yes, I promise,' said Easy and crossed his heart with his finger.

After they dropped Ryan off with a neighbour, Easy took Michelle round the corner where Maxwell was waiting for them in the car. After introductions they drove back down to the High Street and parked at the rear of the flat.

Easy took Michelle upstairs to where JT was waiting. 'Hello Michelle, come on in,' he said.

'Where is he?' Michelle asked as she looked around.

'He is across the road in the bookies.'

Michelle looked out of the window and saw the launderette opposite. The memories filled her with disgust but it was quickly replaced by a burning desire for revenge. 'Take me to him, I'm going to kill him,' she said with a cold and level voice that belied what she felt inside.

'Hang on a second,' said JT.

'You know what he did to my son, what he made me do?' she asked him.

'Yes, I do,' said JT.

'I swore that day that I would kill that animal for what he did. I didn't know how or when but someday there would be an opportunity, and I would take it.'

'I understand,' said JT, he'd made similar vows himself. He thought of the war lord they'd thrown from the roof in Pakistan. The old man had hurt a boy that JT barely knew. He couldn't imagine how it would feel if it was your son.

'Then take me to him,' said Michelle firmly.

'Look Michelle, killing someone, or watching someone be killed, is not an easy thing. It stays with you, forever.'

'What he did will stay with me forever, now, just take me to him, please.'

'Ok, but if you change your mind, we'll take care of him for you,' offered JT.

They walked together in silence across the road and round the back of the bookies to enter via the rear door. Stepping into the basement level corridor Michelle caught her shin on the open lid of a toolbox. She stumbled and JT caught her arm then quickly withdrew it when he felt her go rigid and saw the look on her face.

At the top of the stairs the door was shut and Michelle paused with her hand on the doorknob. The door was solidly built and there was no sound from within that could be heard over the hammering of her own heart.

JT waited patiently behind her on the stairs. He was torn between letting her go through with this, she thought revenge would give her closure, but he knew the weight that had to be carried. He had killed many people. Killing a combatant in war meant nothing to him. His first kill was followed so swiftly by the second and third that he didn't have time to process them. He could recall the incident, the contact and the feeling that it was kill or be killed, but he couldn't see their faces. If he tried and forced the memory to come, he could see the old war lord's face. The missing teeth and henna in his beard but the face was that of the man sat drinking tea around the fire. Not the face of the man as he fell to his death from the roof. The face that came to him easiest, too easily was that of the woman. He saw her in fine detail. Her dark pleading eyes, red from crying. Her pale face. Her mouth twisted in anguish. He could see her slender fingers pulling back her coat. She knew she was going to die. She knew and her last act was to warn him. To save him. Her eyes burned into him even as he pulled the trigger.

The sound of the door handle's faint squeal brought him back, he watched as Michelle used her shoulder to slowly push open the door. She stopped in the doorway and looked in to see Taff and Cooky stood watching her. The door was only halfway open and it hid what she had come to see. Trying to control her breathing she hesitated in the threshold.

JT impulsively reached a hand out to reassure her but before he could touch her, she stepped forward and into the room. He watched her eyes widen and her recoil slightly as she took in the scene. Not for the first time he had to admire the way she steadied herself before taking the next step. She was obviously scared but her need for revenge kept her moving forward.

Michelle stood in front of Igor's massive form without speaking and she tilted back her head to stare in his face. Igor seemed to sense the anger and hatred from her and turned his face away from her. She took a step back and looked at his massive shoulders and arms taking in the cords lashing his wrists to the handles. She saw two cords were used on each wrist, one long and one short. Her eyes followed the line of the cables to the pulley system at the top of the multigym. She stepped toward the right hand stack and traced the cable path with her fingertips to the top of the weight stack. From the pulley wheel attached to the top of the weight stack, she ran her fingers back along the thin steel wire before stepping back and looking down at the man's genitalia. She noted to herself that it didn't match the huge bulk of the man and that he was shaved completely bald from the neck down. So much preening and self-care, but you are still an animal, she thought.

'I assume that if those pieces of wood are removed then...' she made a chopping action with her hand.

'That's the plan Ma'am,' said Cooky.

The use of the formal term made her turn and look at him. 'Will it be over quickly?' she asked.

'Depends on whether the initial shock kills him. He'll bleed. A lot. If he could get himself to hospital after stopping the bleeding then he might survive. Otherwise, he will bleed out. He'll be unconscious after 4 or 5 minutes then lights out in under 10.'

'How would he stop the bleeding?' she asked, turning back to look at Igor.

'Good question. Probably the only feasible method would be to cauterise the wound.'

Michelle looked around the room and her eyes fell on an open cupboard where she saw an ironing board stacked against the wall. She walked over and opened up the cupboard. When she turned back around, she was holding an iron.

'Please, no, please.' Begged Igor, 'There is more money, my money. In the ceiling, in the toilet, move the panel, please just take the money!'

Taff walked out and into the toilet.

'Something like a hot iron would do the trick, right?' Michelle asked Cooky.

'If it was hot enough, yes, that would probably do it,' he said, looking at JT with a questioning look that was answered with a shrug.

Michelle found a socket and plugged in the iron turning it the highest heat setting.

Taff returned with two canvas bank bags and placed them on the desk. 'Got to be £150k in here.'

'Two hundred thousand, and I can get more, much more if you let me go,' Igor blurted out.

'We need to be getting out of here soon,' said JT looking at his watch.

Cooky stepped forward and cut the shorter cords between Igor's wrists and the handles. He pushed each handle into Igor's hands. 'Get ready to take the strain now big man.'

Michelle licked her finger and tested the iron which was already getting hot. She picked it up and stood in front of Igor. 'Look at me,' she said, 'Look at me!' Igor reluctantly looked down at her. Then closed his eyes, unable to meet her stare. 'Oh, you don't like looking at my face do you!' she said, 'maybe this is the only way you like to look at women?' she knelt down in front of him. 'Now look at me, remember this?' she said as she looked up at him to make sure he was looking at her as she put the hot iron against his toes. Igor screamed and bucked in pain as she moved the iron onto his thigh. The smell of singing flesh filled the air and she rocked back looking at the red and already blistering flesh.

'Time to go,' said JT as Michelle got back to her feet.

Cooky handed her the two ropes tied to the sticks wedged beneath the stacks of weights. 'Ready?' she said to Igor then pulled on the ropes.

Igor grunted as the sudden drop of the weights wrenched his shoulders but he managed to keep a grip of the handles to prevent them falling completely.

Michelle looked at him and saw the taut muscles of his forearms and shoulders working to hold the weight.

'He'll get tired soon enough,' said Taff.

JT handed Michelle the canvas bank bags full of cash. 'This should allow you to start a new life for you and your son,' he told her.

'I don't know how to thank you,' she sniffed as she started tearing up.

'You can thank us by putting all of this behind you. I don't know who saw the video Igor took but you and your son might be identifiable. Do you have a passport?'

'Yes, we both do,' she said.

'Well, I'm told Poland is a lovely country, and you can live very comfortably, with that money.'

'You know about my husband?' she asked, confused.

'Easy told us, I'm sorry for your loss,' said JT.

'I don't even know who you men are,' she said looking around the room. 'You're the protectors?'

'Right now, we're not too sure either.' said JT.

She walked back up in front of Igor. 'This', she said tugging at the wire and making Igor grimace, 'this is for what you did to me. But this,' she unplugged the iron and picked up scissors from the desk, 'this is for what you did to my son.' She cut the electrical cord from the iron in two then hurled the iron at the wall smashing it.

Michelle followed the others through the basement door and as she pulled it shut behind her, she heard the start of a scream and the metallic clang of weights hitting the floor.

CHAPTER SEVENTY-SEVEN

'We're done here then?' said Maxwell as the team started packing up.

'Yes, we're going to decant all this stuff back to mine and then re-convene with Hamilton tomorrow.' He handed Maxwell an envelope of papers with a smile, 'How'd you fancy being a Laird then Rory?'

'Sounds lovely!' he replied with a chuckle. 'What the hell are we going to do with this lot?'

'That's a problem for tomorrow, tonight we're celebrating. You fancy grabbing enough Chinese for us all and bringing it with you?'

'No problem, anything in particular?'

'Make it a banquet, in fact, make it 2 banquets I'm starving!'

'Me too!' said Taff on the way past with his hands full of bags.

'I've been thinking about this place,' said Cooky.

'Go on,' said JT.

'How about we give this money from across the road to Uncle Samir and let him do some good with it?'

'To do what?'

'I don't know, a food kitchen? Maybe help out some homeless folks, that sort of thing.'

'Sounds like a good idea to me,' said JT, 'Any objections?' he asked the others in the room.

'Gets my vote,' said Joe.

'Mine too,' said Rambo, 'he's a kind old soul, he'll make sure it goes to the right people.'

'Then that's what we'll do,' said JT.

'How much is there?' asked Maxwell.

'I stopped counting at £175k. That'll fill a fair few hungry bellies, so it will,' said Posty, 'I could get used to this Robin Hood stuff!'

'Michelle called us the Protectors, maybe that's who we are now?' said JT.

CHAPTER SEVENTY-EIGHT

Maxwell struggled into the Mayfair flat with two big boxes of Chinese take-away.

'Did you bring this from the Jade Palace in Chinatown?' asked JT, taking the top box from him.

'No, I ordered a delivery and met them down stairs, I wanted to have a quick swim before I came over.'

'Get it out of your system?' JT asked looking at his old friend.

'Sort of,' said Maxwell, placing the box on the kitchen worktop and starting to lift out cartons and bags. 'This whole thing has been a head fuck, you know?'

'Oh yes, my head has been well a truly fucked,' said JT emptying the other box. 'It's been a head fuck for weeks but it's reached a whole new level now.'

'Do you think we can trust Hamilton?' asked Maxwell.

'I hope so, he's next door,' said JT.

'Ah, I thought we were meeting him tomorrow?'

'He turned up here half an hour ago with a bottle of very nice Scotch and said he was looking forward to Chinese. I thought you'd invited him.'

Maxwell laughed, 'Is there anything that man doesn't know?'

'He doesn't know what we're going to do after this. Largely because we don't know ourselves yet,' said JT as he picked up the 1st tray loaded with food. 'Come on, we're eating on the floor.'

Maxwell picked up another tray and carried it into the lounge where he found the team all sat on the floor with plates, cutlery and chop sticks in front of them. He sat down his tray of starters and was immediately handed a crystal tumbler of scotch.

'Macallan,' said Hamilton and clinked glasses with him.

'Ahem,' said a deep Welsh voice, 'Lordy, you have some hungry souls grateful to be alive, and grateful for this food in front of them, keep them that way until it's time for you to serve them dessert alongside our comrades passed. This we ask in some bugger's name, Amen!'

A chorus of 'Amen' and the clinking of glasses ensued.

Hamilton cleared his throat and offered another toast, 'To the Ultimate Protectors.'

Everyone grinned and charged their glasses to 'The Ultimate Protectors', before they set upon the food like ravenous vultures.

After everyone had eaten their fill, they sat back and waited for JT to do his debrief.

'Ok, even though we're not writing any of this up, let's see what we've learned. Taff?'

'Not the usual planning opportunities Boss, but we achieved our objectives, without serious casualties and so far, it looks as if it's been clean,' said Taff.

'So far?' asked JT though he knew the answer.

'I count 2 civilians who could identify us; Uncle Samir and Michelle. All of the others only saw us in ski masks. The Russians will be the focus of any inquiry, both Police and Albanians.'

'You're discounting Easy?' asked JT, teasing out the opportunity for discussion.

'Yeah, the kid's good. He took out the guy on the roof so I'm comfortable he's tied himself in, even if he were to have an attack of conscience.' Taff looked around at the team and received nods of agreement.

'Michelle?'

'She's in the same position. Might have been better if she hadn't seen our faces but she'll be in the wind soon enough, and has a new life waiting for her, so she'll keep it to herself.'

'Dionne?' he asked the question of Taff but knew Maxwell would have a better view on her.

'From what Easy said she was in a mess and a bit incoherent. She knew Easy already but I don't know what she saw of Rory.'

'She certainly saw my face but she was pretty out of it, I doubt she'd be able to pick me out of a line-up,' offered Maxwell. 'I have a suggestion re Dionne and her family. I think we could provide them with a new start somewhere. They have a crumby life here in a cramped flat, so I'm sure the offer of a house elsewhere would be well received.'

'Yes, I like that idea too. We have twelve million opportunities to help,' said JT.

'Maybe we set up a charity or something?' said Taff.

'Gentlemen, before you give all of the money to good causes, laudable as that is, I would ask you to consider your own futures. I know it is the elephant in the room and we'd agreed to discuss this tomorrow but there is no time like the present,' said Hamilton.

'Ok,' said JT who had hoped to have another night to sleep on it, 'let's finish the debrief and then we can make some decisions about the future. Taff?'

'All about planning and intel boss, we were using a lot of borrowed kit but the lads performed up to their usual high standards.'

'Agreed,' said JT.

'I reckon Easy was a real asset too boss, his tech back up was as good as we usually get in the field, if not better. I know he's a kid, but he's not, if you know what I mean. The lad has been here before as my old Mum would say.'

'Agreed, he was an asset, and I'm sure there's a role for him in MI6, or wherever,' said JT looking at Hamilton who sat expressionless other than one raised eyebrow.

'You want me to mention our guests?' asked Taff.

'Yes, I think we should, how about Hamilton first?' said JT as if neither Hamilton nor Maxwell were in the room. He glanced at Hamilton who had allowed the faintest smile.

'He acquitted himself surprisingly well at Palmerston House. Obviously, his intel has been top notch, and his flying skills were a godsend. I am always mindful that we don't really know who our Mr Hamilton is,' he said with a nod to a slightly amused Hamilton. 'We're used to spooks out in the field and we never know who they really are either, but that's usually the concern of the Brass.'

'Hamilton?' said JT, 'care to add anything?'

'Well now, thank you for the positive appraisal of my field skills, I thought I was perhaps a little rusty but thoroughly enjoyed getting my hands dirty again. As for my identity, I have shared what I can and what I believe is essential. I will say that my role does not fit neatly within parameters and language that you are acquainted with, but suffice to say, I serve my country in the best way I can. I am answerable for my actions in the same way all of you are, my position might afford me a little more protection, but I operate on behalf of Her Majesty's Government though not always with their blessing.'

'So, you don't work for the Government?' said JT.

'There are some things that need to be separated from the Government of the day and party politics. As I said, my role, and indeed our role, does not fit neatly within the parameters of the norm. That has its challenges from a legal perspective, but also grants the freedom to actually get things done.'

'You're not above the law then?'

'Heaven's no, my neck is as ripe for stretching as the next man's. You know Abraham Lincoln, that bastion of libertarianism, when he became President back in the 1860s suspended Habeas Corpus. It was during the American Civil War, and he argued that in time of war the right to a fair trial should be suspended. He effectively gave the right to be Judge, Jury and Executioner to his army. When the war ended, he eventually got round to reinstating the rights of the citizenry. I believe we are at war gentlemen, both domestically and internationally. There are forces who are waging war against our country and our citizens. They are, I fear, currently winning. Our legal system, despite being among the best in the world, is cumbersome and not currently fit for purpose. There are those of us who wish to do something to turn the tide and take the battle to our enemies.'

'And you want us as your personal army?' asked JT.

'Not mine per se, I am not alone in my endeavours but you would be serving your country, much as you had been doing.'

'Had? You seem terribly certain of our fate with the Regiment.'

'Sadly, yes. I believe you are victims of a Machiavellian plot. I have come to believe that pressure has been applied by Washington. You rather upset the CIA when you took out their pet War Lord,' he smiled when he saw the surprise on JT's face. 'Yes, I know about that too. It seems he was considered a rather valuable asset and they believe several US personnel lost their lives due to the gap in intel you created. Now, I don't know if that is the case or whether the CIA are doing what the CIA do and covering their arses by trying to hide their own shortcomings, but your fate could be said to have been decided the day that buggering old man discovered he couldn't fly.'

JT sat trying to take it all in and felt every eye in the room on him. 'Taff, what about Rory?' he said to divert attention.

'He's done very well, for a plod,' said Taff winking at Maxwell and trying to lighten the mood. 'He let the old girl Matriarku swallow some pills but apart from that, and allowing himself to get captured by the bent coppers, he's done pretty well. He also does a mean Chinese takeaway!' He smiled at Maxwell who took a mock bow.

'Rory?' said JT.

'Where to start? It's been a crazy few days, I've shot a colleague, albeit a bent one, and broken more laws than I can count. I don't think I can go back to being a cop after all this. 25 years I've given to the job, but the corruption and letting people down rather than doing our job and protecting them, has made me rethink my future.'

'You could be the Laird in Scotland after all and retire to your castle?' said JT, cocking his head.

'I don't think I'm quite old enough to hang up my boots just yet,' he turned to Hamilton, 'If there's room for me in the team you're creating, then I'd like to put myself forward. I'm not as ninja as these guys but I think I could add some skills to the mix.'

'Most certainly,' said Hamilton, 'of course without these gentlemen there won't be a team, but we await their decision.'

'Can't you just set up a team from retired SF guys? There's plenty out there plying their trade as PMCs, some of them are shit hot too,' JT asked Hamilton.

'I had considered that of course, but I don't wish to create a team of mercenaries, I wish to form a team who will do the right thing and for the right reasons, not just for money. You have all proven to me that you are made of the right stuff. You didn't need to undertake any of the actions you have over the last few days, but you did and at considerable risk to yourselves. You didn't do it for money, or else you'd have left with the millions in your offshore account. We are all of a like mind and I believe have the same purpose.'

JT sat thinking and the weight of the silence spread over all of them.

'Boss, the lads have been talking and we know the situation with resigning or court martial. I think we're ready to take a vote on it,' said Taff.

'I can't guarantee they'll accept our resignations and they can still go after us as civilians,' said JT.

'I can confirm that I have spoken with some senior people at the MOD and despite the political clamour they would rather this was all dealt with, as quietly as possible.'

'Bully for them!' said JT shaking his head. He sat looking at the fire for a few moments before he sat up straight and said, 'Ok, no point in putting it off any longer, show of hands, who is in?'

All of the team with the exception of Rambo and JT raised their hands.

'Rambo, you're a no?' asked JT.

'Sorry Boss, I want to stay with the team, obviously, but there's an issue of honour for me.'

'What do you mean?'

'My family were over the moon when I passed selection. It's the ultimate honour as far as Gurkhas are concerned and brings prestige to my family. If I just quit then I will bring dishonour to my family. I can't do that to them.'

'Yes, I see,' said JT.

'Rambahadur,' began Hamilton, 'the last thing I would want is to see you bring dishonour to your family, but I fear that any dishonour might be worse if you face a court martial that has been set up to reach only one conclusion.'

'That would be better than quitting,' said Rambo, looking crestfallen.

'How would they feel about you having a medical discharge, if that could be arranged?' asked Hamilton so quickly JT thought he had come prepared for this eventuality.

'Well, I suppose that would work,' said Rambo, 'but there's nothing actually wrong with me.'

'I'm sure we can work something out,' said Hamilton. 'That just leaves you JT, what do you say?'

'Like everyone else the Army has been my life for a long time, the Regiment especially. In other circumstances I'd have stayed until I retired, or they delivered me in a box. However, it's increasingly clear that there's no place left for me. I'm sorry that it's come to this and I know it's all my fault. If I hadn't decided to take out that war lord none of this would be happening to you guys.'

'Boss, if you hadn't done it, we would have made the same decision,' said Taff, 'we couldn't just leave him to rape that wee boy, whether the CIA thought it was ok or not.'

'Thanks Taff, but I still feel responsible.'

'The team needs you, Boss,' said Cooky.

He looked at them all in turn then made up his mind.

CHAPTER SEVENTY-NINE

Two days later they reconvened in JT's flat and Hamilton delivered his news. 'Gentlemen, I have spoken to the Defence Minister in person and as he owes me a favour, I have arranged for you all to have the option of medical discharges, complete with commensurate pensions!' He smiled at the group who nodded appreciatively and patted Rambo on the back.

'Just like that?' asked JT

'It was rather a large favour he owed me. His son got in a spot of bother backpacking the Far East and I managed to have him brought back safely home, at considerable expense and not without some difficulty,' said Hamilton

'But not a big enough favour to make the threat of our court martial disappear?' asked JT studying Hamilton's face.

'Sadly not, the Americans wanted their pound of flesh. I doubt they'll be particularly satisfied either, but that's for the politicians to hash out.'

Hamilton took an envelope from his briefcase and placed it on the table. These are the deeds to Eilean Subhain, it is an island within Loch Maree in North Western Scotland. The island does indeed have a castle which is in a state of minor disrepair and three habitable buildings on its 112 hectares. It also has its own small self-contained lochan of fresh water. Quite idyllic,' he said spreading out several photographs. It also has a new owner or perhaps I should say Laird, a certain Rory Carmichael Maxwell.' He shook the hand of the surprised Maxwell. 'I have arranged that the property was bequeathed to you according to the records by a long lost 4th cousin. The Albanians bought it from her estate after putting pressure on her executor and he was more than happy to see it go to a more deserving recipient.'

'What exactly am I supposed to do with an island in the middle of nowhere?' asked Maxwell.

'It is precisely its remote location that I think makes it a perfect training base for our team. No-one to disturb and no-one to question shooting on private land etc.'

'In that case, on behalf of the team I thank you, and dear old cousin Morag!' he laughed as JT shook his hand.

'There's more,' said Hamilton, bringing out another sheet of paper onto the desk. 'Mrs Harper, wife of the erstwhile Superintendent Harper plans to put Palmerston House on the market just as soon as it's no longer a crime scene. I approached her this morning and offered her £250,000 for it.'

'What did she say?' asked JT.

'She declined my offer saying it was ridiculously low even with the bomb damage to the main building. So, I reminded her that as part of the police enquiry they would be looking into the finances of herself and her late husband. Suffice to say she is liquidating assets just as quickly as she can and moving to a little place she apparently owns in Venezuela.'

'I don't get it, you just wanted to scare her?' said JT.

'No, I think you should invest some of the cash you have into property. It is in a wonderful location and the intact smaller house and stables will provide excellent accommodation and a base for you all when you're not in Scotland.'

'You've thought of everything haven't you?' said JT.

'I certainly am trying to,' said Hamilton. 'One last piece of news, Ezekiel has taken up an apprenticeship with my people at GCHQ; he will receive the very best training available. He will be free to join in any training exercises either in person or from my office at the log cabin, which will also function as our command and control centre as and when required.'

'When do you think that might be required?' asked Maxwell.

'There's something in the pipeline now actually, early stages but I'd suggest weeks rather than months.'

'Care to share any details?' asked Maxwell.

'There's plenty for you all to be getting on with and sorting out at the moment, I'll brief you all when I have more information. How did it go with your Commissioner?'

'I didn't even get to see him. I was directed to a Detective Chief Superintendent instead. He wasn't in the least surprised, said I'm the fifth resignation in the last 6 months. He said if it wasn't for his pension, he'd be joining me. With time accrued I will be officially a civilian in 4 weeks, they'll pay me for my annual leave due.'

'Then are congratulations in order?'

'I'm not sure yet, but it doesn't feel real yet to be honest,' said Maxwell, shrugging his shoulders.

'And you JT, when do you see your Colonel?'

'Friday afternoon. There's a new batch passing out on Friday morning so we'll see him after that. Out with the old and in with the new so to speak.'

'Have you made plans immediately afterwards?' asked Hamilton.

'I think the lads are planning a bit of a holiday. Thought we might go see something of France without the motorhome or having to swim the channel.'

'Sounds like a good plan. I would suggest Bordeaux, all of the beauty and refinement of Paris but without the tourists and rude waiters.'

'One of my favourite cities,' said JT, 'always fancied having a holiday place there.'

'Then might I also suggest Sunday breakfast at the Orangerie in the Jardin Publique.'

'Ha, I used to go there with Esmé, it was her favourite place,' he looked at Hamilton, there was that eyebrow again.

CHAPTER EIGHTY

Six men stood at the side of the parade square at Stirling Lines Barracks in Hereford, or as everyone in the Regiment knew it, Home. They felt incongruous in their civilian clothes while those on the parade square wore their uniforms. All were lost in memories of their own times on that parade square.

16 new troopers were receiving their berets, a distinction earned only by the best of the best. These men had endured weeks of the most gruelling and testing training among the world's elite fighting forces. They put the special in special forces.

An adjutant approached them after the parade was over, 'Good morning, Gents, good to see you all, shit circumstances but you know what I mean,' he was addressing JT as the most senior in rank but JT was lost in thought.

'Cheers Mackie,' said Taff, stepping in to fill the silence.

'Colonel Dalgleish asked me to convey that you're all invited to join the troopers in the mess.'

'Not sure I'm in the mood for that,' said Taff.

'I don't think the Colonel was 'asking' Taff,' said Mackie, with a grimace.

'In that case, please tell the Colonel we would be delighted to accept his kind offer,' said Taff, with a small curtsey.

They watched as Mackie marched back across the parade square and retook his place behind Colonel Dalgleish.

Taff nudged JT shoulder to shoulder, 'You ok Boss?'

JT slowly let out the breath he'd been holding and puffed out his cheeks. 'Still hard to get my head around all this,' he said quietly.

'I know, I can't quite believe it myself. I'm trying to focus on the future but that feels all up in the air too.'

'Our future is definitely uncertain. What is certain though is that this is the last time we'll be in here,' said JT dejectedly.

'We'll always be part of "here" boss, and it will always be a part of us.'

'That's the thing Taff, it's been such a huge part of us, all of us, I'm struggling to work out what's left.'

'Some R n R will help with that. I'm looking forward to Bordeaux. As soon as I get off that plane tomorrow, I'm heading for the swankiest wine place I can find. I've never had two shillings to rub together since my divorce and I'm ready to eat some pukka food and drink nice wine without having to order the cheapest thing on the menu.'

JT put his hand on Taff's shoulder, 'I know just the place, I'll book us all a table,' he set off around the edge of the parade square and his team fell in behind him.

JT walked first into the mess and was momentarily stopped in his tracks. Taff and the others filed in behind him and fanned out to flank him. What looked like the entire Barracks were gathered in the mess and waiting for them. The six men glanced at each other not sure what to do or say.

Colonel Dalgleish stepped forward with Paddy and shook each of their hands in turn. 'Gentlemen, this is a truly sad day,' he nodded to his regiment assembled behind him. 'They wanted a chance to say their goodbyes to you. You are part of this brotherhood, and as far as I'm concerned you always will be. Now come on in, say your farewells and then I'll see you in my office in 30 minutes.'

'Will do Colonel,' said JT.

Colonel Dalgleish turned and declared to the room, 'The next round is on me!' Then with a smart about turn, he left them to it.

A rush of uniforms swarmed forward with hands shaken and shoulders grasped, there were even a few hugs and tears. They found themselves pushed forward to the bar and glasses thrust into their hands.

'Colonel says I've to drive you to wherever you want to go, so you're free to have a drink,' said Mackie.

JT sipped at the vodka in his glass but didn't have the stomach for it. He watched the others downing their shots and laughing as they were handed another.

'Any idea what you're going to do in civvy street?' asked Paddy, as he moved to stand beside JT.

'Irons in the fire Paddy, we'll see what opportunities come up I guess,' said JT.

'Well, at least you're getting a proper pension out of the bastards, that'll keep the wolf from the door until you find something.'

'We'll be fine Paddy; I don't think money will be a problem.'

'You're going to France again I hear. Didn't you get enough of it last week?'

'This time it's a holiday, feet up and time to get our heads straight.'

'With some nice vin rouge?'

'Lots of very nice vin rouge,' said JT, and smiled at his old friend.

'Just thinking, if you or any of the guys need a reference, and I don't mean one of those generic MOD numbers, then let me know, I'll happily tell them you guys were the elite.'

'Cheers Paddy, I'll bear that in mind,' replied JT. He hated not being honest with Paddy. They'd always been upfront with each other, but he knew that from now on this was how it would have to be.

\#

'Come in!' called Colonel Dalgleish from his office when JT knocked at the door. The six men marched in and stood at attention side by side in front of the big desk.

Dalgleish was at the sideboard and turned round holding a tray of crystal tumblers each containing a decent measure of a pale amber liquid. 'Stand easy gentlemen,' he told them, and placed the tray on his desk. He picked up the glasses one at a time and looked the men in the eye as he handed each of them a tumbler. Lifting his own glass, he held it to savour the aroma. '21 year old Macallan, a gift from an old friend that I've been saving for a special occasion. These are not the circumstances I envisaged opening it for, but here we are. I wanted to take the opportunity to thank you all for your service, and also to tell you once again how bloody sorry I am to be losing you. You will all be receiving full pensions, and I've arranged that you can keep the two 4x4s you've been using. I'm calling them a severance payment and the comptroller will just have to live with it. Anyways, cheers Gentlemen, to Her Majesty the Queen,' he lifted his glass to toast her portrait on the wall, 'and to the finest of her Regiments.'

They all raised their glasses to the Queen, then in unison said, 'The Queen and her Regiment.'

'Now, gentlemen, I will need a couple of signatures from each of you,' he pointed to six piles of paper on a side table. The lurid pink tags showing where to sign looked out of place in their surroundings.

'I'll go first then, shall I?' said Taff who never failed to volunteer for the jobs nobody really wanted to do.

They each signed their forms in turn with JT signing his last. He had to fight down the lump in his throat as he turned back to the Colonel. 'Well, that's it done then Colonel.'

'I wish it were that simple,' said Dalgleish. 'As we discussed previously, there is still the possibility that they will come after you if they think they have a strong enough case, and the political will to pursue you.'

'Do you think that's likely?' asked JT.

'I bloody well hope not, but there are snakes slithering in the corridors of Whitehall trying to make a name for themselves.'

'Like Symmons you mean?'

'He is admittedly a relatively lowly snake but still, a snake all the same. I have heard a whisper that there is an issue with the Afghan witnesses, they are making all sorts of demands of the Foreign Office. Apparently, they would like asylum and to bring half of bloody Helmand with them.'

'What if the Foreign Office say no?' asked JT

'Then I think it is just possible the witnesses may be struck down with collective amnesia, or at least that's their bargaining chip.'

'Let's hope so,' said JT, as he considered this new information. 'Pity they waited until now.'

'I also think it's no coincidence that it's our American cousins who are controlling these people. The CIA are another nest of vipers.'

'That they are,' agreed JT.

'Listen Gentlemen, sorry to have to cut this short but I'm expecting the head of Legal Services and our friend Symmons shortly, probably best for all concerned if you're not here when they arrive. I have to break the news to them that you've all been Medically Discharged, and I doubt they'll be very happy,' said the Colonel with a smirk.

'Oh dear, my heart bleeds for them!' said JT.

'Mine too JT, mine too. Look, all of your personal belongings have been packed up, if you'd rather, I can have them sent on so you don't need to lug it around today. I'm told you have an early flight tomorrow.'

'That would be ideal Colonel thanks,' said JT, wondering, and not for the first time, how the Colonel was so well informed.

On the way out of the administration block they met Symmons and an official in civilian clothes coming into the building.

Symmons stopped in the doorway blocking their exit, 'Gentlemen, how lovely to see you all together.'

'We are due in Dalgleish's office in 3 minutes,' said the man with him looking awkward in a pinstripe suit and carrying a battered brown briefcase.

'You carry on up old chap,' said Symmons, 'I'll have a quick word with these Gents and then be right behind you.'

'Aren't you supposed to have your head up his arse?' asked Taff.

'I think you mean, 'head up his arse *Sir* or *Major*,' Taff,' said Symmons with a sly smile.

'I know what I meant, and it's Mister Taff to you,' said Taff, stepping close to him.

'Mister? Don't you prefer Sergeant?'

'Not anymore I don't,' said Taff.

'I don't understand, what is it you're trying to say?' asked Symmons, looking perplexed.

'As of 10 minutes ago, we are civilians thanks to snakes like you,' said Taff, who turned his head to make eye contact with JT. JT nodded his assent and Taff punched Symmons hard in the solar plexus, the man folded in two and was wheezing as he steadied himself against the wall, 'There now, that's a much better angle to get your nose nice and brown again now, isn't it?'

The six men walked out and onto the parade square for the last time. It was strictly forbidden to walk across the parade square normally but they walked unmolested to where their vehicles were parked. After saying their goodbyes to Paddy, they drove out of the Barracks, out of The Regiment and into a whole new beginning.

Symmons sat opposite Dalgleish nursing his stomach and trying to regulate his breath.

'Did you take that too far, do you think?' asked Dalgleish.

'Taff has a helluva right on him Sir, but I think it was worth it,' said Symmons with a weak smile.

'Well, I'd rather you than me,' said Dalgleish as he picked up his phone, 'Get me Hamilton please Mackie.'

Mackie dialled the number as instructed and waited for it to be answered, 'Mr Hamilton, I have Colonel Harry Dalgleish for you.'

'Good stuff,' replied Hamilton.

Mackie patched the call through to the Colonel's phone, 'Colonel, I have Mr Hamilton, putting you through now sir.'

'Harry, how did it go?' asked Hamilton.

'All went as planned, Hamilton. Not enjoyable in the slightest, but it's done now.'

'Excellent, and they don't suspect anything?'

'Not at all, Symmons did an excellent job.'

'I knew he was the man for the role,' said Hamilton in a self-congratulatory tone.

'You had better take good care of my men Hamilton, or else friend or not, you'll have me to answer to.'

'Harry, I give you my word, I will take the very best care of them.'

'Just make sure you do.'

'Of course. Oh, and Harry, they're *my* men now,' said Hamilton and hung up.

CHAPTER EIGHTY-ONE

JT finished with the clippers on his beard and looked at the mass of hair in the sink. The dark mass had spread itself over the white porcelain and he used a tissue to clear out as much as he could into the bin before turning on the hot water and filling the sink. He looked at himself in the mirror as he worked up a lather with his shaving brush and painted himself a white foam beard. Esmé had called this a Sunday shave, first run with the razor with the grain, then fresh foam before shaving slowly against the grain to leave a perfectly smooth face. He knew he needed a haircut but that could wait until he returned from Bordeaux; it wasn't as if he was out to impress anyone.

As he pulled the razor down his face, he realised just how tired he was. It was more than the fatigue of being in the field of combat, he knew the mental strain of the last few weeks had gotten to him. A big part of that was now over and he knew a comfy bed at the Hotel de Quinconces awaited him.

When he'd finished shaving, he felt the smooth skin on his face and thought back to when Esmé used to do the same to check he hadn't missed any bristles. Shaking the memory from his head, he stepped into the shower and felt the hot water on his face. He stood for a few seconds with the jets beating on his head and the water running down his face enjoying the sensation. The usual faces appeared in his mind with Esmé merging with the Afghan woman and then disappearing altogether, to be replaced by the little boy they'd saved from the War Lord. He shook his head and refused to dwell on the images.

After he had dressed, he fastened on his Maurice Lacroix watch. It had been his wedding gift from Esmé and they'd always referred to it as his civilian watch; he hadn't worn it in some time.

'Boss, the taxi is here!' called Joe.

'Coming,' he said, 'and you can stop calling me Boss now,' as he grabbed his bag from the bed.

'Whatever you say *Boss*!' laughed Joe as JT walked out of his bedroom.

'You scrub up well!' said Taff with a grin from the already open front door, 'Those Mademoiselles are going to love you!'

'Very funny, now let's get a move on, we've got a flight to catch.'

On the way to the airport JT's phone rang, he answered with his headphones in, 'Good morning, Hamilton.'

'Good morning!' said a happy-sounding Hamilton, 'Just checking in, thought I'd see how you chaps were doing after yesterday.'

'We're all good thanks, we're just on our way to Heathrow.'

'Ah yes, of course. Well, I will see you in a week when you're back, we'll have some things to discuss and plan.'

'Yes, we'll see you when we get back.'

'Excellent, oh and don't forget to try the Orangerie for breakfast tomorrow, it's a magical spot.'

'It's in the diary and I'm looking forward to it.'

'Perfect, well, bon vacance!' said Hamilton cheerily and then hung up.

CHAPTER EIGHTY-TWO

The next morning JT sat in a deck chair sponsored by *Veuve Clicquot*. He sipped espresso and watched families playing on the lawns in front of *L'Orangerie du Jardin Public*. The park was already busy with people out for a wander in the warm weather or sitting sharing breakfast on the grass.

Waking up early, he'd joined the joggers and cyclists along the *Quais*, sweating out the last of the weariness. He felt quite at home here, relaxing in the anonymity of a big city, while enjoying the comfort of familiar surroundings.

It had been a good night last night, the food at *Le Bouchon Bordelais* as exquisite as he remembered. They had ploughed through an eye watering amount of wine, with Kate the Sommelier enjoying educating them on the delights from her cellar. JT had left them to it as the guys went off in search of more of what Bordeaux had to offer late at night and instead wandered along the bank of the Garonne river and had slipped off his socks and shoes to stand in the ankle deep water of the

Mirroir d'Eau on Place de la Bourse. The water mirror was a major attraction and he'd taken a photograph for some Japanese tourists who couldn't get quite the right angles with a selfie.

He saw Taff walking across the grass toward him, his usual smile looked sheepish and his dark sunglasses were obvious hangover protection.

'Good morning,' said JT as Taff approached.

'Good morning to you too.'

'Suffering?'

'That would be an accurate description for how my head feels, yes,' said Taff, wiping the sweat that was beading on his brow.

'Want some coffee?' JT asked him.

'Yeah. good idea,' said Taff as he waved over one of the staff, 'Another one?'

'Please,'

A waitress approached, 'Monsieur?'

'Deux cafés, s'il vous plaît,' said Taff, in his broad Welsh accent.

'Oui Monsieur.'

'Impressive language skills there Taff,' said JT with mock applause.

Taff didn't answer and instead was looking over JT's head and toward the patio.

'The toilet is round to the right of the bar,' said JT.

'Eh, yeah,' said a smiling Taff distractedly.

JT watched as Taff removed his sunglasses and his face lit up, 'You ok there Taff?'

'Listen Boss, just remembered, something, I've got something I have to do!' He shook JT's hand and clapped him on the shoulder grinning.

'You don't want your coffee first?' asked JT, as Taff was walking away.

Taff just waved his hand without turning back and kept walking.

JT was contemplating this odd behaviour when a voice, with an unmistakable Canadian accent, sent shivers down his spine said, 'Hello Jonny.'

The End

Also By

Coming soon, **Hacked** a thrilling page turner and the second book in the SAS: *VIGILANT* series.

Sign up for free content, deals and information on future releases at simondaleybooks.com

Subscribers will receive a free short story featuring a character from the upcoming second novel **Hacked** as a thank you for joining **Team Vigilant**.

I hope you enjoyed reading *RETRIBUTION* as much as I enjoyed writing this my first novel. The characters became a big part of my life while writing, they were with me every day for many months, and good company!

I would be extremely grateful if you could leave a brief review of RETRIBUTION. Reviews will help other readers find my books, but from a purely personal point of view, I am really keen to know if you enjoyed what I've written.

Writing a book is a labour of love and all consuming. I am proud of the work I have produced and always happy to discuss the characters and plot. There are links to my social media platforms at https://www.si mondaleybooks.comand I'd love it if you want get in touch!

Thanks for reading and for your support,

Simon

Acknowledgements

Writing can be a reclusive and individual pursuit. The space, freedom and push for me to get words out of my imagination and onto a page only come with the support of my amazing family.

To Caroline, Erin, Bobby and Frank, my eternal thanks for putting up with me when I've been completely self absorbed.

Caroline deserves another special thanks for her excellent cover design.

ABOUT THE AUTHOR

Simon Daley lives and writes between Scotland and the US. He worked in law enforcement for over 30 years. His experience in Counter Terrorism and working with numerous agencies has given him an insight that he uses in his writing.

Simon has previously had short stories and poetry published but *Retribution* is his first full length novel.

His favourite hobbies away from reading and writing are his dog Frank, tennis and soon to be marathon training.

Printed in Great Britain
by Amazon

34439099R00267